UNDER THE CLOCK

BY

KATE BLACK

Disclaimer

For Colette

ACKNOWLEDGEMENTS

Kate Black is a pseudonym that was used by the late Angela Doyle (1968-2009) when she penned *Under the Clock*. This publication is an acknowledgement of Angela's commitment to her writing. Also my promise to Angela in the weeks before her passing that I would publish this manuscript, her most precious work. However, it was not until the summer of 2017 that the time felt right for me to address my promise to Angela, my beloved partner from 1997 to 2009.

Angela Doyle, a talented journalist, was Deputy Editor of two newspapers based in County Roscommon in Ireland. She had a distinguished career firstly with *The Roscommon Champion* and finally with T*he Roscommon Herald*. While with the latter, Angela Doyle became the ESB Provincial Journalist of the Year (2000).

While Angela was writing *Under the Clock*, at times typed sheets would be randomly flung across a table for me to read aloud. This was for editing purposes and testing against Angela's own exacting standards. I was honoured to have this work dedicated to me.

The journey of this publication brought me from the East to the West of Ireland and, finally, to Mayo, Angela's birthplace. On this most memorable journey, I felt supported by Colette Glynn and Anne Quirke; by Ann Marie Keenan and Dr. Julia Richter; and finally by Marina Tuffy and Cynthia Silva, all true friends and confidantes to us both.

I re-connected with two dear friends of Angela's: Maureen Ahearne and Peti Buchel while in Achill Sound where this project was discussed and fully supported.

I also wish to acknowledge the following: Liam Conroy, Chris Casserly, Berni O'Neill, Cathy Clear, Martina Kavanagh, Sally Keane and Murty Keegan for their friendship to us over the years and their belief in this project.

I wish to thank authors Angela Garrigan and Jean Cross who generously made their time available and answered questions about the process of publishing.

Professionally, I wish to acknowledge the considerable design and formatting work, technological talents and kindness of Dora Murphy in assisting with this publication and the fact that it has now come into the light.

My personal thanks to Conor Fallon designer, for his art work, considered advice, patience and expertise that led to the excellent cover design.

Of course I am greatly indebted to Jean Mc Grath and Rachel Garvey for their assistance, feedback and support during this process.

Finally, in gratitude for our precious time together, I acknowledge the strong unit that was our family consisting of Tadhg and Conor Fallon, myself and Angela Doyle. Her love and dedication to our family knew no bounds. We all miss her.

Colette Byrne
Partner

FOREWORD

This isn't a true story, but it could have been. It doesn't contain facts, but it does contain a certain kind of truth. One of the real truths of Ireland now is that despite lip-service and tokenism it still isn't as easy to be comfortably gay in Ireland as it is to be comfortably 'normal'. One of the real truths of today's Ireland is that, if it was that easy, I would be able to tell you my name, to tell you who I really am.

Words like 'dyke', 'queer' and 'lezzer' – no matter how we try to reclaim them – can still cut enough to make us bleed silently, particularly in small communities where understanding of difference exists in parts, but is still largely unspoken. All over this country, there are women like the characters in this book; women who live stereotypical double lives. They are Irish; they are women who were born in this country, who grew up in this country, who live, work and pay tax in this country... yet they are still treated as the Invisibles... the women who don't exist. Their relationships are not recognized nationally, in law, or in their own communities. Their difference is not celebrated or accepted: it is just endured.

These women laugh, love, create and maintain friendships, work, look after parents, children and siblings. They build careers, buy homes, cut lawns on Sundays and drill holes for picture hooks. They feed pets, enjoy social lives, relate to bosses and subordinates, start their own businesses and go to bed early at night because they're tired. I am one of them. I will never be ashamed to be one of them.

Still, I am a stranger in my own place. Newspapers, television programmes and advertisements – even when they try – and conversations with members of my own community do not reflect my reality because I am one, and they are many. Their power comes only from their number; mine comes from myself.

The main characters in this book, Helen and Catherine, are creations of my imagination but they are based on real people. They are parts of many people I know or have known; they speak expressions I have heard from the mouths of a diverse range of people; they have thoughts that are not my own. But they could be real.

This isn't a true story, but it could have been.

Kate Black

CONTENTS

CHAPTER ONE

ALMOST STRANGERS

Hurling down her pen in utter disgust, Helen bundled three closely written sheets into a crumpled envelope. She stuffed the letter into the bulging back pocket of her holdall. Helen hated writing letters by hand: it was too slow and laborious, but then typewriting was excessively impersonal for this. Her head buzzed pleasantly from the effects of two swift bottles of Heineken and the adrenaline rush of a high-speed drive across the country from Dublin.

Despite what she thought of as her advanced years and her obvious lack of testosterone-induced machismo, Helen drove ridiculously fast and took appalling chances. She thought of it as being symptomatic of a headlong emotional rush through life, or even as a contradiction to her normal practice of physical methodical plodding. Her relatives despaired of her reaching forty unscathed. But what the hell. Helen loved the high of pushing her concentration to the limit. She hadn't been given even one speeding ticket in her life, even though the local Gardai threatened from time to time. With a sweet smile and an innocent promise not to do it again, Helen usually got off. The press card helped, though.

She was suddenly weary, eyes closing as she leaned back, her booted right ankle resting on her left knee. Stirring herself enough to brush her teeth desultorily, Helen thought ahead to Monday and its usual yawning deadline, including the hangover of work that had been lurking on her desk since before the weekend.

Those two days had been a little different from her usual bustling, chore-filled Saturday and long, lazy Sunday with nothing more challenging to do than carry home hefty Sunday newspapers from the corner shop. She'd met Linda under the clock at Eason's on Saturday and had driven north to Balbriggan, concerned at the unusual silence of her pale and uncommunicative companion. Although she was habitually and maddeningly unperceptive, Helen observed that Linda was in a bit of a state and concluded that she was still a little too close to the rough edge of the end of her long, bickering relationship with the enigmatic Catherine. Mind you; she also thought that Catherine took the enigmatic bit a shade too far: Helen looked on it more as a pose than anything else, and if there was one type of person she disliked intensely, it was a poser.

Helen and Linda talked of something and nothing during the drive, filling in the highs and lows of the five years since they'd met previously. Nothing much had really changed, apart from the obvious. Helen had returned home from the States, fed up at last of a rat-race pace of life that left her mentally out of breath; Linda and Catherine had broken up, with a characteristic quota of slime and one-sided bitchiness.

The prospect of a Saturday evening threesome made Helen want to gag; she could never quite understand this lesbian partiality for ex-lovers remaining friendly. There was something masochistic about it, she thought: something very odd indeed. It was as if the parties concerned endeavoured to surround themselves with exes, as if having a rake of trophy ex-wives without the alimony headaches was trendy. In truth, instead of the proposed Saturday evening arrangement, Helen wished for the dubious privilege of covering a four-hour county council meeting in Castlebar or the conventional routine of fending off questions about her eating habits from her mother in Sligo.

Linda and Helen spent the afternoon shopping, drinking coffee and avoiding the non-issue of each other's love lives in favour of small talk about who was shagging whom on the incestuous Dublin scene. Later, they stood uneasily together at the station, waiting for Catherine's train to arrive. The train pulled in ten minutes late. Helen turned away to hide her mental puke reflex at Linda's sick-making enthusiasm for the new arrival. Wan September sunlight glittered sporadically on dirty train windows. Helen glanced quickly at the approaching back-packed and vaguely familiar figure, taking in the neat shape and shock of dark hair before glancing down at the suddenly interesting toe-caps of her own black shoes. She only realized she'd been holding her breath tightly when Catherine's inappropriately warm hug expelled it for her.

During the course of the evening, Helen heard her internal stranger – that part of her muddled intellect that wasn't quite her and yet was, at the same time – tell cruel tales of life in a narrow country town and watched herself smoking after seven nicotine-free months. The same cloaked stranger laughed during an Italian dinner and a game of cards for three, and wrestled Catherine to the ground raucously, in playful imitation of a textbook rugby tackle. When it was very late, the stranger in Helen lifted suspicious eyes to meet Catherine's; pale grey eyes, so unlike her own, narrowed in unmistakable appraisal. Helen blinked and looked away but her eyes guiltily followed the whorls of smoke from someone's cigarette as they spun upwards. Calm pale eyes held her through the haze and a sudden heavy silence. Linda coughed. Helen gathered up the cards and counted out three sevens.

On Sunday, Helen drove slowly through country lanes and over potholes, stopping at a ruin on some godforsaken hill near the coast. Saturday night's mute stranger was gone, and she could smell the sea anyway. Helen loved the sea. She pottered off discreetly and left the others to their own devices. Back in the car a cold and windblown hour later, Helen glanced at Catherine in the rear-view mirror through queer-edged silence and turned on the wipers by accident. Catherine laughed.

'What are you trying to do… prove the wipers on this rust-bucket actually work?'

'It's a long walk back to the train station for a cheeky Wicklow girl of my acquaintance,' Helen informed a passing tractor.

'Ooh, it bites,' Catherine remarked, sticking out her tongue. Silently, Linda rooted in the glove box for a recognizable cassette.

After a quick lunch in Balbriggan, Helen addressed an electrical appliance, her tone deliberately neutral. 'I can drop you in town if you like. It's sort of on my way.'

'Thanks, that'd be great. Those trains are mental on Sundays.' Catherine chewed her lower lip.

Linda's goodbye was chilly enough for Helen to leave them to chat at the door while she warmed up her recalcitrant car engine. She and Catherine sang their way into Dublin; the mood gradually thawed and they ended up flippantly assessing the talent standing at Northside bus-stops. Catherine favoured long-haired bohemians while Helen maintained that fair-haired sophisticates were much more her own style.

'Want to have a cup of coffee?' the driver asked, crashing gears at Connolly Station. 'It's a long drive home for me without at least one intravenous coffee injection.'

'Yeah, I could do with something before tackling the Sunday afternoon horrors of the DART. How 'bout Bewley's?'

Miraculously, an empty parking space materialized at Eden Quay. Helen parked gratefully and, as always, laboriously, and then fumbled her keyring into the gutter while Catherine waited, hands in pockets. They devoured mugs of coffee and sandwiches in Bewley's, bitched about being in the non-smoking section and contributed smutty jokes to an uneven conversation.

On Westmoreland Street, as afternoon turned imperceptibly into early evening, Helen searched her pockets for the keys, suddenly and unaccountably embarrassed. 'Thanks very much. That was a laugh.' She cursed herself for unaccustomed inanity.

'Yeah, it was the high point of my weekend.' Catherine glanced at the sky sourly. 'Thanks for the lift and do come up again soon.'

Helen watched her internal stranger raise her right hand and gently touch her palm to the side of Catherine's face. 'I will,' she said, removing her hand rapidly.

Catherine spoke no more but turned away and walked towards Pearse Street DART station. Helen drove like a nutcase down the Quays, the dual carriageway and the motorway, and only just hit the bumps on the decrepit Roscommon stretches of the N5 before reaching the Mayo border. By the time she arrived back in Castlebar, she could almost hear the car panting from exertion.

'My poor Ophelia, I do treat you badly sometimes… well, most of the time,' she said apologetically to the steering wheel, then barrelled out of the car, threw her bag in the hall, yodelled to her housemate and hammered upstairs to write a letter in scrawled and impatient longhand.

'Goddamn that man.' Helen flung the telephone receiver away venomously. Her colleague chuckled and stuck his head around the office partition.

'Politicians are such fucking hypocrites,' Helen moaned to herself. She stormed out of the office and came to a premature halt at the coffee machine.

Philip followed and poured Guinness-black coffee into two mugs. 'It was time for a break anyway,' he said, grinning. 'Let's hear it, before I have to go and hit the ladies in the planning office with my undeniable charm.'

'Richard O'Donnell, councillor and award-winning asshole, has been drip-feeding me this fucking story about the quarry. I've finally got to the bottom of it and he wants to pull it in case the shagging party big-wigs will find out it came from him. And he's threatening to pull his auctioneering adverts as well, the blackmailing son of a whore. What the fuck do I care for fuckstick politicians? They're only a shower of weak-willied bigots with one eye on the fucking parish pump and the cross-eyed one on the pulpit,' she ranted.

'One sugar or two today, darling?' he asked mildly. 'And that will be eighty pence for the Christmas swear box. 'I'm charging you for the "weak-willied" but count yourself lucky you're getting away with the "asshole".'

She flung a particularly diseased-looking tea-towel at him and walked away, laughing. Back at her desk, Helen ruminated briefly on her decision to return home from Boston. She loved this country town, the people and the guys – well, some of the guys – she worked with, but there were times and this was one of them when she hated being a tabloid newshound for the upbeat, unashamedly commercial and controversial *Mayo Recorder* instead of the respectable *Connaught Telegraph,* loved and regarded mostly for its sober reporting and sheer longevity. Most of the time, working with Philip O'Conor made it fun: she enjoyed his quirky tales of strange court cases and hilarious newspaper blunders that were as much hoary legend as fact. Helen liked this fifty-minus settled and very married granddad-reporter. He made full use of the advantage rule in his reports and was a popular face around the town and county. Helen sighed and went back to work.

That odd, half-ignored internal stranger waited anxiously for the morning post while she got back to boring end-of-week duties and skimmed through another ungrammatical press release from the local IFA. Frustrated by one too many upper-case letters where they clearly didn't belong, she screwed the sheet into a tight ball and aimed it at the bin. It was an unusually woeful miss: she hit Colm, the boss, neatly on his golf club tie-pin. He glanced at her quizzically and dropped a small pile of envelopes on her desk.

'Philip gone out, hmm? You might tell him I need his expenses sheet before lunch if he wants a cheque, which I presume he does. I'm off to the fairways for the afternoon while the weather's still in it.'

'Yeah, I will. Hope you make par at the nineteenth.'

He paused at the door. 'Two sheets work best,' he whispered mysteriously. Helen raised her eyebrows. 'It adds weight, you know.' He indicated the ball of paper on the floor.

'I'll remember that. Oh, and have a good weekend,' Helen said, turning pink. 'I'll need to talk to you about that quarry story on Monday.' 'No problem.' The door was already swinging closed behind him.

Helen paused for two heartbeats and flicked through the unopened post with a single fingernail. It was there, all right. It was, in a slim white Dublin Corporation envelope: two pages bursting with sheer mischief. Helen read quickly, already composing a reply in her head. '*It's an awful pity you didn't manage to pick up – and yes, I do mean that ambiguous-ly – any buxom hitchers on the way home... But be consoled, I didn't have any better luck'* The typing was immaculate; the signature scrawled and tiny. Helen folded the letter thoughtfully and slipped it into her backpack. Smiling, she screwed up two blank sheets of paper, aimed carefully and scored a direct hit.

Six weeks and at least as many letters later, Helen sat at home over a late lunch and dialled a nine-digit number she'd learned off, repeating the extension number three times for the bored switch operator.

'Good afternoon, Tenant Purchase.'

'Hello, Ms Purchase, it's Helen. I know you're probably busy running the country but I'm just ringing to make arrangements for Saturday.'

'Great stuff. So it's The Gate at eight... hey, it's rhyming time!'

'Wonderful, Oscar. I thought we could meet for a meal or something first, if you'd like?'

'Mighty. I'll meet you under the clock at Eason's so... that's probably the best place. What time d'ya think you'll get there?'

'Is five okay?'

'Fine by me. Speaking of fine, pick up any fine things yet?'

'Nah, ye olde fine things are fierce scarce on the ground around here.'

'Yeah, right. You might have better luck up here then.'

'I might.' A pause, too short to be significant.

'You never know. Gotta go – hey, another cheap poetry line – the boss, also known to his friends as Herr Goebbels, is calling. Drive slowly and I'll see you Saturday.'

'I will. See you Saturday, that is. Bye.'

'The day you drive slowly is the day I give up on womankind and join the nuns! See you then.'

Helen picked up her sandwich and went straight back to the letter page of a copy of the *Independent* that she'd sneakily purloined from the office. She sometimes wondered if the correspondents actually existed.

Half the city seemed to meet under the clock on Saturday afternoons. Every thirty seconds, Helen walked down the steps and studied the simple round clock attached to the façade. It was twenty minutes past five but she suspected she might break her personal rule of never waiting for anyone for more than half-an-hour, just this once.

Ten minutes later, she had stopped searching the oncoming river of faces on O'Connell Street and was considering chasing up an old college friend to pass the remaining time when a breathless, pink-faced Catherine raced up the steps.

'Christ, I was sure you'd be gone. Linda rang and I missed the DART. I told her some kind of mad crap to get her off the 'phone. She'd have a fit if she knew I was here, not that it's any of her business. Where're we going for tea… or would you prefer a drink? I could just murder a pint,' she said, all in one short breath.

Helen laughed. 'It's fine. I would have waited.' A lie. 'What did Linda want?'

'To talk, same as usual. I keep telling her that I want to be left alone but all she wants is to know if I've slept with anyone yet, if I've had the opportunity, if I'm planning to or if I intend to at any stage over the next hundred years or so. Chance'd be a fine thing. Westbury all right?'

Helen nodded, still laughing as they started walking South among the throng of November shoppers. She finally gave up any attempt to hold a decent – or even remotely private – conversation around bald heads and punk haircuts, not to mention harassed mothers wheeling loaded push-chairs.

The Westbury Hotel was an island of well-heeled if slightly unctuous professionalism; the kind of oily place that usually left Helen feeling gauche, self-conscious and slight-ly suffocated from the smell of crisp new money. Ensconced in two wing-backed chairs redolent of old cigar smoke and tweed jackets, she and Catherine sampled their pints, unan-imously pronounced them fit to drink and watched the bet-ter-off glide by soundlessly on grass-deep carpets. Cathe-rine, allegedly a non-smoker, accepted a cigarette with blunt, no-nonsense fingers and smiled apologetically as she reached across the table for a light.

The conversation was whispered. Helen remarked on how easy it is to be intimidated by surroundings sometimes: Catherine cracked a joke and laughed loudly to prove she wasn't. Two pints later, they were back where they belonged, according to Catherine; the cold Dublin street, with only the prospect of a bag of chips each and perhaps the extravagance of a shared sausage to look forward to.

While they waited outside the Gate Theatre for the box office to open and provide press tickets for an obscure play by an even more obscure Mayo playwright, Catherine stood uneasily shifting her weight from one foot to the other. Hel-en leaned against the wall and watched the traffic, relatively comfortable in uncommunicative silence.

Inside, while Helen diligently took daft-looking short-hand notes on the wayward proceedings and wondered just how much faint praise she could possibly get away with, her internal stranger was sharply aware of Catherine's slow, even breathing and of the shirt-sleeved arm just touching hers on the shared arm-rest. She steeled herself to say goodbye and turned to Catherine as the first and last wave of tepid appreciation faded and the curtain closed.

Helen resolved to be honest. 'That was absolutely appalling and you'd have a right to murder me for dragging you to it. Fancy a cup of coffee as a peace offering?'

Eyes met her carefully but confidently. "Great idea, young hack."

It turned out to be Bewley's again, a different branch this time but with the same faintly warm French smell of roasting coffee beans.

'D'you want a lift home?' Helen babbled, stumbling over the words, when the last dregs had been consumed.

'To Bray? Are you mad? It's miles out of your way.' Catherine raised one eyebrow in surprise. Helen, who had always lusted after the ability to raise just *one* sardonic eyebrow like that, glanced away. "I mean, you have enough miles ahead of you driving in this pea-soup in the middle of the night,' Catherine continued, waving a hand towards the door that was keeping grim, icy fog outside. 'Pity you can't stay over.'

'Duty calls at eleven in the a.m., unfortunately. Ploughing championship, God bless the mark. What's another few miles between friends and, anyway, the DART must be finished by now.' Helen glanced at her pocket watch.

'Okay so, if you're sure you don't mind?'

'I'm sure. Now shut up or I'll dump you in the canal!'

The silent drive south was broken only by Catherine's crisp and accurate directions. Helen climbed out of the car at a terraced house on a poorly lit street, both to say goodbye and to check that the fog lights were working. They weren't. Catherine stood on the footpath, suddenly businesslike, one hand in a pocket.

'Thanks very much for the lift and I'm sorry to bring you so far out of your way. Want another cup of coffee before you go?'

'Thanks, but no thanks. I'd better get going now if I'm

going to get home before first Mass.'

'Not that you'd ever be in a rush for Mass, you heathen. Listen, thanks very much, and I'll see you again when you're up.'

'Sure thing… Of course, Dublin is roughly East-South-East of my town so I'm sure you mean down rather than up.' Helen paused. 'Catherine, I know the play was desperate but thanks for the company anyway. I'd have cracked up if I'd have had to sit through that shite on my own. Be seeing you.'

Helen thought she was turning to go but observed that she was, in reality, reaching awkwardly to put her arms around Catherine's shoulders. Catherine unselfconsciously returned the hug. Helen leaned down slightly, noting the slight difference in their respective heights and softly kissed the corner of Catherine's mouth. Meaningful glances weren't in it with the pair of them. Helen left without saying goodbye.

It was a long drive home and she should have been tired, but at the end of it sleep was crowded out by too many faces from the past and too many slow-motion replays of her mother's tears dripping with the weight of candle wax onto the dinning-room table at home. In the slow dawn, Helen saw Clare – the textbook First Serious Adolescent Crush – right through to Joan, the last – the mad, dark-haired, bohemian, pseudo-leftie she'd hungered after for years and couldn't feel much for when the unexpected finally happened far away from Ireland. Helen was conscious of each silent, separately ticking moment pulling her along, and of that maddening mental stranger pushing her towards a place to which she never had any desire to go.

With the chilly sense of emotional dislocation learned from years of practicing journalism, Helen disliked trawling through her past experience in the early hours. It was infantile and ultimately pathetic, she suspected, and it clearly wasn't hers. Someone else, some other less certain and more disjointed Helen had actually lived it. Unwillingly, she remembered the cracked and fissuring life of some other nineteen-year-old Helen… the psychiatrist's chair, his boring monotone voice asking long intrusive questions, and her own crude, rude and monosyllabic non-answers.

She remembered her mother's silent grieving; the puzzled eyes that turned her way and, not finding her, then searched for the Helen that used to be. Nora's view that a seemingly carefree, academically-lazy student and absent-minded daughter had been stolen and replaced by someone else's stranger reeked of the turgid rightness of the high moral ground. As she lay in bed, Helen's jaw clenched as she remembered one single word, the drumbeat and keynote of uncountable angry confrontations. In Helen's view, no-one ever had the right to question her existence, to regard her compromise with living as simply a phase. She was ten years older than she had been then and she was tired of attempting to please the people she tried to respect most, tired of silently undertaking to be someone else to suit someone else and, above all that, tired of brief, casual and almost cruel affairs played out repetitively, like scratched, overly familiar records.

Lying in bed, Helen remembered Catherine's voice, muted by the fog outside Bewley's, telling her she had found a foreign cutie and was already half-dead from time-consuming attempts at seductive chivalry. It might have been a joke but it certainly didn't sound like one. Helen realized she was only half relieved.

'Colm, I know I should have asked in advance but I'm feeling a bit under the weather and I'd like to take a few days off next week… I think I must need some of the mother's home-cooking and a good sleep or something.'

He looked surprised. 'If you want to, go ahead. You're due the time off and, anyway, we've a couple of final-year journalism students coming in on work experience tomorrow. As you'd say yourself, hopefully one of them might be able to write a full paragraph with less than three spelling errors.' He checked the diary. 'No-one else's booked anything. You can have a week if you want, I suppose.'

'Thanks, C.P., a week will be fine and I really appreciate the offer. I've got a couple of stories lying around that I can pass on to Philip or one of the others … Georgie should be able to sort them out by now.'

'Whatever you think but just let me know who you're giving them to. Do you want holiday pay before you go?'

'Ah, no, sure I'm rolling in it: a single girl like me hardly needs paying! I'm sure Chris'll drop it into the bank for me just in case I end up in the red and out on the side of the road for not paying the mortgage.'

'Suit yourself. Don't forget to leave a list of what's in your diary while you're gone.' He surveyed the front page of a crisp new copy of the Recorder. 'Good story on the political links to the dodgy quarry, Helen.'

High praise indeed, she thought. 'Yeah, but my friend Dick O'Donnell, councillor and asshole, will blow a gasket when he reads it,' she said. 'And you wonder why I'm leaving town?'

Helen telephoned home and packed a bag on Friday evening. She was already attempting to start Ophelia's engine when she changed her mind. Back in the house, Niamh looked up from *Coronation Street*.

'Car won't start?'

'I didn't hang around long enough to find out. Just gotta make a couple of telephone calls.'

'To find a mechanic?'

'Oh, you're hilarious. At least I'm the proud possessor of my own mechanized transport, even if Ophelia is a little irritable in Winter. Hey, Niamh, I mightn't be back until the end of next week so is there any chance you'd pay the 'phone bill… I know it's one of my household duties but I'll swap you something.'

'Okay, but only if you put out the bin for an extra turn.'

'Christ, Doctor Rodgers, you drive a hard bargain. I don't know why I put up with you; you take this division of labour thing far too seriously,' Helen chided gently.

'I dunno. It must be love, I suppose.'

Helen deliberately folded the sheets of the alarming telephone bill and slipped them back into the envelope. Turning around and leaning against the kitchen table, she returned Niamh's speculative look.

'And what, pray do tell, is that supposed to mean?' Silence.

'Out with it. If you've something to ask, ask. You've been fishing around for weeks. Nothing better to do since Matthew boy stopped calling around, eh?'

Niamh flushed at the cruelty of the barb and turned back to the television. Helen grabbed her keys and ran one hand through her short, habitually tousled hair in frustration.

'I told you when you moved in that I wanted someone to pay the mortgage and the bills and treat the place like home, not a fucking Siamese twin. Don't make assumptions and quit speculating, whether it's out of curiosity or boredom. Get a goddamn life, for fuck's sake. I don't waste my time wondering what you get up to with the strawberry-flavoured condoms I find underneath the toothpaste in the bathroom cabinet from time to time because it's none of my business. With the hours you work up in that hospital I'm surprised you have a spare moment to wonder what I'm doing. Now I'm going to my den to make two telephone calls: one to my mother to tell her I won't be home after all and one to an East coast number that you'll find on the bill in two month's time. Is that okay?'

'For God's sake Helen, I didn't mean anything. It was just a throwaway remark. Don't be so touchy if you've nothing to hide.'

'That's the blessed limit! I don't have anything to hide from you because what goes on in my world is none of your business. I'll be touchy if I damn well please, and I consider myself to be remarkable restrained, given that you're provoking me. You hardly have a word for a dog these days apart from smart comments that have more between the lines than a football field. What the hell is going on?'

'Ah, it's nothing… Matt and I aren't speaking. Again. It's not your fault and I'm sorry if I upset you.'

Niamh looked so miserably contrite that Helen softened instantly, her anger dissipating fast. 'Me too. Oh, bugger it, Niamh. Work's been tough for the past few weeks, hence the couple of days off. Maybe I'm just tired or maybe I'm genetically programmed to bite people's heads off.' Helen walked to the door. 'Corrie's nearly over now. I suppose I'd better get out of your hair and make those calls.'

'Why tell me? After all, it's your own business.'

Helen stuck her head back through the doorway. 'Watch it, Rodgers, or you'll be in grave danger of developing a good sense of humour,' she said, wrinkling her nose and squinting maniacally.

'Yup.'

'It's me. Your telephone-answering manners are appalling.'

'Thanks very much and hello. What d'you want now?'

'Nothing much. I've just eaten the head off Rodgers the lodger; she thinks I'm turning into a neurotic spinster who might have strange tendencies; I've a few days off and I was wondering if you're doing anything vitally important tomorrow that could be cancelled in favour of advising me during a Christmas shopping expedition. Alternatively, I could just shoot myself, I suppose.'

'Wow. Could you say all that again, without stopping?'

'No, I bloody well couldn't. Well?'

'Touchy, touchy.'

'You're the second person to use that word in relation to me in the last five minutes. A girl could get paranoid.'

'Sounds like an interesting disease.'

'Catherine! Are you or are you not doing anything else tomorrow?'

'Nah, just some shopping of my own. I was thinking of dropping into that den of iniquity up near Christchurch tomorrow night. The cutie dropped me and I could do with a night out and a few pints among the Great Leather-Jacketed Ones.'

'Christ, I haven't done that for ages. What about that place in George's Street? It was such a kip but it used to be the best venue when I was in college.'

'Closed absolutely years ago, darling. Where have you been?'

'Working.'

'A likely story but I believe you.' Catherine was gently sarcastic. 'D'ya want to come straight out – hee, hee, I'm such a punster youngster – to the house or shall I be gentlemanly and meet you in town?'

'I'll drop out to the house if I can remember how to get there. Knowing me I'll get hopelessly lost and you'll get a telephone call from West Kerry at three in the morning.'

'Now that I don't believe,' Catherine chuckled. 'Do you want to stay the night? There's loads of room in the manor.'

'I might just take you up on that. The weather's so fuck-ing unpredictable and I don't think I'd get through an evening with those Great Leather-Jacketed Ones of yours without serious quantities of heavy alcohol,' Helen thought for a few moments. 'Okay, why not?'

'Brilliant. I must away now to inform mother that we have a guest. Must break it to her gently or she might have one of her turns, you know.'

'Jesus Christ!'

'It was a joke, Helen. You know, one of those witty things that most people laugh at except serious journalists with no sense of humour and odd bogger accents.'

'At least I didn't get dropped from a hockey team for turning up drunk at training nor did I get dumped recently by any "foreign cuties",' Helen retaliated swiftly.

'Touch, wagon. See you tomorrow,' said Catherine cheerfully. She hung up.

Catherine's mother had the same grey eyes along with a melodic Cork accent undercut with harsher Dublin tones, but she could easily have been someone else's parent, so slight was the physical resemblance. She also had an endearing aversion to the word Missus and a fondness for being called by her name, Maggie. Helen was charmed by the time her only daughter bounced down the stairs, swinging hard enough out of the banister to make it creak.

'Well, will you look at what the neighbour's cat's gone and dragged in?' she drawled.

'Whatever you're selling, we ain't buyin'. No, ma'am. Want some lunch?'

'Thanks, but no. I got some on the road.'

'Rather a strange place to eat one's meals, I would have thought. C'mon, I'll stick the kettle on – even though I'm sure it won't suit me! – and you can drop your bag in the rather grandly named Blue Room. The colour scheme's a bit over-powering, especially in the early hours when one is langered. You have been warned.'

They pottered around a frigid pre-Christmas Bray for the afternoon, poking into ships and sneering at varying standards of tacky festive decorations before strolling as far as the seafront for coffee in a semi-deserted pub.

'Why don't we go for something to eat tonight before we hit that den of iniquity you seem to know so well?' Helen suggested when they were settled at the one table next to a window. 'Know anywhere nice in town?'

'Nice, nice, nice. What an overused word. Let me see. There's a great little pizza place on Stephen's Green that's worth trying if the garlic doesn't kill us. We'd better hope all the Great Leather-Jacketed Ones are eating Italian tonight too, or we'll have no chance of getting a dance, never mind anything more… um… interested.' Catherine sniggered lasciviously.

'I'm not looking and I'm not really interested. Sleeping with someone complicates things.' Helen squirmed as soon as she'd said it.

Catherine regarded her frankly, amazed amusement shading her eyes a cloudier grey. 'Not always,' she said simply.

'Well, maybe not but I've got to concentrate on the job. Colm's fifty-five and he could be retiring at sixty. Philip's the deputy but he's not interested and in five years I should be just about qualified for a decent shot at it.'

'We could all be dead in five years, Helen. Don't forget about wine, women and song while you're hiding behind stacks of gutter-press newspapers and a by-line down there in the bogs.'

'I'll manage the wine if it's brought for me and the song if it's sung by someone else, thanks.' Helen rubbed the condensation on one small window pane with her thumb. 'I'll leave the women to professionals like you.'

'Are you calling me a prostitute?' Catherine's eyes glinted with devilment.

'Of course not. Prostitutes get paid for it.' Helen paused. 'In your case, I'm sure it's the other way 'round.'

'Bitch!'

'Tart!'

They both looked out the window, laughing.

'At least tonight you'll get to see a professional in action, dearie,' Catherine ventured.

'Did it take you that long to think that line up?' Helen retorted. The look in Catherine's eyes stopped her next quip. 'A professional? Hmm, I hope so.' Helen's gauche words hung in the air. She felt Catherine's eyes on the side of her burning face and glanced at the square hand resting easily on the edge of the table. Her internal stranger considered. As if Catherine had read the hidden thought, the hand moved closer and tugged at her sleeve.

'Penny for them.'

'No way, cheapskate. A penny isn't as valuable as it used to be.' Helen reached for her watch, noticing the growing dark. 'Fuck. Is that the time?'

Catherine failed to hide a smile as she watched Helen frantically search her pockets for the car key that couldn't be there. 'You left them at home, Hel. We're on foot, remember?' She shrugged on her coat and walked away, chuckling.

'I knew that! I was looking for my wallet and don't call me Hel or I'll tell your mother about your sordid secret and then your days of hot dinners will be over forever. Your hear me? Forever!' She followed Catherine, her emotional stranger noting the tapers of a youthful, athletic shape with an artist's eye that Helen had never possessed. She walked out into the freezing Wicklow dust and watched Catherine as she gazed across the narrow beach with eyes the same colour as a rustling winter sea.

'I love the sea. Don't you?' Catherine said quietly. 'It only whispers most of the time and yet it's so powerful.'

'Yes. It's powerful alright but only when there's an angry storm about,' Helen replied. She shivered. 'Let's go, Catherine, Empress of all the Sandhills. I'm cold.'

Helen dressed with unaccustomed care, using a wet hairbrush with vigour on unmanageable, wiry kinks with minds of their own. She hated the waves in her short dark hair and the functional, wire-framed spectacles that gave her a slightly puzzled expression. Her month-long trial – and it was a *trial* – with contact lenses ended when the twenty-third person asked her if someone belonging to her had died: the twenty-third person was the district court judge in Westport. After that, Helen disposed of the contact lenses permanently.

She wasn't exactly bad-looking, she thought. She was tall and fairly slim with reasonable proportions. Helen sighed and threatened one wayward curl with the handle of the brush but she knew the threat was ineffectual and would only make her bad-humoured. Surveying her full-length reflection in the mottled mirror on one side of the Blue Room, she sighed impatiently.

'You look like a frigging vampire, Helen Dunne,' scolded her pale, black-clad reflection. She finished struggling with a shoelace and threw on her trench coat when Catherine roared up the stairs that she'd like to get going before closing time if at all possible.

'You look nice,' Catherine remarked airily as they walked towards the local DART station companionably.

'Nice, nice, nice. What an overused word. Humph. It's easy to say that when it's pitch black out.'

'A very ungracious way to take a compliment. Don't they teach you people any manners down there in the bogs? Anyway, my night vision's so good I could've been a pilot.'

'So how do you go about explaining why you are, in

fact, a civil servant specializing in local authority tenants buying their corporation flats?'

'That's easy. With my looks and brains and all 'round charisma, I'm practically a national treasure so it wouldn't have been right to work for the mere private sector.'

'Oh, right. That's a great explanation. And by the way, they do teach us manners in the bogs, as you so poetically put it. At least we don't suffer from big heads, superiority complexes, insufferable accents and West Brit attitudes.' Helen's steel-topped boot-heels kept time.

Catherine glanced at her sideways, hissed through her teeth and acknowledged the attack with a smile.

'At least there's more talent here than in any Connacht boghole... C'mon, you lazy bog-trotter, or we'll miss the train.'

Apropos of nothing at all, Helen asked: 'So you and the "foreign cutie" are definitely finished?'

'Yup. Never got started really. I'm not cut out to be a cradle-snatcher because it takes for too much energy. That one was old enough to be a confirmed flirt and young enough to be either a tease or indecisive. Are you indecisive, Helen?'

'Sometimes. It depends.'

'On?'

'Circumstances.'

'Very mysterious... Ah, here we are,' Catherine said, borrowing twenty pence to make up her train fare.

After the meal, they sat facing each other across a narrow table in a dark, packed and cavernous bar, listening to outdated hits from some other decade played at a level that made conversation almost impossible.

Helen looked around curiously once they were settled, content to observe with a crisp sense of detachment that was part nature and part requisite professional disengagement. Disco lights periodically cut a swathe through the gloom, alternately illuminating tight, tribal groups as well as the eloquent clasped hands and familiar kisses of seemingly impregnable couples. Some women stood at the bar, drinking long-necked beers and waiting for someone to approach them with a chat-up line or for an opportunity to approach someone else. The worst chat-up line Helen ever heard came up in a similar bar, years before.

'Have you twenty pence? Ring your mother and tell her you won't be home tonight,' the butchest woman she had ever seen on this side of the Atlantic had whispered in her ear after five minutes' discussion about the local gay scene.

Helen smiled at that particular memory: she'd extricated herself neatly and, as she walked towards a taxi rank alone that same evening, she'd sworn she'd write a book some day and include that particular pick-up line. Helen always said that underneath most journalists, there's a frustrated writer. And she even had the sense to admit to herself at the time that it wasn't just the writer in her that was frustrated that night. Still smiling to herself, Helen relaxed but still felt the sharp pull of desperation that scented the atmosphere. These places were all the same. Some people had friends; some didn't. That was the way of the world, yes, but there was something bloody lonely about being alone in a place like this. In her view, there was no loneliness quite like it.

Turning back to face her companion, her internal stranger observed those blunt fingers cupped around a pint glass as Helen noted that Catherine was chatting to a tall woman with shaven hair and a nose-ring. Oblivious to the noise, Catherine was deep in a shouted conversation. Catching Helen's eye, she smiled and mimed a hockey stroke before pointing to the newcomer and introducing them. In the ruckus, the tall woman's name sounded something like Lily but was probably really Billy. Helen mimed back, flexing her arm at the elbow and indicating her pint. At Catherine's vigorous nod, she stood up and shouldered her way to the bar to buy another round. A short woman sitting at the bar asked for the time and tried to catch Helen's eye when she answered politely. Helen braced three pints in both hands and turned away guiltily, feeling heavy eyes on her shoulders as she manoeuvred her way back to the table.

After closing time, the tall woman – who was actually called Milly – went back to her lover at the other end of the bar. Catherine and Helen left and strolled slowly in the general direction of a taxi rank, joking merrily about Helen's refusal of a fifth pint. Helen's refusal had, she said herself, a lot to do with the fact that a four-foot-ten middle-aged biker-type tried to buy it for her. She argued her case with the outrageous verbosity of the seriously tiddly, pulled the laughing Catherine out of the gutter and threw an arm around her shoulders to keep them both steady. Catherine fell easily into step and slipped her hand into the pocket of Helen's coat to keep it warm, remarking on the lack of small change that was the usual residue of a night on the batter.

'Fuck!' they sang in chorus when they saw the length of the taxi queue. Helen, sobered by the contact, pulled away and reached for her cigarettes.

Back in a warm and blissfully silent house, they sat up talking for hours, one on either side of an old-fashioned high-mantled fireplace. Catherine stretched her booted feet towards the hearth. Helen, ankle on knee in her customary pontificating pose, waded through three small bottles of Heineken in an attempt to get either drunk again or sleepy. They talked softly of their families, backgrounds, childhood pets and schooldays. At around four in the morning, they compared awkward teenage crushes on unobtainable but infinitely fascinating P.E. teachers.

Finally, Catherine yawned, stretched and decided it was time for bed. 'I'm knackered,' she announced. 'D'ya want a hot water bottle? The rooms upstairs'll be freezing at this hour. We don't call yours the Blue Room just because of the paint, you know.'

'In that case, yes, thanks. If I go to bed cold, not to mention stone cold sober, I'll never get to sleep.' She waggled her empty bottle. 'This Heineken's awful shite. What did you do to it, distil all the alcohol out and put it on your Weetabix?'

'What? A complaint from the great drinker of Connacht? You have some nerve. Any woman who couldn't finish four pints has no right to complain about my bottles.'

Helen followed her into the kitchen and leaned against a breakfast table set for six while Catherine, yawning, filled the kettle and plugged it in. 'Great night, Helen, apart from you letting the side down,' she commented, turning and restlessly swaying first one way and then the other.

The ensuring silence was broken only by the rising sound of rapidly heating water. Helen vacillated, eyes down. 'I suppose a hug would be out of the question,' she said haltingly, searching for words.

Catherine smiled, arms already reaching. 'How could I refuse when you ask so politely, bog-trotter. A hug is never out of the question when you ask.'

Helen held her breath and slid her arms around Catherine's waist; buried her flushed face in the gentle curve between neck and shoulder and held on tightly. The kettle boiled and switched itself off, gradually leaving an oppressive silence unbroken even by breathing. Catherine began to pull away but Helen held on until breathing deeply was imperative. They talked about nothing in whispers, arms still around each other, Helen's eyes fixed on a point somewhere above Catherine's left ear. Her legs were in danger of collapsing like radio aerials and she was grateful for the support of

the kitchen table. In contrast, Catherine was relaxed and curious, trying to make eye contact and failing.

So close, Helen could smell clean hair and skin but her
internal stranger was sharply aware of an underlying, undeniable bitter spiciness as unique as a fingerprint. Her brain
murmured incessantly, desperately seeking an escape route
that would entail minimal embarrassment. As always, she
took refuge in humour – although afterwards she couldn't
remember what she had said – and the laughing Catherine
looked away. She peeked back quickly, just as Helen's eyes
slid weightily across her mouth. Catherine leaned imperceptibly close, then stopped and flushed as their lips touched
with the lightness of childhood circus candy-floss.

Helen went to bed alone, unsettled and cynically re-
flective before she fell into an exhausted and dreamless but
restless sleep. She had kissed Catherine with unaccustomed
decorousness. Despite the courteous nature of her advances,
her restraint had left every raw nerve bloody and exposed
from the pull of new and half-remembered sensations. Her
body tingled as she recalled the questions asked and answered without recourse to words in the silent kitchen, and
the depths of Catherine's stormy eyes. There was no denying
that Helen had been aroused – mentally stretching in warmth
like a half-asleep but still wakeful kitten before an open fire
– as the kisses went on and on, seconds stretching into minutes. Catherine's confident and almost complacent responses
were unnerving, as if she had predicted that it would happen
just so, on that night, after that day.

Helen's arms had stayed resolutely around Catherine's
waist, her thumbs gently circling, feeling skin through the
soft white shirt. Helen's reticence was unusual and she was
puzzled by it: normally, with someone else, these kisses
would have led to more intimate discoveries without much

delay. By the time she fell asleep, she had steeled herself for the awkwardness that would come with morning. She was resolved to be up, dressed and armed with a good excuse prepared for a swift departure before Catherine was even awake.

She woke to a dim December morning. Catherine was kneeling beside the narrow bed, one hand outstretched, playing with a wayward lock of hair at Helen's temple.

'Mother and the devilish brood have gone to the Mass and to the shops to buy Christmas presents for me… God alone knows how many pairs of socks I'll get this year. Robin wanted to know why you weren't up yet and if you're buying him a present. Jesus, Helen, it's freezing out here… Let me in.' She tugged at the quilt and snuggled close, promising not to put her icy feet near the two cosy ones. Helen's heart beat too fast in the silence and her brain itched with words.

'Catherine, what d'you think you're doing?'

'On the basis of the evidence available to me at this time, I strongly suspect that I'm having a morning cuddle,' she said, tickling the unresponsive initial occupant of the bed. Pausing and thinking hard, chewing her lower lip and musing speculatively, she asked: 'How long has it been since you slept with someone?'

Helen gaped. 'How long has it been since your tact was amputated or were you just born that way?'

'I was born without any. I have no shame. Don't change the subject. I'm waiting.'

Helen sighed and started calculating. 'Over three years,' she said finally, her tone tinged with faint surprise.

Catherine whistled. 'Christ on a bike with the windows down, how did you manage? I'm sure you've a grand little engine when you get it revved up for you by someone who knows how to turn it on…' she said, a smile softening the crudeness of the analogy.

Noting the past tense but deciding to ignore, Helen replied: 'I didn't notice after a while. I burned someone else's feelings once too often and I suppose I've just got used to it. Anyway, I was never that enthusiastic about it… It's too bloody complicated.'

Catherine leaned on one elbow, looking down into her face. 'On the basis of last night's degenerate, if disappointingly polite behaviour, you little tart, I'd say you've just perjured yourself and any jury in the land would agree with me. This court, reclining in the Blue Room of the manor, sentences you to one kiss.'

She bent and kissed the tip of Helen's nose, pausing to smile into her eyes. 'Jesus, Mary, Holy Saint Joseph and the blessed donkey, it's hot in here all of a sudden,' she said. For all the world like a cabaret stripper, she pulled off her night-shirt and flung it over her shoulder in one movement. Helen's frantic heartbeat sent warmer blood pounding along constricting veins. She froze and looked directly into Catherine's amused eyes, staying silent through a warning stare.

'I see,' said Catherine. 'We're pretending to be a consecrated nun, are we? Have we taken vows since last night, young novice? Oh, Helen, you're such a fraud and I can see right through you.' She snuggled close again, rested her head on Helen's shoulder and played with the top button of her dark silk pyjamas.

'Can you?'

'Of course. It's obvious you want to but you're afraid of something. It couldn't possibly be me because I'm a sweet little thing really, very innocent and not at all the marauding dragon I see reflected in your rabbit eyes.'

'Charming.' Helen smiled. 'And if I'm a rabbit, doesn't that make you a complete pervert or something?'

'Without a doubt but at least I got the first smile of the new day for my trouble.' The top button of Helen's pyjama jacket opened but it was no accident. Catherine was suddenly serious. Her head still nestling on Helen's shoulder and one hand stroking the hollow between Helen's collar-bones, she whispered: 'Don't be afraid. I like you. I won't hurt you.'

'I'm not afraid. It's just… oh, I don't know… it's just…'

Catherine slid the pyjama top off one shoulder and looked at her sideways, exasperated, then quickly leaned over and kissed, teasing the corner of her mouth with subtle warmth. Helen shivered. Conscious at last of the warm, naked body joined to hers like matching pieces of the same perfect jigsaw, she lodged an acquiescent arm around Catherine's neck and pulled her closer. She saw a flash of relief in Catherine's eyes before she closed her own and kissed open, seething lips. Feeling the sharpness of teeth and soft wetness with her own tongue, her lower abdomen began to pound with the dull, nagging ache of physical desire. She began to strain upwards, mouth frantically exploring the planes and curves of an unfamiliar face.

Clinks of light streaked through the curtains as Catherine flung back the quilt and trawled her body with gentle and forgiving eyes. Helen turned a ferocious pink when Catherine removed her night clothes without haste. She avoided invading thoughts by reaching out one hand and drawing long, narrow fingers across one honeyed breast. Catherine inhaled quickly, her breath catching as she exhaled. Fascinated, Helen and her internal stranger, united for once, watched the rise and fall of Catherine's chest and watched her fingers follow the easy curves that led to waist, stomach and a round, even thigh.

Her insides contracted pleasurably and she felt the beginnings of hungry dew seeping between her legs. Helen surveyed Catherine's square hands with their shorter, blunter fingers and wanted those fingers inside her body, as deep as they would go. Her one desire to be the receptacle shocked her into activity. This had never been her way. Grabbing Catherine by the hair roughly, she looked right into her eyes and slowly pulled her down, kissing her frantically. Their deeper breathing remained unbroken by any whispered words. December clouds rolled in from the sea. The room darkened.

Suddenly strong and with a new determination to fuck the living daylights out of this gorgeous creature, Helen wrestled Catherine onto her back and looked down on her with humourless severity. Slowly lowering her head, she ran her tongue lightly over one anxious nipple and felt it grow hard and urgent in her mouth, swelling to a round, cylindrical shape. Snaking her thigh slowly between Catherine's legs, she waited until she felt wetness and the brush of crinkly dark hair before pushing hard. Catherine arched, groaning, pushing her wetness tighter against Helen.

Helen slid her arm into the small of Catherine's back and roughly pulled her closer, staring into the eyes so close to her own for a long time before letting go. Instinctively, she knew this was going to be good. Mute, she slid one tremulous hand between their bodies across undulating skin, hungry finger-tips tingling in anticipation. She moved her fingers through coarse dark curls gently, slowing and teasing until the silent appeal in Catherine's breathing broke through the fog of self-indulgence. Helen's fingers roamed intensely into the slippery hot velvet of Catherine's body and began to trace long, slow strokes of loving. Catherine growled and stiffened, fingers clutching at Helen's shoulder, nails scoring vivid, uneven crescents.

Helen paused. 'I'm going to fuck you now. Do you her me? I'm going to fuck you the way I want and the way you want, Catherine Mary Lacey. I know what you want but I want to hear you say it,' she said then with more menace than gentleness in her tone.

'I hear you, Helen.'

Reaching down and grasping Helen's wrist, Catherine

whispered: 'I want you to put those wonderful long fingers inside my body, right now. I want you to fuck me, right now. I want you to fuck me until you can feel me coming all over your fingers and my cunt closing around you. I want you. Fuck you, Helen, but I want you.'

Helen pulled Catherine's hand away and lay across her body, nipple to tight nipple, her full weight pressing Catherine down. Seizing her around the shoulders, she pushed her fingers forcefully into Catherine's body and held her while she groaned. Using her thumb to gently polish the smothering wetness, she began thrusting and rotating her fingers, lifting her own body to create space and to enjoy the musky, spicy scent created only when women make love together.

Catherine, surfacing temporarily from the depths of her own pleasure, took her chance. With neither panache nor restraint and hand-cuffed by her own desire, she sank her fingers into Helen, smoothing wetness before sliding demandingly inside. Helen gasped and thrust into Catherine's body with new energy. A long moment shattered into a thousand silvered shards. Then, knowing now what they wanted and both giving and getting it, they fought each other. Lips caressing outraged breasts and teeth nipped skin too sensitive to feel the hurt. Fingers probed, questioned, explored, soaked. There was anger but they were hypnotized by the rhythmical tones of their vicious bodies as they lay together in a hot silence cracked by an intimate but wordless vocabulary.

Catherine came first. Oblivious to her own cries as she was thrown over a long edge by Helen's skilful advances. As Catherine's body closed and opened and closed again along her lover's fingers, just as she knew it would, Helen felt her own body rising, climbing steps of stairs in response. Catherine increased her pace, thrusting in and out, her mouth fixed to one nipple that was attached directly by an intense, red-hot wire to Helen's heart. When Helen came, screaming obscenities, she began to cry, but hid her face and bit Catherine's shoulder so that she wouldn't see.

Later, she lay in wandering calm, the drowsy Catherine cradled in her arms.

A door slammed and feet pounded on the stairs. 'Are you pair of drunks not up yet? It's after twelve. D'you think you might get up before dark and bring those empties down to the bottle bank.'

Catherine was in her night-shirt and at the door before Helen reacted. 'All right, Mother, we're up. I was just giving the lazy, good-for-nothing bog-trotter a shout.' She turned and winked. 'Fancy some breakfast sweetie? Your extraordinary transformation into a grade A sexpot has left me starving. Get thee to a shower while I be a good little wifie and check you the victuals.' She crossed the room, kissed Helen's ear and dashed off, whistling.

In the afternoon, when the rain cleared and a brisk wind blew from the East, Catherine suggested a drive. Helen, grateful for a chance to leave a suddenly claustrophobic house and escape from Catherine's insatiably curious youngest brother, Robin, chivalrously opened the car door.

'Not only do you fuck like an Amazon but you're also a perfect lady… With that combination, I'll be spoiled in a week,' Catherine remarked, patting her cheek in full view of the living-room window.

By unspoken agreement, they walked the rutted paths and climbed the uneven stone steps of Killiney Hill, pausing often to catch shortened breath and savour the view. In December, Killiney had a down-trodden bleakness that pleased Helen. Catherine, who was not fond of their desolate surroundings, described the Summer sun twinkling through heavily laden trees and the view of a ferry, minuscule and insignificant, crossing the level blue pond to Dun Laoghaire.

Without thinking, they walked hand in hand, ignorant of the puzzled, embarrassed glances of the other Sunday strollers. At the top, Helen found a level stone near the obelisk and sat down, reaching for her cigarettes.

Catherine scolded. 'They're bad for you. Why not enjoy the fresh air?' Helen smiled and patted the stone beside her. Catherine sat. Neither spoke for a time. Helen smoked silently, eyes on a distant horizon and, when she did speak, her words were harsh and directed more to herself than to her quietly waiting companion.

'I'm truly fecked if I know what's going on. I was having a nice, boring and uncomplicated little life. I didn't think this was going to happen but now it has and I'm shagged if I know what to do next. Why did you have to come along and make a fucking application to be number six in the depressing, lengthening list of my failures? I've never had an experience like this, never. Every other time, when morning came, I just made the bed, pulled down the shutters, shut up shop, said goodbye nicely with a decent quota of manufactured regret and pottered on my merry way. I can't seem to do that today; not with you. But where's the shagging point in asking for more? I mean, look at the geography, for fuck's sake... I live on the other side of this bog island. I work in a job with irregular hours like you wouldn't believe. And don't even mention telephones, the fucked-up postal service or Iarnrod fucking Eireann... It would never work...' Her voice trailed away into a hard silence. She flicked her cigarette butt away angrily.

'We got this far, didn't we?'

'Yes, we did, damn it all to hell and back on a pony-trap. I've been having myself on for the past three months, kidding myself into thinking I was looking for a friend, a laugh, a drinking buddy. Bollix. Absolute and utter bollix. I knew exactly what I was doing. I wanted to get into your knickers. I wanted you and I got you.'

'God, Helen, your language is outrageous. Convent girl, my eye.'

'Don't change the fucking subject.'

Catherine sighed. 'So?'

'Exactly.'

'But I thought you weren't interested in me.'

'Personally, I was convinced it was the other way around. Jesus, but you know how to play it cool. I have this passion for chasing after unobtainable skirt – or tight trousers, in your case – because it's safer that way. What you can't catch can't do your head in. What the fuck am I supposed to do now?'

'I think that should be "what the fuck are *we* supposed to do now?".' Catherine reached into Helen's pocket for a cigarette, shrugging. 'If you can't beat em, etcetera, etcetera, blah-de-blah blah. Promise me something.'

'Oh, good Christ, no. don't ask me to promise you things or I swear I'll get hysterical, jump off this fucking hill and swim to England.'

'Don't be such a drama queen, Helen. Just promise me you won't disappear into the wilds of bog-trot land, never to be seen again. Don't pop out for a packet of cigarettes and send me a postcard from sunny Australia weeks later. Don't break your back trying to pull down shutters when there's really no need. Let's just potter along for a while and have great times together. I'll try not to put any pressure on you. That's Linda's specialty, not mine, remember?'

'I remember.'

They fell silent, each remembering their respective entanglements with their difficult mutual ex. Helen had stuck her for three weekends more than ten years previously before giving Linda what she charmingly referred to as 'the flick'. Linda, the rubber-ball of the Dublin scene, had bounced back and eventually into baby-dyke Catherine's arms.

'You must be nearly due a visit there, even though I don't know why you bother,' Helen whispered.

'Don't remind me. I promised to meet her for lunch next week. I haven't seen her since that weekend in September when you and I met. Well, I know I'd met you before then, but I think of that day as being the day we really met.'

Helen turned and smiled. 'I never thought a game of cards could be so erotic... and with a chaperone, too. Please, Catherine, don't say anything to her over the grapefruit cocktail... it'd suit her to see herself as betrayed by both of us.'

'I haven't a notion, but you know how perceptive she can be. She can smell funny business and recent shagging from fifty miles and, anyway, I'm a bad liar. I wouldn't be surprised if she tried to hit me a belt.'

'Ah, give over, she wouldn't.'

'She already has.'

'What?' Helen felt her skin beginning to crawl. 'When?'

'When I told her I couldn't take any more of her tantrums and that it was over. It took me hours to convince her I was serious and, when I finally did, she walloped me so hard I hit the wall. It wasn't the first time. She's so much smaller and slighter than me and I just couldn't bring myself to slap her back. That day, I should have seen it coming and ducked but I was being a big, brave and very stupid dyke.' Catherine's eyes were dark grey, shadowed by lowered eyelids.

Helen turned and hugged her, squeezing warm breath into the air. 'Catherine, if I'd known that I wouldn't have been so rough with you this morning. I just didn't know. You have to believe that I could never do that to you. If you don't, there's not much point, is there?'

'There's a world of difference between being roughed up by the girl of your dreams in bed and being battered around the place by a tiny, half-mental asshole. I believe you,

Helen. Do you honestly think I'd have climbed into your bed if I could see that in you? But then, I didn't see it in her either, at first…'

'Ah, c'mon, Catherine. I'm not saying what happened wasn't wrong, but you can't judge me by her standards or blame me for what she's done to you. I'm so scared of touching people with intent that I can't play contact sports anymore.'

'You're not always scared of touching people with intent, you appalling little slut.' Catherine was smiling. She hesitated for a moment, then sighed. 'You're a journalist; I suppose you know the meaning of the word probation?' she said.

'It's part of the criminal justice system. DPOA… dismissed under the Probation of Offender Act. We hear it in court for minor offences all the time.'

'Be serious. I suggest we do some probation.'

'Oh. For how long?'

'I thought maybe twenty years or so, but that's just for starters.'

Helen stood, frowning and rooting around in her jeans pockets. Then she smiled crookedly and said just one word, holding out her hand.

'Okay.'

Chapter Two

ALL RELATIVE

At home on Christmas Day, Helen looked at her ageing father who was seated in his customary place at the head of the table. Through the window behind Frank she could see snowflakes still falling softly in the approaching dusk, adding to the thin blanket of hushed white already covering the garden. The snowman's carrot nose had fallen off again. This was the first white Christmas for years, an unusual event in what Helen usually referred to as 'this wet hole of a country'. Finally, Nora sat down. In the soft candlelight illuminating the table, Helen could see new grey in her mother's hair.

'I'd like to propose a toast,' Helen said, reaching for her wine-glass.

'Go ahead,' said Frank. 'You're the wordsmith in the family. If anyone can find the right words, it'll be you.'

The shadow of Helen's only sister Caroline, killed by a drunken-driver four years previously, fell across the festive table. Caroline would have been three years older than Helen, had she lived. Caroline had been the brilliant one in the family; an environmental scientist based in California for years before homesickness brought her home. Helen missed her still. She had been witty and sensitive and a damn good friend. The driver got a suspended sentence.

Before Helen could speak, her older and prematurely balding brother Andy, leaned across the table to pull a knife out of his daughter's hand.

'How many times have I told you not to put that in your mouth? How many?'

'Loads, Daddy.' Four-year-old Maria was near to tears. Her Christmas ribbon was attached to wiry curls but it was already lopsided.

'So why do you keep doing it then?'

'I dunno, Daddy. I forgot.'

'I can't understand why Santa bothered to bring lovely toys to such a bold little girl. There are plenty of other good girls who should have got them. I think I'll write to Santa and tell him to take them back.'

Maria bent her head and hiccoughed as only a tearful child does, tears dripping silently onto tiny, twisting hands. Helen felt an unreasonable surge of irritation: she often wanted to beat Andy about the head for no logical reason. She put her arm around her niece, squeezed gently, and raised her glass.

'To those who are no longer with us, especially Caroline, and to absent friends. May those who are gone and those who are living, but not with us, find peace and happiness wherever they are today.'

Her mother's eyes held Helen's over the rim of her glass for a moment. Then Nora burst into activity. 'Frank, will you carve the turkey please? Andrew, pass me Helen's lighter… this candle's gone out again. Maria, put that down, child! Didn't you hear what your Daddy said?'

Maria giggled and turned to her aunt. 'Auntie Helen, what's an Amazon?'

Helen caught Mary's eye in a silent plea for guidance

but Mary hid a smile behind her napkin and indicated with her eyebrows that, this time, her sister-in-law was very much on her own.

'And why does my Tinkerbell want to know?' Helen asked.

'I heard it on the telly… It's a nice word.'

'Let me see. Oh, yes, the Amazon is a huge forest made of lots of big trees.'

'Can we go an' see it after dinner?'

'No, 'fraid not, Tinkerbell. It's a long, long way from here. And I'll tell you something else: because the Amazon has big huge trees and because they grow in the earth in the same way as little girls live with their mammies until they grow up big and strong, sometimes really strong women are called Amazons too.'

'Wow!' Maria's eyes were round with amazement. 'Are you an Amazon, Auntie Helen?'

Nora started to choke. Mary sniggered behind her napkin. Andy just glowered at her and Frank cleared his throat nervously, a little uncomfortable at the turn the conversation had taken.

'Hardly, child, but you might grow up to be one if you eat up all your dinner,' Helen replied. Maria immediately applied herself to mashed potatoes with enthusiasm. Mary applauded silently from her end of the table; Nora sighed with relief and Frank patted his daughter on the shoulder approvingly. Andy glowered on but that was nothing unusual. Wine flowed freely and the massive meal disappeared slowly.

'Andrew, did you hear that John Holmes – you remember him, you went to school with him – won't last much longer,' Nora said. 'It must be a poor Christmas in that house today. That poor lad and his poor mother. I remember you and he used to pal around when you were teenagers and he was such a polite lad.'

'Really, Ma? Do they know what's wrong with him? Is it cancer or what? I thought he'd gone back to America after he was over in the summer.'

'Oh, he did, he did indeed, but he came home again six weeks ago… came home to die, I suppose. His misfortunate mother is in an awful state altogether. I met her at Mass the other day and she was telling me… well, it was in confidence but I know it won't go any further… that he's in the serious stages of Aids and has developed pneumonia, it seems. The house is in a complete uproar. Of course, he's an only son too, not that that really makes it any better or worse.'

Andy's face hardened. 'Jesus, did you say Aids? I was going to say I might pop around to see him but I couldn't be bothered. Aids? God Almighty, I should have guessed he was one of those limp-wristed perverts. That explains why he never married, the queer. I have no sympathy for him. All those bloody faggots should be locked up for spreading that disease instead of the country spending money on medical treatment for them.'

Helen's glass froze midway between the table and her mouth during this unseasonal tirade. Gently and deliberately, she put the glass on the table and lowered her head to eye Andy over the rim of her spectacles. It was her customary don't-fuck-with-me-and-expect-to-survive pose. Nora recognized it and struggled to fill the uncomfortable silence.

'Ah, now, Andrew, don't be so hard on the lad. Sure isn't it little enough he has now and his life slipping away before his family's eyes. He'll probably be dead in a year or so. It wouldn't hurt to be a bit more Christian about it.'

'What's a faggot, Auntie Helen?' Maria looked at her trustingly, balancing a sliver of turkey on her fork precariously.

'It's a little stick that some people use to light the fire with, Tinkerbell.' Helen paused, looking her brother in the eye. 'Drop it, Andy. Drop it now.'

'Ah, Helen, for Jaysus' sake, don't be so hypersensitive. I was only speaking the truth.'

'And I'm saying drop it. Now, Andy. You're an ignorant bigot. You don't even know how Johnny caught it. It could have been drugs or a blood transfusion or a woman and you know it. Even if he *is* playing for the other team, what difference does that make? He's still Johnny. At least most gays have sense these days and use condoms, unlike some drunk breeders after their Christmas staff parties. And what faggot ever did you any harm, anyway? Is there something interesting from your past you'd like to share with us?' She sneered openly.

'Listen to me, the likes of you and your ultra-modern attitudes would turn this country into a moral cesspool. Anything goes in this new liberal Ireland, is that it?'

'It's Christmas. Leave it!' Frank's courtroom voice, little used at home, silenced them both. 'I think we all know the views of both of you on that topic well enough by now without hearing the same boring argument rehashed today at this table. I will not have this bickering in my house on Christmas Day or any other day. Get outside if you want to behave like children, the pair of you.'

'Sorry, Dad. I shouldn't have lost my cool,' Helen said, quickly repentant.

Mary touched Andy's arm in encouragement but he stared resolutely at the ceiling for a long moment. 'Oh, all right, I'm sorry, Dad,' he said finally.

'That's all right, then,' said Frank. 'Now, Nora, where is the traditional trifle lurking? You know how much I love your trifle and even though you've been threatening not to make one this year, I know you made it while I was out walking this morning. You had the time, the opportunity, the weapons and the motive. Where is it? Come on, woman, out with it or you'll be had up for contempt of court!'

Nora grinned girlishly, lowered her eyes and then bustled off to fetch the dessert. Helen admired her parents and their relationship. Frank and Nora had been married for forty years but his eyes still lit up when she came into a room. Nora thought there was no husband and provider quite as wonderful as Frank. It would have been corny if it wasn't so damn sweet.

The telephone rang at seven while Maria was showing her aunt how to make a helicopter with a wing and only two rotors from her new Lego set.

'Helen, it's someone called Catherine Lacey. Are you in?'

'Everyone's in on Christmas Day, Mother.'

Nora handed over the telephone and flicked at her daughter's legs with a wet dishcloth on her way back to the kitchen where Frank was making heavy weather of filling the dishwasher.

'Hi, sweetheart. Merry Christmas. I'm lonely without you.' Catherine's voice was wishful and her words slightly slurred.

'A likely story and Merry Christmas to you too, you drunken bowsie. How many did you have for dinner?'

'Well, we could only fit two of the neighbours in the cookpot so there wasn't really enough to go around.'

'Catherine! Okay. I'll rephrase the question to suit the master of the double meaning. How many people ate their Christmas dinner in your mother's house?'

'Ten. Why d'ya want to know, anyway?'

'Ten. Ten whole people. And you're lonely without little old me?'

'You're fishing for compliments, madam, and I just won't have it. You know why: they're all here and you're not.

I must be just missing you, I suppose, unlikely as that may seem to you. And how is Christmas proceeding in the Dunne household down the bogs?'

'Truly stupendous. Maria's been asking for my definition of an Amazon and Andy's of the opinion that all faggots should be locked up and left to die for spreading Aids.'

'I beg your pardon?'

Helen explained, making the story seem funnier than it had actually been at the time.

'Excellent definition of an Amazon, darling, but forgive me if I say that your sweet brother sounds like a complete pillock.'

'He was a prat at birth but that's what teaching adolescent gougers in Cork for 13 years does to a person, I suppose.'

'I'm telling my Corkonian mother you said that!'

'Go right ahead and then I'll be forced to beat you to death with your very own, if sadly underused hockey stick,' Helen replied sweetly. 'And how's the festive season going at your end, now that we've established that you didn't in fact eat the neighbours?'

'Awful. Robin ate too many sweets before the dinner and puked on the cat. Mother nearly had a fit. T'would have been bad enough normally, but the cat was sitting on the holy father home from the missions at the time, so she was rightly mortified.'

'Where did he come from?'

'The missions, dimwit. He's a cousin of my late lamented father but at least he's keeping up the family trait... bent as a safety pin, you know, but would deny it to his Maker.'

'Not like some I could mention who are in favour of borrowing a megaphone and shouting the odds from the town square.'

'Ooh, you bitch! Leave me alone, you awful cow. Hey, sweetheart, I really, really miss you. Is there any chance at all you could escape that undoubtedly claustrophobic household for a couple of days before you go back to work? I know you're going to say it's snowing and I don't really expect you to start cross-country skiing up the bogs. I've learned the train timetable off by heart for you. I want my Christmas kisses and I want them now, not to mention other, more unspeakable intimacies. Did I ever tell you how much I like the shape of your left tit? I like the right one too but, to be honest, the left one is really adorable.'

'Will you knock it off, you fuckwit,' Helen replied, laughing. 'Honestly, anyone'd think you were sex-starved or something, but you can't fool me because I know you're not. I'll see what I can do. It should be all right because Andy and Mary are staying here for a few days with Maria so I wouldn't be missed as much. How are you fixed for the day after tomorrow?'

'Better than good. I can't wait.'

'You can and you will. I'll get the morning train and you can get up out of the scratcher and meet me at the station to carry my bags, if you can tear yourself away from playing happy families with the holy father, the cat and the puking brother.'

Maria pulled at Helen's sleeve, pouting. 'C'mon, Auntie Helen, we haven't finished the hellocockter yet.'

'Sweetheart, I have to go. The niece is obviously considering mechanical engineering for a career. We're making a hellocockter from Lego.'

'Okay, okay. How can I compete with that? I'll see you the day after tomorrow. I'll start crossing off the hours now…' Catherine said, adopting a melodramatic Southern belle persona.

'Get a life, you fool,' Helen interrupted. 'a happy Christmas to all your tribe, pet.'

'Okay so. See you. Take care, Helen.'

'Only if you promise me you'll do the same.'

'Don't ask me to promise you things or I swear I'll get hysterical, jump off this effing stool and crawl into your knickers.'

'Get lost, Catherine!'

'See you in less than forty-eight hours, wench.' Catherine said and hung up.

Catherine was wearing a red Santa hat when the Sligo train arrived at Connolly Station, and that more or less set the tone for their couple of days together. The crowd staying in Lacey's for Christmas meant they had to share a room, an inconvenience that Maggie Lacey apologised for profusely but that neither Catherine nor Helen minded at all, for obvious reasons. They spent two long, lazy mornings in the faded grandeur of Catherine's chaotic bedroom on the second floor of the ramshackle old house.

Undisturbed, except occasionally by the huge, lazy and impossibly fat cat called Bob – short for Roberta, no less – they murmured and kissed and cuddled. Sometimes, they were simply silent, listening to each other's heartbeats, and watching snowflakes fall through the panes of the one high window in the room.

In the afternoons, they walked for miles, once taking the Dart as far as Dun Laoghaire to walk the slippery pier and watch the moored boats, tied up for Winter, bobbing peacefully in the harbour. The pier was popular and hundreds of people walked along briskly, trying to shake the effects of an excess of festive cheer. It was cold too but they were well wrapped up. Helen wore boots, gloves, a scarf, her new long coat – Catherine's Christmas present to her – and the trilby hat she didn't have the courage to wear at home, not to mention two sweaters. Catherine said her bright red cheeks and all the layers of clothing made her look like a thawed snowman who'd been on the piss. Catherine wore a black leather jacket over a sweatshirt and jeans, as well as fluffy pink mufflers over her ears. The mufflers were a present from the holy father cousin. Catherine loved them because they were so twee and looked so ridiculous teamed up with her short biker jacket. The mufflers meant their chat was full of half understood words and a painful *non sequitur* or two.

'I really need to get fitter,' Helen puffed as they reached the first elbow in the middle of the pier.

'Fish? Are you mad? Fish? Where? What d'ya want fish for?' Catherine said, lifting one pink pom-pom away from her ear. Helen doubled over at her bewildered expression, laughing enough to wheeze, her breath condensing in the bitter Winter air.

They were half frozen by the time they got home that afternoon but thawed out later playing Monopoly with Catherine's three brothers. Gerry was eleven and beginning to lose patience with being constantly shadowed by his nine-year-old brother, Paul. Poor Paul, anxious to please, kept swapping streets for less than they were worth and ended up owning only the electricity company and two train stations. Robin, aged seven, didn't really understand how to play but he muddled through, assisted at various times by Catherine and Helen. The difference in the two women's personalities were obvious from how they played the game. Helen took calculated risks, made wise investments, put her money into property and stayed out of jail. Catherine, on the other hand, spent money like it was going out of fashion and ended up with nothing left for that rainy day when she landed on Mayfair. It was owned by Helen and included a newly constructed red hotel.

'That's it, I'm fecked,' she said. 'Of course, I could offer to pay you in kind.'

'What do you mean? You have to pay her and if you

haven't got the money you'll have to mortgage Oxford Street and Pall Mall or you're out of the game.' Gerry was suspicious, thinking that perhaps his sister was going to pull a fast one.

'No way. Pay up or you're out,' Helen agreed, laughing and giving Gerry a thumbs-up sign. 'She's history now, boyo.'

'Fine. I don't want to play with you anymore anyway. I bet you cheat,' Catherine said, sticking out her lower lip petulantly for effect.

'It's all right, Catherine. I'll help you. I have money here you can have if you really need it.' Robin looked up at his sister adoringly.

'No thanks, Robbie, you keep it. I have a feeling you're going to need it to pay off one of these sharks,' she said, getting up off the floor and picking up the new acoustic guitar that was her Christmas present from Helen. 'I must practice my cords anyway.'

The game, punctuated by whoops of triumph, groans of despair and the odd mangled guitar chord, lasted about three hours before Maggie called a halt for dinner. The turkey had finally been sent to its last resting place in the composting barrel down the back and the chips, bangers and beans went down a treat with adults and youngsters alike.

That last evening of their time together was a Saturday so Helen and Catherine went back to the club near Christchurch. Catherine, who knew dozens of people on the scene, never left Helen's side all night. They held hands all the time, even when they were having conversations with different people. They were still at the stage of learning something new about each other every day and they were happy. It was Christmas, after all.

As they waited at Connolly for the Sligo train, Catherine presented Helen with her Santa hat and three bottles of Heineken.

'Some sustenance for the journey, darling,' she said. 'If you drink the bottles, put on the hat and start singing, the passengers might throw you enough coppers to pay your fare.'

They parted on very good terms, thrilled at the prospect of seeing each other again within a week. As the train pulled out and the dregs of December edged into January and another year, Helen noted that Catherine stayed on the platform, one hand raised in a signal of farewell.

Helen struggled up from sleep to the shrill fire siren of an unfamiliar alarm. Feeling an even more unfamiliar arm reach across her body towards the bedside table, she grabbed it and held on tightly, fighting back with all the unconscious ferocity of a dream-chaser. In the struggle, the clock was knocked to the floor, its final ring a hollow, off-key wail against bare varnished boards.

'Helen, wake up, it's just me. You're okay. Wake up, Helen!'

Helen opened her eyes and stared suspiciously at the face hovering in near darkness just inches from her own without even a flicker of recognition. She reached out and switched on the bedside lamp.

'Helen?' Catherine was puzzled but warmth flooded back into Helen's eyes at the tone.

'Good morning. What's that your name is again? For a second there, I didn't know who you were or, more to the point, what you were doing in my bed.' She grinned.

'No kidding, Sherlock. Now that you do know, would you mind letting go?' Helen relaxed her tenacious grip and freed Catherine's forearm, sighing remorsefully at the pink-and-white imprints of her fingers on finely-haired, honey-tinted skin. 'I'm so sorry. I must have been still half asleep. I just didn't know...'

Catherine looked up from massaging her arm. 'I didn't realise you're so strong. It's okay, sweetie, but I'm warning you, next time I'm sleeping next to the alarm clock or else I'll get a certificate showing that I have a right to be here without being molested by a Mad Thing.'

'Molested? Oh Lordie. I could be arrested.' Helen yawned. 'I can see the headline now… *Molester arrested in dawn lesbo swoop.* What time is it?'

Catherine performed contortions, leaning over Helen's body to read the alarm clock upside-down. 'I do believe it's seven hours and thirty-two minutes after midnight.'

'Shite. I'm really sorry. The new clock was a great idea for a present but unfortunately yours truly forgot to set the alarm for a time more befitting a Saturday. And as well as waking you up at this ungodly hour, I've been and gone and attacked you as well. I'm sorry. It's just that I've never had to share a bed with anyone. Even when we were kids me and Caroline had separate rooms. I was asleep and I just wasn't expecting anyone to be here. I suppose I must have been having a dream and then I panicked or something.'

'Will you give it a rest, twit, although I'm sure you'll understand why I'm going to graciously refuse if you ever challenge me to arm wrestle. In my case, cowardice is definitely the better part of valour.' Catherine smiled and lay down on her side, one arm around Helen's waist, lips just touching one bare shoulder.

Yawning, Helen stretched, dislodging the lips and nearly knocking Catherine's head off with her elbow. 'Oops. I'm making a habit of beating up the wifie,' she said. Helen snuggled back down under the duvet, closed her eyes for five seconds and then started mooching around the bed. 'Fuck it, I'm wide awake now. What would you like to do today, lover?'

'Work up the energy to leap out of bed, brush my teeth,

make coffee and then leap back into bed again. Then I might have my wicked way with you. I think it's time to get to know a little more about you, strictly in the biblical sense.'

'Ah, be serious, Catherine. The daylight hours are so short at this time of year and it might be nice to see what you look like without the aid of artificial lighting. Do you even remember me? I'm about five foot six, I have dark hair, impossibly kinky – a bit like my morals – my eyes are blue and …'

'But I am serious. I'd like nothing better than to stay here with you all day, you fascinating creature.'

Helen gave her a playful dig in the ribs. 'C'mon, let's get up for an early breakfast and go for a walk. C'mon, lazybones, all you ever want to do is stay in bed and get up to no good.'

'Ah, Helen. Let's stay here.'

'Why?'

Catherine paused for a long time, chewing her bottom lip. 'Well, because it's the only time I hear you say anything.'

'Like what?'

'Like what's going on for you, for us. You never really talk about us except when we're in bed. I can't get anything out of you otherwise.'

'There's the pot calling the kettle black-arse. You're not exactly full of chat about us either.'

'That's because I promised not to put pressure on you, remember?'

'I remember. So Catherine, Empress of all the Bedsheets, now that we're here and awake and not shagging each other's brains out, what's really going through that alarmingly attractive head of yours?'

'I just need to hear you say things, sometimes.'

'What kind of things?'

'I don't know.'

'Catherine? Come on, my little cabbage, give me at least a slight idea of what you're on about. You're doing more flutin' around than James Galway this morning.'

'Well, I can tell you this… I find you very difficult to resist, Helen. I just wonder if you know that I live for the times I can lie cuddled up with you like this, with nothing between your kin and mine. I wonder if you know I'm quite besotted with you, that I already love you a little.'

'What?'

'I said I already…'

'I heard what you said but I'm not sure I believe what I'm hearing. You must take me for a right eejit. You hardly know me, Catherine, and here you are spouting on about love as if this was a grand passion in the great French tradition. I like you, bean-face, but half-a-dozen weekends together and a few telephone calls do not a grand passion make.' Helen's voice was harsh, even unkind.

Catherine bristled. 'Take it easy. You asked me and I told you. I didn't mean anything by it. I didn't mean that you have to say it's all reciprocated. I was just stating a fact and if you can't hack it then don't take it out on me. What's happening? Why do you always do this whenever I hint at an L word that isn't lust?'

'That's not the only L word I have a problem with: I'd much rather be a has-been that a lez-bean.' Helen tickled Catherine under the ribs, desperately trying to tighten the mood.

'That's all you ever do. You change the subject or crack a joke every time there's the slightest hint of trouble or mention of feelings that have nothing to do with bedtime fun. Why can't you just talk to me?'

Helen flung back the duvet and climbed out of bed, reaching for her bathrobe. 'All right, you want to talk, so talk. What the hell do you want to know? What do you want from me?'

'I can't talk to you when you're like this. It's not a question of what I want. I'm just wondering if we should start looking at this as something a bit deeper than you're pretending it is, but you won't even give me half a chance to explain.'

'I see, you've changed your mind. Now you don't want to talk. What is it you want from me? A lifetime commitment? You're always asking how I feel but I don't bloody know. I like you and I care about you but it could be different tomorrow. Nothing's permanent, not me or you or this house or this street and you can't predict the future any more than you can predict which small African state will have a coup d'état next or whether or not Mayo will win the Connacht championship in the Summer. Now get off my back, Catherine. I told you before that I don't bloody know how to do relationships. I'm thirty years of age and I'm flying blind here, so stop pushing me.'

Helen walked away and Catherine let her go. She lay in bed, waiting anxiously for the sound of the front door after the kiss of the shower and heavy feet on the stairs. It didn't come.

An hour later, she went downstairs and found Helen sitting at the kitchen table, reading Emma Donoghue's novel, *Stirfry*, and chain-smoking, judging by the number of butts in the ashtray.

'Good book, this. Thanks for getting it for me. I wonder which of us is the Ruth and which is the Jael. Bet I'm the Jael one: she's the mad hoor who doesn't know when she's found a good thing in life.'

Catherine ignored her and walked across the room to switch on the kettle. A breakfast tray was set neatly for two. She leaned against the worktop, breathing deeply, then looked across at Helen who was, once again, engrossed in her book. 'What's all this then?' Catherine asked.

'It was supposed to be breakfast in bed,' Helen replied, eyes glued to the printed page, 'but I couldn't figure out a way of getting through the door without being hit by flying foot-wear and the entire contents of my bedroom. I'm not much good at those sort of logistics and I thought the cornflakes would have made a really alarming mess.'

'Not my style, sweetie. I'm not angry with you. Well, I am angry with you; just not that much. I worry that I'm going to get hurt; that maybe you'll get tired of me.'

Helen looked up and reached for another cigarette. 'My best prediction is that your scenario is unlikely.' She paused to blow smoke into the air. 'I'm so stupid that sometimes I think Chinese checkers are Oriental train conductors,' she informed the ceiling. 'I suppose this is where a repentant lit-tle personage apologises for being a prat and promises to at least try to be reasonable henceforth?'

'I suppose it is.'

'I apologise, Unreservedly.'

'Apology accepted, although I'm tempted to extract a promise that you'll talk to me about this some other time. Apology accepted unreservedly, I suppose, but only if you bring breakfast upstairs. You might need to know that I like warm milk on my cornflakes.'

'Your wish is my command, petal. Begone to bed while I heat the milk.' Helen caught Catherine's arm as she passed. 'I promise.'

'Promise what?'

'That we will talk about this but I don't think now is the time. We've only been together a few months so there's plenty of time for it. I promise we'll talk about it when we're both feeling a little less raw and maybe we can come to some arrangement.'

'Arrangement? Now you're making me sound like a mistress.'

'Hmm. What a lovely thought,' Helen said, fidgeting with the lapel of Catherine's dressing-gown.

'Get off me, you perv. About your promise… I'll hold you to it.'

'In an odd sort of way, I hope you will.' Helen pulled Catherine down to her level by the front of her dressing-gown and kissed her gently on the lips. 'I do hope you will.'

They met the gang in Crosbie's that same evening. Catherine was subdued from numerous warnings not to be too obvious. She had argued back vociferously, refusing to lie to protect the neighbours' old-fashioned, fuddy-duddy sensibilities, as she put it.

Helen stuck to her guns. 'Christ, Catherine,' she said, 'this isn't Dublin and I have to live here. Do you really want to make it even more difficult for me? I'm not asking you to lie, just to keep your mouth shut and your hands to yourself for a couple of hours. Chris from accounts will be there and she has a mouth on her like a half door. Telling her my personal business is the same as telling half the country, and she's only dying for a go at me because she thinks I'm way too big for my boots since I won that fucking award. This is the West, Catherine, it's not a big anonymous city. I choose to live my life here, even if it is a form of half-arsed compromise.'

Catherine responded to this tirade by being uncharacteristically quiet, politely saying hello to the usual Saturday evening crowd of Helen's colleagues, casual acquaintances and friends of friends. A natural and cheerful loner, Helen had very few close friends.

'Are you mad at me? Helen asked quietly when Catherine placed an unlit cigarette back on the table between them after Michael Byrne, Helen's old accountant pal from the Department of Finance, had left. Mike and Helen had shared Dublin digs during their college years and Helen liked nothing better than to meet him occasionally to catch up over a couple of pints, just the two of them. Their paths didn't cross often but when they did, there's was no room for a third in conversations composed almost entirely of nostalgic reminiscences about the *bean a ti's* appalling stews.

'Of course. Well, I should be but I can't seem to stay mad at you, especially when you have a point,' Catherine whispered back. 'This is your place and you've every right to your closet if that's what you want. It's just not my way but, when in Rome…' She placed the unlit cigarette back in the box. 'No, thanks. I hadn't smoked for fifteen months before I met you. Do you always have such an effect on people that they do silly things?'

'No, but I could say the same about you. Niamh's been going mad around the house with air fresheners since I went back on them and my mother's absolutely disgusted with me. Here's Philip,' she said, waving towards the door and pointing at the spare stool she'd been keeping her foot on for twenty minutes.

'Sorry, I'm so late. Jack's home with Sean and we couldn't get the little gossoon to sleep. It's terrible being a grandfather when you want to get to the pub on a Saturday night and your offspring's offspring wants yet another *Thomas, The Tank Engine* adventure read to him at half-past ten. How're you, Chris? Nice to see you again, Dave. Chris must be treating you well, hey?' he said, nodding at the rest of the group and running a hand through thin and greying blond hair. 'Time for a drink?'

'Nah, thanks, Philip. We've full ones here but rest yourself and say hello to Catherine while I get you one,' Helen said, clambering over Catherine's knees to get within striking distance of the bar. 'Catherine, this is Philip from the office.'

'Pleased to meet you, Philip From The Office, 'Catherine said, grinning and sticking out her hand.

'Oh, no, not another joker,' He sighed. 'Helen, where'd you get this one?'

'Dublin, where they're all mad and incapable of sorting out the ewe hoggets from the rams. At that graphic design course I did last Autumn in Bolton Street. A pint of black for you as usual, I suppose,' she said, winking at Catherine.

Helen found herself unable to get a word in for most of the evening. Catherine and Philip compared notes about city life, local government and housing policy. Long after normal closing time, Helen caught Catherine's eye as she defended the latest round of public sector pay increases. 'But Philip, those of us at the lower end of the scale deserve it and, anyway, they got a productivity deal in return,' she protested, while he illustrated the contrary view with statistics on private sector pay.

'Enough,' said Helen in the end. 'I'd better get this one home before a row breaks out. Philip, you'd better finish that and get out of here before the peace officers come calling in the course of their duty… I'd truly hate to report your "found on" case but I'd do you anyway, you know that.' Helen helped Catherine into her jacket.

'Thank you, James. Is my carriage outside?' Catherine whispered.

'Out, bitch, or I'll tie you to a tree on the Mall on the way home.'

'Promises, promises,' she murmured. Speaking in her normal tone, Catherine continued: "Night, Philip O'Connor from the office. See you again soon, I hope. 'Night, Chris… I don't know why you bother paying this one at all. She's useless.'

Philip caught the cuff of Helen's jacket before she could leave. 'Nice girl, that Catherine. Lively but nice,' he said quietly.

'Yeah, she's an awful messer,' Helen relied levelly. ''Night, Philip. Enjoy the match tomorrow.'

He groaned at her retreating back. 'Shag it, I'd almost

forgotten about that. Enjoy? Hardly likely… have you seen the weather forecast?'

'The joys of sports journalism, eh? Nothing like it. Think of me reading the papers in a warm house while you're being pissed on by Her Upstairs,' Helen's voice drawled back from near the door.

They walked home, hands in pockets, Helen bemoaning her lack of a spare shoelace with which to carry out her threat when they reached the Mall, a green circle ringed with trees and bisected by a long pedestrian path. Catherine grabbed her jacket.

'You never told me you were into bondage so much, darling, but I'm willing to try anything for you,' she mumbled into Helen's ear before dashing off across the park.

Helen caught her before she reached the other side. 'I'm the one who smokes but you're the one badly in need of a fitness regime,' she slagged, patting her gasping companion on the back.

No windows were lit in the neat terraced house on McHale Road, just a couple of hundred yards from the county's biggest GAA ground which bore a similar name. The street was hellish on match days: Helen was sick and tired of collecting empty chip bags and Coke cans from her front garden after they were deposited there by delighted or forlorn football fans. Sometimes, just to irritate the neighbours, she stuck a Sligo flag out through one of the upstairs windows and endured the subsequent slagging with good-humoured composure.

It was late and the street was deserted. Helen slid the front door key into the lock, opened the door, turned around, grabbed Catherine by the lapels of her jacket and pulled her inside. Shoving her up against the closed door in the dark, Helen kissed Catherine roughly, breaking away when she felt arms slide around her waist inside her jacket. 'That was letting Philip – a mere man and a happily married grandfather at that – monopolise you all night.'

She kissed Catherine more gently, pausing so that their lips were just touching before pulling away a little. Helen delayed, feeling Catherine's warm breath, redolent of beer and vinegary chips, on her face. 'And this… this is to let you know how much I enjoy your company, how much I like kissing you and how much I want to explore that narrow hollow that runs down the centre of your back… with my tongue. Again.'

Still holding Catherine's jacket tightly and standing so close that their glacial noses were almost touching, Helen waited. Then, leaning forward and tilting her head slightly, she pressed closed lips delicately against her lover's, waiting a moment before parting Catherine's with her tongue.

'I want you upstairs and in bed in fifteen seconds,' Catherine whispered when, minutes later, she finally broke the kiss for good.

'Not so fast, slut. I'll teach you to discuss local authority affairs with my friends instead of discussing affairs of the heart with me.'

'But you said I have to behave myself when we're out together. And, anyway, after this morning I assumed you really hate talking about all that mushy stuff.'

'Um, you assumed correctly, but then again, I'm a woman and I'm entitled to be unpredictable and change my mind.' Helen pulled away and swaggered down the short hallway, switching on the light in the sitting-room. She smiled. 'C'mere. The fire's still alive and the rug is soft. Niamh's away on an A&E course or something. I've got a gorgeous double malt hidden in the study and a spare duvet in a colour that will contrast with your skin.' She walked into the room, then turned and looked directly into Catherine's eyes.

Catherine ambled down the hall, eyes down, and stopped in the doorway. Hesitantly, she raised her eyes to meet the lively blue of Helen's. 'Helen, I think I might...'

'That's a first. You think what?'

'I think that's a very good idea.'

The next morning, Catherine woke to find Helen propped on one elbow, gazing into the space where the fire had flickered during the previous night. Squinting against a narrow bar of watery March sunlight peeping through the curtains, Catherine stirred a little and watched Helen's expression change slightly as she became aware that she was under quiet observation.

'Morning, Honey,' Helen said quietly. 'Yes, indeed, it is in fact a morning. We have confirmation of that fact due to the expected rising of the sun. It's a morning thing.'

Catherine stretched, yawned and snuggled back under the quilt. 'Already,' she whispered hoarsely. 'How could it possibly be morning when I'm wishing it was still last night?'

'So am I,' Helen murmured, smiling down at Catherine's upturned face but not quite meeting her eye as if embarrassed at her memories. She twitched, easing her neck. 'D'ya know, I'm suffering from a severe case of Parquet Floor Law.'

'And what's that, sweetwit?'

'Parquet Floor Law... the immutable set of facts which decrees that the floor shall always feel so much more unyielding and uncomfortable the morning after.'

'I can't say I've had the opportunity to notice,' Catherine replied, turning away from the sunlight. 'Do I take it you've done this more than once, then?'

Helen ran her index finger slowly along her lover's chin. 'Hmm. Looking for information, eh? Ah, stop fishing, tadpole, you know I haven't. I was just making a casual observation.' She coughed theatrically to draw attention to the lie.

The telephone rang. Helen climbed across Catherine towards the receiver. 'Yell-o, ze Dunne rezidenze. Oh, hi ya, Ma. Yes, you are getting me out of bed. It's Sunday, ze day of rezt. What time is it?'

Catherine dug deeper into the quilt and listened with half an ear to half a conversation.

'Oh, that would be lovely but I've got a visitor… Catherine Lacey… No, you haven't met her… We hit if off at that graphic design course last Autumn and she's down for the weekend… I don't know… Oh, for heaven's sake, hang on and I'll ask.' Helen covered the mouthpiece with her hand and sighed heavily. 'We in the plural are invited to Sunday lunch at my parents' place. Andrew's down for the weekend as well. D'ya fancy it? What do you think?'

Without turning, Catherine asked: 'Would you like to?'

'I don't have very strong feelings about it either way. I just don't know if we're ready for this yet. It could be a fucking disaster but, on the other hand, it will save me from rooting out something to cook.'

'If you think it's okay, I'll do it.'

Helen shrugged, stuck her tongue out at the corner of her mouth for a second and put the telephone back to her ear. 'Okay, Ma, but we'll have to leave early to catch Catherine's train back to Dublin… Yes, I know she could go from Sligo but she's got a return ticket so she has to go from here… Okay, so… What's for dinner? Great, I'll bring a bottle of red; Catherine can have some even if I can't… See you at one then… Is Maria there….? Oh, well, tell her I hope she said lots of prayers for me and I'll see her later… Okay… 'Bye then.' She hung up and tossed the telephone onto the nearest armchair.

Catherine turned and opened one eye sleepily. 'If they guess, will they throw me to the lions for seducing their only daughter and refusing to make an honest woman of her?'

'Nah, they're very civilized. We don't keep lions at the

family pile. They'll just bury you alive in the wild corner down beyond the compost heap… and even David Attenborough wouldn't venture down there without an armed escort.'

Catherine smiled. 'I'd better be a model of decorum so. Better also get a paper so I can swot up on some current affairs and then I can bewilder your dad with my incisive insights into Irish politics and the Law Reports.' She paused, reached up and kissed Helen on the lips. 'Last night was like a fairytale. Well, the kind of fairytale that's strictly for adults, at any rate. It was magical. You were wonderful. I feel so close to you sometimes that I'm often taken by surprise by it. You're such a messer. I know you're really a kind-hearted woman behind all the crusty bachelor-girl stuff and I consider myself very lucky to be the one who sees it.'

Helen blushed and after three attempts at starting a sentence, gave up. Kissing Catherine gently and slowly on the lips, she said: 'Christy almighty on a crutch, you say the sweetest things to me and I never quite know what to say in reply.'

'You don't have to say anything but, if you feel you must, then how about saying what you feel, like you did last night in the firelight?'

'Ah, would you get a grip, you eejit,' Helen chuckled, shoving Catherine away playfully. Then she shrugged, serious again. 'That wasn't me. Something takes me over when I feel your skin against mine in the dark and hear you breathing so close to me.' Helen blushed again. 'It was good though, wasn't it?'

'The best yet, my love and I'm sure things can only getter better in that department,' Catherine smirked. 'If I promise not to ask your sister-in-law out over the Sunday joint, will you make me some coffee? I think someone's been weaving a carpet on my tongue in the night.'

Helen nodded. 'If coffee is what my darling desires

then coffee she shall get. 'She looked Catherine in the eye. 'And thanks.'

'For what?'

'For… um… well, I just wanted to thank you… em… for putting up with my poor performance in the communications department.'

'You make it sound like a disease. That's okay. No thanks necessary. I'm just being a gentleman, saving some poor lesser-equipped woman from a fate worse than being beaten up with a toilet brush.'

'Very complimentary. And there was I actually thinking you were getting something out of this relationship too. Anyway, I'd say you're quite well equipped enough for the task.'

Helen let her gaze wander towards Catherine's breasts, gently rising and falling underneath the quilt. She cleared her throat. 'It's getting a bit too late for more of the same, I suppose. Oh, well, coffee will be a good substitute. I shall head for Brazil immediately and pick some beans.'

An hour later, Helen sat on her bed, quietly smoking while Catherine dressed. She was enjoying the comfortable silence. She was good at silence and so was Catherine. She liked that. Helen ended up thinking that wet hair was quietly erotic in an odd sort of way. She crossed her legs at the ankle and admired her own red Argyle socks. She loved socks, the madder the better. It was a contrast to her usual choice of sensible clothes.

'Catherine, are you nervous?'

Catherine's head popped through her polo-neck sweater, her expression resembling that of a very surprised turtle. 'No. Should I be?'

'I don't know. Maybe you're better off not being nervous. I'm a bit jittery myself. Andy hates gays and my sainted mother is particularly observant in a scatter-brained sort of way. She lets on that everything just passes her by but I know it doesn't. She's noted your name when it popped up in conversation several times over the last couple of months and she looked a little amazed when I openly stood up to Andy about Johnny Holmes at Christmas in front of my father.'

'Johnny who again?'

'You remember. The guy from the estate down the road who's got AIDS.'

'Oh, yeah. How is he doing anyway?'

'Ah, he's in a bad shape, to put it mildly. Everyone thinks he'll shuffle off soon but he's been hanging on gamely since Christmas. It's a horror for the family, though. I'm sure it's getting to the stage where they'd prefer him to be gone just so they wouldn't have to look at him suffering. Oh, yeah, the mother was telling me that his English lover, Nick something or other, visited from San Francisco last month and was welcomed with open arms by Johnny's parents.'

'Lord, but isn't that wonderful. I would have expected the bog-trotters to eat the poor bastard on toast.'

'True, it was wonderful for Nick and for Johnny. I'm sure they were both relieved. Of course, the tearful reunion happened much to the disgust of some of the more bitchy neighbours who were expecting a major brawl, not to mention the exciting sight of Johnny's four sisters riding out in a posse after the poor black Protestant gay naturalised American.'

'Jesus, Hel. What century are they in down there again? Maybe I should get out my Victorian cravat?' Catherine smiled, lacing up a shoe.

'Same century as everywhere else, sweetie. There are small minds everywhere, not just in small town, but they're not all like that. Johnny's mum walked arm-in-arm down the main street with Nick the day after he arrived and, allegedly – I have this information from the mother, who is normally a good source – introduced him to the parish priest as "my Johnny's friend" after Mass on the following Sunday. That's real courage. It doesn't take much bravery or strength of character to gossip behind that family's back. Anyone who does it must feel so unkind and petty.'

'Thank Christ I won't be needing that breed of courage just to meet your Ma, Da, intolerant brother, sexy sister-in-law and delightful niece,' Catherine joked, combing her still-damp hair. Helen watched, feeling awkwardly possessive. Sneaking off the bed and across the room, she put her arms around Catherine from behind and rested her chin on one shoulder.

'We'll be fine,' she told their mirrored reflections. 'You're my friend and you'll be a guest in my parents' home. What Andy thinks, or thinks he knows, is neither here nor there. My parents aren't thick, however…. They just hope I've got over this phase of fancying skirt and that's why we never talk about it. In ten years, we've never had a second discussion about what's probably the most important part of my life but I get the impression that, deep down, they know I'm not going to get married and have babies. If they suspect you're my lover, I guarantee you they won't react because they're too courteous. No friend of mine will ever be embarrassed or treated badly in their home. And that fucker Andy is too blind to see what's in front of him and too wary of me since that row we had at Christmas to ask me for the right time. All right?'

'Absolutely.' Catherine turned in her arms and looked her straight in the eye. 'I know this is important to you and I promise to do my best. I will try not to make a fool of you in front of the people you love. I will be so good you won't even know I'm there… but while we're enjoying that nice bottle of wine you've unearthed from that hell-hole under the stairs, I hope you'll toast us silently and think about what we got up to in front of your hearth during the early hours.'

Helen snorted in exasperation. 'You're incorrigible,' she said, pulling away and picking up her keys from the dressing table. 'We're going to my mother's and you're alluding to the fact that I have immoral carnal knowledge of every inch of your skin.'

'And I of yours.'

They locked eyes for a long moment before Helen broke the contact and turned to go. 'C'mon, you slag. Ophelia's getting impatient,' she said.

'Hi, Dad, as the teenager said to the bishop.' Helen kissed her father on the cheek. 'This is Catherine.'

'So I'm led to believe although I've no proof worth a damn,' he quipped in return, shaking hands with the visitor and introducing Nora, Andy, Mary and little Maria. Maria was captivated by Catherine's accent and insisted on sitting beside her at lunch. Oddly, Helen felt slightly jealous and ruminated about how stupid it was to feel envious of her four-year-old niece. It was a bit ridiculous, really. She sat across the table, noting the matching expression on the two faces as Catherine bent to hear yet another story from the big, bad outside world of junior infants. Andy, chatting with his dad about insurance, was uncharacteristically subdued. He was anxious to get lunch over so that he and Mary could get some way towards Cork before dark.

'Frank, are you going to pass the vegetables this side of Whit weekend or are you going to talk about public liability all day?'

'Oh, sorry, love.' he smiled at Nora and hoisted the vegetable dish. 'Catherine, would you like some carrots?'

'Carrots are good for you, teacher says,' Maria piped up.

'Indeed, so they are,' agreed Catherine, helping herself to plenty of the steaming vegetables.

'Teacher says we should eat loads of spuds and carrots and cabbage and apples.'

'Not all at the same time, I hope.'

'No, Catherine. Now you're just being silly. You can't have apples with your dinner. We never do. Teacher says we'll all grown up an' have happy hearts if we eat loads of spuds and carrots and cabbage and things.'

'A happy heart?' put in Helen. 'What's that all about?'

'We're doing a projek on happy hearts. A lady came in from the hostkipal and told us all about happy hearts and sad ones. Teacher says that the sad ones are in people that are fat and don't run around the playground at break.'

'Is that a fact?'

'Is so. Teacher says that fat people and people who don't run around or play football have sad hearts and then their hearts get sick and they go all funny an' die an' go to heaven an' all.'

'I don't think that's all true, Maria,' Catherine said firm-ly. Helen looked up from her dinner, surprised, and noticed Catherine's fingers turning white on her fork.

''Tis so. Teacher said,' Maria said truculently.

'Well, it's not true.'

'Is.'

'Busybody teachers sometimes think they know everything but they know f… damn all about it!' Catherine muttered.

Maria's lips started to wobble. Helen reached across the table to fill Catherine's wine glass. 'Ah, leave it, sure she's only a child and they're trying to teach them about healthy eating and Happy Heart Weekend to stop them turning into uni-versity students who survive on crisps, chicken vindaloo and fourteen pints of snakebite a night,' she said.

'I will not leave it,' Catherine said very quietly. There was an embarrassed silence. 'I will not leave it because it's perpetuating something that isn't true. My dad never smoked or drank; he played golf and swam twice a week and was fitter than I'll ever be. Pity he fell dead of a heart attack on the living-room floor while we were in the middle of a conversation, despite all the fruit and veg.'

A further silence was broken only by the sound of Maria's feet banging nervously on the bars of her chair. Helen false-started: she just didn't know what to say.

'God, love. That must have been really hard for you,' Nora broke in. 'It's awful having to live with a memory like that. I remember when Caroline died and the worst thing was the sight of her poor, bruised face against white sheets on a hospital bed. We all have memories we'd rather forget. Sometimes, I think they come into our minds for a reason.'

Helen looked at her mother, new respect in her eyes. Nora settled back into her chair and picked up her cutlery, looking a little surprised at herself. Catherine glanced up, blushing.

'I'm so sorry. That was awful. I'm a guest in your home and now I've embarrassed you all. And I've been nasty to you, Maria. I didn't really mean what I said about teacher.'

'Not to worry,' said Frank, clearing his throat.

'Forget about it,' Andy added.

Mary smiled warmly and patted Catherine on the back of the hand. 'It's all right, Catherine. People, even little people like this one, can be very good at pushing buttons they don't even know are there.'

Maria pulled at her sleeve. 'What's embarrassed?'

'I'm not smart enough to put it into words for you, Maria. Perhaps you'd be better off asking your Auntie Helen. She's very good with words... sometimes.'

Helen looked her in the eye sharply, acknowledging the dig. 'That's a really tough one, Tinkerbell... How about we eat up all these blessed carrots and look it up in the dictionary when we're finished?'

'Okay, but we'd better remember to tell Catherine about it too, jus' so's she'll know it for the next time. And I want to know why the carrots are blessed too.'

'I think it's a great idea for you to find out and then tell me,' Catherine said, smiling down at the little upturned face. 'That way I'll be able to tell my little brother about it too.'

'What's his name.'

'Robin. He's seven. He'd like you but he hates carrots.'

'I love them,' Maria commented. 'Auntie Helen says if I eat lots of them I'll be able to see in the dark when I grow up. Like Jane, you know.'

'Jane, the cat,' Maria said with a touch of exasperation, indicating the ginger-and-white ball currently sleeping in a small wicker basket in the corner of the room.

'Oh, that Jane!' Catherine lowered her voice to a conspiratorial stage-whisper. 'Did you ever ask Auntie Helen how come she wears glasses then?'

Maria considered this question carefully and then looked quizzically across the table. Helen sighed dramatically. 'Because I don't know what's good for me, Maria. I suppose I mustn't have eaten enough of them when I was a little kid like you.'

'Eggzactly,' said Maria, seemingly satisfied with this explanation. She began drawing designs on her little mound of mashed potato with her fork.

Catherine smiled at Helen and turned to Frank. 'So Mr. Dunne, I've been meaning to ask you, d'you do much work on tenant purchase for the county council at all?'

'Indeed we do, Catherine, but I leave most of the conveyancing to my junior partner now. I'm getting far too old to be worrying about site layouts, extinct rights of way and percolation areas. Ground rent is another area that can cause plenty of problems…

The beach was deserted. Maria skipped ahead, her long curls trailing, sand kicked up by her heels. Catherine and Helen walked side by side in silence without touching.

'Careful, Tinkerbell. Don't go so near the water… you might get your feet wet and then you'd have to walk back to the car on your hands!' Helen called.

Maria turned and waved, abandoned trying to pull a stubborn piece of seaweed from hard wet sand near the water's edge and scampered up the beach.

'That one's a tomboy,' Catherine remarked. 'I wonder if she'll turn out to have more in common with her favourite auntie than mere blood relationship.'

'Fuck, no. Christ help her if she does. I'll have to spirit her away to another planet or else set her up with someone big and butch enough to beat the shite out of her father. Mary would be cool enough about it, I think… but you never know with people; you never know how they're going to react when stuff like that comes in their own hall door. Anyway, Andy would simply have a stroke and launch into a no-child-of – mine play in five acts.' Abruptly, Helen stopped walking.

'Whashappnin?' Catherine bawled ludicrously, stopping three steps further on.

'Are you feeling okay now?' Helen said, walking towards her.

Catherine looked down, scuffling sand with the toecap of her boot. Turning into the wind and shoving her hands deep into her jacket pockets, she muttered: 'I'm sorry for making a fool of myself. I really didn't mean to make a show of you in front of the folks.'

'I didn't ask you to apologise. I asked if you were feeling okay now.'

'I'm okay. That "teacher said" stuff just got under my skin. You'd think I'd have learned not to let it get to me so much after six years. Jesus, Hel, I was only twenty. I was three weeks away from leaving the secretarial course and we were talking about safe jobs in the civil service when he simply dropped dead in the middle of a fucking sentence. He was dead before he hit the floor. It was such a mess. Gerry cried for six weeks straight. Paul didn't speak one word for a month. Robin didn't notice, he was so young. I just settled down to looking after everyone else, out of a sense of guilt, I suppose.'

'Some experiences cut a lot deeper than others,' Helen observed dispassionately. She raised a hand to Catherine's cheek to soften the words. 'I used to feel like that about Caroline. We were so very close. She was my hero and I worshipped her. She looked after me for years and I just couldn't forgive myself for not being with her before she died. I didn't get the chance the rest of them had to say goodbye. By the time I got a flight home, everyone else was here and she was dead, laid out on a mortuary slab for a post mortem. I was the last to arrive and, by the time I did, it all seemed so fucking pointless. For ages, even the mention of her name made me feel cold… It reminded me of all those endless hours waiting on standby for a 'plane home. For a while, I forgot the warmth that was her, and the way she used to smile at me and call me "little sis", even though I was the taller one.' Helen's eyes, looking out to sea, turned a deeper blue. 'There's no-one alive who hasn't had to learn how to live with loss. We all learn differently. There's nothing to apologise for.' She took Catherine's arm companionably. 'C'mon, sexpot. We'd better be getting back or you'll miss the train and your darling mother will think you've been dyke-napped by the muck savages from Connacht.' She looked around 'Jesus H. Christ on a shopping trolley! Where's Tinkerbell. Maria! Maria!'

Maria appeared from the sand dunes, minus one shoe. 'Oh, fuck, I'm dead,' Helen groaned. 'I can just hear the humourless bastard. "For God's sake, Helen, can you not be trusted to take the child for a walk without being so irresponsible'" she mimicked. 'Maria, darling, we have to go now. Don't worry about the shoe. I'll explain it to mammy when we got home.'

Maria limped theatrically ahead of them. Catherine dug her hand into Helen's pocket as they walked. 'Hel, d'you know, that's the longest speech I've ever heard you make about the F word.'

'Eff off yourself. What's the F word?'

'Feelings.'

'Really?' Helen stiffened slightly. 'Maybe you don't know me as well as you think you do. Or maybe you're figuring out a sneaky, devious way to get under my skin.'

'Maybe.'

In the cool half-light of a March dusk, they waited together for the ponderous train that runs from Westport through Castlebar to Heuston Station in Dublin. Most of the passengers were students or migrants, the kind who made a living in the city from Monday to Friday and a life in Mayo at weekends. Helen nodded to one or two acquaintances as they walked to the quieter end of the platform. She hated the Sunday evening sound of the Eastbound train, a sound that carried for miles in still evening air. When they stopped walking, Catherine dropped her bag off her shoulder and leaned back, hands in pockets, against the platform wall.

'When will I see you again?' she asked.

'Next weekend, I hope, but it depends on work. If I'm free I'll go up to you.'

'Okay, Helen. I won't be able to come down next weekend anyway. It's Robin's birthday on Saturday and he would be really upset if his big sister missed the party. Mother certainly wouldn't be impressed with me either. She likes us to do all that family stuff together.'

'Ah, I know. Mothers are the same all over this bloody country, not to mention all over the world.' Helen shivered. 'I knew I should have brought a warmer jacket.' She caught the first click of the train in the distance and checked her watch. 'Why is this fucking train always on time on Sunday evenings and always late on Fridays?'

'I dunno. It's a mystery to me too, a bit on a par with the Immaculate Conception except it's not quite so widely debated in clerical circles.'

Helen smiled. 'Have you got your ticket?'

Catherine checked three pockets and came up with the required cardboard rectangle. 'Yes, mammy.'

'I'll miss you,' Helen said, her eyes on the concrete plat-form. 'Thank you. That was really a wonderful weekend.'

'You're welcome, wench.'

The driver of the approaching train announced its im-minent arrival, the powerful sound reverberating in the air. Catherine smiled sadly and looked into Helen's eyes. 'It's not too easy, is it? Hmm? One of us always seems to be leaving on Sundays.'

'And one of us is always left behind with a house full of reminders… like the upturned coffee mugs on my drain-ing board or the pleasant, tired ache between my shoul-der-blades,' Helen observed, smiling the slow crooked grin that always made Catherine want to kiss her. 'I'll 'phone you tonight.'

The train pulled into the station and the intending pas-sengers moved, largely reluctantly, into action. Catherine de-layed. 'Take care. I'll miss you too. Let me know about your plans for the weekend as soon as you can so I can tell Robin you'll be at his birthday party. Or not, as the case may be.'

'Thursday afternoon, at the latest.' They walked to-wards an open carriage door. 'The best thing about being at the second station on the return trip is that you get a seat.'

'Yeah, but it's a small compensation for leaving you alone here.'

Catherine moved to step onto the train but Helen caught her arm. 'It won't always be like this,' Helen said.

'I know.' Catherine climbed the steps, turned and stooped to kiss Helen on the cheek. 'See you Friday.'

'See you.'

There was silence for a moment and then the conductor began his mournful litany, advising passengers to stand clear of the doors. Catherine stood back as the door began its slow automatic progress. She waved when the train began to move. Helen waited, as she usually did, until it rounded the first bend on the four-hour journey that would take Catherine home, then strode towards the car park, the steel tips of her booted heels ringing on concrete. It was so cold that she could see her breath in the air and she wished she'd been able to find her woolly gloves in the tangled mess of her bedroom. The chaos in the normally tidy room was already the established legacy of weekends spent there with Catherine.

The finality of the single click when she turned the key in Ophelia's ignition brought her back to reality. The starter had gone, finally, after a long month of idle threats.

'Fuck.' Helen said reasonably.

She checked the glove pocket and then remembered that her mobile was at home, under the bed and switched off. '087 me arse. Fuck, fuck, fuckedy fuck,' she swore, slamming the door and heading for a telephone box to ring a mechanic.

CHAPTER THREE

FIT TO PRINT

'Helen, I'm off now. D'ya want me to get some petrol for Ophelia…? You'll wreck her driving around on empty all the time.'

'Yeah, you might get me twenty quids' worth of best leaded. There's money in my briefcase somewhere.' Catherine thumped up the stairs and stuck her head through the doorway of Helen's study, a tiny, uncharacteristically untidy boxroom partly shelved from floor to ceiling along one wall. 'Are you sure you don't want to come with me? Can I really be trusted to buy the makings of a truly demented lasagne all on my own?'

Helen turned from her computer. 'I'm sure you'll manage. And get a haircut, for Christ's sake. You're a disgrace. Now, for the love of all that's pagan, get the feck out of here and let me get on with this. You're so much of a distraction that I never get any work done when you're in the house.'

'Gee, thanks, and I think you're just great for concentration too. See you in a couple of hours when I will be suitably shorn and bearing the fruits of my expedition into the great outdoors. I wonder should I bring a little spear with which to kill my sweetheart some dinner?' Catherine blew a kiss and was gone.

Restlessly, Helen stood by the window and watched Catherine start the aged Ophelia and pull away from the kerb, forgetting to indicate as usual. She sat down in front of the computer screen, closed a file containing two-thirds of a feature story on landfill dumping and opened a new one. After thinking for a few moments, staring unseeingly at the flickering cursor on its white background, hands poised over the keyboard like an absent-minded concert pianist, she began to type.

She wrote: *I'm waiting for Catherine. She's just left in my car to do the shopping and get a haircut. When she gets back, she'll potter around downstairs and cook dinner while I try to work. It's never easy to concentrate when she's around. She whistles and sings and bangs things. Even when she's quiet, when there's no sound downstairs, I know she's there.*

She's not here now and I still can't concentrate because I'm waiting for Catherine. The muscles in my back are aching and my eyes are tired because we spent most of last night in my bed, in the half-light of candles, trying to become each other. Last night was a wonderful timeless battle-like encounter with no winner, no loser. Each battle is both like and unlike the last. Last night, Catherine cried in my arms and I thought I was going to burst; I was so full of some queer feeling I can neither define nor express.

Even now, when I'm sitting here thinking about her and drugged with last night's thoughts of her, I desire her. Every time I see her, even in the distance, my hearts starts going funny, beating faster and I can feel my mouth going dry with that weird metallic taste of longing.

I'm waiting for Catherine. All I can do is wait. I can't think of any way to show her the depth, the length of the moment when we're alone together, wrapped up close in my bed or hers, giggling with relief at being together again before basic blind need of her makes me serious.

It's eerie sometimes, but there's always something, some awkward neurotic something in me holding me back and it's never quite as tangible as I would like. If Catherine ever knew how much I long for her; how much awful breathless impatience there is in me; how much I want to possess her over and over and over... again and again until she drowns and disappears in me... If she knew, then she would hover and hesitate. I hover too and I'm afraid, but I'm waiting for Catherine.

I wish she was here now. It's always simpler when she is. If she was here, I could switch off this ticking machine and go downstairs; make small talk about the price of tinned tomatoes and sneak lascivious looks inside the collar of that sexy white shirt she's wearing. I could help her with dinner and watch the way her hands move; feel myself smile at last night's memories of those same hands. I could run my hand up the back of her head; call her "Prickles, the house hedgehog" and laugh at her kind mock annoyance before giving her a hug.

If she was here, she might come upstairs and put her arms around my shoulders while I write, in that way she does sometimes that means I can feel the shape of her breasts against my back. She might tickle the nape of my neck with her tongue and watch the fine hairs rise there; watch me blush and grow warmer while I pretend to work. She might kiss me then and we might end up cooking dinner a lot later than we'd planned.

But Catherine's not here and I'm still waiting for her. She's a complex character but she's simple too. She's simple, in the same way that we all know two plus two adds up to four but we can't explain how the sum really works. One of the simplest things about her is the way she looks at me. She never looks at anyone else like that. Just me. So I'm waiting for Catherine.

She'll be home soon. I'm glad. This house, this half a home is so quiet and dark when she's not in it. Catherine lights

*up each room. Tomorrow, both of us will wait for the train
that takes her away from here on Sunday evenings but that's
tomorrow. It's nearly Summer now and there's a lot of light in
one day.*

*I'm waiting for Catherine and I know she's coming home
now. I can hear the sound of Ophelia turning the corner at the
top of the road because Catherine always drives through that
junction one gear too low. She's pulling up outside now and
she'll probably hit the kerb. She usually does.*

*Catherine's whistling. It's a tune that's all her own, the
one I can never put a name to. I can hear her whistling over
the rustle of shopping bags and the slamming of Ophelia's wonky door. And there, I can her that too. That's the hard, met-
al-on-metal sound of her key in my lock.*

*Listen. She's dropping the bags in the hall and that means
Catherine's coming straight upstairs. That makes me happy.
She's in a hurry. I know that because I can hear the buckles on
her jacket jingling and she's taking the stairs in twos.*

*Maybe Catherine's been waiting for me while she's been
away.*

Most Fridays were very odd in the newsroom. With the
office diary boasting two blank pages except for the inevitable sports markings, the five reporters held their collective
breath every time the telephone rang. It was so often like that
on Fridays.

Colm was in rough humour this morning. The door to
his office was open so the newsroom was uncharacteristically
quiet, given Friday was the day when the pay and expenses
cheques customarily led to an outbreak of silliness among
the reporters. Impromptu basketball games using a tiny hoop
clipped to the top of the cabinet used for useless file pix were
not uncommon.

The office junior, Georgie Lennon – aged twenty and

still not finding it necessary to shave every day – was still stinging from his early morning encounter with the boss over his habit of leaving 'the boring bits' out of Urban District Council reports. Georgie was diligently typing up a twenty-five par feature story on the birthday celebrations of the latest hundred-year-old pensioner. The story would be published complete with the usual pictures of a wrinkled old dear lying in a Sacred Heart Home bed, surrounded by allegedly adoring and only slightly less wrinkled younger relatives.

Liam Sullivan, a reasonably experienced reporter in his late twenties who had a penchant for pin-ups, had taken two days off to make a four-day weekend. Helen took the opportunity to pull the bare-breasted page-three beauties off the back of his computer. Again. Paula Coogan, affectionately known as "The Cougar", a forty-plus virago with a headache, four kids and a drink problem, was in court. Laurence S. McNally, the sports hack who'd joined the *Recorder* from a UK regional paper for a hugely inflated salary with which to massage his equally hugely inflated ego, was nowhere to be seen. Some surprise. Larry worked precisely the thirty-five hours a week demanded by the National Union of Journalists' house agreement but somehow always managed to take time off in lieu of overtime on Fridays.

Helen, the Mother of the Chapel – that's the weird title journalists use for a female union shop steward – and he shared a mutual antipathy that usually seethed uncomfortably below the surface but occasionally erupted into short verbal exchanges vicious enough to make even Philip wince.

Philip was at his desk, reading the *Independent* and occasionally humming the theme tune from *The Twilight Zone*. Helen was rooting around her desk, catching up with paperwork. Someone had to send back contributed pictures to their owners once a month and it was usually her. It was irritating; one of those awful, pointless, routine chores that just had to be done. Well, no-one else would do it anyway despite her best efforts to brow-beat the men into it on a rota.

'Helen, would you grace me with your presence for ten minutes of your undoubtedly valuable time?' Colm disappeared through the door as quickly as he had arrived. Philip hissed through his teeth, wagged a finger at Helen, grabbed a notebook and left for his afternoon assignment. Helen shrugged, picked up a notebook and pen and headed for the office.

'Shut the door and sit down. We have trouble and you might be in it. Does the name Jimmy Kennedy mean anything to you?'

'No, but I get the impression it should.'

'He was up at the district court in town a couple of months ago for assaulting some McNamara man outside a chipper.'

'Oh, yeah, I half-remember him now. He's from Claremorris, right?

'That's the one. You might be interested to know that he's alleging that our report – well, your report, to be precise – contains… hang on, let me get this just right… "gross libel, misrepresentation and an inaccuracy that has severely damaged his reputation". He intends to sue for thirty big ones in the circuit court if we don't come up with a satisfactory financial offer and front page apology within seven days.'

Helen sat down, colour draining from her face as she swallowed one of her worst night-time fears. 'Do we know what his precise grounds are?' She asked weakly.

'We do,' Colm answered, looking at the second page of the solicitor's letter on his desk. 'He claims there was no evidence that he kicked McNamara in the stomach as you reported. There's no mention of that in any of the other papers, his solicitor is at pains to point out. Helen, it'd be a first but, be honest, did you up fuck this one?' Colm's use of the expression was unusual, to say the least.

Helen thought quickly, trying not to panic. 'Jesus, Colm, I know my memory isn't perfect but Kennedy is recent. I remember telling my mother about that one. I have a clear recollection of Garda… what the hell is his name?... Holland, I think, telling the judge that McNamara gave a statement alleging Kennedy kicked him while he was in the gutter with his lights practically punched out. I'm sure the Guard read the statement but I can't remember if McNamara said it in evidence. It certainly wasn't picked up on cross, maybe because Kennedy's legal eagle didn't want to make too much of it. You know the judge, he's one of those old-stock types who thinks a toe-to-toe between a couple of lads outside a chipper is acceptable but use of the boot or a weapon isn't. Helen fell silent.

'Can we prove any of that? Do you still have your notebook? And, now that I think of it, is this the same solicitor?' He held up the letter. Helen scrutinized the letterhead.

'Haven't a clue but I should still have the notebook somewhere. Will I look for it now?'

'I should fucking well think that would be appropriate.'

She was back in his office in five minutes, leafing through one of the hardback A4 notebooks she only used for covering courts. 'Okay. No, damn, that's not it. Hang on… here we go. March 12th. Let me see. Right, DPP v James W. Kennedy was contested so it would have been after all the plea cases.' She flicked through a few more pages. 'Here it is. His solicitor on the day was Mick Furling. Who's the letter from?'

'One Judith McGrath, Dublin.'

'That's good, isn't it? I mean, if his local solicitor isn't the one sending the fireworks and none of the other local solicitors have a hand in it, maybe it's because they think there's something funny about it. Either that or they don't want to piss us off and fuck up all the free publicity they get for defending the wankers around here. This McGrath woman could be a no-foal-no-fee ambulance-chaser who is just trying it on or who knows nothing about Kennedy's previous,' she reasoned.

'Possible.' Colm fell silent for a moment. Helen continued reading, muttering to herself. He grew impatient. 'What about your evidence notes? Any solace for us there?' She read on, then turned the notebook around, plopped it on the desk and put her finger on a line half-way down the left-hand page.

'There you go. That's Holland reading McNamara's statement of complaint and, if you turn the page... there's McNamara's own evidence.'

'What the fuck is this? How do you read this shit?' he growled, passing the book back to her. 'It looks like a drunk spider on a walkabout. Read it to me.'

Helen picked up the notebook and, still standing, read: "He punched me once in the stomach and twice in the face. I think I remember hitting my head as I went down, your honour, but I'm not sure. While I was down he kicked me in the stomach, not very hard."

Colm compared the spoken words with those printed in the relevant edition of the *Recorder*. 'I hope your shorthand is like a bloody textbook so someone else can read that scrawl but this makes me feel a whole lot better. Can you explain why this little detail wasn't in any of the other papers?'

'Maybe their court reports aren't written as comprehensively and accurately as mine,' Helen said, risking the quip but Colm was clearly not in the mood to be amused. 'Let me check something,' she added. She left his office, scooped up the newsroom diary and browsed through the pages.

Georgie looked up. 'Trouble?' he asked.

'The worst.'

'Anything I can do?'

'Not unless you've been called to the Bar since I was talking to you.'

'Oh, shit.'

'Yep.'

Helen found what she was looking for and returned to Colm's office. 'Good news of a sort. March 12th was the day of the big bash for the President in Breaffy House Hotel hosted by the Chamber of Commerce. Free food and drink for all invited guests all afternoon. You went to it with Georgie and The Cougar and came back at five o'clock well oiled, along with most of the reporters from Mayo and Galway. There were only two reporters in the district court that morning: me, who drew the short straw for once, and Colin Harper from the *Courier*. The other papers couldn't publish it simply because they weren't there. I bet our friend Kennedy conveniently neglected to mention that to Ms Judith B. McGrath, solicitor.'

Colm was beginning to look relieved. 'Any chance we'd have a copy of that week's Courier lying around?' he asked hopefully.

'I can check. Georgie's been elected master of the back issues by general acclamation… at least since Philip cut GAA logos out of two of the October editions,' she replied. Colm picked up the 'phone.

'Mr. George Lennon, this is Colm P. Bolton, your boss and the man you will have nightmares about if you don't find the last two March issues of the Courier and bring them in here.'

'Now?'

'Now, Mr. Lennon, right now.'

Together, the three of them skimmed both issues without success. 'Jesus H. Christ, George, it's hardly on the fucking farming page!' Colm growled impatiently, grabbing a

newspaper from the junior's hand. 'Colm growled impatiently, grabbing a newspaper from the junior's hands. 'Let's start
again and do it right.'

There was no sound but the rustle of pages for about
two minutes. 'Bingo,' Colm said quietly. 'Back to work,
George.'

'Oh. Rightio, then.' George reddened and left the room,
almost knocking over a rubber plant in his eagerness to make
an exit. Colm and Helen silently compared the reports.

'Fuck it, Colm,' she said, after a while. 'I know they
don't mention the kicking business but look at it… my report must be thirty pars and Colin's is only ten. He's fucking
summarized it.'

Colm leaned back, made a steeple of his fingers and
propped it under his chin. 'Okay, Helen. Let's leave it at that
for now. Don't take your notebook or the diary and put
markers in both at the relevant pages. I'll brief the MD who,
I might mention in passing, is seriously pissed off about other matters, and I'll have a chat with the company solicitor
this afternoon. Superficially, it doesn't look as if there's much
of a case but there was no official stenographer there and if
Kennedy pushes it towards court we may have to settle. Our
friend Garda Holland is hardly likely to come to the rescue
after that business about the checkpoint that never was. On
the basis of what's here, I'd say it couldn't be worth more than
a couple of grand, but I'll let you know what tack we'll be
taking on Monday.'

'Two grand is two grand too much for that fucking chancer,' Helen sneered, then held up her hands to still
Colm's protestations. 'I know, I know. You don't have to say it.
If it goes to court the best we can hope for is a massive costs
bill, with the very remote possibility that he might have to
pay our costs as well as his own if the judge rules the claim to
be vexatious. We're talking serious shillings, right?'

'Too right,' Colm replied. 'You know yourself it's impossible to predict what the doddery old wig will do when Joe Put-Upon Upstanding Citizen is doing a David-and-Goliath against Corporate Entity with a perceived heap of ill-gotten gains in the petty cash. Oh, fuck it, just leave it with me and we'll do what we can. We might have to settle with the stupid fucker. If it goes against us you might get a rap on the knuckles from Fleming… you can take that as a friendly warning. He's really pissed off with this stuff since Sullivan's last fuck-up cost us eight thousand.'

'Rap on the knuckles? Yeah, right. He might run this place as a hobby but I know I'm in the right and if he tackles me on this one he'll be left with the very strong impression that said rap on knuckles is totally unjustified.' Helen caught Colm's expression and hurried on. 'Moving swiftly off on one of my usual mad tangents, d'ya know am I wanted this weekend or not?'

'Not to my knowledge. Off to Wicklow again then?' Helen raised her eyebrows and he coughed before continuing. 'It's just that Chris has been telling me you've been spending a lot of weekends outside the provincial boundaries these days. She seems to be under the misguided impression that I give a tinker's curse what my hackettes do in the time I'm not paying for.' He cleared his throat. 'You're not getting off that easy. Bring your mobile: it occurs to me that you're on call this weekend just in case the town might be burned down or all the inhabitants of same be put to the knife before Monday morning.'

'Okay, C.P.. And don't call me a hackette. You know it irritates me.'

He grinned, delighted with himself. 'Ah, you feisty wimminy types need a firm hand now and again.'

'That's harassment. I could sue.'

'I think you've had your fill of litigation today.'

'You're not wrong, but that doesn't affect my rights.'

'Rights, rights, rights. What about my rights to a little peace and to get some work out of you for what's left of this day?'

'Point taken, boss, and thanks'

'For what, precisely?'

'For hearing me out instead of shooting first.'

'Judgement, Helen.' He tapped his forehead. 'That's what separates experienced editors like me from dizzy little girl reporters like you.'

She didn't bite. 'Hopefully, I'll develop some of that highly admirable quality before you retire… Not that I'd like to see you go because you're such a wonderful boss,' she said sweetly.

'Out of my office now, you youthful idiot. You couldn't do my job for a week without dropping yourself in it.' He paused, smiling. 'Anyway, you'll be delighted to hear that McNally's already been softening up the management on that score.'

'Thanks for the unsolicited info, C.P.. Must be off now to sharpen me daggers. If Laurence S. McNally, the one man in this place who couldn't organize a nun-shoot in a nunnery, takes over, the *Recorder* will, point one, have a lazy megalomaniac for an editor, and point two, lose its brightest reporter.'

'Put those sentiments on toast and feed them to the MD when he's giving you a gentle dressing down and he'll probably fire you,' Colm said, grinning, 'and wouldn't that be such a sweet relief which would leave me free to serve my limited time until retirement with a blissfully quiet little newsroom. Now go, before I change my mind and make you type local notes all weekend.'

Helen scampered off, singing *you are my sunshine, my only sunshine* loud enough to be heard.

A single candle burned in the middle of the table, the black candlestick stark against starched white and gleaming silver plate. It was May day, a birthday, and the first of Helen and Catherine's relationship.

'Medallions of beef for me, please, and can we have a bottle of the Nederberg Pinotage as well?' The waiter nodded politely, scribbling on his little pad. Catherine relaxed, the trial of ordering over, and looked around. 'Now then, dearest, isn't this nice?' she asked.

'It's wonderful, really wonderful but are you sure you can afford it? We could go Dutch if you like?'

'Oh, shut up, Helen. It's your birthday and I'm taking you out to dinner to celebrate. Can you not be gracious, even once? Go on, say thank you nicely and stop worrying.'

'Sorry.' Helen grinned madly and unrolled her linen napkin with an admirable flourish, blushing when the waiter appeared at her elbow with a freshly uncorked bottle of wine poised over her glass. 'Ah, no, sure I wouldn't know what I'm drinking. She'll taste it,' she said, gesturing to the other side of the table. The waiter moved sideways silently on crepe-soled shoes and expertly poured just a thimble-full of wine into Catherine's glass. She made a fuss of the tasting, much to the brown-eyed waiter's delight. He filled both glasses.

'So,' Helen continued, 'what's the other part of my present, if you have any money left after paying for this blow-out?'

'Patience, you slapper. I think I'll make you wait until we get home. To be honest, it's a little too personal to just peg out on the dinner table in public. And you might get gravy on it.'

'I would not. I am not the messy eater in this relationship. You are the one who ends up wearing the dinner on a regular basis!'

Catherine laughed heartily.

'And what do you mean that it's too personal to just throw out on the dinner table? Jesus, Catherine, don't tell me you've gone and bought some French knickers or handcuffs or something? You know how bloody conservative I am.' They locked eyes for a moment and the stranger in Helen softened, gazing into the illusion of warm grey space in the eyes across the table.

'I love you,' Catherine said conversationally, using the same tone she often used to tell the time or compile a shopping list. 'That's a bit matter-of-fact, isn't it?' she added bemusedly. She held Helen's eyes for a long moment and then averted her gaze to a middle-distance point in the choking space between them.

Helen said nothing. Catherine sighed heavily. 'I'm sorry. That isn't quite how I planned it… I didn't quite mean for it to just pop out like that.' Helen, still silent, shifted uneasily. Catherine added: 'Don't be angry. Please, sweetie, don't be angry. I just simply love you.'

'I'm not angry. I'm in shock. Jesus, Catherine, what the fucking Jesus hell is happening to us? We've only been together for a few months – and you know that that's a record for me – but I find myself starting to day-dream about what it would be like to be with you all the time, not just at weekends or the odd day here and there when we manage to link up. I just don't know what…' She paused impatiently while the waiter placed immaculate, massive platter bearing the main course on the table.

Helen leaned across the table, speaking quickly, her internal stranger urging her on to unfamiliar and painfully brusque territory. 'Catherine, look at me, I don't know what love is… For fuck's sake, I've never been in love enough to know what it's like to carry a broken heart around. I've only been infatuated once and that was nothing to write home about in the end. I don't really know about any of it. All I know is that it feels like there's a long string of elastic between you and me; as if I'd rather be unhappy myself than to see you hurt…' Helen stopped and fidgeted with the edge of the tablecloth while part of her stood outside, observing while she searched for words with some form of legitimate meaning.

'Sometimes I feel as if I've champagne running through my veins instead of blood or as if you fit me like a very old, very woolly and very comfortable sock. Fuck it, Catherine, if that's love; if that's what it's really like then I suppose I do love you. But I'm fecked if I can really figure out why you – of all the women I've ever met in my life and, God knows, I've met some humdingers in my time; of all the women I've wanted or who've wanted me – should have that effect on my brain.'

The meal was growing cold. Helen sighed heavily, gazing sadly and intensely into Catherine's eyes. 'But damn it all to hell, I can't deny it to you like this, face to face, any more than I can really deny you anything. We've been and gone and done it now, haven't we? We've crossed some kind of fucking Rubicon or ended up at some half-arsed watershed over a bottle of South African red on my fuckhead of a thirty-first birthday. There's no going back, is there? Not without at least one broken heart.' Answering her own question, the bitterness in her tone was evident. Helen sat back, lit a cigarette and, with something that was close to anger in her eyes, sat back and exhaled furiously, filling the distance between them with a blue-grey haze. Dragging indignantly on her cigarette, she went on: 'Now what do we do, hmm? Get a fucking ladder and elope, is it? Pledge undying love, run off to Sweden and get married? I'm damned if I know what to fucking do.'

In the ensuring prolonged silence, both seemed to recognize the agelessness of their predicament and the comic aspect to what had been said. Catherine, smiling indulgently and with not a little bemusement, remarked: 'That's all right, then, but what was all that about a ladder? I hate heights.'

'Don't you, oh wise woman of the world, already know that all self-respecting secret lovers require (a) one two-storey house and (b) one ladder with which to elope from same? Convent girls are usually entrusted with this valuable and useful information by doddering old nun-types who assume they would never consider such an immoral course of action,' Helen replied, relaxing. 'They also lost the run of themselves entirely and advised us never to wear particularly shiny shoes – you remember those patent-leather ones? – under a skirt in case the boys from the college or, worse still, the "tech" would have the opportunity to see the reflection of one's presumably virgin-white knickers. I took their advice so much to heart, in my inimitable fashion, that I gave up wearing skirts altogether, seeing they were such a serious threat to my poor immortal soul.'

'Jesus, Hel, community school was so very boring by comparison,' Catherine said archly, enjoying the mood and encouraging Helen to further revelations.

'You bet, sister.' Helen nodded expansively while her internal stranger stayed silent, cocooned in the incandescent half-light trickling from Catherine's eyes. 'The older ones, the ones still in the long habits, used to come up with the most ridiculous spakes.' She paused, examining the barely tepid contents of her plate as if it had just appeared and began fiddling with her cutlery as she spoke. 'Of course, we learned young, but only in theory, that boys just can't control themselves, God love them. Mother Mary Therese Alphonus Benedictus Concepta – not her real name! – presented me with a copy of a wonderful book called The Guide to Modern Living. An admirable gesture, apart from the fact that it was published in the Year of Our Lord 1937. Mother M.T. also seriously suggested – in a roundabout fashion without using the actual words – that if we were ever in the unlikely and obviously dangerous position of actually dancing with a boy, there should be room between us for the Holy Spirit to pass through. And the evident corollary of this advice was that if you ever found yourself in the very stupid and totally irresponsible situation of actually sitting on a boy's knee, then there was no help for it but to make contraceptive use of the handy telephone directory or pile of old newspapers that one was always likely to find in the corner of an average 1980s discotheque.'

'I'm sure you've heard of the phrase, "particular friendships", Helen continued. 'Well, particular friendships with our peers of the same gender were always discouraged, not that we were ever given a reason. Mind you, given that we weren't supposed to have particular friendships with the opposite gender either, I don't know what the bloody hell we were supposed to do with our time. Anyway, I must thank the good sisters for the decorous and excellent work they put into nurturing my inquiring mind so that I could find out for myself why the old "particular friendships" were persona non grata, so to speak. If I didn't know better, based on my personal experience, I'd say convent school are secret dyke recruiting centres!'

Catherine rocked with laughter, imagining a spindly-legged teenage Helen aloud. Helen half-agreed with the portrayal. 'Dead right, except I was so bloody conservative I thought everything was immoral. Politically, I was probably a little to the right of Margaret Thatcher, not that I even knew at the time what the word "political" actually meant or who Margaret Thatcher was, for that matter.'

'I suppose people must see a change in you then, given that you're now a little to the left of Fidel Castro.'

'Not quite, bunny. I'm still a believer in the hang-'em-and-flog-'em philosophy when it comes to the criminal justice system and laissez-faire when it comes to suggesting to piss-heads on the dole that all they need to do is get a job. I've been an extremist since the day I was born. I'm a regular pendulum, swinging too far one way or the other, depending on the weather.'

'Well, at least you're swinging my way this time, and isn't that lucky for me.' Catherine raised her glass. 'Happy birthday, sweet stuff.' She surveyed the ruined meal. 'We can always have chips on the way home.'

They strolled home together from the DART station, holding hands, not saying much. Helen had the feeling that enough had been said for the moment. She felt no need for idle chatter simply for the sake of it and was content to luxuriate in comfortable silence. Back at the gloriously empty Bray house, Catherine teased her a little before producing a home-made birthday card decorated with two childishly-drawn teddies and numerous slightly lop-sided hearts.

'What's this then, a civil suit for that CD I scratched?' Helen asked as she opened the envelope. She was smiling and not really expecting an answer.

Inside the card, along with heart-warming hand-written sentiments was another, smaller white envelope. Inside that was a simple but stylish gold-embossed card bearing the words: "You'll have a ball at "Radclyffe Hall" and the dates of the following weekend. Helen frowned, trying to figure it out silently while Catherine waited, grinning. Eventually, when no words came from Helen, she lost patience.

'Guessed it yet, sweetie?' Catherine asked, kneeling in front of Helen and putting arms around her waist.

'Radclyffe Hall… em… I dunno. Isn't she the one who wrote that ancient dyke book we all read… what's it called… is it *The Well of Something or Other*? What's she got to do with next weekend?'

'*Loneliness.*'

'Eh?'

'*Loneliness.* It's called *The Well of Loneliness.*'

'Oh, right. But what's that got to do with us?'

'Maybe I should let you wait until next weekend and then you can find out for yourself. Yes, I think that would be a very good plan.'

In mock rage, Helen grabbed her shoulders and shook them. 'Tell me now, bitch, or I'll tickle you half to death and I won't let you into my knickers for a month,' she threatened.

'Yeah, right. You wouldn't last a fortnight and you know it!'

They grinned at each other. Helen kissed her gently, tasting her lips with calm, unhurried sensuality. 'I've a better plan. Tell me now and I'll let you into my knickers twice as often as heretofore.'

Catherine slapped her knee, laughing. 'Jesus, sometimes you talk like an old book, you do. You're the only person I know who can use the word "heretofore" in the same sentence as the word "knickers" and get away with it.'

'You're changing the subject. Tell me. Please, Catherine, tell me what's this about?' Helen begged.

'Okay, you heartless tart. This is the deal. Radclyffe Hall is an exclusive women-only but mostly dyke B&B buried in darkest Galway. It's so discreet very few people know about it and a booking is only accepted if you have a recommendation from a trusted regular guest. It's run by this half-mad couple who've been together for absolute yonks: one of them is an earth mother who makes breakfast and the other one tinkers with antique cars and chats to the guests about current events in what is quaintly called the common room. We're going there next weekend. I've even been in touch with your boss and I've arranged the time off for you. In addition, I'm driving you and you won't have to lift a finger for the whole weekend. Well, are you pleased?'

Helen's reaction was slow and considered. She kissed

Catherine's forehead and pulled her close. 'Pleased, yes, and also truly amazed at my luck in finding someone as thoughtful, generous and inventive as you.' She ran fingers through Catherine's hair and held on tightly, then spoke her next thought aloud. 'Let's go to bed. The scent of you is actually addling my brain. The only way I can think when you're this close to me is to…'

'Is to what?' Catherine asked, her voice muffled against Helen's shoulder.

'You know already,' Helen murmured.

'I know that. Tell me anyway.'

'Is to see your body with my fingertips in the dark.'

Catherine stood up, leaned over and looked directly into Helen's eyes. 'Darling, you can be so oblique sometimes. What you really mean is that you want me in your arms, naked, sweating and breathing hard,' she said.

'Yes. All that. And more. And over and over and over again.'

Catherine straightened and smiled, the corners of her mouth turning upwards in the way that made Helen's stomach muscles tighten with simple craving. 'You've got to catch me first,' she hissed and was gone.

Radclyffe Hall was hilarious. Helen thought she had stepped into the pages of a period novella, such was the comedy of manners going on in the three-storey townhouse just a few streets sway from Kennedy Park. Wearing the end of Spring's foliage, Galway city breathed the promise of Summer evenings in the softest of breezes carrying the scent of Western sea salt. The usual vagaries of May weather gave way to unbroken tepid sunshine on their Thursday journey, so they walked the city streets and wandered into nooks in the long dusk of evening. Back at 'the Hall', as Helen persisted in referring to the six-bedroom B&B, Margaret Dawson, who was the earth mother half of the partnership, invited them both to join her for a nightcap in the common room. She even called it a nightcap. They agreed.

'Very good. Whiskey all right?' Lisa's got a delightful Scotch around somewhere. She hides it, you know,' Margaret informed them. 'Lisa, dear, where are you?' she called down the hallway.

A tall, taciturn woman with an air of landed gentry in her bearing and an accent to match materialized. Lisa Swift looked about five-foot-ten in her stockinged feet and gave the impression that she would unashamedly peg any time-wasters or trouble-makers out into the public street without even taking a breath.

'Whiskeys all round for the girls, dear, and I'll have a very small one myself' said Margaret.

They chatted informally around the turf fire. Helen was mesmerised, both by the flames and by the conversation. Lisa had been to a finishing school in Paris and had spent most of her youth in English boarding schools while her parents were overseas, both on diplomatic postings for the Foreign Office. Originally an Anglican and now a Methodist, she converted to Catholicism and joined an enclosed convent at 21 after graduating with a first from Cambridge, just to exasperate her parents. It worked; her father had a heart attack. Her mother never spoke to her again but that suited Lisa well. Just after taking her final vows, she jumped the convent wall – literally – and moved to Ireland. Within forty-eight hours of abandoning her habit, she met Margaret in a train station. Margaret, a psychiatric nurse from Edenderry in County Offaly, was with a gaggle of other nurses on a wild, beer-sodden weekend. They were waiting for a train to Galway when Lisa asked her for the time. That was it; it was love at first sight. They'd been together ever since and Margaret's inheritance of part of the family farm paid for Radclyffe Hall.

Eventually, Helen's attempts to stifle yawns were noticed. 'Sorry and no, you're not boring me. I'm just completely knackered. I think I'll make my way to the theatre of dreams,' she said. Catherine moved to rise but Helen placed a restraining, possessive hand on her shoulder. 'No, Bubbles, stay. I'll be fine on my own and you're enjoying yourself.'

'I know,' Catherine smiled, 'but I can't possibly run the risk of you being waylaid on the landing by some gorgeous woman with precious little on her bod and devilment on her mind.'

Helen scowled. 'As if that's likely.'

'Nonetheless, indulge me in my little daydreams of being chivalrous and protecting your honour. I think the atmosphere in this place is getting to me.'

Margaret and Lisa looked at each other knowingly and chuckled quietly. 'Goodnight,' they said in unison. As Helen and Catherine left the room, Helen caught a glimpse of Lisa reaching for Margaret's hand and she could still hear them murmuring softly as she ascended the stairs behind Catherine.

Later, as they lay in lazy, purring half-sleep, Catherine murmured: 'Isn't it odd that there's always one lover and one beloved in a relationship?'

Helen raised one droopy eyelid to half mast and growled: 'What are you on about?'

' Margaret and Lisa just got me thinking. You'd never guess because they're so stereotypical in other ways, but Lisa is obviously the lover half.'

'And how does Doctor Jung know this?'

'Didn't you see the way they look at each other? When she thinks there's no-one else looking, Lisa has an expression like a homeless puppy desperate for a kind mistress. If the beloved so much as stirs, she's all over her.'

Helen shifted position and rooted under the bedclothes, snorting softly. Catherine tapped her on the arm. 'Would you mind telling me what in the hell you're doing? She asked sweetly.

'Looking for something soft to hold onto in the night.' The grin on Helen's upturned face was that of a bold school-girl, minus the marks usually left by sticky sweets. 'And I've found it,' she added, sliding her hand around the curve of Catherine's breast. 'You're such a great lover, you know. To-morrow, as your just reward for services rendered, I shall show you my beloved West of Ireland, the place where even the quality of the light seems to seep from the ancient bogs and where the air carries a faint whimper of the pain of our collective past.' She snuggled closer. 'Now, be a dear and switch off that infernal light before I go blind.'

Catherine did as she was told and they lay still. She murmured: 'You're almost a poet. I want for nothing when I'm in your arms. You're good for my body, mind and heart, you know.'

'Now who's the poet? Goodnight, love, and dream of me.'

They slept.

Catherine and Helen spent two days pottering around Connemara, venturing as far as Clifden for lunch on the second.

'There it is. Next parish: America.' Helen gestured at the heaving grey ocean as they strolled near a headland, keeping a wary eye out for droppings left by scrawny and bedraggled mountainy sheep. She pondered aloud about whether or not she needed a haircut. 'I leave it so long between cuts some-times that it's more like a ceremonial quarterly sheep-sheer-ing in the hairdressers than anything else,' she joked. 'Hey, what's up?'

Catherine, who had been lagging behind, finally

stopped. 'Isn't it great, Helen, this kind of peace, this kind of contentment?' she asked.

'Yeah, it's great but I love getting back to my life after a welcome few days in a rustic idyll. I love the peace but I miss the buzz at work.'

'Your life? Doesn't that include me now?' Catherine asked, raising her voice slightly to be sure of being heard over the strengthening sea breeze.

Helen brushed a lock of hair off her forehead and shrugged. 'Of course it does. Do you really need to ask me that anymore?' Catherine did not reply. Helen walked towards her and added: 'You've got a funny little look on your funny little face. Tell me, Bubbles, is there something going on here that I know nothing about but that I might need to know?'

'Yes. No. Possibly.' Catherine paused, drew another breath and paused again before she spoke. 'It's just that when I go back to my life without you, nothing seems to fit right anymore. It's like it's all out of focus or something. I assumed you felt the same but perhaps I should have had the manners to check with you first.'

'Out of focus, you say. Mmm. Maybe you need spectacles or something.' A look from Catherine stopped Helen. 'Sorry, not a good joke, okay.' She held up her hands, palms outward. 'Pax,' she said. They touched fingertips. 'I do feel like we're a couple and if it seems to you that I don't then I can only apologise,' Helen went on. 'The easiest way I get along with the hole in my life when you're not around is to ignore it. Sometimes I'm so god awful at finding the right direction with you that it seems I'll only be on course if I turn left at the planet Twit. Pax?'

'Pax. And thanks for saying it. At least now I don't feel like a freak of nature just because I miss you.' Catherine looked out to sea. 'It's really beautiful here but all this open space is beginning to do my head in. Can we go back to Galway now? I've got £300 for new clothes burning a substantial hole in my pocket. Just let me loose in the shopping centre and I'll be fine, and I promise I won't spend all day preening in the changing rooms while you lurk outside with all the husbands and boyfriends.'

Helen took her hand and they walked back to the car, arms swinging like school kids in the middle of a two-by-two convent-school crocodile on an outing. 'Your wish is my command, petal and even vice versa, when I'm in the mood,' she said.

'Christ, Helen. Look at this!'

'Mmm?' Helen didn't even glance up from the sports section. 'What is it, sweetie?'

'Look. The *Chronicle* is looking for a senior news reporter with five years experience and the job is based in Dublin. It's perfect.' She passed the newspaper across the table.

'Hey, mind my egg! Mmm, computerized design and layout skills… tight deadlines… attractive remuneration… It looks all right. Oh, 'morning, Lisa.'

Lisa stood beside the table, hands in pockets, feet planted firmly about a foot apart. 'Good morning, Helen. I do hope you both slept well. It's been nice having you stay and Margaret and I hope you might come back again or that you might tell some of your very good friends about us. Of course, that's only if you're pleased with us; otherwise, we'd rather you tell us.'

'This is a lovely place and we've enjoyed it immensely. You've created a rare atmosphere here and it's very comfortable for us,' Helen responded.

'That's excellent news. Margaret will be pleased: she's always nervous when we have new guests to stay. Travel safely, both of you.'

'We will, and thanks.' Helen caught the fury in Catherine's eyes as she followed Lisa's progress to the next table in the long conservatory that doubled as a dining room. 'What? What? What did I say wrong?'

'"All right". What do mean by "all right"? You might like to show a little enthusiasm. If you applied for the job in the *Chronicle* you might actually get it and then we could live together.'

'Whoa. Hold your horses. Just hang on a second there…'

'No, I won't hang on just a second. I applied for a transfer to the Department of the Environment in Ballina weeks ago but your lack of enthusiasm for the idea of us being together leads me to wonder whether or not I should have bothered. I have to pack. Let me know when you're ready to leave.' Catherine stood up to go.

'Catherine, listen to me… '

'For what? To hear you rationalize? No, thanks, not now.' She grabbed the room key off the table, knocking against Helen's coffee cup hard enough to make it jangle against the saucer.

The rest of Sunday passed in cool silence. Helen, fiery-tempered but loathe to row with someone who really mattered, drove home quickly and decided to let Catherine stew until she was ready to talk sensibly and calmly. They kissed perfunctorily before leaving for the train station in Castlebar in the evening.

'We need to talk about this,' Catherine remarked. 'Giving me the silent treatment isn't going to achieve anything.'

Helen shrugged and turned away. 'I wasn't giving you the silent treatment. We don't have time to go through this now and I need more time to think before I talk.'

'All right, so.'

'Thank you for the weekend. It was a lovely, generous

gesture and so typical of you. I hope I'll have the same imagination when it comes to choosing a birthday present for you.'
Helen smiled her special slow grin and whispered: 'Pax?'

'You'd charm your way out from under a nuclear mushroom cloud.' Catherine held up her hands. 'Okay, okay, pax. Now come on or I'll miss this train and you'll be stuck with me then while I look for gainful employment.

'Niamh, you haven't seen a brown manila folder with "job stuff" written on it, have you?'

'Ah, Helen, for God's sake, I've been at a hen party. I couldn't find my way out of the loo at the moment and now you want to know if I've seen one of your hundred-and-one identical folders. What's so important? Oh, Jesus, my aching head.' Niamh leaned against the doorframe of the boxroom.

Helen extracted her head from the wardrobe where a series of half-finished shelves were filled with piles of paper and wood-shavings. She sneezed dramatically. 'My CV. I've got to finish these effing shelves soon. This clutter is driving me batty.'

'Never mind the shelves. What about the plug on the microwave that my rack-renting landlord has been promising to fix for three weeks? And the blocked shower head that's so bad I can only wash half my hair at a time?'

'Get a fucking haircut then,' Helen growled. Niamh felt her forehead gingerly. Helen ran one hand through her hair and dived back into the wardrobe.

'Your CV? What do you need that for, anyway? Has the lord and master of the *Recorder* grown tired of your cheek and pitched you out on your ear to earn a living as a tenement landlord?'

'My home is not a tenement, Niamh Rodgers, and you know it. Any more cheek and you'll be getting notice to quit over supper.' Helen's voice was muffled as she rooted through the mess. 'There's a job in Dublin I was half-thinking of applying for but if I can't find my CV in the next five minutes I probably won't bother. Be a darlin' and make us a cuppa, will you? I'm parched.'

Niamh went off, muttering. 'I'm the one with the raging hangover and that cow upstairs won't even make the coffee. Ouch, me head! I'd be fine if everyone would just shut up for 24 hours.'

'Mine's a coffee, no sugar, just milk,' Helen roared. Niamh turned and looked back up the stairs where Helen stood in the doorway, red-faced and tousled, triumphantly brandishing a manila folder. 'Eureka, as the needle-hunter said to the haystack,' she crowed. Niamh was still applauding silently and Helen was bowing dramatically at the top of the stairs when the telephone rang.

'It's Philip here. Is Helen around?'

'Hello, Philip. Last time I checked she was in the wardrobe. No, I tell a lie. She's now out of the wardrobe and is at this moment approaching me with what looks like murder in her eyes.'

Helen took the receiver gently, smiled sweetly and whispered: 'Where's my coffee, you lazy git?' Niamh grinned and scuttled off. Helen propped the telephone between her ear and shoulder. 'Philip O'Conor, the footballer's football, how are you on this fine Sunday evening?'

'Great. Niamh's been telling me that you were upstairs auditioning for the role of Wardrobe in *The Lion, the Witch and the Wardrobe*.'

'It'll be *The Lion Puts Bitch in the Wardrobe* if my tenant doesn't learn her place and stop taking the piss,' she replied, winking at Niamh.

'Nice to hear you have good, clean fun in that house. Listen, have you time to meet me later for a pint?'

'How much?'

'Eh?'

'How much later?'

'About ten. I'll call 'round to yours and we might stay there if you're not mad for out tonight. There's something I want to talk to you about in private.'

Helen caught the edge in Philip's tone. 'Anything wrong?' she asked.

'Well, yes, but I can't really talk now. Hey, did you see that *Chronicle* job ad in the *Trib* this morning? Interested?'

'If one more person of my acquaintance asks me that today I shall just scream and scream and scream. Mother was on the 'phone to me half-an-hour ago and Andy rang earlier. He was his usual charming self and stressed that he had my best interests at heart. I just held the 'phone a foot from my ear and said "yeah" every thirty seconds through his snide references to sleazy tabloids and respectable broadsheets. I pretended the house was on fire to get rid of him.'

'Oh, that's very sisterly of you. Helen, are you interested in the job, though?'

'I dunno. Everyone seems to think I should be and maybe they're right. I just haven't had much time to think about it between Catherine leaving on the train and Niamh arriving back from a Letterkenny hen night with the mother of all hangovers.'

'What an interesting life you young people lead, especially in that house.'

'Yep. My life is just full of a whole big pile of steaming, warm…'

'I get the picture and I'd empathise but I've troubles enough of my own at the moment.'

'I gathered that. You sound rough, Philip. I was just trying to cheer you up some.'

'Thanks anyway. I'll see you later?'

'Ten pee em. I'll be here.'

Niamh was on her way out, picking her steps and avoiding Philip carefully when he walked up the narrow path. She nodded at him very slowly. He turned and watched her retreating back. Helen, leaning against the open door, explained: 'She's off for a hair of the dog that took the bit with him last night. Come in.'

She studied his face as he brushed past her in the doorway. 'Philip is this glass of wine trouble or double Jack trouble?' she asked softly.

'Double Jack,' he said shortly, dropping into an armchair in the living room and examining his hands. She poured two very stiff measures of her favourite Jack Daniel's whiskey, surreptitiously took the telephone off the hook and sat opposite him, depositing both drinks on the glass-topped pine table between them. It was very quiet. Helen waited.

Philip took his drink, sipped it and put the glass back on the table. He looked up. 'Patti's leaving me.' Helen didn't flinch. 'We've been married for 28 years and now she's leaving. She was my only girlfriend and we were twenty when we married, four years after we started going out together. Now I wonder how I ever could have been stupid enough to think I knew her at all. There's no reason; well, she's not giving me one. She wants me out of the house because she says she's earned the right to stay there. She said that because the kids are grown up and provided for there's not enough between us now to keep us together. She says there's no third party. I wanted to tell you myself because she told half the town herself this morning after Mass and I didn't want you hearing it from someone else, complete with whatever bloody spin she's putting on it.'

'Did you see it coming, Philip?'

'Ah, sort of, I suppose. Things haven't been really good between us for a while but I expected us to stay together. I'm old fashioned. I come from the you-make-your-bed-and-lie-on-it school of matrimony. I believe in forever. You didn't guess, did you?'

'No.' Helen looked into her glass sadly. 'Apart from my demented parents, you and Patti seemed like the most solid couple I know. Jesus, Philip, you went everywhere together. I hardly ever saw you apart, except at work or when we were out for a point.'

'Appearances can deceive.' He said simply. 'I'll be moving out as soon as I can find a place to live although I haven't decided yet whether to fight her for the house or not. I just can't stand to be in the same room as her so I'd better find a place. At least the bloody thing is paid for but I don't see why I'm not entitled to something out of it. I did pay the fucking mortgage, after all.' He drained his drink. 'I rang Colm this evening. I won't be in for a few days. I thought you should know about this before you went back to work tomorrow.'

'Is there anything I can do?'

'Two things. Pour me another bigger one of these and rack your brains for the name of a very good family law solicitor… preferably one from out of town. Otherwise, I'll be okay. Now that the sword has finally dropped on my neck it seems to have been almost inevitable.'

'What about the kids?'

'The kids – well, they're hardly kids anymore – are devastated, much as I expected. They didn't see it coming either. I suppose once they see we're going to sort it out in a civilized fashion they'll get over it. They have their own lives to lead and enough troubles of their own not to waste time worrying about ours.'

'I don't think that's necessarily true. Talk to them. They're adults; they'll understand eventually.' Helen paused. 'Philip, if you think I can help, ask. I'm no expert on this stuff and I won't moralise or give you my mother's homespun wisdom but when you want to talk, I'll listen.'

'I appreciate that. Thank you. You've a very cool head when you don't let your temper get the better of you,' Philip smiled, started on his second drink and changed the subject with a visible effort. 'So. How was Galway and how is the fair Catherine?'

'Galway was bliss and Catherine is in great form.' They looked into each other's eyes, Philip with eyebrows raised interrogatively. 'What? No, really, it was great.'

Silence. Almost before she had time to formulate the thought, Helen said the words. 'Oh, for Christ's sake, Philip, we're lovers.'

He grinned like a Cheshire cat. 'So? What do you want? A medal or a papal blessing?'

Philip slept on the sofa next to the half-empty bottle of Jack Daniel's and Helen was the one nursing a monstrous hangover the next morning as she quietly force-fed herself some breakfast. After two cups of coffee and three cigarettes, she left a note for Philip offering to meet him for lunch and, as an afterthought, left a spare house-key with it.

Throwing on a jacket, she left for work, nodding at Eamonn, her middle-aged next-door neighbour. He was the one with the most irritatingly impeccable front garden in the entire street. For about the fiftieth time, Helen glanced with a sense of defeat at her own small patch of moss-strangled grass. Gardening would never be her forte.

She got moving but was seriously late for work. Kate, the efficient control freak at reception who considered a request for new Biros as a personal insult, let her know all about the time of day.

'Two calls already this morning; three messages for you on the answering machine over the weekend and Mr. Fleming wants to meet you in the Royal at eleven... which is exactly thirty-three minutes from this moment.'

Helen took the slips of paper off the desk without comment, mentally counting to ten to avoid uttering a stinging retort. She tapped on Colm's door and struck her head inside. He was alone. 'Morning, Colm. Are you in on this meeting with Fleming or is it just me?'

'No, sorry, not invited. Come in for a minute.'

Helen closed the door and leaned against the wall, her briefcase held across her chest like a shield.

'You look pale,' he said. 'Are you sick?'

'Yeah, but it's all self-inflicted. That's why I'm late. Sorry.'

'It's nothing that hasn't happened to the rest of us from time to time. Don't worry about it but mind your liver. We don't want to lose you to a drink rehab programme.' Colm looked down at his keyboard and fidgeted. 'Have you been speaking to Philip?'

'Yes. Last night. Hence the hangover and the lateness,' she replied guardedly.

'Rough deal for the poor fellow.'

'And then some.'

'Look after him. He likes you.'

'I know. I'll try.'

Colm blinked and went straight back into business mode. 'You didn't hear this from me but McNally's threatening to leave and he's been telling tales about you to Fleming without going through the proper channels, i.e. me. I'll deal with that end of things in my own way, but dot those i's and cross those t's this morning, okay? Apparently McNally's been saying you have an attitude problem and you're impossible to work with. Keep the temper under wraps this morning or Fleming'll go for you.'

Helen sighed angrily. 'Duly noted,' she said shortly.

Helen picked up the telephone on the second ring.

'Helen Dunne,' she said briskly, fingers still typing and head cocked on one side to keep the receiver in place.

'Afternoon, sweetheart. I just rang to apologise for yesterday's slight over-reaction and to see how you're doing today.'

'Not great, actually.'

'Ah, the poor bunny. Have you given any thought to applying for that job at all?'

'What job?' Silence. 'Oh, for fuck's sake, Catherine... Philip slept at my house last night because his wife's leaving him and I've a sick head as a result. I spent half-an-hour this morning arse-licking because I have allegedly behaved unreasonably towards a more experienced and better regarded colleague, and now this. I've enough on my plate without looking for a job on the other side of the fucking country. Get off my back, Catherine,' Helen spat.

She kept the receiver pinned between ear and shoulder as she spoke, watching Georgie get up from his desk, clear his throat nervously and head for the door. Paula 'The Cougar' Coogan continued typing but Helen knew she was listening intently.

'Who the fuck rattled your cage, Helen? I just asked a civil and very simple question. A plain "no" would have been enough.'

'Wrong question at the wrong time.'

'No kidding. I wondered what had happened last night. I usually ring on Sunday nights – as you might recall if you had your head screwed on halfways straight today – but your 'phone was off the hook all night. Is Philip all right?'

'Another stupid question. Don't be ridiculous. The man's devastated but he's doing his best. Like all self-respecting Irish men with emotional problems, he's turning to drink.'

'Okay, okay. Helen, I hate it when you're like this. Will you at least think about the job when you get the chance?'

'No, Catherine. I don't want it. I'd die up there. Dublin's no place for me anymore.' Helen replied with the sharpness of certainty in her tone. 'No way. It's just not going to happen.'

'I see.' Catherine's voice was distant. 'And that's it, is it?' You make the decision and don't worry about even making a pretence of consulting anyone else or taking my feelings into consideration.'

'That's rich coming from someone who applied for a transfer without saying one word.'

'It was supposed to be a surprise if it worked out.'

'Surprises like that I can do without. Anyway, it's my career; I decide. The answer's no. I need to get back to work now... I've eight stories to write and a court in the morning.'

'I won't delay you so.'

'Don't.' Helen hung up and eyeballed The Cougar angrily. 'Well, Ms. Coogan,' she said acerbically, 'did you hear enough of that or would you like me to relay the other half of the conversation?'

'This is a newsroom, Helen. We all work here and it's not my fault if you shout your perverted business around the place.'

'Fuck off, Paula. Get out of my face. You holier-than-thou fuckwits make my head ache.'

'I don't have to take that shit from you, you bent little twerp.' The Cougar's eyes narrowed.

'Guess what? I don't give a flying fuck. Why don't you go home to your four snot-nosed brats and drink another farm this evening, eh? Or, better still, go and get yourself laid by someone who knows the difference between an orgasm and a sneeze.'

'You little shit! I'll fucking have you for that!'

'I think not. I wouldn't touch you with a forty-foot disinfected barge-pole, you big girl's blouse. Now fuck off before I say something I might actually regret.'

'Fuck you.'

'Jesus, there's an inspired insult if ever I heard one.'

Paula fumed silently, beaten in the word-game again. Helen went back to work, pounding the keyboard as if it was an antique Remington in need of oil.

By evening, Helen was feeling guilty enough about her conversation with Catherine to add the price of an Interflora bouquet to an already alarming credit card bill. It was an empty gesture and she knew it: there was no real thaw to her mood and she was fit to fight with her own toenails.

After work, she went home to find a note of thanks from Philip and a £320 telephone bill. The fridge was empty bar one wrinkled tomato and some out-of-date milk. Helen slammed the door of the fridge with temper, muttering angrily to herself then, and put her jacket back on and strolled to the little supermarket in the middle of the street, breathing deeply and regularly to calm herself down.

When she got there, Helen realized she had fifty-three pence and one thirty-pence stamp in her pocket. She smiled apologetically at the slightly dykey assistant, got some cholesterol-soaked food on tick and walked back to the house, singing *My Momma always told me there'd be days like this* under her breath to lighten her mood.

The 'phone began to ring as she turned the key in the door. Helen recognised Catherine's number from the caller ID unit in the hall and ignored it.

'Enough for one day,' she said conversationally, addressing her remarks to the kettle as she slung her bag of shopping onto the worktop. 'Enough. This is where I exit the day. Exit, stage left.' Heading upstairs for a scalding shower, Helen let the telephone ring.

Chapter Four

Foreign Affair

Rolling up socks in pairs neatly, Helen put them into the gaps in the suitcase tidily. The tickets, two small ring-boxes, her passport, E111 form and foreign currency were on her bedside locker. Folding her new silk pyjamas carefully, she put them on top – even though she knew it would be too hot to wear them for long – and closed the suitcase. It wasn't full. Helen always travelled light. She sat down on the bed and looked at the tickets for the twenty-first time that evening. Four nights in Paris. Helen had won Catherine over with tales of the most romantic city in the world and a promise of an ice-cream in a café on the Champs Elysees. With the tickets still in her hand, Helen's mind wandered.

The argument over the newspaper job in Dublin had petered out eventually, but the central issue still lay unresolved. Helen dug her heels in very hard like a stubborn ass and refused to be moved by promises of togetherness and descriptions of future urban bright lights. Catherine eventually gave up. After a couple of weeks, they returned to an uneasy peace, each fearful of upsetting the other. Helen knew one thing for sure and absolute certain: she was lost. She was madly in love. She knew she would do almost everything to make her lover happy, but city living was one of the few things she would not do; it was one of the few changes she could not make to her like because that change would break her and, in the end, them too. Catherine accepted it reluctantly.

The Summer had been a simple matter of almost somnolent routine that, to Helen, reeked of the old sock nature of a love that was settling down from the bubbly champagne high of infatuation to something a little more substantial but also more satisfying, like home-made apple tart. She was very happy. They spent the Summer months travelling across the country, stealing days to be together, both hoping that Catherine's transfer to Ballina – the lively second-biggest town in the county – would come through. Helen probably hoped most: she knew that. Catherine was nervous about moving to what she called 'the country'. Helen vowed she'd learn to love it, and that there was nowhere on earth quite like the rocky fields, cloudy skies and lonely windswept mountains of Mayo.

It had been, in many ways, an uneventful Summer. The wheels of the Kennedy v recorder Publications Limited libel action ground very slowly and Helen was, in the intervening months, becoming accustomed to occasional bouts of professional worry about it. In other ways the Summer had been a little mad.

One night, they were curled up in sleep on one of the nights Niamh was on holidays and the house was their own. Helen woke to a dripping sound. It was raining heavily outside and she was drifting away again, half-thinking of cleaning the eaves, when a drop hit her squarely on the ear. Initially she thought she was dreaming but the first drop was quickly followed by another. Screeching like a banshee, she leapt out of bed and switched on the overhead light. Catherine sat bolt upright in bed. Her hair was mussed from sleep and her eyes were rolling in her head from fright when she beheld her lover, naked as the day she was born, prancing around on the head of the bed and staring frantically at the ceiling.

'What? Jesus Christ, Helen! What's wrong? Have you lost your mind?'

'No, but I think I might be losing the roof over my head,' Helen replied, eyes still glued to a growing stain on the ceiling about the size of a dinner plate. 'I think the fucking roof is leaking.'

'Right. Let's move the bed and get a basin to put on the floor. We can investigate in the morning.'

'Are you mad? We will like fuck. The whole ceiling could come down on top of us and I'm sure wet plasterboard could be very heavy. We'll investigate now.' Helen jumped off the bed and flung open a drawer so hard it popped out of the wall and hit the floor with a crash, just missing her bare toes. 'Shite,' she said.

For a moment, Catherine pulled the duvet over her head in exasperation and then got out of bed. 'Hang on. What time is it? Listen to me. We can just sort it out down here now and call a roofer tomorrow. There's nothing to be gained from losing your head.'

'A roofer? Where the fuck do you think I'll get a roofer in this town at less than three weeks' notice. This shagging place is collapsing around my head,' Helen said, pulling on a t-shirt and tracksuit bottoms from the mess on the floor. 'Get dressed. I'm going up into the attic. I'll get the ladder. Bring the torch from downstairs. I'll need you to hold the ladder in case I break my neck.'

'Will you get sense? You are not going up there at this time of night and that's final. Stop panicking; I'm sure it's only something small.'

'That's easy for you to say. This isn't your house and you haven't invested every shilling you have in it. I won't be able to sleep until I know how bad it is.'

Catherine sighed and reached for the clothes that she had discarded in haste earlier when she came to bed and found Helen sitting up, stark naked, reading a book of erotic lesbian tales by candlelight. 'All right, all right. Let's do it then.'

In the attic, Helen tracked down the leak, rolled back the insulation and found a fair puddle on the ceiling plasterboard. 'Mother of fuck!' she exclaimed. 'Catherine, are you there?'

'Yes, sweetie.'

'Right. Get me two black plastic bags from under the sink and half a dozen tea-towels.'

Catherine fecked the stuff across to her from the trapdoor, visible only from the shoulder up. 'Is it bad?' she asked.

'Not critical, I don't think. I haven't a fucking clue. I'll just clean it up and line the ceiling with plastic until the morning.' She mopped up the mess, laid the plastic bags between the joists and left dry tea-towels on top to soak up the water coming from the hole in the roof. Casting the torchbeam around, she called: 'I think it's just the one spot. Will you go into the bedroom and see if there's still a drip falling where my head usually is?'

Catherine's voice, calling the all-clear on the drip front, was muffled. Helen waited until she came back to hold the ladder and swung down to floor level, panting. Catherine started laughing.

'What's funny?'

'You look a sight. You're all panicked and red in the face, your hair is standing on end, you're covered in cobwebs and your t-shirt is inside out and back to front. I just love you.'

'And I love you. I love you. I don't honestly know how you put up with me,' Helen said, smiling broadly and relieved that she'd temporarily solved a practical problem.

'Because you're so entertaining. Come here to me 'til I give you a big kiss.'

They kissed quietly on the landing for ages, Helen leaning back against the step-ladder while Catherine pulled strands of cobweb from her hair. Eventually, Helen closed the trapdoor and they shared a bath. Then they shared Helen's bed with one pillow less than usual.

Next morning, Helen went outside early to investigate the roof tiles from the back of the rear garden. She had a symmetrical eye. Returning to the house with her steaming mug of coffee, she announced confidently: 'It's only a loose tile up near the ridge and I'm going to fix it.'

'Hang on,' Catherine was grilling rashers and tomatoes for breakfast. She looked tired. 'Get an expert. You could fall off the roof and even if you make it up there you won't know what you're doing.'

Helen was already flittering through the contents of the under-sink cupboard. She emerged waving a hammer. 'All I need is a couple of these and a mallet. Honest, I saw someone doing it once.'

'Yeah, and I've seen people driving articulated trucks but I wouldn't chance it myself.'

'Just watch me. Watch and learn. Watch and admire. You might find it a turn-on.'

'I don't need any more turn-ons where you're concerned,' Catherine noted, running one finger along the line of Helen's jaw.

'So I've noticed. See you later.'

'Where're you going?'

'To Mr. Perfect Eamonn next door to borry a hammer.'

'Helen, please don't.'

'Give it up. I'm having a go. I'm not waiting for three weeks and then paying some condescending make fucker one hundred quid to shift a tile.'

Within ten minutes, Helen had climbed up via the boiler-house roof and was crawling on all fours along the ridge, two hammers stuck into the back of her jeans belt and the handle of a mallet between her teeth. Catherine waited in the garden. Eamonn was in the garden next door, watching the operation that had required the loan of his claw-hammer.

'Okay, Catherine,' Helen called, placing the head of the mallet on a tile near her. 'Make like a crossword clue. How many across and how many down?'

'Two down and…' Catherine counted silently.

'Seven across,' Eamonn added helpfully.

'Thank you, kind friend and kind neighbour,' said Helen, standing up and making a wobbly bow.

'Be careful, Helen!'

'No, Catherine, I will not be careful. It is my greatest ambition to career off the roof of my own house and split my skull on my very own patio near your feet. O course I'll be careful. Now stop hallooing or I'll lose my concentration and end up doing an unassisted skydive.'

She sidled down slowly to the row containing the misaligned tile, testing each tile with her foot before leaning on each one after every step. Positioning herself below and slightly to the left of the faulty tile, she reached left and then right, levering the claw of a hammer under the row of tiles on each side. With the mallet in her right hand, she leaned hard on the hammer handle to her left and used her right knee to put pressure on the other hammer handle. The row of tiles lifted a couple of inches. She administered three sharp blows to the bottom edge of the tile with the mallet. When Helen pulled the two hammers away, the row fell back into place, as symmetrical as an expertly built wall. Shuffling back up to the ridge, she reached the chimney and slid down to the boiler-house on her rear end.

Gaining her feet, she faced the garden. 'Standing ovation and something strong in a glass, please, lady and gentleman. Eamonn, get over here and join us for a celebratory beer,' she said, as the two below applauded.

They still laughed over it, Helen thought as she remembered, fingering the plane tickets in her hand. And, in a way, that was what she enjoyed the most: all the laughter. They were getting on well, better than she'd hoped, but there was a hole in Helen's heart when they just couldn't find the time to get together. She was at the stage where she could no longer bear her own company. She couldn't stand to be alone and wandered restlessly from room to room in the house when she had time free and Catherine wasn't there. Helen knew it couldn't go on for much longer like this without something breaking. She banished the thought. Time enough to worry about that after Paris.

The little hotel in rue Notre Dame de Lorette struck Helen as being quintessentially French, although she'd never stayed there before and had only visited Paris once previously. The little lift only went to the fifth floor and from there they carried the cases up the final stretch of the little winding staircase. Their room, lit by top-floor skylights, was suffocatingly hot at midday but featured stained oak beams and twin beds light enough to push together easily. Standing on a chair, Catherine was tall enough to stick her head out through a skylight to see the surface of the city spread before her. She was totally and utterly captivated, mesmerized by Helen's knowledge of the Metro system as much as by the architecture, the rudeness of the citizenry and the sheer class and reeking history of the place. They walked the streets hand in hand, dyke-spotting for hours. There was plenty to spot.

Helen made Catherine learn off the address of the hotel and provided her with an emergency fund of currency for a taxi fare from the farthest reaches of the city – not to be spent otherwise – and the two green rectangles of light cardboard that were here emergency Metro tickets. Helen made Catherine agree that if they were separated in a crowd, they would each make their way back to the hotel separately. Catherine, who had travelled widely on her own, including a month-long trip to Mozambique in south-East Africa, thought these precautions were hilarious and called her partner a control freak but she acquiesced when Helen sternly insisted in that special tone she used when all arguments would be ultimately futile.

During the days, they visited the usual sights. In the Louvre, Helen whispered into Catherine's ear that the Mona Lisa's smile indicated she'd just had a shag. Catherine nearly fainted from laughter and they kissed in front of the painting, still laughing while German and Japanese tourists affected to look the other way. While they had a beer in a sidewalk café near Notre Dame one afternoon, Catherine cocked her head. 'Am I raving or do you hear singing?'

Helen listened, tuning out the surrounding interference of traffic and slurred conversation. 'No, you're not. I hear it. Where's it coming from? Will we go and find out?' They paid and wandered towards the island church, the harmony growing stronger all the while. Noting the signs, Helen took off her baseball cap on the way in and Catherine joked that she must have been a Catholic man in a past life. Helen snorted dismissively. At the other end of this vast place of worship, close beneath the famous window, a choir was practicing. Helen and Catherine sat quietly, entranced and holding hands, for over an hour. The sound of mixed voices and the atmosphere of the undeniably holy place itself spliced imperceptibly to create a temporary state of something close to contented hypnosis.

Later that night, they took seats on the Bateaux Mouches and hummed about the bridges of Paris to each other, eagerly taking up the guide's invitation to kiss for luck under Pont Neuf. The air was warm and the lights of the city, bouncing intermittently off the dark waters of the Seine, made Catherine's eyes glow. Helen's, turned away from the lights, were in shadow.

They had planned a special picnic in the Jardins du Luxembourg for the next day. Helen, who had been to Paris before, picked the place and they checked it out for ages first. Catherine murmured her agreement that it was a perfect setting. Leaving the park for a while, they walked the perimeter, hands joined. There was a photographic exhibition on display, each massive print tied to the high railings. Helen would always remember one print in particular. It featured impossibly blue sky and, about a third of the way down, a single silky undulating line. The bottom two-thirds was composed of sand dunes rippled with inconceivable tide marks. The print looked both like and unlike a beach fading into a blue Indian sea. Together and puzzled, they stood in front of the photograph. Helen backed away, uncomfortable with the lack of scale on the huge fourteen-by-nine print. She was halfway across the street, marooned on a traffic island in the midst of manic Parisian traffic, when she gave a shout of triumph. Catherine, who had stayed closer to the picture, looked around only to be surprised by a view of her lover doing a frenzied reel using a traffic bollard as a partner.

'Helen, for Jaysus' sake, you'll be arrested!' she called.

'I will not. I've figured it out,' Helen roared back, jaywalking through Citroens and Renaults at the junction. Marching up to the photograph, she put a finger on one spot, near the bottom left of the print, bringing her face close to a tiny blot about an inch high. 'There it is. A person. Walking. In the desert. It's a fucking desert, Bubbles, a veritable ocean of sand!' Catherine laughed and Helen turned to her to grin in triumph. 'Hey,' Helen said suddenly, 'it's getting wodjous hot. I need shade and a drink. Let's go buy something for the picnic.'

They crossed the street and wandered among the shops and capes, stopping once to buy Helen a pint. It was 11.15 a.m. but she was thirsty and incredibly nervous. She went to the loo four times before they left. Catherine was anxious too: she smoked three cigarettes and drank two espressos strong enough to take the enamel off her teeth, or so Helen said.

As they strolled by the premises next door, Catherine pulled her hand away and pointed at the window. 'Look! It's bread. French bread. It's still steaming. Let's buy some.'

'Would you look at the style of the wans,' Helen replied, viewing the neat uniforms of the sales assistants. 'I'm not going in there. They'll have me lifted for a knacker.'

Catherine kept going but Helen was carrying their joint funds in her backpack so she had little choice but to follow. Helen spoke a little schoolgirl French but she was easily intimidated by the Parisian chic of a simple Left Bank bakery shop. Catherine gave her a slap on the arm, wrested her wallet from the backpack and pointed to what she wanted, shouting the words in English as if the sales assistants were deaf. Helen was mortified and stayed by the door, hidden under her cap and behind dark glasses until Catherine bounced over, bearing a warm loaf wrapped in brown paper.

Outside, Helen looked up at the scorching sun. 'Will we do it now?' she asked.

'Jesus, I'm shaking,' Catherine said.

'Me too. We don't have to.'

'Yes, we do. This was the whole point of the trip. We can't go home without it done. Let's just do it.'

Helen took her hand and smiled tremulously into her eyes. 'It'll be all right, you know. I used to be a girl guide. I know how to do a picnic.'

Catherine grinned. 'It's not the picnic I'm worried about.'

'I know. C'mon then, follow the leader.' Helen pulled Catherine into the traffic and they returned to the gardens.

Inside the railings, they commandeered enough green metal chairs to make a table under the trees overlooking the fountain and the gingerbread Palais de Luxembourg for their simple meal of crunchy fresh bread, cheese and new Beaujolais. The wine was warm from being carried in Helen's backpack in the sun.

Before they ate, Helen deliberately took the two black ring-boxes from the pack and placed them carefully, side by side, on one of the chairs between them. She took off her cap and mopped her brow with a handkerchief. 'Are you really sure you want to do this? You know how seriously I take it but I don't want to do it if you're not sure.'

'I'm sure. Get on with it,' Catherine replied nervously.

Helen opened both boxes, placing them back on the chair. In each was heavy silver Claddagh, shaped like a wedding band. They gleamed occasionally in flickers of sunlight filtering through the leaves as Helen and Catherine looked at them. Helen picked up the one nearest her and examined it. It was slightly smaller and narrower than its counterpart. On the inner surface, on the side which would rest on Catherine's skin, Helen's name was inscribed in Ogham characters. She fingered the design slowly, took Catherine's left hand and looked into her eyes. Her words were simple. 'I honour you,' she said, after clearing her throat twice. 'I honour you. This ring has no beginning and no end, no visible join. Like us sometimes... most times. I love you. Wear this for me.'

She slid the ring onto the third finger of Catherine's hand and kissed her lightly on the cheek. Catherine held up her hand, examining the ring, then smiled right into her eyes. 'That feels good,' she said simply. Helen smiled back.

Catherine took the second ring and held it up to catch the occasional sunlight. She placed the ring on Helen's finger and held Helen's hand between her own. Looking directly into her eyes, Catherine said: 'There is no truth but this. The room is warmer when you're in it… I stole that sentence from a book but it fits you. It fits us. We fit together the way this ring fits your finger. Perfectly. I love you. I hope you'll wear this for me.' She kissed the ring on Helen's finger.

They said nothing more but sat on under the trees, feet up on chairs, munching their picnic and sipping tepid wine from proper glasses they'd brought from Ireland wrapped in towels for just this occasion. Neither wanted to leave. They watched passing Parisians on their lunchtime strolls, commenting on each one that passed their little hideaway.

'Would you look at the cut of the jib on that,' Helen said, indicating a dapper, middle-aged man approaching, still about twenty-five yards away and heading straight in their direction. He looked like a diplomat. The tall, thin man had greying temples and a neat black-and-grey meg. He was impossibly handsome in a gentlemanly, world-weary, chivalrous sort of way.

Before Helen had time to think, Catherine had taken the camera from the bag and was bounding across the thin sand of the park to intercept him. Much shorter, she smiled up at him engagingly and indicated by gestures that she wanted a photograph taken. He inclined his head slowly and walked towards where Helen was sitting, carrying the camera. When he reached Helen, he bowed again, this time from the waist. 'Mademoiselle,' he said. It wasn't a question. Helen nodded and muttered her 'bonjour' in a poor accent.

Catherine rearranged the chairs so that they were sitting side by side. Helen, speaking out of the side of her mouth as the Frenchman set up the shot, commented: 'This is going to look well: me half-steamed at lunchtime and wearing a

Mayo Recorder t-shirt into the bargain. Are you batty?'

'No. Not really. I just wanted a memento of a wonderful occasion.'

The Frenchman called something incomprehensible to them and Helen smiled dutifully, holding Catherine's hand. When the picture had been taken, the photographer rapidly covered the ground between them and returned the camera to Catherine before she could rise. Bowing to them both in turn, he took Helen's hand.

'Enchante, Madamoiselle,' he said slowly and distinctly and then he addressed them both in clear but heavily accented English: 'You are very beautiful. I hope you will be very happy.' He walked away swiftly. Helen was still alternately gaping and giggling fifteen minutes later.

They spent a long afternoon whispering and kissing under the trees; strolling the dusty paths of the gardens and watching Frenchmen play their version of outdoor bowls, work-day jackets discarded, ties loosened and sleeves rolled up over dark forearms, listening for the click of the bowls echoing sharply in the stillness of approaching evening. In the evening, they ate mussels and chips at a crazy place near the Opera House. It was packed. The tables were crammed close together like tinned sardines and the waiters practically flung crocks of steaming, fragrant mussels over customers' heads to reach the tables. Catherine and Helen got completely and deliberately rat-arsed on cheap local wine and Irish coffees that were more whiskey than caffeine. Later, they danced close together in a gay club in the Marais, turning tight circles on a small dance floor with eyes for no-one but each other and no words worth saying. They barely made the last Metro home to the little room on the top floor of the hotel near the Pigalle end of the ninth arrondissement.

On their last day in Paris, they breakfasted as early as

possible and returned to their room to shower and pack. The room didn't have to be vacated until noon and their taxi wasn't due until four. It was very hot. Helen packed most of their stuff while Catherine showered. Helen amused herself by giving out through the open bathroom door about the amount of rubbish Catherine had bought in the tacky Montmartre souvenir shops. Catherine threw a soapy sponge accurately and it hit Helen right in the face, leaving clouds of suds and bubbles on her spectacles.

'Right,' said Helen gravely, advancing towards the door. 'Now you're in trouble.'

'Ooh, I'd be shaking in my boots if I had any on,' Catherine returned, turning away and soaping the back of her neck. She jumped when Helen touched her shoulders. 'Jesus, where'd you come from?'

'That faraway country known as the twin bedroom, lover,' Helen replied. 'Turn around.'

When Catherine did so, she laughed out loud. Helen was standing fully clothed in the shower: shorts, t-shirt, spectacles, sandals, the lot. Helen placed a hand on the tiled shower wall on either side of Catherine. Leaning forward, she kissed the nook where Catherine's collar-bones met under her chin, and then emerged soaked from beneath the warm spray. Helen blew water out of her mouth amusingly before speaking. 'I would like to see my wifie on the flat of her back just at this precise moment,' she observed calmly.

Catherine took off Helen's spectacles and left them on the shelf with the shower gel. 'No thanks, I'm busy.'

'Doing what, pray?' Helen asked, raising her arms to allow Catherine to pull her t-shirt over her head.

'Undressing my wifie.'

'Mmm. I had hoped you'd say that. I have a confession to make.'

'What?' Catherine nibbled her lips.

'I have designs on you. Did I ever tell you that I have this really odd fantasy about a shower, practically a fetish, I'd say' Helen said, nibbling back and blushing.

'Design away then.'

'Say no more.'

Neither did. Helen shed her clothes and footwear and threw them on the bathroom floor. She closed the shower door, eyes still on Catherine's. Without a word, she backed Catherine against the cool white tiles and circled her waist, kissing fiercely and without preliminaries. Catherine gasped and attempted to pull away but there was nowhere to go.

Helen smiled with her eyes. Using the advantage of her extra two inches in height, she leaned against her lover, pressing her tighter against the tiles, still kissing. Without warning, she reached one hand between their bodies, searching. Catherine was warmer and wetter than the jets of water falling between their faces. Leaning away, Helen let her fingers slide in slowly, satisfied with the easy familiarity. Catherine groaned. Helen fastened her lips around one raspberry-red nipple and sucked, occasionally circling the nipple with her tongue and flicking it quickly over the sensitive, cylindrical top. Catherine groaned louder. Helen sank to her knees, gasping for breath in the flowing water. With her elbows, she nudged Catherine's legs until they were apart and planted firmly. Darting her tongue into Catherine's dripping wet navel, she continued stroking her, pausing only to look up through the falling water.

Catherine rested her hands on Helen's shoulders and nodded slowly. Helen roamed lower and slid her tongue along the cleft that led to the hidden location of Catherine's greatest pleasure. Catherine jumped at her gentle touch, but then a small bud expanded slowly in her eager mouth. Catherine moved one hand to the back of Helen's head encouragingly. Helen sucked gently and stroked more gently until

Catherine's legs began to shake and the pressure of her hand on the back of Helen's head grew harder. Helen knew she was on the plateau, admiring the stunning view. Standing up abruptly, she smiled into the mild anxiety in Catherine's eyes.

'Turn around,' Helen whispered.

Catherine braced her body against the tiles with her palms as Helen leaned into her back. Both hands caressed Catherine's nipples for long moments until Helen slid one hand down along her belly. Helen paused before entering. 'Open for me, sweetheart. I'm coming into you,' she whispered, mouth close to Catherine's ear. There was no reply. Helen slid three long fingers into her lover's body. Catherine's knees buckled and Helen quickly slid her free arm around Catherine's waist to hold her up. Helen fucked her slowly, measuring each movement, keeping calm time like a metronome or the beating of a quiet heart. Catherine's face, one cheek against the tiles, at last bore a rising flush of colour. Her eyes closed slowly and she moaned. Helen tightened her grip around Catherine's waist and increased the speed and force of her fingers' movements, matching them to Catherine's breathing, increasing the pace imperceptibly until the change was finally obvious. Catherine's fingers, resting against the tiles, formed tight child-like fists in the moments before she came. With her fingers deep in Catherine's warm body, Helen felt the last long rise before the fall approaching as if it were her own. Catherine's body tightened hard and powerfully, her wetness lubricating unyielding, demanding fingers. She collapsed and cried out Helen's name, just once, the sound echoing around them as she came. Helen fell to the floor with her, still holding on with slowing determination until the aftershocks were over.

When Catherine's ragged breathing finally slowed, Helen turned off the water, opened the shower door and pulled a towel off the rack. She knelt in the bath and spread it around

Catherine's shoulders. 'Come, love, come and lie down for a little,' she said. Catherine staggered to beds that were still joined together and lay face down for a few moments, groaning. Helen lay face up on the other bed, one outstretched hand just touching Catherine's hip, enjoying the sensation of her skin drying naturally from the warm breeze through the skylight above. Catherine turned to face her and lay silently, regarding Helen's profile in repose. Helen's eyes were closed.

'Helen, do you know how beautiful you are?' Catherine said.

Helen's only response was a snort. 'Would you ever get down off the horse and drink your milk. I've been described as many things in my lifetime, Bubbles, but beautiful is a rare term.'

'Well, you are to me. You're not pretty but…'

'Gee, thanks. Same goes for you, ugly-mug.'

'I didn't finish! You have a really handsome face, kind of ageless and strong. It's mobile and expressive. Those angles sit well on you. You look really stern most of the time but when you smile, sometimes it touches every part of your face.'

Helen ran one hand through her damp hair. It was growing longer since they'd met and Catherine loved its sheer unkempt and dark wildness, especially when it was wet. Helen turned her head and opened her eyes. To Catherine, they held Helen's character and often their blueness was startling in her pale face. 'I love your face,' Catherine continued softly.

'What about you then, sweetie, hmm? Let's see.' Helen narrowed her eyes to feline slyness. 'You're not pretty either. Your face is all curvy and soft and you look a lot less than your twenty-six years. I will be raiding your attic shortly because I'm sure you have an ageing portrait of yourself hidden up there, my darling Dorian. You must have. You look impossibly young. I'm sure people think I'm a cradle-snatcher.

You could be jail-bait.' She paused, opening her eyes wide and looking closely in to the Winter grey of Catherine's. 'Your eyes are captivating. They remind me of a moody, truculent ocean, hiding dangerous currents and darker depths.'

Helen raised her left hand and examined her Claddagh ring, shiny from the soap and water of the shower. 'This means a lot to me' she said. 'I never liked anyone enough to bother before. I know it's not a wedding ring but I suppose I consider it a gesture of intent. It's a promise of a future promise, the beginning of something, not the end.' She snuggled across the join between the beds and wrapped her body around Catherine's, kissing her gently on one bare shoulder. 'Thanks for agreeing to wear one for me. I just wanted to brand you as mine. It's not pretty and it sure ain't politically correct, but that's what it is. You're branded. You're mine. You're my big fluffy woolly white sheepy thing, you are.'

Catherine kissed her back softly and slowly, willing Helen to temperate arousal. Helen responded. Sometimes she didn't. Sometimes, she gave so much to the loving that she had nothing left to be loved. Their passion was very different. Catherine loved the giving as much as the receiving: Helen often found more deliverance in the active. It was occasionally a touchy point between them. Catherine hated the distance that Helen retreated afterwards, claiming convincingly that she simply didn't feel the need to be an open vessel for Catherine's ravenous and occasionally rough lust.

Unwillingly, Catherine had to accept that Helen simply didn't need he as much as she needed Helen, not in that sense anyway. She didn't like it and would have preferred Helen to have the dependable all-consuming desire that she experienced herself. It had been somewhat of a surprise to gradually learn that Helen, so capable and physically strong for her size, had the stereotypical butch leanings that Catherine had previously suspected didn't really exist at all. Helen found it hard to let go and often a simple noise outside or a stray thought would bring her back and spoil the moment despite Catherine's intuitive technical expertise. Helen said that, physically, she was the lover and Catherine was the be-loved. Her cut-and-dried attitude to the corporeal facet of their affair was irritating to Catherine. Their passion was very different. Sometimes.

Catherine pulled away, noting the tell-tale softness in Helen's eyes as she pushed her shoulder to leave Helen lying on her back. Their bodies were dry now. Catherine looked along her body, gently massaging one small breast with her palm. Helen's breast fit her hand perfectly with nothing to spare. She loved this body and often burned with a simple desire to make it bend to her will, as if by complete physical appropriation of this cocoon of skin she could possess what-ever lay inside.

Helen smiled encouragement. 'Do I see a devilish glint in those delightful eyes?' she asked.

'You do.'

'I don't know if we have the time,' Helen said, craning her neck to see the little square alarm clock on the dressing table.

'We have time.' Catherine's tone did not invite further debate on the point. Propped on one elbow, she continued massaging Helen's breast and lowered her face to Helen's. When Helen lifted her head to meet her lips, Catherine pulled back, a sequence that was repeated many times until Helen, wanting nothing but those lips against her won, grabbed her hair and thrust her tongue between Catherine's teeth, growl-ing softly. Catherine growled back and Helen giggled like a schoolgirl. Her giggle faded into a soft, breathy groan when Catherine fastened her lips tightly around the nearest nip-ple, her fingers stroking the line below Helen's waist where translucent white skin met wiry tangles. Helen shivered in the heat.

'What do you want?' Catherine asked, raising her head and tantalizing Helen's nipple with her hot breath.

'You know.'

'I know I know. But I want to hear you say it.'

'I can't. I'd be embarrassed.'

Catherine resumed her attentions, pausing occasionally to ask the same question. Helen demurred more than once. Catherine eased her body gently on top of her lover and held Helen's wrists with less than gentleness. 'Fuck you. Tell me,' she said impatiently, with a hint of crossness in her tone that was immediately cut by a sensuous, teasing kiss on the mouth. 'Come on. Don't hide. You don't have to hide. Give it up, sweetheart. Tell me.'

Helen closed her eyes and breathed slowly, shifting her hips gently when Catherine began licking the other nipple. 'I can't,' she said, after a couple of false starts.

'You can. You will or I'll tease you until our 'plane leaves and thin I'll keep teasing you until you can't stand it and lose your mind forever. I'll tie you to one of those beams and tease you for hours.'

Helen flushed at the bold image that took shape in her head. Catherine continued: 'Oh, I see. I wondered about that. Maybe that's an aspect of our relationship we might explore a little more at home where it's safer. Now tell me. Tell me what you want from me, what you need from me.' She kissed the special tender spot below Helen's ear and ran her tongue along its outer edge.

Helen squirmed and a single tear emerged from beneath one of her closed eyelids. 'You win. I'll tell you.'

'It's not winning or losing. It's asking and giving. Ask.'

'I want you to fuck me.'

'Be specific.'

'Until I break. I want you on me, all over me, in me.'

'More.'

'I want it hard, so hard that I can't bear it. I want it fast and strong and basic. I don't want any frilly time-wasting. Just a strong, basic fucking until I feel that there's nothing else in the universe except me and the only reason I'll exist is because of your fingers.'

Helen's body shook and her eyes opened. She laughed nervously. 'Jesus, I'm wringing wet just thinking about it.'

'Hmm. Let's see just how wet you are. Oh, yes. You've been a very good girl and I think it's time I rewarded you. See these fingers? See all four of them? You're going to open wide for me and I'm going to put each and every one of them inside your body. Together. I'm going to move them inside you, following your breathing for speed. See this thumb? That's going to be outside, bathed in pinkness, driving you on. You will come for me. You will.'

'Do it.'

Catherine parted Helen's thighs with her own, and bathed her fingers in oily wetness before pushing in, going on even when Helen shoved against her in almost-pain. When her fingers were completely sheathed by Helen's body, Catherine kissed her dry mouth, drooling soaking saliva onto suddenly parched lips. Helen sucked in another rasping breath as Catherine began to move inside her, holding the upper part of her body off the bed and against her own with unaccustomed strength. There was no distance between them.

Catherine's thrusts were slow and deliberate, each long and probing. Each and every breath began to catch in Helen's throat: she panted like a woman in labour and she was deafened by the kango-hammering of her own heartbeat.

When next she was conscious of what was outside herself, Catherine was moving faster but with the same long, intrusive thrusts, each one filling her and making her body grasp hungrily for the swiftly retreating fingers. Helen rose quickly in short stages, a magenta flush creeping up her rib cage until she spiralled, out of control and unable to stop it herself, into a place where there was nothing but sensation and pure panting animal need. Catherine rose onto her knees and fucked her harder, ignoring Helen's tears and moaned please to stop, please stop, please let her breathe.

Before she realized it, Helen careered past the point of no return and fell head-first into bursting emptiness, crying and writhing, her rising hips nearly flipping Catherine off the bed with their sudden but anticipated violence. She tightened and released unwillingly, over and over, but Catherine didn't stop, even when she begged. Helen's innermost channel, elongated by orgasm, swallowed Catherine's still-moving hand. The thrusts became deeper and ever swifter and Helen realised that there was nothing, nothing at all but her battered body and that long, accelerating movement.

Falling from an impossible height, she hit a hard, rough ledge just below the peak and started to climb again, rapidly and with a safety rope weaved only from glinting sand that she couldn't catch or hold. Catherine calmly measured the distance to the second pinnacle and, just as Helen began her ultimate leap, thrust her fist as deep into Helen as it would go. Finally, it was enough. Helen's scream lay silent, strangled in her throat by simple inability to articulate what she couldn't comprehend. She lost consciousness swiftly.

When she came to, Helen was lying on her stomach in the classic first aid recovery position. Catherine lay beside her, smoking, a whirling grey cloud around her head. At Helen's first movement, Catherine looked down on her with relief. 'Jesus, you're back. If you weren't breathing I'd have thought I'd killed you,' she said.

'You did. I'm a born-again dyke.' Helen's voice was a weak croak. She smiled, her expression reflecting inner fragility. 'That was a once in a lifetime experience. Did I dream it or was that two for the price of one?'

'Yup. I knew you could. I hate you holding out on me. I just want it all from you. You need to know that if you won't give it, sometimes I'll just take it.'

'Well, you got it.' Helen lips felt strange and she eventually realised what was missing. 'Kiss me,' she whispered. They kissed and cuddled for several minutes, whispering words that, afterwards, neither would remember. It didn't matter.

Catherine and Helen hardly spoke on the journey home. For once, the air between them wasn't filled with idle chatter or dry wit. The silence between them was full and complete. If she had to speak, Helen wouldn't have known what to say. In some situations, she believed, words were truly redundant.

Catherine's silence was of the maddening self-satisfied variety. Possessively, she felt a sense of achievement and savoured it in silence on the 'plane and on the drive to Bray, her fingers gently cupped n the curve of Helen's thigh. It was a gesture of ownership, more than affection. Helen had been sold to a new owner and she knew it.

Before Helen returned to work, they spent a couple of days mooching around the Bray house. It was quiet during the days because the boys were at school and Maggie often went shopping or called down to the Apostolic Work crowd to make vestments for mission priests. One mid-morning, Helen made breakfast while Catherine snoozed in the room they usually shared out of habit. Every time Helen stayed, they set up a creaking camping bed on the floor beside Catherine's single bed and decorated it with fresh sheets and a pillow. It was never used.

While Helen was waiting for the eggs to boil, she wandered the downstairs rooms and finally noticed a family portrait in a little office room she'd never been in before. The picture included a younger Catherine and just two of her brothers, along with their parents. Catherine looked a lot like her dead father. Helen realized she knew almost nothing about the dead man, apart from his name, occupation and age at the time of death. Bryan de Lacey – being a Labour Party member, he dropped the Norman 'de' before Catherine was born – had been a fitter with Bord Gais and played the drums at night and weekends when he wasn't playing golf. He was sixty-two when he died of a heart attack two years after Robin was born.

The eggs boiled and Helen scooted back to the nearby kitchen, made toast and set the tray. Upstairs, Catherine stirred and sat up in bed. They munched eggy soldiers happily, Helen bouncing up and down on the creaking spare bed.

'You never talk about your father,' she said conversationally.

'He's dead.'

'I know that. What was he like?'

'I loved him. He didn't want a girl and I was the first to be born so I grew up knowing I was a disappointment to him. He should've stayed a bachelor. He was never here and there was never enough money because he wouldn't work overtime or do nixers. He wouldn't let me go to college because he hated educated women, which is why I ended up in the Civil Service. He fought with my mother a lot. There was a big age gap between them. Mam was only 18 when I was born. After that, she couldn't have kids for ages or maybe it was that she wouldn't. When I was growing up, he was constantly bemoaning the lack of a son so she started again with Gerry. I was fifteen myself then and she was thirty-six. She was terrified Robin was going to be Downs Syndrome because she had him at forty. The pregnancy was a nightmare. Dad just kept playing golf. He was good at it too. It was a mediaeval marriage but she stuck it out.'

'That was tough.'

'Yeah. The trouble was that as I grew older he knew I was like him. He hated that. I loved him but we used to have terrible, bitchy rows. He threw me out of the house once for expressing an opinion but my mother begged me to come back so I did. I often think I should have stayed away. I remind her of him so she looks on me as a replacement. I pay some of the bills and do little jobs around the house and badger the boys into shape. Fuck it, sure I'm nearly old enough to be a mother to all of them. Sometimes I think I am their mother. I'm nearly a surrogate husband.'

'What did you fight about? Sometimes fighting like that is an indicator of love.'

'Not in his case. We fought about everything. I should have told you this before, but we were fighting the day he died.'

'What about?'

'Me.'

'Eh?'

'He'd found out I was gay. He saw me coming out of *The George* one night with an androgynous woman – God, was she a walking stereotype or what? – and put two and two together. He told me to leave and threatened to tell Mother. I told him to fuck off and we had a right set to for about twenty minutes. I screamed all the appalling obscenities I could think of. I rubbed his nose in it and said I'd never be like him, bringing children into the world and leaving them to grow up without love, without a real father. He hit me across the face and I hit him back. Then he turned blue and keeled over. I couldn't leave then, could I?'

Catherine's eyes were dry but angry. Helen put the breakfast tray on the floor and touched her cheek. 'It's all right, love. It's the past. I shouldn't have asked. You're entitled to a past and you can tell me to mind my own business in future, if you want.'

'Ah, there's no secret to it. It's over and done with, but I should have told you the truth before. In the end, I was glad he died because it meant I had one person less in the world to fight against. Still, I hate him for leaving, for leaving this unresolved.' She smiled. 'Let's get up and go shopping. I promised Mam we'd cook a special dinner tonight, to say thank you for all the times you stay. I know you put a few quid in the kitty but she likes nothing better than a meal, a glass of wine, a video and no washing up.'

'Great idea. What're we cooking?'

'I said you'd do your amazing spaghetti with home-made garlic bread for starters and apple crumble for afters.'

'Apple crumble? I don't have a fucking clue how to make that! Get up, you stupid wench, I need to buy a cookbook this instant! If you were going to volunteer my services you could at least have picked something I know how to make, like jelly and ice-cream.'

Catherine picked up a pillow and belted her across the shoulders with it. There was foam on the floor from a torn pillow by the time Helen finally gave up and cried for pax.

The apple crumble Catherine made was a huge success, especially with the boys. After they'd left the table to tackle the homework, Catherine got up to clear the dishes. Maggie touched her shoulder.

'Sit down, Catherine.'

'No, Helen cooked so I'm doing the dishes. That was the deal.'

'Leave them. I want to talk to you two.'

Helen met Catherine's eyes across the table and swallowed nervously.

'What about?' Catherine asked.

'How was Paris?'

'We told you all about it.'

'Not everything.' Maggie paused and pointed at the ring on Catherine's left hand, then glanced to her right and turned her eyes to Helen's ring.

Helen met Catherine's eyes again, sending a silent, fervent message that it was her mother and therefore her call. Catherine sighed. 'Oh, you mean the rings.'

'Yes, I mean the rings. They're Claddaghs. They're the same, they're unusual, you both wear them on the same finger and I don't think you got them in Paris,' she said, looking from one to the other interrogatively.

Helen looked down at the table, tasting a ferrous stain in the atmosphere. She lifted her eyes to find Maggie still looking at her. 'That's a good story. I'll let Catherine tell it,' she mumbled.

'Well?' Maggie's head swung to the left and Helen could see the tell-tale crinkling of wrinkles that indicated narrowing eyes.

'We saw them in a jewellers' in Mayo a couple of weeks ago. We liked them so we bought one each. They weren't expensive.'

Helen cringed at the triple denial of reality. The rings had been specially designed and custom-made for them by an Austrian master jeweller in Leitrim. They were atrociously expensive for silver and were chosen with care and after much discussion

'Why do you wear them on the same finger?' Maggie asked.

Catherine shrugged. 'Don't know, really. It's just the way it happened. They were the sizes they had in stock.' She smiled an apology at Helen. 'At least it means we spinsters don't get hit on by scummy men in nightclubs. They look like gold in disco lights. Isn't that right, Helen?'

Helen nodded through a faint feeling of sickness. There was a long pause. The kitchen clock ticked on in the silence.

Maggie looked from one to the other.

'You hang around a lot together, don't you? I never see you bringing any other pals around when Helen's here.'

'Yeah, we get on well.'

'Maybe you hang around with each other a bit too much.'

'What's wrong with that?'

'Well, it's good to keep in touch with other friends and that goes for both of you. You're both over 21, I know, but the older you get... people might start to think it strange.'

'Strange how?' Helen asked. Catherine shot her a clear warning look. 'No, Catherine, I know she's your mother and all, but I'd like to know exactly what she's circling around.'

'Don't get me wrong, Helen. You're welcome in this house. You're hard working and sensible and you know how to have fun too. You're polite and kind to the boys and Catherine likes you. You're very welcome. It's just that people are curious. Your auntie Bridget was asking about you the other day, Catherine, asking if there was a boyfriend on the scene. I just realized there hasn't been one for years. There's nothing wrong with that but I just wonder if the two of you being stuck together like twins is putting the fellows off.'

Catherine spluttered her drink over the side of the glass. 'Would you ever tell my Auntie Bridget to feck off and mind her own business.'

'Catherine, no language, please.'

'Sorry, Mam, it's just that you know she's an interfering old busybody with a head full of conspiracy theories. She'd just love to see me married off and living in a semi-d in Templeogue with two screaming brats. She hates anyone to have a bit of crack.'

'Be that as it may, look at the pair of you. You're not getting any younger, either of you. I know you may not have any interest in settling down now, but what happens in a few years time when maybe you want to have kids of your own?'

Helen broke in. 'Hang on, Maggie. I don't think I should be here. This is a private conversation and I've got caught up in it.'

'No, you're all right. We're all adults here. Sometimes I forget that Catherine isn't just one of the kids. You're twenty-six, Catherine, and I'd hate to think that I'm holding you back. Maybe it's time you started thinking about moving out and living your own life.'

Catherine looked into Helen's eyes, drinking in courage. 'You're right, Ma, I've been thinking that myself,' she said at last. 'I'm thinking of leaving Dublin altogether. I've looked for a transfer and I'm hoping it will come through soon.'

'To where?'

'Mayo. Ballina. Department of the Environment.'

Maggie tapped her dessert fork against her plate, playing for time. 'Why Mayo? Why so far?'

'Because Helen's there. At least I'd know somebody and I'd have somewhere to live.'

'You'd live in her house?'

'Yes.'

'People would talk.'

'Let them.'

Helen shifted uncomfortably. 'Maggie, it's not unusual for unattached women of a certain age to share a house. It doesn't mean anything. I rent a room to another woman already.'

'Hmm.'

'Mam, please. Will you spit it out, whatever it is?'

'I'm not saying anything. Just be careful. People aren't always kind or understanding.'

'Understanding of what? We haven't done anything. We're not hurting anyone. We just hang around together and we're going to share a house to split the bills. It makes sense if we're both working in the same county.'

Maggie sighed heavily. 'Ah, Catherine love, you're your father's daughter. He was headstrong too. Do as you like.' She got up from the table, the legs of the kitchen chair clattering starkly against the tiled floor. 'I'm off to watch that video. You picked it, Helen, so tell me, will I need a hankie?'

'It's *Beaches,* Maggie. It rates about nine-point-five on the hankie scale. Bring the box just in case.'

'I will. Enjoy the washing up.'

When she left, Helen and Catherine sat on in silence. 'Jesus fucking H. Christ up a skyscraper, what the fuck was that?' Helen breathed eventually.

Catherine looked up. 'We're sussed,' she said quickly.

'Are you sure? I thought she was just fishing around. She didn't seem certain.'

'She knows, Helen, trust me.'

'Well, she's not my mother. What do we do now?'

'Keep schtum and say nowt is the best bet.'

'Is that fair? I mean to her?'

'What's the alternative?'

'Tell her the truth. Lies have a habit of back-firing in the end,' Helen said.

'I can't.'

'Won't.'

'Can't. She'd go mental.'

Would you give her credit, for fuck's sake! You're her daughter and she loves you. She might throw a fit but it'd all blow over.'

'No. We're just going to have to be a bit more careful.'

'Careful? Are you cracked or drunk or what? I love you and it fairly sticks in my craw to deny it like that. I don't think we can keep it up forever. We have to face up to stuff like this sooner or later.'

'Yes, but not now.'

Helen pulled off her spectacles and propped them on top of her head. With her elbows on the table, she leaned across and eyeballed Catherine. 'Listen to me, you. Denying this will wreck us in time. It's soul-destroying and you know it; look what happened to Peter.'

'Who the fuck is Peter?'

'Peter in the bible.'

'That's it, Helen. You've lost your mind. I'm calling Dundrum. Stay there, the men in white coats will be along with a strait-jacket presently.'

'You know what I mean. She gave you an opening and you... you who normally shouts shit from the rooftops, you didn't have the balls for it.'

'And you do with that crowd in Castlebar? Would you ever fuck off and leave it be. I don't see you taking ads out in your precious newspaper to call the fucking banns, do I?'

'Banns? Banns? No, you don't,' Helen replied angrily. 'Maybe that's something I need to think about. Ah, fuck this, we're getting nowhere as usual. You're impossible to argue with. Maybe that transfer will come through and we can just get on with it. I'm doing the dishes.'

She cleared the table and was elbow deep in suds when Catherine sneaked up behind her and slipped her arms around Helen's waist. Helen's hands, scrubbing dishes, stopped moving.

'What do you want?' she said.

'Pax.'

'Pax isn't the answer to everything.'

'It'll do for now. She hopped it on me, Helen. I need time to think. We need time to think.'

'Oh, all right, pax then,' Helen said. She turned, grabbed a tea-towel and stuffed it up Catherine's polo shirt impudently. Both took a fit of laughing and Catherine held her hand over Helen's mouth to stop her giggling being heard.

Helen went home, laden down with bottles of cheap French plonk, on the day before she was due to return to work. After the holidays, she felt well rested and sure of herself. She made the obligatory duty telephone call home, did some shopping and put on the washing. The grass needed cutting, probably the second last of the year. Helen made a mental note to ring her usual but unreliable grass-cutting service. The house was colder than it should have been, despite weak autumnal sunshine: Niamh was notoriously miserly with the heat because she paid half the oil bill. Helen was sitting in the kitchen in the late afternoon, mindlessly watching the washing machine drum roll around rhythmically, when the doorbell rang.

A long-legged teenager, all elbows and taller than herself, stood on the doorstep, hands jammed into the pockets of jeans that were ripped at the ankle.

'You're Helen Dunne?' he asked.

'Correct. And you are?'

The teenager blushed. 'I'm Adam.'

'How biblical for you. Adam who?'

'Adam Murphy. I live up the road.'

'Oh, yes, I've seen you hanging around. At least, I think it was you in the middle of a crowd. You all look alike to an old lady like me.'

He giggled nervously. 'It might have been me. I've seen you around too.'

'Well, what can I do for you?'

'I'm looking for work. I'm doing a Young Entrepreneurs Scheme project. Y'see, what we have to do is set a business and …'

'I know. I've reported on the regional finals for the *Recorder* before. What kind of work?'

'Well, four of us have set up an odd-job business. So

I'm looking for odd jobs.'

'Such as?' Helen asked, leaning against the doorframe and folding her arms.

'Maybe washing your car.'

Helen looked over his shoulder at the mucky old silver VW Golf that was her pride and joy. 'I think we can do business. Do you cut grass? The only problem is that I don't have a lawnmower.'

'I can borrow Dad's.'

'Right so. Let's talk terms.'

Adam turned to survey the mottled front lawn and the dusty car. Helen smiled to herself while he wasn't looking. There was something inexpressibly camp about her young neighbour. As he turned back to her, she schooled her features into seriousness.

'What do you think, Mr. Murphy?'

'I'd say maybe six quid for the lawn and seven for the car, inside and out. It's very dirty. I'll need to get into your kitchen for water.'

'Too expensive. I'll give you a tenner for the two but I want them done properly and today.

'Done.'

She took a fiver out of her pocket and handed it to him. 'Half in advance and half on completion of the contract. Deal?'

'Deal.'

'Off you go and get your bucket then.'

Adam cut the lawn first, neatly piling the cuttings into the wheelie-bin that Helen brought around to the front to avoid him traipsing grass all over the house. He was soaping the car out on the street and Helen was at the door, drinking coffee and warning him to be gentle with Ophelia when Philip pulled up. Wandering up the path, Philip called: 'Who's yer man?'

'That's Adam. He's auditioning for the leading role of Man About The House, aren't you, Adam?'

Adam blew air though his short fringe. 'I suppose so if I can stick it. You're very fussy.'

'Cheeky brat! Keep working, Adam from the Garden of Eden. I'll be out later to inspect the results of your labour before handing over another hard-earned fiver. Enter, Philip, and be seated for coffee. I'm in an expansive mood so I might even put a drop of something nice and warming in it.'

When they were seated on the patio, enjoying the diminishing sun, Helen commented: 'So, what's the goss? I presume you've come around to fill me in on all the office politics that's been politicked since I've been away.'

'Nah, not really. I just came to get my present.'

'Present?'

'From Paris.'

'Oh, right.' Helen disappeared and returned moments later with a little parcel, tied neatly with ribbon. When she handed it to him, Philip laughed: 'I was only joking!'

'I know that. But I couldn't go to Paris and not bring you home something.'

Philip opened the package and chuckled over the contents. Helen had notoriously naff taste in souvenirs. A set of coasters featuring major Parisian sights was accompanied by a ballpoint pen complete with an Eiffel Tower logo, and a paper knife, the handle shaped like Napoleon's head. 'You never lost it for tack,' he said.

'You're welcome,' she smiled sweetly.

They sat in silence, sipping coffee laced with smooth French brandy. 'Anything new in the office: any new undercurrents I need to know about before I put my foot in it?' Helen asked.

'Yes, that's really why I came. I don't quite know how to put this…'

'That doesn't sound too good. Do your best.'

'Paula's been spreading a rumour about you around the office.'

'I don't suppose I need to ask what kind of rumour,' Helen said, looking into the distance.'

'You suppose right.'

'How bad is it?'

'Bad enough. The front office is abuzz. There's been a lot of talk about lowering the tone and how the advertisers will react. Laurence nearly spits every time your name is mentioned and Coogan's very self-satisfied.'

'What about Liam and George? Jesus, and C.P.?'

'Jesus doesn't seem to be too bothered, given that the place hasn't been struck by heavenly lightning since you left. Liam, I think, finds it a turn-on but then he would. Georgie's hard to figure out. I honestly don't know what he thinks but he's half afraid to open his mouth to ask for the time anyway. As for Colm, well, you know Colm: he never lets much slip. I don't think he knows but he doesn't miss a trick in that place, even though he swans in and out as if he notices nothing. I've been under a bit of pressure myself. Everyone keeps asking me what I know because I'm closest to you.'

'And what have you been saying?'

'Fuck all, really. Just that I don't know anything. They don't believe me. Chris – from accounts, not the advertising one – is convinced it's true on the basis that you don't have a boyfriend but then, she's never without some man or other on her arm. Desirable doesn't come into it as far as she's concerned, as long as he's got a prick.'

'Philip, that's gross!'

'Gross, but true.'

The doorbell rang. Helen went out onto the street and first surveyed Ophelia from distance, then brought her nose close enough to the paintwork to see stars.

'Well, what do you think, Adam Murphy from up the road? Have you earned your fiver? Answer honestly now.'

The teenager gaped, perhaps thinking Helen was going to fiddle him. 'I did my best. I can't do anything about the scratches and that grunge just won't come off the bottom of the door.'

'Gunge, gunge. What a nice word. Of course it won't. You'd need a specialized tar cleaner for that. I'll have some ready for the next time,' she said, handing him a fiver and two pound coins.

'The next time?' he asked, trying to hand back the two coins and spluttering an explanation that she'd overpaid.

'Consider it a tip for a job well done, Mr. Murphy. Ophelia will need a bath every month. Preferably on a Thursday evening but that will have to be flexible so I suppose I'll ring you when the great day arrives. And a wax in the Winter. Can you manage that?'

'Done, Mrs. Dunne.'

'It's Ms. Not Mrs., Adam. I've killed people with my bare hands for less. The name is Helen. Now get off my property and report for duty at ten-past-six on Thursday week if you don't hear from me before then. No excuses or you're sacked. You her me?'

'I'll be here... em... Helen,' Adam said sincerely, unsure whether or not to laugh. 'There's just one other thing.'

'What? More extortion?'

'My mother likes your column. She said to be sure and say.'

Helen sighed heavily. She wrote an opinionated weekly column full of manic observations on life, feminism and the behaviour of the next-door neighbour's Yorkshire Terrier, Aphrodite. The column was designed to appeal to younger readers but, for some reason, the blue-rinse matrons and the county's ladies-who-lunch brigade absolutely loved it. Therefore, Helen reckoned she was doing something very, very wrong. 'Tell her I said thanks. It's nice that people notice.'

'Oh, they do.'

'Hmm. I wonder what else they notice?' She asked, half to herself.

'They think you're cracked,' Adam blurted. Noticing the alarming change in Helen's features, he hurried on. 'I don't mean cracked exactly. Oh, I can't think of the word. It begins with "egg".'

'Eccentric.'

'Yah, that's it.'

'You just saved yourself a hammering, Murphy. Eccentric is good, cracked is bad but for your information, I am cracked. Now get out of here before I call the police.'

Adam displayed a hugely attractive grin and backed away. 'Okay, okay. See you on Thursday week.'

'Be sure you do,' Helen said, slamming the door for effect.

Out on the patio, Philip was at ease, feet up on a spare plastic garden chair.

'I think that youngster's gay,' Helen said when she was seated.

'You think everyone's gay.'

'I do not. We have radar and it's very accurate.'

'Yeah, right.'

They sat on in silence for a moment. 'What should I do?' she asked.

'I don't know, weather it, I suppose. Or ignore it. You're such a lunatic they're hardly likely to say it to your face.'

'Except that bitch Coogan. And she's bound to sing out when the place is packed. She just gets right up my nose and I can't help myself.'

'Try.'

'Why should I? They can't sack me for it.'

'No,' Philip said slowly. 'They can't. But they could make life so difficult for you that you'd just leave anyway.'

'Fuck that. That's constructive dismissal. I'd sue.'

'And then what. It'd be all over the bloody newspapers.'

'Shit. You're right.'

Philip looked at his watch. 'Listen, I've really got to go. Sorry. I've to meet Patti to discuss whether or not we're going to go into mediation to split up the joint assets arising from the marriage. What a lovely prospect.'

'Feck, Philip, will you be all right? Here I am, raving on about my problems and...'

'Will you relax? It's fine. I'm good at the practical stuff.'

'Don't I know it. Ring me later for a chat.'

'I will. I'll see myself out.'

'Okay. See you.'

'Bye.'

When he left, she leaned back and closed her eyes, breathing slowly and deeply and dreading the inevitable passing of time which would bring the morning. She didn't have a plan and couldn't think of one. Helen decided to wing it.

Chapter Five

Split Ends

Catherine fairly bounced off the train on Friday evening, grinning like she'd just won a couple of million quid on the National Lottery.

'Have I got a surprise for you!' she told Helen, grabbing her by the sleeve of her coat and marching her at speed down the platform towards the car park.

'What? What? What is it? Will you let go of me! I just got off work and I'm too tired to run a sprint.'

'Later, wenchie. This news will put big-time pep in your step. You'll not need any vitamins this Winter by the time I'm finished with you.'

'I don't think I like surprises. Is it a good surprise or a bad surprise?' Helen asked, stopping short.

'Good. Very, very good. I would even stretch the point and says it's excellent. Now come on and take me home. Actually, I'll take you home. I need the practice.'

Helen piled her with questions during the very short drive to the house but Catherine refused to divulge a word, covering her mouth with her hands, her eyes twinkling with devilish humour. Niamh was cooking lunch in the kitchen when they arrived: she was on nights in the hospital for a few weeks and cooked the oddest concoctions at the oddest times. Two days previously, Helen had found her cooking porridge at three in the afternoon.

'Tell me, tell me,' Helen demanded.

'Not yet,' Catherine said, rooting in her bag and producing a bottle of champagne packed in ice and clear plastic bags. 'First, we need glasses.'

'Spectacles, like? Sure I've got them already,' Helen quipped.

Niamh raised her eyebrows. 'What's the celebration?' she asked.

'Fecked if I know,' said Helen, taking three wine glasses from a shelf above her head, 'but we might as well drink the free plonk anyway. Join us.'

'Nah, you go ahead. It's still morning to me and I can't put stitches in you after drinking anyway.'

'Ah, c'mon Niamh, this concerns you anyway,' Catherine said.

'You what?'

'Well, indirectly,' she added, handing the bottle to Helen who looked at her quizzically before opening the back door and popping the cork in safety. It hit the wooden garden shed door with a wallop and Catherine quickly galloped across the room to put a glass under the foaming waterfall. They clinked glasses and drank, Catherine grinning and trying not to burst from the effort of withholding information.

'Is three a crowd?' she asked conversationally, looking around the room but not at the other women.

Niamh and Helen just looked at each other. Niamh shrugged. 'What is she on?' Helen whispered to Niamh.

'Damned if I know but whatever it is, I'd like some,' she replied.

'Okay, that's it. Out with it or I'll crown you with the

bottle,' Helen threatened.

Catherine pulled an envelope from the back pocket of her jeans and opened it, pulling out one sheet of paper. She passed it to Helen who read the letter silently. Folding it up neatly, she handed it back without a word, avoiding Catherine's eyes.

'Well, Niamh, it looks like I'm getting another lodger,' she said eventually.

'What?'

'Catherine's been transferred to Ballina and call me Sherlock but I suspect she's going to suggest moving in here with us. I wouldn't have done it this way if I had a choice, but how do you feel about that, Niamh?'

Niamh said nothing. Catherine grinned from one to the other. 'Ah, go on, Niamh, let me move in. It'll be cheaper and I'll take my turn at the hovering and lighting the fire.'

Niamh turned back to the cooker. 'Helen, this is a two-bedroom house. Where would she sleep?'

Helen eyed Catherine sharply and shrugged. 'In my room,' she said. There was a protracted, edgy lull to the conversation.

'I see.'

'Do you?'

'I'm not blind or brainless, Helen. I get the impression that this wasn't as spontaneous as the two of you are letting on.'

'It was and wasn't. I knew she was looking for the transfer, I suppose, but I had no idea when it might come through, if it ever would. I should have said something before this happened.'

'You should.'

'Sorry.'

'It's all right. It's your house. A little notice would have been nice though.'

'I know. I apologise.'

Niamh continued stirring the contents of her saucepan. Catherine leaned back against the worktop, sipping champagne and looking from one to the other. 'I'm sorry,' she mouthed at Helen silently. Helen waggled her head from side to side, easing the tension in her neck with her free hand. 'Niamh,' she said.

'What?'

'I hope you'll stay too. I don't want you to leave,' she continued. Glancing at Catherine, she continued: 'We don't want you to leave. Catherine moving in here doesn't mean you have to go... unless you want to.'

'I like it here.'

'Does that mean you'll try it? That you'll stay?'

'Might as well.'

Helen put an arm around her shoulders, squeezing lightly. 'I don't think you'll regret it. We'll get on okay.'

'There'll have to be some ground rules.'

'Won't there just. She'll change her mind when we tell her about the bin rota,' Helen smiled.

'I didn't mean that.'

'Oh?'

Niamh swung around. Helen joined Catherine at the worktop across the little kitchen from her. 'If this little ménage is going to work at all, I don't want to see you pair canoodling in front of the television.

Caught unawares, Helen sprayed champagne down her shirt front and wiped her mouth with the back of her hand. 'Canoodling? Where in the world did you get a word like that, you Seventies reject? What makes you think I'd be canoodling with her? She's dog ugly, for a start!'

'I mean it. You can do what you like in your own house but I'm not putting up with coochy-cooing. Is that clear?'

Helen was on the point of responding when Catherine interrupted. Quietly, but in a firm, level voice, she said: 'That's fair enough.'

Niamh looked directly at Helen, immense satisfaction written large on her face. 'I fucking knew it. You're gay.'

'I am. We are,' Helen said decisively, glaring at Catherine and then at Niamh. 'We are and we're together. Is that going to be a problem for you?'

'Not unless there's obvious canoodling in the communal areas of the house.'

'Good. That's settled then. House rule number one, Catherine: no nooky in the sitting-room, please, or you're evicted.' Walking over to stand beside Niamh again, she asked softly: 'How did you know?'

'I'm a doctor, Helen, I've done the psychology module and studied the texts. We get all sorts at the hospital. We had one fellow in a month ago with a ketchup bottle stuck up his bum, the fecking eejit. If it was a shampoo bottle, at least he'd have been able to use the standard explanation that he'd slipped in the en-suite.'

'Jesus, that's disgusting!' Catherine piped up.

'Ah, Niamh, seriously now, how did you really figure it out?' I need to know so I can work out how to keep it quiet outside,' Helen said.

'Let me see, mmm.' Niamh turned off the cooker and moved the saucepan away from the hot ring. 'How can I put this and still be thought of as a sensitive person? You look like a dyke, you walk like a dyke and, when she's around, you look like a pair of dykes. There's a connectedness that only some women notice. Most of them wouldn't know what it was. The rings just confirmed it.' She transferred the contents of the saucepan onto a warm plate she'd taken from the oven. Helen said nothing and drained her glass. 'When are you moving in?' Niamh asked Catherine.

'In about a month or six weeks, I think.'

'I look forward to it.' Niamh took a knife and fork from the cutlery drawer, picked up her plate and opened the kitchen door. 'I'm eating this in the front room so you can talk about me when I'm gone.'

Later that night, Helen and Catherine cuddled up on the sofa, breaking house rule number one.

'No, it's too much. She can't pay that! You're going to have to come down at least a couple of hundred. Sure that piece of crap'll be due a service shortly. Look at the mileage, for fuck's sake!'

'Ah Helen, you're trying to rob me. Will you take pity on me and let me make a living?' Dan spluttered.

Helen looked out the window of the Opel dealership to the forecourt where Catherine sat poking around in a four-year-old Corsa, talking to herself. 'What about the tax? When's it due?'

'Not until March.'

'More money.'

'That gives her four months to save up for it, for Christ's sake! And it's not that much; the engine's small.'

'Hmm.'

'And you said yourself her mechanic gave it clean bill of health,' Dan protested.

'Apart from the wonky central locking and one of the stereo speakers.'

''I'll knock off seventy-five. I can't do better.'

'And I don't like the colour, Dan. It's canary yellow, for Jaysus' sake. Who custom paints their car canary yellow?'

'At the end of the day, you're not buying it. She likes it.'

'I know. All right, she'll give you five for it and not a penny more. And she wants a year's warranty on the engine and gearbox.'

'Five-three.'

'In your dreams. Five-one and the warranty or no deal.'

'Okay, okay, split the difference. Five-two. And the warranty.'

'Shake.' Helen held out her hand. 'You'll have the money this afternoon as soon as she gets insurance sorted out. Fill up the paperwork and she'll be back later today to sign.'

The salesman raised his eyes to heaven before taking her hand. 'I'd like to say it's been a pleasure doing business with you, Helen, but as usual it has been nothing but a feckin' nightmare.'

'That's a compliment, Dan. Thanks.' Helen stood up. 'How's the wife and when's she due?'

'Fine. Any day now. It could be a boy, you know.'

'Bet it's a girl. I can tell by the shape of the bump.'

'That's an old wives' tale.'

'No, nowadays it's a politically correct young spinster's one. Give her my regards.'

'I'll tell her. How's your own crock holding up?'

'How dare you! Ophelia is far from a crock. She's wonderful but I might trade her in shortly.'

'For scrappage, I presume.'

'I'll be going elsewhere with my business if you continue that line of thought.'

'That's what I was hoping.' Dan got up. 'I'll get the paperwork sorted and I'll see you at about…?'

'Four-ish.'

'See you this afternoon then.'

'Bye, Danno.'

Catherine got out of the car as she approached. 'You're smiling. Does that mean it's mine?'

'Yes, ma'am. Five-two. Not too bad considering.'

'That's great, but you know I could have negotiated for myself. I's all growed up.'

'You could surely but Danno knows the form. I screwed

a bit more out of him than you would have on your own. Let's go.'

'What now?'

'Insurance cover and money. I said we'd sort it and be back around four to pick it up.'

'Wonderful. My first car. No more scrounging lifts and buses and hitching. I'm thrilled,' Catherine said as they walked back towards the town centre.

'You won't be when you see the insurance bill.'

'I will so. She's a beauty.'

'What are you going to call her?'

'Nothing.'

'Funny name.'

'I don't put names on things the way you do, Helen. It's just a car, a means of transportation, an A-to-B kind of item, not an actual relationship.'

'Not so. My darling Ophelia is a slutty courtesan with an attitude problem, and I love her.'

'You're mad.'

'Yeah, and I'm getting worse. Stretch those legs and speed it up, Catherine, I need to get my heart rate up higher or my dreams of supermodel-dom will come to naught due to obesity.' They increased their pace, keeping step easily. 'And let me do the talking in the insurance office; I know the manager.'

Catherine chuckled and shook her head. 'I never would have guessed.'

Catherine moved in over a long weekend. The yellow Corsa – nicknamed Tweetie by Helen – arrived from Wicklow packed to the roof. Helen was shocked by the sheer amount of stuff and amused by the choices and the items Catherine had forgotten or left behind to collect on another trip home. Catherine had brought eight hockey medals, 50 compact discs, a pile of books and her shocking pink dressing gown but no socks and only one spare pair of shoes. Helen hated personal disruption and became more easily irritated as the afternoon wore on and more and more of Catherine's belongings appeared in her room and around the house.

'You moved my gong!' she said accusingly in the sitting-room at tea-time.

'Only a bit, to make room for the CD's.'

'A bit? It's on the wrong shelf.' Helen got up and rearranged the items on the built-in shelves so that her one and only journalism award was back in the middle of the top shelf. 'Leave it alone.'

'Helen, there's no right or wrong shelf,' Catherine replied indulgently.

Helen grumbled and sat down, propping her feet on the coffee table. 'I like my stuff the way I have it.'

'I know, love, but if I'm going to live here with you, you're just going to have to shove over and make room. In lots of ways.'

'I never thought of it like that.'

'Maybe you should have. If it doesn't work out, I can always move and rent somewhere else.'

'Don't be thick. You're gorgeous and charming and very sexy, and I don't want you to move out. Sure, Jesus, you've hardly moved in yet and here I am picking on you. I suppose I just need a chance to adjust.'

Catherine hopped up and plonked down beside her on the couch. 'So do I. Let's be nice to each other. It might be difficult to get used to this living together bit.'

'Yeah, I mean, I know I was angry about you looking for a transfer without talking to me first but I really wanted you to get it. I've been looking forward to this but maybe I didn't think about the reality of it. Old married couple and all that. Not that we're married or anything. Oh, feck, you know what I mean,' she added hastily when Catherine grinned.

Catherine kissed her on the lips. Helen pulled away and snickered. 'Stop that immediately. No canoodling in the sitting-room. Break the rules and you're out,' she remarked.

'How's it working out with Patti?' Helen asked Philip over morning coffee in Crosbie's. They sneaked out from work together at least twice a week to avoid the front-office gossips in the tea-room, and this was one of those days.

'It's getting there. We're going for a judicial separation and I'm hoping the judge will order the house to be sold. It's worth enough to buy two smaller ones a bit out of town. I'm sick of renting. It's a pure balls.'

'Yeah, I remember that rootless, flatland feeling. You could have moved in with me and Niamh temporarily, but now that Catherine's here it's a bit crowded.'

'How's it going so far?'

'Okay, I suppose. You won't believe this but she leaves the feckin' top off the toothpaste and she's grumpy in the mornings because she has to get up at half-seven to be in Ballina for nine. It still takes her three-quarters of an hour. Can you believe it? Forty-five minutes to drive twenty-four miles? I'd walk it quicker.'

'And you're the paragon with no bad habits?'

Helen exhaled smoke and twirled her cigarette against the ashtray to loosen the half-centimetre of ash at the end. 'I know, I know. I just hate having to account for my movements all the time. I keep having to leave notes saying where I am and what time I'll be home. It's like living with my mother and it's driving me nuts.'

'And does cohabitation not have any advantages at all, then?' he asked smiling.

'A few.' Helen smiled back. 'I'm just grouching for the sake of form. It's wonderful being with her *most* of the time and that's all a person like me could expect. We'll settle down into it after a few months. I suppose I'll just have to live and learn, as usual.'

'Good. That's the way. You'll get the hang of it as you go along.'

'That's life.'

They slurped coffee companionably and Helen chided Philip for eating a cream slice. She loved those flaky cream slices but was trying to control her weight. She complained to Philip that she could taste it and suggested he should just hurry up and eat the blessed yolk.

'Things seem to have settled in the office,' he commented through the last mouthful.

'A bit, anyway. At least the usual ones are talking civilly to me and the others never did before, so they don't count.'

'C.P. never commented, did he?'

'Not a word. Coogan keeps dropping hints wider than the blue Danube but I'm doing my best to let that shite run off me. She's fecking cute enough to start up only when you're not around. My hero. Hey, did you notice that Liam's pin-ups have even bigger tits lately?'

Philip struggled manfully, juggling a mouthful of hot coffee against the impulse to laugh. 'He probably thinks you'll be distracted by them and he can take over your column when you're not looking,' he said when he'd recovered.

'Not fucking likely. I'd burn the place down first,' she growled amicably.

'I think it's all blowing over, to be honest.'

'Yup, and that's great, but it's a long-term nuisance, though.'

'What is?' 'Always having to watch what I say and who I say it to. It was easier when I was more or less on my own, but with Catherine in the house, it's going to be more difficult to be discreet. And I absolutely hate having to be. Discretion can be a dirty word. Sometimes, I feel like a fucking criminal. Or a freak.'

'I know, Helen,' he said, his sympathy for her very human predicament obvious.

'People can be so bigoted about things they know nothing about. You'd think I was doing something I ought to be ashamed of but I'm not. I don't know why we can't just get on with living the way we please without the town fuckwits poking their narrow-minded noses in.'

'Do noses have minds? Helen, look, I know how you feel. When the news broke about my separation it was the talk of the town. People stood in the street, whispering about me. My personal affairs became public property for a while. But it's like everything else: it's a nine-day wonder and it only lasts until the next new sensation comes along. That crowd in the office don't know about you for sure, and they'll get tired wondering eventually. Life will go back to normal.'

'Counselling, that's it. You should give up reporting and go into counselling. You'd be brilliant.'

'Feck off.'

Helen looked behind the bar at the mahogany grandmother clock mounted behind the optics. It was always set to run five minutes fast. 'Right, we'd better be getting back.' She put on her coat and they headed for the door. 'Hey, Philip, d'ya know something? We spend so much time together they probably think we're having a hot affair!'

Philip agreed, adding that a scandal like that would do wonders for Helen's reputation and also for his if it was thought that he'd converted a dyke back to the one true way. They strolled back towards the office, parting company when he went into the newsagents to buy a packet of Polo. Waiting in the cold outside, Helen decided she was sick of the whole miserable scene.

The next Sunday, Catherine drove Helen to Sligo in the yellow car to show it to Helen's parents. Helen had another agenda and she told Catherine about it on the journey. Catherine, working hard at concentrating on driving, was not in favour.

'You should have told me this before I agreed to come with you. That wasn't fair. Why can't you just leave it as it is? You should at least think about it more.'

'No. I would have told you but if I did you'd never have come with me. I need you for this in case it all goes pear-shaped.'

'Helen, please, please, don't do it. Not today. We'll talk about it, but don't do it today.'

'No. There's only one kind of talking I want to do. I'm pig-sick of this messing and I want it sorted. I want it sorted now.'

'Have you even worked out what you're going to say?'

'Nah. I shall fly high on a wing and a prayer, my love. I'll just wait for a chance and then I shall open my gob and see what comes out. If it's bad language, I suspect we'll have to leave.'

'That's not funny. This isn't funny, Helen' Catherine's words were almost muffled by the accent of straining gears. 'Shite, I can never get it from fourth to fifth without it revving like that. What am I doing wrong?'

'Try it again and I'll see,' Helen said, an instruction that was followed by a protesting screech from a labouring engine. 'Okay, it's simple. You've got a bad habit, the first of your driving career. Congratulations.'

'Thanks. Now how do I get rid of it?'

'Depress clutch. At the same time as you move your hand to change gears lift your foot completely and quickly off the accelerator... all the way off. What's happening is you're leaving your foot on it while you're changing up and the revs are high anyway.'

'Thanks, Helen.' Catherine tried again and accomplished the manoeuvre correctly.

'Excellent. That's an A-plus for my pupil. Now will you turn down the fecking heater before my shoes get scorched.'

'But it's freezing out there.'

'Indeed, and it's like the Sahara in here, my darling.'

They argued constantly about temperature. Helen liked to be cool and preferred being too cold to being too warm. Catherine loved heat and practically sat on the open fire in the evenings. Helen said that it was better to be too cold because then you could put extra clothes on. With the house too hot, she'd added, there wasn't much else she could do when she was down to her knickers.

Catherine turned the dial a couple of points and the air around them cooled slightly.

'Thanks. I thought I was going to suffocate.'

'Helen…'

'Leave it be, now. I'm not ashamed of you and I'm not hiding you anymore. Not from them. I've made up my mind, child. All I need you to do is sit there and smile and get me out of the house and away if there's a bad scene. Can you do that?'

'You know I wouldn't leave you in the shit.'

'Yeah, right. Next left and then third right.'

'I know. I've been here four times before.'

'Oops, sorry.'

Catherine turned the car into the drive, engaged the handbrake, disengaged the gears and switched off the ignition, all in the right order. Helen clapped.

'Okay, love-bomb. Let's eat lunch and see if later I'll be eating my words,' she said, waving through the window to her mother who was already in the process of opening the front door for them.

Lunch was delicious. After the meal, Helen and Frank installed themselves in the conservatory at the back of the house, a room constantly warm even in thin Winter sunshine. Helen disappeared behind a Sunday newspaper, eavesdropping on the conversation she could hear from the kitchen through the open door. Nora and Catherine were filling the dishwasher and nattering on and on about each other's families. Helen squeaked and rustled the paper threateningly when she heard her mother tell Catherine about the time she'd mitched school and been caught by Frank while she was sitting eating her sandwiches in the graveyard. Helen only mitched the once; she could never understand what the hell her father was doing up the graveyard halfway through a Circuit Court day. He never told her.

When the dishes were done, Nora joined Frank on the bamboo couch and Catherine took the other armchair.

'That's a nice ring,' Nora said, pointing to Catherine's hand. 'Can I have a look? It looks very familiar.'

Helen folded her newspaper and threw it on the floor beside her chair. 'It should. It's identical to mine,' she said quietly.

Her mother looked up from the piece of jewellery sharply. Frank lowered his newspaper, still holding an edge in either hand, until it was a crumpled pile in his lap. He stared at Helen.

'It's very nice,' Nora said quietly and handed the ring back to Catherine who slipped it discreetly onto her wedding finger.

'I've something to tell you both,' Helen began, hoisting herself up in the armchair until she was upright. Looking at a point between her parents, she continued: 'Catherine's moved into my house.'

'Oh, and has Niamh moved out?' This was from Frank.

'No. She's still there too.'

'You converted the study into a bedroom then,' he said softly, not asking a question.

'No. Catherine shares my room. Our room.'

Nora put her hands together into her lap. Frank looked at Catherine who was examining her shoes in minute detail. He folded his newspaper and settled himself more comfortably. 'And?' he asked.

'And what?'

'And I assume there's more.'

'There is. Mam, Dad, I think it's important for you to know that Catherine and I are together and we're in it for the long haul.'

'More important for whom, you or us?' Frank asked. Nora started to weep silently.

The question took Helen by surprise. Struggling for words, she replied: 'For all of us, I suppose. It's not enough for my relationship with you to be based on a lie.'

'Why are you gracing us with this information now? You think we don't have enough to worry about, is that it?'

'There's nothing to worry about. I just wanted to tell you because I've met someone who's important to me and I don't want to be constantly hiding it; cleaning out my room when you're coming to visit and coming home on my own in case you guess.'

'You've upset your mother.'

That short sentence made Helen's teeth grate. Over the years, she'd heard it too many times to count. It was always the same and it was always going to be the same.

'I didn't mean to but this… us… me and Catherine… it's important to me.'

'Important! I honestly thought, at your age, that you'd outgrown that stupid phase. You're taking a long time to develop a mature and responsible attitude, my lady.'

'Dad, don't. I'm thirty-one. I'm never going to change.'

'Hrrumph. So what do you want from us? It better not be our blessing because you can forget about that.'

Helen sighed, suddenly tired. Looking across at Catherine, she said firmly: 'I don't need your blessing. I'm over twenty-one so what I do is really my business, but you're my parents and I expect a bit of tolerance. I don't need it but I expect it.'

'Expect a bit of tolerance,' he repeated. 'Your head seems to be full of expectations. Who else knows about this?'

'Niamh. A couple of friends. Philip O'Connor.'

'From the office? You idiot! You could lose your job and who'll pay your mortgage then?'

'It's not like that anymore, Dad. I just want to be able to come home and be the person I am, not the person you expect me to be,' Helen retorted, a little sadly. Nora was still sitting, calmly weeping and looking at her hands. 'Mam. Mam, please don't be upset. I'm just like Johnny Holmes. You like him. You like his partner. I'm still your baby girl. I'm still Helen and I love you.'

Nora stood up, smoothing her skirt over her hips. 'Get up, Frank, we'll go for a walk. Let Jane out when you leave, Helen.' The fat ginger-and-white cat lay inside the conservatory door, asleep in the sun.

Frank rose. He hitched his trousers up over his stomach and tucked in his shirt neatly. Looking Helen straight in the eye and hardly blinking, he said slowly: 'You're not the only one who had expectations. You're our only daughter now. Think about that while you're parading your lifestyle around the place. Stay away from here until you hear from us. You've had plenty of time to think. You'll give us plenty too.'

As her parents walked from the room without saying goodbye to either of them, Helen spoke again. 'Wait. Can't you stay we can talk about it? This isn't as awful as you think. I can't explain it but you might understand eventually.'

Frank left the room without responding. Nora turned in the doorway. 'You're my daughter, Helen, but I don't know who you are. As long as I live, I will never understand.'

Helen froze in her seat until the front door slammed, staring at Jane who was calmly washing her front paw, the white one with the ginger freckle. At the sound of the door, Catherine looked up. 'I tried to stop you,' she said.

'Yeah.' Helen got up and carried the protesting cat to the conservatory door. Jane bit her on the thumb, earning herself a clatter on the head and a kick in the rear end for her trouble. Jane scooted down the garden, ears flattened in irritation, looking for all the world like someone walking on high heels. 'Thanks for your support.'

'Don't start looking for someone to blame, Helen. You did this on your own.'

Helen went into the kitchen for their coats and gloves. Returning to the conservatory, she stood over Catherine, holding out her coat. 'Come on. I'm going home. Give me the keys.'

When Catherine looked into her eyes, they were dead in her head: glassy machine-gunners' eyes complete with the quintessential thousand-yard stare full of no real emotion.

They drove home by a slow, circuitous route, calling to see two friends of Helen's in Foxford. Over tea at the ramshackle farmhouse a mile from the town where Madeline lived with Anna, their combined total of seven children, three dogs, five cats and four goats nicknamed, inexplicably, the Three Degrees, Helen began to defrost. When they arrived home, Niamh mentioned that she'd taken three messages from Andy. Helen disappeared upstairs, and after a while Catherine heard the sound of the bath being filled. She waited for about twenty minutes, chatting to Niamh about her wonky knee. It was occasionally troublesome, a four-year-old legacy of a massive belt with a hockey stick earned when she told her marker during a game that she fancied her sister, just to distract her from the oncoming ball. Catherine was never as good a player after that, having lost the ability to change direction at the last moment to skirt around opposing players with a smile. Niamh had little sympathy when told the circumstances but she recommended a sports injury specialist in Galway.

Helen was soaking in a ferociously hot bath when Catherine tapped on the door.

'It's me. Can I come in?'

'Yeah.'

The fog in the bathroom was heavy enough to make condensation run off the tiled walls. Helen was submerged to the shoulders, leaning her head against the edge of the bath, a dripping face flannel over her face. 'What's up?' she asked, her voice muffled.

'Nothing. I just thought you might like me to scrub your back.'

'Sounds good.' Helen removed the flannel from her face and sloshed into an upright position. Her skin was pink from the heat. Catherine rolled up her sleeves and picked up Helen's favourite bath stuff, a blue concoction smelling of salty sea. She played with the top of the bottle and perched on the edge of the bath.

'Are you all right?' she asked.

'Of course. I didn't expect it to be easy. They'll calm down eventually. My mother being upset doesn't mean the sky's going to fall in and Dad's just pissed off because he won't get to walk me up the aisle in St. Mary's Cathedral in front of all his legal friends,' Helen replied sarcastically.

'I think they were a bit shocked.'

'Not at the fact of it, I bet.'

'What do you mean?'

'They knew; they just can't believe I had the neck to say it. It's always been the same: maintain the status quo and sweep the shitty bits of our family under the carpet. Like Uncle Paddy.'

'What happened him?'

'He's a drinker and a philanderer. He left his wife for someone younger than his oldest daughter. Dad paid him to emigrate to Liverpool twenty-five years ago. They haven't spoken since. Dad doesn't know I know. I only found out when I met Paddy on the street once in Dublin. I recognized him. We keep in touch.'

'Hmmm.' Catherine picked up the flannel and began to soap Helen's back slowly. 'Families can be a nuisance sometimes. I hope you understand now why I didn't want to tell my mother.'

'Your mother: your choice. Nothing to do with me.'

'I know that but I'd prefer if you understood it.'

'Nothing to understand.'

Catherine rinsed her back and Helen threw pint glasses of water over her hair swiftly, making the little yellow duck at the end of the bath bob around. Catherine smiled at it. 'I still can't believe you have a rubber duckie,' she said.

Helen pouted as she shampooed her hair. 'I like my duck. If you marry me, my duck makes three. That's the way it is.'

'There's a word that crops up a lot recently.'

'What, duck?'

'No, marriage.'

'It was a joke.'

'Was it?'

Helen threw more water on her hair to wash away the suds. 'Yep, I'm getting my hair cut.'

'Why? I like it longer.'

'It's driving me batty. I'm going down this week to get a number two short-back-and-sides.'

'Ah, don't Helen.'

'Will so. If I'm going to be the most notorious dyke in town I might as well look the part. When they see my new haircut, there'll be a stampede as the good men of this parish rush to lock up their daughters.'

'You're spoken for.'

'Don't I know it.' Helen wiped her face and opened her eyes. 'I'd better get out of here and ring the bastard brother.'

'What do you think he wants?'

'My head on a plate, at a guess.'

'So don't ring him.'

'I'm in the mood for a screaming match. We'll go for a pint afterwards. I told Philip we might be in Crosbie's later.'

Mary answered the phone; her voice warm as she inquired how things were going. Helen was noncommittal. Catherine puttered around the kitchen, making tea and deliberately staying within earshot.

'Hang on, I'll get him. Em, Helen?' Mary said.

'Yes.'

'He's a bit upset.'

'That doesn't come as a surprise.'

'Right, as long as you know.'

Andy started as soon as he had the receiver in his hand. 'I've had my mother on the telephone about you, crying her head off.'

'And?'

'And I want to know what the fuck you think you're doing. My mother is upset. You don't seem to give a shit about anyone but yourself. Could you not have kept your fucking mouth shut instead of rubbing their noses in your private perversions.'

'Don't say that, Andy. You don't know what you're talking about and it's none of your business.'

'It is my fucking business when my mother is upset.'

'Fine, suit yourself.'

'What are you going to do about it?'

'It's nothing to do with you, but what do you suggest?'

'I suggest you get that woman out of your house and get yourself straightened out. Get a fucking psychiatrist.'

'You made a pun and that's amazing for a man with no sense of humour. I don't want to be "straightened" out.'

'That's a good measure of just how sick you are.'

'Watch it!'

'Listen here, you. What you're doing is wrong and if you don't know that you're worse than I thought.'

'It's not wrong and if there was a pill to cure it, I wouldn't take it.'

'Stubborn bitch. You don't know what you're at.'

'Yes, I do. I know what's wrong with you. You don't really give a fuck about me at all. All you're worried about is how it might look to people I don't give a tinker's curse about. That's what this is: a classic case of what-will-the-neighbours-think.'

'Would you grow the fuck up.'

'I would if I was left alone without you constantly on my back trying to pull strings you have no control over. Remember, sunshine, I'm a free agent and I don't need your approval.'

'You won't get my approval for what you do. Jesus, Helen, it's unnatural, women together doing what men and women should be doing. You disgust me.'

'It's mutual, you backward ape.'

There was a long, strained pause. Andy continued. 'So you're not going to change your mind.'

'About what?'

'Don't play fucking word-games with me. Get your house in order and apologise to my mother and father or this will be the last time you hear from me.'

'That would be a blessing.'

'And you won't be hearing from Maria either, or seeing her again.'

Helen said nothing.

'Did you hear what I said?' her brother continued. 'I'm not having my daughter corrupted by you or that other pervert.'

'You can't do that, Andy; she's my niece.'

'Oh, yes, I can because I'm her father. I don't want you around her.'

'You shouldn't use a child as a weapon to try and get what you want. Fuck you, you bastard, you always knew how to push my buttons when we were kids but it won't work this time.'

'That's your choice. I'm going now. Talking to you is making me want to puke.'

'Ditto.'

Andy hung up violently. Helen took the offered cup of tea and sat down, breathing heavily.

'Well?' Catherine asked, stirring her own tea while making an effort not to let the spoon tinkle against the side of the cup.

'He won't let me see Maria. It's an ultimatum: get straightened out or I'll never see her again. I won't bore you with the details. I must look like Uncle Paddy by now.' She stirred her tea relentlessly, a habit that amused Catherine no end. Helen didn't take sugar at all. 'That's it then. Auntie Helen's off the visiting list. But, Hey, every cloud has a silver lining: I won't be hearing from Andy again either. Yip-fuck-ing-ee.'

'You'll miss her.'

'I just love the little mite as if she was my own. The only revenge I can have is that she's so like me when I was that age: precocious and a tomboy.'

'Gay or straight then, she's going to be a looker when she grows up. Irresistible,' Catherine said.

Helen looked up, half-smiling. 'Thanks for the compliment. And the tea and sympathy. You'll have to stay with me now. Otherwise, I'm rightly fucked.'

'I'm not going anywhere.'

'Don't. Ever.'

Helen was very busy as it got closer and closer to Christmas. It was the busiest time of the year in the newspaper business and taking days off during late November or during the month of December was a definite no-no. She hated all the stupid Christmas shopping ad-features which involved writing paragraphs and paragraphs extolling the retailing virtues of one-horse towns at the back end of beyond. She worked late about three nights a week. For Catherine, on the other hand, December was a long, tiring round of State-sponsored after-work parties. She even stayed in Ballina on a couple of nights when she'd been drinking. She badgered Helen to go out and enjoy the approaching festive cheer, but Helen almost always cried off. Occasionally she got her shit together enough to go for a few pints. For a couple of weeks they barely met, passing one another by in the house with shouts of 'back at ten, I'm working late' or 'see you tomorrow, I'm staying over.' In the middle of it all, Helen was lonely. Most of all, she hated sleeping on her own.

'For the first time this week, we are breaking bread together,' she noted, serving Catherine and Niamh their dinner late on a Thursday night in early December. Both agreed that it was indeed becoming a rare event for all three of them to share a meal.

'What're you doing for Christmas?' Helen asked Niamh around a mouthful of Mexican chilli hot enough to strip paint from old skirting boards.

'Bloody working. The staff rota for Christmas went up this morning. As far as N. Rodgers, nearly M.D., is concerned, Christmas has been cancelled. It should be quiet though. They clear all the walking wounded out of the place and send them home to the bosoms of their families to be minded on the day before Christmas Eve. I'm on casualty duty on Christmas Eve and Christmas night. I'll be keeping a count of the number of pump-outs and split skulls as usual.'

'I always thought doctoring was such a glamorous job,' Catherine observed. 'Or maybe it was just the thought of nurses in those cute uniforms.'

'It's not cute when they're cleaning up vomit.'

Helen spluttered. 'Niamh, for the umpteenth time, will you not do that when I'm eating? You do it on purpose, you bitch.'

'I do surely. It's fun watching you go green in the face.'

'Feck off.'

Catherine continued shovelling chilli into her mouth, eating with just a fork. 'This is just gorgeous, Helen, but I can't understand why you make it so hot when you've an ulcer.'

'Latent masochism. Give us more milk, will you? I'll be dying in an hour.'

'What're you doing for Christmas?' Niamh asked.

'Haven't thought about it,' Helen replied, the fork rattling against her plate.

'Jesus, it's only two weeks away. We should think about it,' Catherine commented.

'Yeah, suppose. Oh, I forgot to tell you, dad rang me at the office this morning to invite me to Christmas dinner.

Well, it wasn't exactly an invitation. He just said he presumed I would be joining them. It was definitely "I" and not "us".

'What did you say?'

'Fuck all. Said I'd think about it. Jesus, I'm popping out in a sweat from this grub.'

'Helen, my mother thinks I'm coming to Dublin. I thought you'd come with me.'

'You could've asked.'

Niamh picked up her empty plate and dropped it on the draining board. 'Oooh, I sense a domestic on the horizon. I'm off to see Matt,' she said. 'Don't do anything that requires stitches because I plan to get scuthered tonight.'

'How is Matt?' Helen asked.

'Gorgeous.'

'Back on again then.'

'Better than ever. Might last it out this time.'

'Good luck.'

'Same to you guys. If I notice any broken windows and scattered lumps of destroyed furniture in the garden on the way back, I'll be staying at Matt's tonight,' she said, leaving the room.

Helen twiddled her cutlery on her plate. 'So what will we do? You're expected and I'm expected. I think it's too late to do anything about it.'

'That's it so. You've made up your mind the way you always do.'

'Not fair. You assumed I was going to Dublin without asking me.'

'But I don't want to spend Christmas without you.'

'Me neither.'

'Then don't.'

'Ah, for fuck's sake, Catherine, what am I supposed to do? Fire the olive branch back in their faces? It's only one day, one dinner.'

'It's Christmas, and I have a big fucking difficulty with this.'

'I can't solve it. I have to go when I'm asked. Andy isn't coming this year and if I don't oblige, they'll have no-one. It might give me a chance to talk to them.'

'So you're just going to go off and leave me on my own.'

'You'll have your family, your friends, your wild nights out.'

'They're not wild.'

'Maybe, but there's a lot of them.'

'I like going out, and there's not much else to do when you're at work all the time anyway.'

'That's not my fault. Work is work.'

'Fine. I just like to have a life as well.'

Helen frowned and lowered her head, looking at Catherine over her spectacles. 'I think we're wandering off the point here. I can't make two of myself. I'm going home for Christmas.'

'Great. Do you know, this is the second Christmas we're been together and the second Christmas that we've been separated?'

'I know. I can't help it. We'll organize something for next year.'

'Some consolation.'

'It'll have to do.' Helen looked at the kitchen clock. 'Let's not fight. We could go to the pictures. My treat?'

'The pictures. Great . So we can sit in the dark for two hours, not talking.'

'I didn't mean it like that.'

'I don't give a fuck.' Catherine got up from the table. 'I'm going out.'

'Where're you going? It's your turn to do the dishes.'

'Get a fucking life, Helen, for fuck's sake. I'm going over to Colette's.'

'Again? That's the third time in a fortnight.'

'I didn't know you were counting. She's my colleague. I like her. She's good crack. Don't wait up.'

The dishes were done and Helen was feigning deep sleep in bed when Catherine came home.

They exchanged gifts late on Christmas Eve before going their separate ways. They had hardly spoken for a week and were diffident with each other as they sat on the bed, trading colourful parcels. Catherine had bought Helen a new silver pocket watch to replace the old brass one that was becoming increasingly unreliable. The new one had a lid that popped open when she pressed the winder. Helen's name and the date were inscribed inside the lid. She loved it. Helen usually bought practical presents, a habit that the more romantic Catherine could never understand. For her birthday two months previously, Helen had bought her a combined coffee grinder and percolator that everyone in the house used. It was expensive but Catherine had little *meas* on it. This time, however, wanting to make up for not being with her at Christmas, Helen had bought a square, solid silver locket bearing her initials, along with a matching bracelet and a small cuddly toy – a white bear holding a red satin heart. When Catherine opened the locket, she found it contained a lock of dark hair, tied carefully with silver string. Her eyes filled with tears.

'I saved it for you when I got my hair cut off. You said how much you liked it so I thought you should have some to keep.' Helen ran her fingertips along her shaven temple. The stubble of the marine haircut was almost short enough to light a match. 'Just so there'd be a little piece of me with you, wherever you are.' She took the locket from Catherine's still fingers, and leaning over slightly, she fastened it around Catherine's neck. 'It suits you,' she said.

Catherine looked up with tear-filled eyes. 'I don't want to go.'

'I don't want you to go. I'll be here when you get back.' Catherine didn't respond so Helen continued. 'I'm really sorry. Things will get better between us. It's just Christmas and all the happy-families baggage that goes with it. We'll get back to where we were, I promise you. Happy Christmas.'

They lay on the bed, fully dressed. Catherine wrapped herself in Helen's arms. 'Promise me we won't be doing this next year,' she said.

'I promise. We'll sort it out earlier so everyone knows what we're doing, including us. I can't bear to see you so unhappy.'

'I'm not unhappy. Not really. Just disappointed.'

'I know. I am too. Come on, lover girl, we'd better go. It will take you hours and hours to get home in the traffic. I want you to promise me you'll drive safely. I've had a word with Tweetie and she says she'll look after you on the journey.'

Helen brought the two overnight bags downstairs. They clung together in the dark behind the front door for a long time before leaving.

'We won't be doing this again,' Helen said decisively as she put Catherine's bag in Tweetie's boot.' The air carried a faint hint of frost but it was dry and clear. Catherine sat into the car and looked at her sadly before starting the engine.

'Go on, now,' Helen encouraged softly. 'This isn't goodbye, it's simply *au revoir*. I'll see you the day after tomorrow.'

'The day after tomorrow,' Catherine said, closing the door.

Christmas, to Helen, crawled by like a slow, rasping death. Her parents were civil, nothing more. She didn't even broach the subject of their estrangement because she assumed it would be temporary. She didn't really care. She was very tired. Lacking the sheer energy for what was likely to be a fractious debate, she let it be. Helen felt herself growing older in the thirty-nine hours she was apart from Catherine, much older than her thirty-one years. She was surprised when, after a night spent tangling in sheets, the same face looked back at her from the bedroom mirror. There were no new wrinkles and, no, she wasn't sixty. Peeling carrots on Christmas morning while her parents were at Mass – for the first time in her life, she had not been invited or conscripted – her body ached from the effort of missing Catherine.

It was a sombre meal. She cried off dessert and sat in the conservatory, a book open on her knee purely for show. Startled, she realized that she'd only been with Catherine for just over a year. It seemed, somehow, like half a lifetime or three lifetimes. Helen had never been a lover before, not like this. She didn't recognize the vague restlessness that suffocated her even when her body was still, nor did she comprehend the grating uneasiness of their last parting, or the vacant emptiness it left behind like a gaping toothlessness of a derelict house lacking windows. This blatant, maddening longing wasn't even physical and because it wasn't, Helen simply didn't know how to classify it. There was no easy pigeon-hole for this and it irked her, like a minuscule thorn embedded in the soft flesh of a fingertip, slowly turning septic.

With a sudden, piercing flash of unaccustomed self-realisation, she recognized she would do anything to have Catherine. She hated that simple, uncomplicated feeling of need; it was embarrassing, mortifying and shameful. Bereft of the cunning skill of a womaniser who had been converted initially to reluctant monogamy, Helen knew the real, stomach-churning fear of "what if." What if Catherine found someone else? What if? What if Helen was too boring, too realistic, too practical? What if? What if Catherine, during her regular nights out alone, found someone with a less demanding job, a younger outlook, an easier personality? What if it wasn't really forever? What if it was? This last was the truly terrifying question.

Helen had never wanted forever, dismissed it as an unrealistic expectation that would be foiled and trampled upon inevitably by the twisting vagaries of human nature. She despised this new grasping, this acquisitive hoarding of the minutiae of a glance, the casual touch of a hand, a tone of voice; the lunacy of unfounded jealousies based on footing of nothing but quicksand; this miserly calculation of love's currency, as if it could be counted in tarnished pounds and duller pence on the abacus of her life.

She walked alone on her favourite beach, miles from home and close to the Mayo county boundary, fighting for breath against the tempestuous violence of a Winter wind being driven ashore, fuelled by its own angry energy. The afternoon light, lowered by glowering dark clouds, snatched away the bitter sediment of Christmas Day. Helen wished she had a dog. The other few solitary walkers all had dogs, small furry piles of life barking outdoor joy at the gun-metal ocean. She was love-sick and sickened and she felt like a total idiot, walking alone on Christmas Day. It was low tide. She struggled on, walking at the edge of the water where the wind seemed fiercest, her eyes searching the ground for a pretty shell to bring home to Catherine: a sandy badge to be handed over shyly as a cheap token of her craven misery.

Jane was curled up in her favourite armchair when she returned to the house. The television was on, and her father was asleep. She upended the cat discourteously and was rewarded with Jane's special discomfited draw. Jane looked at Helen with murder in her eyes before marching off to the hearth and sitting with her bottom to the room, resentment clear in every ginger inch. Helen dropped into the chair with a sigh. Her mother was knitting. The intermittent click of the needles was irritating. Helen was on edge.

'I'm going home early tomorrow,' she said, helping herself to a very large neat brandy. All she wanted was for Catherine to get home and find her there, to lock the door behind them until the thick wall of itchy, fascinated need faded.

'You can stay as long as you like. This is your home.'

'No it's not. It's your home. I have my own.'

The clicking resumed. Helen coughed through a haze of tears caused by a too-large mouthful of Hennessy.

'You should put a mixer in that.'

'I like it this way.'

'Typical.' The needles were mercifully quiet for a moment.

'What?'

'Typical. Stubborn.'

'Leave it, Mam. Please.'

Nora looked at Frank. He was still asleep, snoring softly. Jane unwound herself from the hearthrug and moved onto the arm of his chair, folding her front paws under her chin and blinking slowly at Helen.

'How's Johnny Holmes?' Helen asked.

'He's rallied a bit. He's in and out of hospital all the time.'

'God love him.'

'He's brought awful trouble on that family. There'll be a body-bag at the end of it, I believe. I don't know how they'll manage to bury him at home…'

'You've changed your tune.'

The clicking resumed. 'And you haven't. Helen, this thing with…'

'Catherine. Her name is Catherine.'

'This thing. Are you just trying to be different, is that it?'

'No, Mam.' Helen swirled the brandy around her glass, blinking back at Jane. 'That's not it.'

'What is?'

'There's no point.'

'Just because you haven't met the right man for you, that doesn't mean he's not out there. It doesn't mean you have to go the other way. You could just be on your own.'

'And be miserable.'

'Ah, it's not like that. You have a good job and your own house; you could be happy.'

'Would you have been? You've had dad for 40 years and more; why condemn me to a life alone because you're afraid what the neighbours and the cousins might think?'

'That's not fair, Helen.'

'Well, that's what it looks like from where I'm sitting.'

The flames cracked around seasoned wood, breaking the silence. Jane yawned voluptuously and curled her tail around her body until it was touching her chin as she prepared to sleep.

'You could think about us,' Nora continued.

'I do, but I can't live for you or what you want. Mam, do you honestly want me to grow older and more dried-up and bitter and twisted? What would happen to me when you're gone? It would be too late for me then. Too late to have the opportunity to squeeze something out of my life. I won't get a second chance. I don't want a second chance. I have her now and I love her.'

'You will never bring her to this house again.'

'Is that the price?'

'What d'you mean by that?'

'The price I have to pay for still being considered part of this family.'

'It's our home. She's not to come here.'

'I'll pay it.'

Stilled needles in her hands, Nora looked up but Helen continued: 'I'll pay what you ask but I won't be coming here as often. That's the price you must pay.'

Frank stirred in the chair and Jane, suddenly alert, opened her eyes at this new disturbance. He changed the television channel without asking, a habit that drove Nora to complete distraction. She often got completely muddled if she was sitting watching one programme and occasionally glancing at her knitting when Frank changed over to another.

He kicked off his slippers and cleared his throat. 'Put that kettle on and put Jane out, Helen, would you?' he asked.

Helen made tea for both of them and went to bed.

It was hardly lunchtime on St. Stephen's Day when Helen got home. Tweetie was parked at the kerb. Passing by the car, Helen put her palm on the bonnet. It was still warm. Catherine was down on one knee at the hearth, lighting the fire and singing some Indigo Girls ballad to herself, something about pretty pretender and negligent vendors. In the moments before she realized Helen was home, Helen had an opportunity to study the back of her neck. Two inches of the collar of her white shirt were twisted. Catherine had a problem with collars and rarely got them settled just right without Helen's assistance. Helen often fiddled with them even when they were straight, just as an excuse to touch her. Against the white, Catherine's skin looked darker than it really was. Creamy. The ends of her hair lay flat on her neck, one piece beginning the hint of a curl. In that moment, Helen smiled; her face felt as if she had never smiled before.

Still kneeling and with one hand twitching the firelighters into place, Catherine's other hand began to slide across the mantelpiece as she searched for the matches. Helen crossed the room quickly and picked up the box.

'Let me.' She knelt down and struck a match, holding it to the fire. The petroleum aroma of firelighters was in the air. Turning her head, she noticed that Catherine had a black coal smudge on the tip of her nose. Dropping the match, Helen dusted if off. 'Hi, Bubbles,' she whispered.

They embraced without speaking, rocking on their knees. Helen smothered her face in the neat space between Catherine's neck and shoulder, breathing perfume through her nose and mouth. She broke away and held Catherine's face between her palms. 'Missing you doesn't cover it.'

'Ditto.'

'I love you.'

'Ditto.'

Catherine smiled slowly. The fire began to catch and they watched the growing flames crawling up the angles of coal.

'What's for lunch?' Catherine asked.

'Me.'

'You don't look much like leftover turkey.'

'Don't taste like it either,' Helen grinned.

'How was it?'

'Truly awful. And for you?'

'Not so awful,' Catherine said.

'Lucky.'

They ate a cold meat salad at the kitchen table, then settled in front of the fire with a video Catherine had bought before Christmas, a long, expansive film about Africa. Helen took the telephone off the hook, leaned against Catherine and gradually lost the plot, mesmerized by the strong, sudden rhythms of the soundtrack. They shared a bottle of wine, slowly sipping and savouring the solitude.

'She's a babe, drool, drool,' Catherine said suddenly.

Helen focused on the television. 'Her? She's a dog. Look at the head on her. You have fuck all taste.'

'Are you saying my lover is ugly?'

'I wouldn't dare,' Helen said, pulling Catherine's arm tighter around her shoulder. Catherine switched off the television. Helen sat up, unreasonably anxious.

'What's wrong? Aren't you enjoying it?'

'Yeah, but there's something I have to talk to you about.'

'Oh, Lord. Go on then.'

Catherine moved away and sat on the edge of the couch. She took one of Helen's hands between her own and fiddled with it, twisting Helen's Claddagh around and around on her finger. 'It's amazing how much thinking you can do in one day, in a house filled with screeching brats and a mother who's demented because the only daughter in the household forgot to turn the oven on. There's a lot of time to think when it's Christmas supper instead of Christmas dinner.'

'I think I know what you mean. Go on.'

'I was thinking about us.'

'Ditto.'

Catherine smiled into her eyes but the smile disappeared just as quickly. 'I was wondering about the way things were going and thinking that maybe we need to make some decisions.'

Helen's stomach heaved once. She sat up straight and scratched the back of her head where the stubble was growing longer. 'I'm lost. Keep going.'

'We keep joking about making things permanent and play-acting and carrying on. Maybe people would take us more seriously if we decided to do something more permanent.'

'More permanent how? D'you mean buy a house between us or something? I'm sure there's a legal way of doing it… tenants-in-common or something they call it. I could check it out. I don't know if we have enough money but we could look at it. It'd take a while though. But it's such a bastard when you're selling one place and buying another. I'd end up in the mental.'

The merest touch of a smile caressed the left side of

Catherine's mouth. 'No, I didn't really mean it like that. That's a good practical idea but I was thinking of something a little more romantic, a little more personal.'

'Eh?' Helen looked at her, confusion plain on her face. Catherine looked back, not speaking, still holding her hand. After a long minute, Helen began to get it. She blushed. 'Oh. Right. I see. I think I see.'

'Do you?'

'I think so.'

'And will you?'

'Will I what?'

Catherine slid off the sofa until she was on both knees. She shuffled forward until she was kneeling in the space between Helen's legs. Still holding Helen's fingers with one hand lightly, she touched her on the face. 'Will you marry me?' she asked, her voice little more than a midnight whisper.

CHAPTER SIX

POISONED CHALICE

They stood side by side in the silence, together watching the spade pass from hand to work-worn hand. A cutting February wind energized by three thousand miles of bare Atlantic galloped ashore unhindered. Even in early afternoon, the shadows were long. Dusk threatened. Catherine shivered as Helen reached for her hand.

They stood side by side in silence, together watching the spade pass from hand to hand; together hearing the muted clunk of sandy soil on pine, picturing sparkling grains besmirching glinting brass. John Patrick Holmes was dead. His mother, clad in black, had brought him back to the place of her birth, refusing to bury him among a community that had treated him, in the end, with the mindless cruelty of ignorance and narrow bigotry. He had been an only son.

They stood side by side in stretching, lengthening silence, together watching the spade pass from hand to hand. It was the custom of the place, Helen had explained, a custom of the place in which her mother too had been born. In Belmullet – farther even, out on a peninsula – it was still the custom. On a sandy hill overlooking beach and ocean, the male relatives of John Patrick Holmes buried him. It was simply the custom. Farmers stood shoulder to shoulder with doctors; fair pale-skinned men next to swarthy dark-eyed cousins carrying Mediterranean remnants of the wrecked Spanish armada on their faces and in their blood. This coastline had always been the same: inhospitable and unkind or welcoming to all, friend or foe. It did not discriminate.

Glancing across the open, gaping mouth of the grave, Helen recognized her mother's grief; her sadness for a young life snuffed out painfully and slowly, her sympathy for those left behind to wield the spade. The last was a pale echo of pain. She saw Johnny's partner, the rather unfortunately named Nicholas Lenin, a pale, handsome, Slavic-faced man with a Yank accent that suited his appearance ill. Unwillingly, she mentally acknowledged the real sadness of her own brother. Andy's face was half-frozen between a lament for a stolen childhood friend and callous hatred of what that friend had become, of perhaps what he had always been. Helen looked away, back to the violent gash in the earth before he could catch her eye.

Drawing a deep breath, she looked out to sea. This was not Helen's first time standing on this particular sandy hillside and she knew it was unlikely to be the last. To her left, her grandparents lay; behind her, a great aunt and, a little to the right and further up the hill, great-grandparents. Along by the wall, small headstones marked the resting places of English soldiers who fell from the sky onto this unwelcoming patch of Europe during the war. And there was always Caroline.

To Helen, this ritual was comforting, suffused with rightness and the natural order. Family buried family in this place as they had for generations. Impersonal paid gravediggers had no place here, and still less had the peculiar American custom of leaving a coffin above ground for strangers to bury.

The last uneven prayers rose and died away… ashes to ashes, dust to dust, silence to silence. Looking around the sparse gathering, Helen saw that the grave had been filled and flowers placed on the concave mound above Johnny's coffin. People were leaving. She twitched Catherine's hand and turned to go.

As they walked away towards the car, Helen felt a touch on her shoulder. It was Johnny's first cousin, Martina. She and Helen had been in the same national school class for a time, many years before.

'There's lunch in the town. Will you stay? Nick said to ask.'

Looking at Catherine quickly for corroboration, Helen replied: 'Tell him thank you. We'll stay. The usual place?'

'Where else?'

Helen smiled slowly and touched Martina's face with her free hand. 'Where else indeed. Martina… I hope he's at peace now. I feel really sorry for Nick, having to leave him here like this.'

'I know. It's not right. If he was a legal husband he'd have a legal say. But he's not so he doesn't. Auntie Kathy and Uncle Marty insisted.'

'Ach, it's always the same but maybe things will change in time for someone else.'

'I hope so,' Martina said, glancing pointedly at their intertwined hands. 'Who's your friend?'

'Forgive me, ladies, I have no manners. Catherine, this is Martina Holmes, first cousin of the deceased. Martina, this is Catherine Lacey, my partner.' Catherine and Martina shook hands, both blushing. 'And now, Martina, we'll leave you in peace. See you later in town,' Helen said before they strolled away.

The Atlantic Hotel was the usual post-event venue for

weddings, christenings and funerals, not always in that order. After funerals, there was a meal of some sort to be eaten, drink to be drunk, songs to be sung and stories to be told about the deceased. Turning from the bar with a mineral water in one hand, a pint of Heineken in the other and an unlit cigarette in her mouth, Helen bumped into her father. They had not spoken since Christmas.

'Helen.'

'Dad.' She put the pint back on the bar, pulled the cigarette out of her mouth and quickly leaned over to kiss him on the cheek. 'Long time, no see.'

'Indeed. We're glad you came.'

'I couldn't not come once I heard. It's a duty thing.'

'Rubbish. You really like Johnny.'

'Yes, I did. He was a gentleman and he was very kind to me when I was growing up, even though he and Andy were the pals and it wasn't cool to be nice to the kid sister.'

'Hmm. Have you spoken to your mother?'

'No, not yet. We were late to the church. I got lost.'

Frank chuckled. 'I don't believe it. I though you knew this godforsaken place like the back of your hand.'

'It's not godforsaken.' Helen bristled in defence of her mother's rural birthplace, then softened. 'It's been a while. Maybe too long.'

'Will you go and speak to your Mam, Helen?'

'In a while, Dad.'

After a drink, Helen leaned over to Catherine and asked if it was okay to leave her with a gaggle of Johnny's cousins for a while. Catherine raised her eyebrow in a question and Helen jerked her head slightly to where her family were seated. Catherine nodded and whispered: 'I have a small white charger under the table… whistle if you need me.'

Helen smiled and rose from her seat, buttoning her long black jacket and surreptitiously shinning her shoes on the backs of her trouser legs. She walked swiftly across the room, through the double doors into the main bar and kissed her mother.

'Howya, Mam. Andy. Mary. Where's Tinkerbell today?'

'At home.' Andy's tone was decidedly frigid. 'Funerals aren't for young children.'

'I wouldn't agree with that. Keeping them away from occasions like this will hardly get them used to the notion of death as being part of the natural process.' Andy began the customary fidgeting that was usually preparatory to an outburst. Helen held her hand up, palms outward in a placatory pose. 'But you're the parent, after all.' She smiled when she realised that he hadn't heard or recognized the acerbic tint in her tone.

'How have you been, Helen?' her mother asked.

'Mad busy, Mam. Colm had a mild heart attack last week so between dealing with the telephone calls he's been surreptitiously making on his mobile from the hospital and trying to fend off the manic editorial ambitions of the half-cut Ms. Coogan, myself and Philip have our hands full trying to get a paper out.'

'Is it serious?' I mean, I haven't heard you mention that he had health problems before?'

'Nah, I don't think so. He'll be right as rain in a couple of weeks. He's so laid back I'm surprised he had it in him to have a heart attack at all. Must have been that story about the meat factory I tried to get him to print last month!'

'And how are things otherwise?'

'Fine, Mam. We're fine.'

Andy broke in. 'I see you're still intent on rubbing our noses in it. I don't know why but I'm surprised at you, bringing her to a family thing like this.'

'Andrew, not now,' their mother said clearly but neutrally. 'Now is not the time.'

Helen looked at the floor for a couple of seconds then smiled brightly at her mother. 'Anyway, I'd better get back to the younger crowd. I haven't seen some of them for years and it's great catching up, even at a time like this. See you, Mam. Mary, give Maria my bestest love ever. She'll know what I mean.'

Hours later, there was still a crowd in the Atlantic Hotel. Knowing that she had to drive the lonely, windswept road back to Castlebar in the darkness, Helen stuck to bottled water. Catherine was getting slightly squiffy and had started trading Kerryman jokes – sometimes substituting Mayo men – with Johnny's cousins. The remainder of a light meal of sandwiches, cocktail sausages and other typical funeral fare was still on the table along with empty glasses, packets of cigarettes, and a soon-to-be-overflowing green Smithwick's ashtray. Helen's parents, brother and sister-in-law were still in the main bar.

Laughing uproariously at some punch-line, Catherine turned to Helen. 'That's a gas,' she said, slapping Helen on the leg and squeezing her thigh just above the knee joint in the special place that always made Helen jump. The squeeze turned rapidly into a caress.

'Yes, it is a gas as you so eloquently put it, my dear, but will you please get your hand off my leg before my brother has a stroke and my 93-year-old great auntie Brigid has a friggin' heart attack,' Helen hissed. 'You're pissed.'

'Am not. Anyway, what're funerals for if not to toast the late lamented and get ossified?' Catherine's voice was just one decibel too loud. Michael, Eddie and Nathan – Johnny's three cousins – sniggered but elsewhere heads began to turn.

'Knock it off, now,' Helen whispered savagely into Catherine's ear. 'You're an embarrassment.'

Catherine subsided, sobering quickly. 'Sorry, I didn't

realise I was so loud,' she said slowly, looking over her shoulder. 'Oh, fuck, Andy's staring at me.'

Helen glanced at her watch and then through the double doors at her brother, who was listening to their mother, head tilted to one side, eyes turned in her direction. 'Right. C'mon, it's time to go. I have to be up early for work tomorrow. Give me the keys of that banana-yellow beast now, Catherine.'

Catherine handed over the keys and they both stood up to leave. Helen shook hands with all the relatives and waved at various other acquaintances. She paused at her parent's end of the bar and leaned over to kiss both of them while Catherine hovered at a safe distance.

Outside, Helen drew in a long breath of cold, salty air and exhaled quickly, searching in her pockets for a cigarette. Catherine, four pints to the good, found the fresh air less than sobering. She started to giggle and leaned against the doorway. Helen sighed heavily. 'Okay, Bunty, c'mon,' she said, catching Catherine's arm and steering her in the direction of the car. The windscreen was frosted over. 'Fuck,' she swore heartily, then deposited the still giggling Catherine in the passenger seat, warned her to fasten her seat belt and then opened the boot to find the defrosting spray for the glass.

She was still rooting in the untidy boot when heavy male footsteps stopped at the side of the car. The street was very quiet. Helen emerged from the boot clutching the blue-capped tin, shaking it rapidly as if it was a cocktail shaker.

'Going home?' Andy asked unpleasantly.

'Yeah. Thank God it didn't rain today or the roads'd be like a bottle,' Helen replied quietly, still shaking the tin.

Catherine rolled down her window. 'Hey, sexy!' she called to Helen. 'What's keepin' you? How about taking me home and shagging my brains out?'

Squinting into her brother's shadowed eyes, for once

Helen was stuck for words. 'Shut the fuck up, Catherine,' she said eventually.

'Ooh, I like it when you order me around, Mistress,' Catherine replied, still giggling.

'Shit,' Helen said under her breath.

Andy slammed the boot-lid shut. 'You'll never fucking change,' he said. 'You couldn't leave her at home, even today.'

'Fuck off, Andy.'

'You don't give a shit, do you?'

'About what?'

'You don't give a shit about breaking my mother's heart and making a show of her in front of all these people.'

'Ah, c'mon Andy, since when did our mother need you to fight her battles? She's well able to say what's on her mind without recourse to the one-man family mafia.'

Andy moved a step closer, his fists clenched at his sides. She gripped the defrosting tin tighter. 'Back off,' she said tightly, a little afraid. Catherine's door opened. 'Get back in the car, Catherine, I'm dealing with this,' Helen added.

Catherine stood out on the road, closed the door quietly and leaned against the car, her breath condensing. 'I'll just stay here then 'til you're done,' she commented expansively.

'Now who needs the mafia?' Andy snorted.

'Back off.' Helen repeated.

Andy moved another step closer and Helen backed away again. 'You listen to me, my little fucking sister,' he said, his voice rising. 'I don't want her near my family and I don't want you near any of us until you get your shit together. Do you hear me?'

'What's this all about, Andy? I'm not the annoying five-year-old that you can bully anymore. You've made your choices. You have your job and your wife and child and your own life. It's all of your own choosing. Why begrudge me the opportunity to choose mine?'

'Choice? What the fuck? What about what's right and wrong? You're mad as a March hare!' he roared.

Helen drew in a long, slow breath, calming herself. 'Andy, let's not do this. Please. It's not worth it. You're just getting yourself into a state for nothing. Johnny is lying dead on that hill. Show some respect for the dead, if not for the living.'

'Respect!' he spat. 'Who the fuck are you to talk about "respect"? You have no respect for anything or anyone, you selfish little bitch. You've always been the same, going your own way without a thought for how it affects anyone else.'

Helen was stung by the unfairness of the accusation. 'Fuck that,' she said angrily. 'Where will that get me and where did it get me? What do you want? Do you want me to play the virgin maiden sister, is that it? Well, you know what you can do: you can fuck right off, sunshine. I could be dead tomorrow. I could be lying in a grave up on that shagging hill next week and you wouldn't give a continental fuck as long as the neighbours turned up to shake your hand and nod sympathetically. You don't care whether or not I'm happy. All you ever care about is fucking appearances. You're a shallow, spiteful, hypocritical bastard.'

'What the fuck do you mean by that, you little cow?' he shouted.

Driven by rising anger, Helen went on, raising her voice to be heard over his protestations: 'You think your little affair went unnoticed, did you? That tawdry, tacky little affairette with the school secretary? We all know, Andy. We're always known. You're a hypocrite and I don't know why Mary hasn't left you. And taken Maria with her. You don't deserve either of them.' Out of breath, she stopped abruptly.

Andy raised his hand as if to strike her. Helen had already stiffened to take the back-handed blow when a female voice rang out. 'Andrew, stop!' His hand froze at the top of the back-swing and Helen saw that he was looking over her shoulder, towards the door of the hotel. She turned slowly. Their mother was standing in the doorway.

Helen turned to face him. 'Goodbye, Andy,' she said evenly. With a struggle, Andy pulled his gaze back to her. 'Maybe you need to work out why you're so angry because I have a feeling it has fuck all to do with me,' she added softly. Helen turned on her heel and walked to the front of the car. She sprayed the windscreen, tore off her jacket and threw it onto the back seat. Sitting into the driver's seat, she waited a few moments for the spray to work before switching on the wipers. Helen rolled down the electric window on Catherine's side. 'Get in the car now,' she said, without looking out. Catherine obeyed. Helen turned the key and pulled away from the kerb without speaking, leaving Andy wreathed in exhaust fumes and their mother still standing in the doorway of the Atlantic Hotel. If the car had been a horse and cart, it would have been a fine tableau from a John B. Keane play.

'No, Philip. That headline stinks and you know it. Fuck off back to the sports section and leave the hard news to the expert.' The department phone rang while she was giving her friend a playful shove to get him away from the compositor's computer. 'Move it, I said,' she added, telling Martin to put the front page lead headline back the way it had been before Philip interfered. She put the phone to her ear. It was Colm on the line.

'Howdy, boss. How are things in St. Monica's male medical ward?' she asked.

'Cut it out, Helen,' Colm replied frostily. 'What's on the front and how close are you to meeting the deadline.'

'We're grand. We'll make it. Martin's nearly ready to ISDN the front. Well, he would be if I could find the caption for the top right pic.'

'What's the lead?'

'"Mackey to run as independent", she replied. 'Two lines, six cols, about 140 point. Big, black and in-your-face Helvetica bold with knobs on.'

'Are you sure?'

'Course. I was talking to his wife on a mobile with a blocked number, after all. He wants the story in, he just doesn't want it tracked back to him.'

'How do you know it was her?'

'Jesus, Colm. She's in the friggin' drama group. I'd know that voice anywhere,' Helen said, gently pressing the speaker button on the telephone.

'Read me the intro.' Colm's voice was amplified to a level that the whole case room could hear.

'Are you sure you're not supposed to be taking tablets or something?' Helen asked very sweetly.

'Read me the fucking intro,' he growled. Martin stifled a snigger.

'Ahem,' she said. '"Maverick Fianna Fail Deputy Tony Mackey is to ditch the party and run as an independent candidate in the flagged General Election, the *Recorder* has learned. Despite his 30 years service to the Soldiers of Destiny, Mackey is reportedly angry at the National Executive's decision not to add his name to the party ticket. Mackey was defeated at last month's convention in Westport by two votes in a controversial secret ballot.'"

'You'd better be sure or he'll go ape-shit.'

'I'm sure. I can feel it in me bones. He's jumping ship.'

'Okay. Pagination?'

'Sixty-four. Eight full colour, six spot colour, five full page ads, two ad features and 20 sport; two motoring, two farming, and two from the council meeting; nice pic of three girl guides from the regional camp on the front and a cute four-page spread on the Papal Nuncio's visit to Tourmakeady. Need I go on?'

'All right, Helen. You've made your point, whatever it is. Just get the fucking thing to bed.'

'I'm turning down the covers now, darling,' Helen quipped. 'How are you doing anyway, Colm?'

'Great, actually. I'll be out of here by the end of the week and the consultant says two weeks rest before I can think about going back to work. Come and see me tomorrow morning.'

'Do you doubt me? Didn't I come to see you the same time last week, bearing in my arms a fresh edition with a front-page exclusive written by moi?'

'Yeah, yeah, yeah. Get back to work and tell that crowd of wasters down the back I'll be back soon.'

'I'm sure they love you too,' Helen said, grinning at Martin. 'See you tomorrow, Colm.'

'Right,' she said, cutting the connection. One of Colm's little eccentricities was that he never actually finished a conversation before slamming down the telephone.

'Your mother rang. I told her you were at work and would be in later.'

'Thanks, Niamh. The telephone still works then.'

'Eh?'

'Nothing. Just family stuff. Where's Catherine?'

'Gone out. She left a note stuck to the kettle.'

'Well, she may not be here but she certainly knows the form. Rule number one for H.M. Dunne: kettle is first port of call after working day.'

'We're out of milk.'

'Fuck,' Helen pulled off her coat and flung it over the back of a chair.

'It was her turn to do the kitty shopping.'

'Did you mention it?'

'No.'

'Why not?' Helen asked, exasperation in her tone.

'I thought you'd look after it.'

'What am I, house mammy or something? If she doesn't pull her weight, tackle her on it.'

'All right, Helen.'

'Any post?'

'Just two.'

Helen opened the two envelopes, read the contents and threw them in the cutlery drawer. 'Jesus, car insurance is going through the fucking roof!' she said contrarily, opening the fridge for a beer.

'Tell me about it. I paid mine last month and it had gone up twenty-five per cent. They think all doctors run around the place for emergencies at night.'

'And journalists do nothing but chase ambulances in the middle of the night while drunk as lords, too,' Helen added, reading the note attached to the kettle before taking a swig from the bottle. 'I fucking hate March. It's the one month of the year that is still Winter and not Spring and there's nothing to look forward to because you think it's going to piss rain forever. She could have at least said where she was going and I could have joined her for a pint.'

'She didn't mention the pub; just something about meeting the girls from work.'

'Right. How're things with Matthew?'

'Great, at the moment. I think we got some stuff sorted out: he feels like we've got through the wall, or something. He's buying a house and he wants me to move in with him but I'm not so sure. He still lives at home and I just wonder if he's looking for a handy replacement for mammy so that he won't have to figure out how to work a washing machine himself.'

'Typical Irish son. Wants another mammy but isn't prepared to propose in case his own mammy doesn't like his choice. Take my advice. Let him move in and live by himself for a few months first. When you see wrinkled shirts you'll know he's learning.'

Niamh smiled. 'Yeah, you're right. I'm mad about him, though.'

'There's no cure for that, I'm afraid,' Helen said, leaning against the worktop and draining her beer bottle. 'Better ring the mammy myself, I suppose,' she added, dropping the bottle in the bin and heading for her bedroom.

Helen was asleep when Catherine arrived home. It was 2.00 a.m. She jerked awake when Catherine dropped one of her shoes on the bare floorboards.

'Jesus Christ, you frightened the life out of me,' she said, switching on the bedside light. 'What time is it? Where've you been?'

'Just out for a few. It got late. Sorry.'

'I thought you'd be here when I got home.'

'C'mon, Helen. I can't hang around the house every evening, waiting for you to finish work and never knowing when that might be. I have to make friends here too. Don't nag.'

'I'm not nagging. It's just that I would have joined you for a drink if I'd known where you were.'

'I'm not tied to you.'

'I never said you were,' Helen said sharply, pulling herself up in the bed. 'I'm talking about common courtesy and manners, not a ball and chain.'

'Oh, fuck, leave it, Helen. It's too late for this.'

'Too late for what?'

'Too late for you to pick a row.'

'Fine. You forgot to get milk. Niamh was thick about it.'

'More nagging. Sometimes you're like a fucking broken record.'

'Fuck off, Catherine. All I'm saying is that this isn't

a hotel and you can't treat me like a chambermaid. I won't stand for it. Goodnight.'

Helen turned off the light abruptly, leaving Catherine to undress in the dark. The next morning, Catherine was repentant, bringing Helen breakfast on a tray before she left for work and waking her with a soft kiss on the forehead.

'Sorry about last night, love, I was just so tired.'

'That's okay,' Helen replied sleepily. 'I was tired too, and disappointed that I didn't speak to you all day.'

'Okay. What time're you finishing tonight?'

'Early. Should be home about half-five or so. You?'

'Flexi-day. I'm off at one. I'll cook for you this evening.'

It was a feast of roast chicken, roast potatoes, carrots and gravy, with a bottle of Merlot to wash it all down. Replete, Helen sat back after the meal, rubbing her tummy approvingly. 'By God, woman, you really do know how to get to a girl. A roast chicken dinner on a Thursday... on the same day as breakfast in bed. I must berate you over not buying milk much more often,' she joked.

'Hey, don't get too full of yourself or you'll be wearing the carcass, wench,' Catherine replied, spooning expensive, unseasonable strawberries out of a large bowl into two smaller ones.

'Em, Catherine?'

'Yes, sheep?'

'I have a confession to make. I've sort of invited my parents for Easter Sunday lunch. My mother rang me three times this week talking in code about Andy attempting to clock me one at the funeral. On one occasion I'd swear she'd been drinking. I think she's a bit sorry this whole thing's gone so far. I sort of met her halfway, I suppose, if a little ungraciously. I mean, I don't want this shit to get out of hand any more than she does.'

Catherine sat down. 'Does this dinner invitation include me and, if so, does she know that?'

'Yes and yes.'

'Wow. That's progress.'

'Catherine, I love my mother dearly but I am under no illusions. She is a psychopath. She is inconsistent. She is seriously demented. She's likely to arrive here and skin us both alive in the sweetest possible way, then swish out and leave us to deal with it. I grew up with a long-play mantra in my head about no-one being allowed to upset mother. I don't know what she's at, to be honest. I can only suppose that Andy trying to belt me was a step too far, even for her. Maybe he's on the shit-list because he's upset her the most at the moment.'

'I think we should go for it. Pull out all the stops. Buy them Easter eggs – even one for that awful cat – and decant the wine.'

'But I don't have a decanter.'

'You know what I mean, Helen. We could just be totally mannerly and show her we're just the same as everyone else.'

'I was thinking of inviting Philip as well, if he's not going to visit any of his kids. A stranger in the room might stop her crossing the line.'

'Good plan. Why don't I invite my whole family as well?'

'Now you're being ridiculous!'

'Ah, Helen, is it such a bad idea? They don't know where I live and I'm sure the boys would love it.'

'They're welcome here any time, you know that, but wouldn't it be too complicated… it'd be a nightmare trying to keep those who know from telling those who don't.'

'Fuck families anyway.'

'Catherine!'

'You're right. It wouldn't work. Philip'd be fine but we'd have to swear your parents to secrecy.'

'And, depending on whether or not my Mam is feeling like a terrorist, she might decide to drop us in it and leave before the carpet bombing starts. Happy Easter, one and all!'

'Okay, just your parents and Philip then. We'll get lamb. I bet your traditionalist mother cooks lamb on Easter Sunday.'

'You bet right, yet again. We could even announce our engagement over the trifle.'

'What engagement? You never did give me an answer, you brat.'

'Do you really need a verbal answer, Catherine?'

'Well, it would be nice to hear it, just once. It's been a long time since Christmas.'

'All right then.' Helen dropped her spoon and reached across the table for Catherine's hand, searching for her suddenly bashful eyes. 'Yes. Yes, Catherine, I will.'

Easter Sunday could have been described as tense but, from Helen's point of view, tension was comparative. Relatively speaking, the parental visit was a walk in the park, with casual and unhurried duck-feeding added in for good measure. She hadn't hoped for much better: keeping her expectations low in many situations had reaped her considerable bonuses. Catherine had been much more optimistic. In fairness to her, Helen thought, she had put in an immense effort both with the practical mechanics of the occasion and with displaying the social graces. Philip had, as always, been a charmer. When Helen explained to him how important the dinner was and his lead role in a film called *Rent A United Nations Mediator*, he launched into thoughtful, funny slagging. Helen was delighted with him: she knew that when Philip cared enough to think up witty puns and poke fun, he was really involved and was taking an event or situation very seriously indeed.

Late that Easter Sunday night, not long after the Dunne parents had headed for Tubbercurry and home, Helen, Catherine and Philip finished a bottle of wine in the sitting room, half-ignoring an old black-and-white film on television. Philip, sprawled across an armchair in a manner unbecoming a grown man of his years, yawned energetically. Catherine was the only one of the three sitting properly. Helen lay on the sofa, shoes off, legs thrown across Catherine's, idly scratching the sole of one foot with the toes of the other.

'Your mother and I had a meaningful chat in Swahili while you two were doing the dishes,' Catherine remarked mildly, taking a long, enjoyable swig from her glass to make up for her promise not to drink at all earlier.

Helen and Philip, like twin marionettes or particularly alert Yorkshire Terriers, jerked their heads around in unison. 'You what?' Helen asked, while Philip hummed scary music and pretended to be Dracula, showing his pointed incisors.

'Stop it, Philip,' Catherine wailed. 'You know that scares the shite out of me.' He smirked in apology. 'I said that myself and your mother had a chat while you were out of the room. I think your father might have been listening too… although it was hard to tell whether or not he was asleep.'

'Bet he wasn't, the sly one. He pretends to be asleep sometimes but you can bet he's taking it all in. I bet he could quote your words back to you.'

'Hmm. Hope not. Anyway, your mother's quite a strong person; what Nora wants, I think Nora is used to getting.'

'Too right.'

Philip joined the conversation. 'Ah, I dunno, girls, I thought she was lovely. If she was just the teeniest bit younger I might fancy her meself. I've always wondered what it'd be like to be called a home wrecker.'

'Give over, you fool,' Helen said, throwing a cushion at him. 'You can't talk about my mother like that. My mother is not fanciable simply because she's my mother. No-one's mother could possibly be fanciable. It's disgusting. You are a very horrible man, sometimes, my esteemed colleague.' She raised her glass to him. 'Now Catherine, tell me what transpired between yourself and the Ma before I stab you with my big toe.'

Catherine squirmed a little to get more comfortable. 'She sort of cornered me in here deliberately, I think. She even sat in the chair nearest the door so I'd have to pass by her to get out. Has your mother ever served with the KGB, Helen?'

Helen laughed. 'No, too rough for them. Now get on, get on.'

'The Gestapo, perhaps? The Special Branch? B Specials?'

'Easy now. You're going too far there, Catherine,' Philip broke in. 'The B Specials? People have lost bits of their legs for suggesting such a thing. Helen, would you ever administer a punishment beating at your convenience.' He tossed the cushion back in Helen's direction. It landed short.

Helen poked Catherine in the side. 'Will you get on with it, for heaven's sake... It takes you half the friggin' night to tell a simple story. You're just dragging it out, you bitch.'

'Okay. Anyway, she started talking about you and how happy you've appeared to be lately.'

'Me? Is she mad?' Philip interrupted again, this time sitting up straight.

'Not you, you self-centered eejit. Me!' Helen said. 'Now go back to sleep. I swear the two of you are conspiring to make sure I fall asleep before I hear anything even slightly juicy. Shut up, Philip.'

He subsided back into the armchair, stretching one leg over the arm of the furniture and proceeded to examine his half-empty wine glass. Catherine smiled. 'As I was saying, your mother was sort of just mooching around and qualifying everything she said. She explained how hard it is for them because you're the only daughter they have now and how Frank had expectations for you... I think they might have included a white wedding and grandchildren but she didn't quite say that straight out. She said they were doing their best to come to terms with it and they were really delighted to see you looking so happy. She went on and on and on about how parents only really want what's best for their child. I was inclined to argue that point based on my own experience but she was on a bit of a roll and I couldn't really get a full sentence in. Oh, and she said a bit about how embarrassing it could be for them in your home town and how we all have to live together and try to get on better. All very uplifting stuff, really.'

'Jesus Christ,' Helen responded dramatically, picking the cushion up off the floor and dropping it on her face. 'Smother me now please before life gets to be too, too much.'

'Ah, will you stop! She was really nice about it.'

'Obviously, but what did she want?'

'How do you mean?'

'She means that the mother always has a hidden agenda, in her view, and she wants to know what was on that agenda on this occasion,' Philip explained while Helen groaned on under the cushion.

'I think she wanted me to promise that I wouldn't embarrass her in front of anyone again.'

'And did you?'

'Well, yes, I suppose I did in a roundabout sort of way.'

'That's it. My life is over. The wedding's off. I couldn't possibly hitch my wagon to someone who makes promises to my mother without my prior knowledge or consent,' Helen said from under the cushion. Catherine pulled it off her face. 'Hey, leave go! Don't dare put a hand on the item I've chosen to put myself out of my own misery,' Helen said.

'I did my best, Helen,' Catherine remarked sourly. 'She put me on the spot and it was such a relief not to be on the receiving end of a tirade that I probably would've promised to have a sex change operation if she'd asked.'

'I know. Ugh. If I'd wanted a man I'd have stolen Philip from Patti years ago.' She looked over at her colleague who was stretched over and feigning sleep. 'He's quite cute and charming, as men go... if a little over-fond of himself,' Helen added. Philip snorted. Helen threw the cushion back at him. 'There, fool. That's what happens to eavesdroppers!'

A couple of weeks later, they began to make plans. Catherine was the more spiritual of the two and fancied lots of candle-lighting and earthy-type faux Celtic mysticism on the top of a hill. Her choice of venue was Rathcroghan, an ancient elevated site near Tulsk in County Roscommon that had been of some significance to the pre-Christian Connacht kings. Catherine thought it was fascinating that you could see all the counties of Connacht from the highest ring fort on a clear day. Helen thought the idea was an absolute hoot and swore she'd never do it, given that Catherine's choice of venue would mean Wellington boots in a fetching shade of farmer green. She favoured something sensible in a small hotel conference room. They had great fun – and a couple of serious arguments – working out the details. Eventually, they decided, on Helen's suggestion, to combine it with a wee-long holiday on the Northern coast of France. They'd have the event in a hotel, have a meal afterwards, stay the night and then head off on holidays the next morning. Catherine, still pining for the half-pagan ambiance of damp Rathcroghan, wasn't one hundred per cent in favour but she agreed eventually. The main argument was over the guest list and it was definitely a case of the twain never meeting: Catherine wanted to invite

half the country and Helen was anti-social. Looked at another way, Helen was miserly, saving for no tangible purpose
and Catherine was throwing money away like there was no
tomorrow when she knew full well that Ophelia was due a
new set of tyres and probably a replacement engine as well.
At one point in the discussion, Niamh opened the kitchen
door and threw them an inquiring glance. Catherine and
Helen called a meddled truce for the evening. They hardly
spoke for two days after that disagreement and even Niamh
finally noticed the atmosphere when Catherine asked her
to ask Helen to pass the salt at dinner one evening. Niamh
kept hacking away at her lamb chop, ignoring them both and
smiling dolefully.

'Lovely evening,' she noted airily, addressing the tablecloth.

'Humph,' Helen grunted agreement.

'Yep,' Catherine said shortly.

'It's great that you two aren't really speaking,' Niamh
continued. 'On the one hand, it's like sitting between two
small brats who've both been given a wallop of the wood-
en-spoon to keep them quiet and, on the other, it's a blessing to be able to enjoy a meal without that chattering and
wittering that you constantly go on with. Sometimes it's like
living in a nest full of boisterous chicks, but not today. Today
is heaven.'

Helen looked up. 'Well, we can't have that, can we? We
can't have Doctor Niamh enjoying her time in this house.
We'll have to do something about it immediately, won't we,
Catherine?' she said, sneaking one hand across the table
while she was speaking and lifting a threadbare chop bone
from Niamh's plate.

'No way,' Catherine agreed. 'I've been saving up lots of
idle chatter and now I have a good store of ammunition to
unleash.'

'Too late for this evening. I'm off to swimming and then to the pub,' Niamh said, finishing her glass of water and leaving the table. 'See you chattering classes later.'

After she left, Helen fiddled with the chop bone in the silence, picking slivers of lamb from its edges with her fingernails. Eventually, she dropped it onto her plate and sat back. 'She's right. We can't not talk to each other. This house is too small for that, isn't it?'

'Yeah, let's buy a bigger one with a bigger garden and thicker walls so we can bark at each other in comfort and privacy.'

'Can't afford it.'

'You surprise me.'

'No need for that sarcasm, given that you live from hand to mouth and never saved anything until I bet the head off you to get you in the credit union door. But that's beside the point. Listen, I've been thinking and I've come up with a compromise that might appeal to you.'

'Go ahead. Sock it to me, baby.'

'Only if you'll think about it seriously.'

'I will.'

'Okay, this is it. A humanist ceremony in a hotel meeting room. Ten guests max. Dinner afterwards. Then off on holidays the next day.'

'Not much difference between that and what we argued over.'

'True, but I didn't quite get around to explaining the real reason why I don't want too many people there.'

Catherine raised her head. 'What reason?'

'I have this thing about not appearing weak in front of you. I like to think I could do anything if I put my mind to it but I can't do this. I can't stand up in a room full of people and say how much I love you out loud. I just can't do it.' To cover her confusion, Helen picked up the chop bone again and surveyed it, searching for a non-existent shred of meat.

Catherine moved around the table to sit beside her. 'Why didn't you say?' she asked, taking the bone out of Helen's fingers and wiping them off with a napkin before interlocking her fingers with Helen's.

'Like I said, I get embarrassed at showing weakness. It's either a particular fault of mine or else it's a general butch thing. I'd pick a row before I'd let you know a situation's beyond my personal capabilities.' Helen squeezed her hand. 'I just thought that, seeing you're taking all this so seriously, I'd better come clean and tell you the truth. I just can't do it. I'd die.'

'Aw, Helen, I'm not going to make you do something if it's that hard for you. What do you think I am, a bitch with a heart of stone? It's supposed to be a happy day for both of us and it wouldn't do much good if you were dreading it so much you couldn't enjoy it. We'll sort something out: there's no real rush anyway.'

'Thanks' Helen smiled ruefully, then leaned over to kiss Catherine on the lips.

'Yuch, you taste of chop, you carnivore,' Catherine said, pretending to spit on the floor.

'I'm a real flesh-eater all right,' Helen responded, sneaking a quick peek at her watch. 'Sorry, love, but I've to go to work.'

Catherine sobbed heroically. 'What's it this time? Your job is driving me to drink, you know. I never precisely know where the hell you're going to be or when we're going to be able to get together for an evening.'

'I know, love, but work's work and it can't be argued with. Tonight, we have a tree-planting in the grounds of the library.'

'In this weather? Are they bonkers?'

'Very probably. The tree is to commemorate some benefactor who donated 1,200 quality tomes to the county library service. He gets a tree and I get to take speeches down in a wet notebook.' Helen got up and washed her hands. 'That reminds me of a story I once did, oh, years and years ago. The Lord Mayor of Dublin was passing through some village – can't remember which one now – and the local community organized a tree for him to plant on the village green or something. Nice story, nice pix of Lord Mayor with spade in hand. The tree disappeared the next day. I was put on the story and, after ringing the sub post mistress, the local national teachers, the village Garda and the priest, I got to the bottom of it: it was the wrong time of year for tree-planting so the community council pulled the tree up again as soon as the Merc disappeared up the road. Yet another Mayo solution to a Mayo problem!'

'Michael?'

'Yah, who's this?'

'Ranger, it's Helen Dunne.'

'Dunne Roamin', how are ya!? Christ, Hel, it must be years, if not centuries since we crossed swords in person.'

'And then some, pardner. How's Silver?'

'She's great. She had triplets two months ago.'

'Triplets! Jesus Christ, Mike, you must have been handing out the cigars for hours after that. How are the babies?'

'Doin' fine, Tonto, jest doin' fine. Near 'bout ready for market 'n'all. Fancy a baby yourself?'

'Thank ya, no, kind sir. God, they must be really cute. Can I come and see them before you give them away?'

'Give them away, nuttin'. Dey's for sale. £140 a pop, God bless 'em, de bitches.'

'Have they got any spots yet?'

'Nah, too young. All white and cute at the moment. The littlest one is a darling. She was so small at birth that she couldn't fight her corner and I've had to hand feed her. Anyways, Hel, where the hell've you been?'

'Busy, busy, busy. Newspapers are like that. One week oozes into another and, before you know it, you haven't seen your old college pals for months and, point two, you've forgotten who you are yourself.'

'Accountancy is somewhat different. I spent most of my spare time calculating my net worth. So what've you been up to?'

'Well, that's why I called. Been getting hitched and I need a witness. You volunteerin'?'

'Helen Dunne, are you majorly shittin' me? You're getting married? Have I lost the plot or what? I thought you were so bent only a plumber could straighten you out? What would that long-haired sweetheart in Boston think of you now?'

'Relax, Byrne. It's not so serious. I'm getting hitched to my lady friend of 18 months acquaintance.'

'Fast work, pardner. Where'd you rope that one?'

'Bray.'

'Sad. None of the local gals suit you then?'

'Nope in spades. This one's special. Are you up for it, Mike?'

Pitch me the deal, pay me in porter – half in advance – and I'll consider it.'

'Okay. Her name's Catherine. She's a bit younger than me. She moved down before Christmas and she's asked me to tie the knot, unofficially. I said I would and we've spent days rowing ever since. Anyway, we've come to a half-agreement: it's a humanist ceremony in Wynne's Hotel, probably towards the end of this year… maybe just before Christmas… but we haven't set a date yet. It should last about 20 minutes and will be followed by din-dins and several pints of plain porter. All you have to do is wear a suit, stand up straight and hand me a ring when I cue you with a kick in the shins. Interested?'

'Honoured to be asked, me dear, truly honoured. Wouldn't let down my old college drinkin' buddy, now would I? Hey, Helen, do you remember that time we got pissed and went playing mixed-doubles pool and we were both so drunk that we tried to pot the white with the black ball in the college league final?'

'No, I don't remember. I hope I never remember that bit. All I can recall is that you left me in the lounge to go shifting that blonde bimbo from second year communications. Jesus, was she some twat!'

'I married her last week.'

'Oh, fuck. Ah, em, Mike maybe I've got the women mixed up… it's difficult, you know… there were so many of them…'

'You can talk. Jesus, if you had to buy a round for all your exes 'twould bankrupt a small South American republic!' Mike paused for breath. 'Naw, I didn't marry her, just enjoyed her charms for the one evening. I am, however, shacking up with the delightful Evelyn Whyte who is currently feeding the runt.'

'How long has that been going on?'

'Oh, a goodish while now. Let me give you some advice, Helen: never shack up with someone who does the same job you do. Balancing our joint account is an absolute nightmare and I can imagine if you and the wan were comparing stories at night instead of getting better acquainted things might get a little boring.'

'Too right, Mike. Say, listen, would you and Evelyn like to come for dinner some weekend soon? I'd love to catch up with you and I think you should meet Catherine before the formal function.'

'Sounds very excellent. I'll have to consult the other half, however, as far as that's concerned. Can I get back to you on it?'

'Yeah, whatever suits, Mike. I'm really delighted you'll consider it… I can't think of anyone I'd prefer to stand up beside me.'

'You sound seriously happy, Tonto.'

Helen was taken aback a little. 'What makes you say that, Ranger?'

'I don't know. You don't sound like yourself. You're different. More settled and more wired at the same time. Softer somehow. Just happy.'

'I am.'

'Well, I'm thrilled for you, Helen. You took some shit times over the years and I'm glad you found someone special enough to make a real difference.'

'Ah, Mike, will you quit! You'll start me crying in a minute.'

'Now that would be something I'd love to see: tough journo Hel in tears. I'd pay money for that.'

'Feck off. Mike, sorry but I've to go. I'll ring you about the dinner invitation and I'll let you know if we set a date in the meantime.'

'Grand. Oh, just one more thing…'

'Yup.'

'Is she good in bed?'

'Michael Byrne, have you no shame?'

'That means she is.'

'You might well think that but I couldn't possibly comment.' Helen laughed heartily and hung up on him.

It was another four weeks before Colm came back to work and even then it was only to tell the staff that he was leaving. Accompanied by Alexander Fleming, the managing director, the mournful editor told them that, for health reasons, he had to take early retirement. He looked a little lost at the prospect. After he thanked them all for their loyal service and the usual other platitudes, Fleming took over the meeting.

Fleming was a dapper, silver-haired charmer, hard as nails, manipulative and adept at playing one member of staff off against another. Formerly a barrister and backed by old money, he fancied himself in the role of newspaper proprietor and, by extension, as The Man Who Formed Public Opinion. Instinctively, Helen didn't trust him, nor did she really like him, although he was friendly enough at the annual staff Christmas dinner. He always wore three-piece suits, starched white shirts with unfashionable but neat button-down collars and square silver cufflinks. Helen thought him slightly vain and Philip had, on short acquaintance, dismissed him as a 'corner-cutting sleeveen'. They were wary of him. He was well known to have his favourites and they knew they were not among them.

'As you will have deduced by now, there will be some changes arising from Colm's decision to retire. Although I regret losing him, I'm sure he is doing what is correct for himself and for his family,' Fleming began.

Sitting next to Philip at the back of the room, Helen hissed very quietly and whispered in her colleague's ear: 'Did he really fall or was he pushed?' Philip raised an eyebrow in response and, with eye contact only, they promised each other a good long gossip session after the meeting.

'This obviously leaves a serious vacancy among the management staff, a vacancy which will have to be filled with a suitable calibre of candidate,' Fleming continued. 'I have consulted the other directors and, having invited Colm also to have an input into the interim decisions, we have decided upon the following. Point one: on the basis of her length of service only – Philip having made it clear in the past that he is not interested in promotion – and as of the end of this month, Helen Dunne will be appointed acting editor for a period not exceeding six months. During that time, the position of editor will be advertised through a recruitment company who will eventually present the directors with a short-list. All existing members of the editorial staff are welcome to apply for the position, if they wish, but there will be no advance guarantees on the matter.' Helen dropped her eyes from the standing Fleming and pointedly looked out the window into the paper's little private car park.

'Point two: arising from point one, there will be a temporary vacancy in the newsroom. It is not proposed to fill that vacancy at this time, pending the outcome of the selection process for the editor's post.'

'Point number three: contracts. George Lennon's contract, which is due to expire shortly, will be extended for one year. He is showing great promise. The contracts of all other members of the editorial, front office, clerical and advertising staff will be renewed for another three years, if they wish to stay, when their current contracts expire.'

'Colm will be remaining with us for a couple of weeks purely in an advisory capacity to assist in a smooth transition of the newspaper production to the new acting editor.'

'For the rest of you, matters will remain unchanged for the moment. I must say, however, that the new editor will be styled as managing editor and will therefore be responsible for the budgeting of the publishing and stationery businesses as well as for the production of the newspaper. The successful candidate may wish to implement changes in staff or work practices in due course, although these will be implemented only following discussions with the directors and consultations with the staff concerned. If anyone wishes to comment, please do so now.'

Most of the twenty-eight heads in the conference room began to shake from side to side. Two remained stationary as the print and clerical union reps tried to assimilate the implications of Fleming's little speech. Helen stood up.

'Mr. Fleming, I'll save my wordy tributes to Colm for his going-away party but I do have a question. In the event that I accept your offer to become acting editor with all the additional duties that entails, we will be left short-handed on the news side, with only Liam, Paula, Philip part of the time and Georgie who, in fairness to him, is still only learning the trade. Will you consider employing a freelance on a fixed-term contract?'

'No,' he replied. 'I appreciate your concerns but I'm sure all the newsroom hands will make extra efforts at this time of change for what is a relatively young company.' Helen began to speak further. 'If you insist,' Fleming continued, and this said with a dismissive wave of one hand, 'we can review the situation on a monthly basis. Privately.' Helen shrugged and took her seat.

'Now,' Fleming went on, displaying his charming shark's smile, 'if there's nothing else, I think we should all get back to work.'

'Call a chapel meeting, now,' Philip said to Helen, the scraping noise of chairs being moved on the wooden floor covering his words. Helen shook her head and indicated she'd talk back in the newsroom.

When the staff dispersed, some pausing to shake Colm's hand and wish him well, Liam, Philip, George, Paula and Helen gathered around Helen's desk upstairs. It being a Friday, Larry McNally, curse his name for an informer git, was on a day off.

'Congratulations Helen,' George said, beaming.

'God, child, but you have a lot to learn,' she told the junior reporter, and then turned to Philip. 'Well, what do you think?'

'I'm not impressed. They're intent on fucking you over

and if you take the acting job you'll be asking for it. The way I see it, they'll knock six months of slave-labour out of you while the recruitment company is picking up someone with management experience, then you'll be thrown back here. That may not seem so bad, but try looking for a more senior job somewhere else and see where it gets you. This business is a fecking small world, Helen, and you'll end up being known as the acting editor who couldn't hack it and had to step back down again. It's a set up. I think they want to get shut of you but I can't figure out why. In the meantime, we'll be short a reporter so we're all going to have to do more work for the same money.'

Helen's eyes were closed. 'Liam?' she asked wearily.

'I agree with Philip. This is a classical poisoned chalice. The problem is that, if you don't agree to six months acting, they'll try to get rid of you anyway and use that as an excuse. He's manoeuvred you into a situation where he wins, either way. I suspect that even if you apply for the permanent job and make it onto the shortlist, they'll find a reason not to give you the job. He already thinks you're too confident and he hates your attitude.'

'Come on, Georgie, tell me what you think now,' Helen turned to the youngster.

'I think I want to work somewhere else,' he said. Everyone else laughed. 'I didn't realize that sort of crack went on.' Georgie finished lamely.

Helen sat back and scrubbed at her eyes. 'Imagine, when I woke up this morning, all I could think about was going for a pint with Philip this evening, along with planning my holidays and paying my ESB bill. A day is a long time in newspapers…' The telephone rang and she scooped up the receiver, listened for a moment, murmured 'okay' and replaced it gently.

Rising from her office chair, she asked quietly: 'Anyone

got a slingshot handy?'

'Why?' Liam asked.

'For the forthcoming battle of Davina and Goliath. Fleming wants to meet me privately in the conference room,' she replied, moving slowly towards the door.

'Helen!' Philip called.

'Yes?'

'Don't commit yourself. And don't sign anything.'

'Understood. Over and out, Captain Kirk.' She saluted, executed a faulty about-turn, and marched away.

'Take a seat,' Fleming said, pointing to a chair on the opposite side of the conference table. Helen took the indicated chair and placed her hands, palm down so he could see they were steady, on the polished pine. Her watch bracelet clicked on the table's surface.

He smiled. 'We have a lot to discuss.'

'We do,' she agreed blandly.

'I probably should have asked you about the acting editor post prior to the staff meeting, but I know how keen you are to get on and I assumed you'd be pleased.' He paused, waiting for a response, although he had not asked a question, either in words or tone.

'I see,' Helen said.

'You will take the job?'

'I haven't had time to think about it. At the moment, I don't know exactly what's on the table so there isn't really anything to think about,' she said, looking pointedly at the *Mayo Recorder* logo inlaid in the centre of the table.

'Of course, of course. We need to discuss money. The other directors and I…'

'Not just money,' Helen interjected. 'You're a realist, Mr. Fleming, and you know that money talks. It's just that, where I'm coming from, money is not the only medium. We also need to discuss conditions, hours, duties and responsibilities. I would also like some indication of how you see my future with this company in the longer-term. Shall we say, longer than six months?' When she stopped speaking, Helen raised her eyes and looked at him directly, her face scrubbed free of everything but innocent inquiry.

'Hmm. First things first. Money. We propose a payment of £200 per week net in addition of your current wage, in consideration of acting editor duties, starting next week. I'm sure you'll agree we're being more than generous, given your lack of experience in a senior management post.'

'Generous, but not "more than generous". Because I'll be tied to the office all week, I'll be losing about £75 a week in mileage and subsistence. Shall we say £275 net instead?' Helen replied.

'£225.'

'£260.'

'£250.'

'I'll consider it.'

'Conditions will be the same as Colm's,' Fleming went on. 'You'll have the same corporate expense and sponsorship account as he had, although all spending over and above £400 a month will be queried by me personally. That would be normal practice up to now. You'll move into his office as soon as he leaves and, should you be required to attend meetings for any reason away from home, you'll be paid a preferential mileage rate.'

'Of what?'

'I'd prefer to leave that until we have an agreement. I wouldn't want it broadcast to the rest of the staff should you spurn our offer.'

'Interesting choice of words. Have you ever heard the expression "pig in a poke", Mr. Fleming?'

'I beg your pardon?'

'Don't mention it. It's nothing,' Helen said, mentally clocking up a one-nil score in her head.

'Moving on, the hours you keep will be a matter for yourself but I suggest you model yourself on your predecessor. The same applies to the duties and responsibilities which Colm will outline to you in full over the next couple of weeks. Most of them I'm sure a woman of your experience and with your powers of observation will already know. Naturally, avoiding defamation proceedings will be one of your main priorities.'

Kennedy. The ongoing Kennedy libel case. One-all. Helen drew in a deep, considering breath and exhaled slowly. 'And my longer term future here?'

'That will be a matter for you, I'm sure. If you choose to apply for the permanent post of editor and are successful, the rest is self-evident. If, however, you choose not to apply, you may return to your current post with our thanks for your help in a challenging period for the company. If, thirdly, you apply for the permanent post and are unsuccessful… well… only you could possibly know what would be the best course of action for you professionally in that event.'

Two-one. 'And your answer?' he continued. 'Obviously, if you refuse to assist us now, we will be forced to look elsewhere for someone willing to take on Colm's position immediately. That process will take, let me see, about six months. In the meantime, you would of course be expected to fulfil the duties you normally would undertake in the editor's absence, for example when Colm has been on annual or sick leave. Speaking frankly, your acting-up duties already include getting the paper out every week. The only real changes would be in terms of title and salary.'

Three-one. Helen knew she had been beaten, but also that this would be a league rather than a championship event. She drummed the fingers of her right hand on the pine surface twice before rising. 'Thank you for your frankness, Mr. Fleming. I will consider the matters we have discussed over the weekend,' she said, buttoning her jacket. 'I'll speak to you on Monday.'

'Before eleven.'

'Before eleven.' She stared down at Fleming through a long pause. He didn't extend his hand for her to shake but then, she didn't extend hers either and simply walked away.

Helen turned in the doorway, her hand on the polished brass doorknob. 'One last thing. Not that it really matters, but why don't you like me, Mr. Fleming?'

He tried and failed to meet her eyes. 'I'm sure I don't know what you mean. I don't know you well enough to make that judgement.'

'A careful answer, but hardly reassuring,' she replied, bowing slightly at the waist to acknowledge his craftiness.

'And what would lead you to assume that I don't like you?'

Helen thought for a swift moment. 'You never use my name,' she said. They locked eyes for a moment before the door closed gently, a slim barrier between mannered and undeclared adversaries.

CHAPTER SEVEN

SMALL WORLD

Helen leaned against the door, weary and relishing the sudden silence. It was after ten, her usual quitting time these days. She dropped her bag at the bottom of the stairs and hung her light jacket over the polished spherical knob that acted as the full stop to a banister sentence. It was too hot. She was too hot. She hated being overheated and the last two weeks of unusually warm weather left her feeling faded, like a photocopy made on a machine without enough toner, or a photographic print short on fixer.

There was a note stuck to the vase on the table. Helen didn't see it until she was sitting down with a mug of strong, black coffee and a stiff shot of Jack Daniel's side by side on the table in front of her. Reading the note, she sipped the whiskey, then crumpled the paper and threw it over her shoulder. Catherine was out. Surprise, surprise.

Helen half-regretted taking Alexander Fleming's terms. Sipping her whiskey slowly, she was conscious of having made a perverse bargain forged out of mutual aversion and sour conceit. With a calculating reticence she didn't really feel, Helen had told him she was gay just after he signed the six-month contract. It was a deliberate manoeuvre; a one-size-fits-all throw of weighted dice. He figured it out too.

'Why are you telling me this now? Why should we have any interest in your private life?'

'I just thought it would be more fair of me to be straight with you.' She smiled moodily at her own unintentional pun. 'I've been around long enough and this is a small enough town for people to talk. I just thought you might have heard some roundabout gossip and I wanted you to hear the truth from me, just to clear the air in case it might become an issue later on.'

'An issue? And why should it become one?'

'I know this is a good place to work and I don't have any worries about being victimized here,' Helen replied, placing deliberate stress on the last two words of the sentence. 'I just wanted to cover myself, in case things change. I wouldn't like you or the other directors to hear about this from someone with a reason to put a pejorative spin on it… around the time of the interviews for the permanent position, for example.'

Fleming had the grace to look alarmed. The dice were still rolling. 'I doubt that would make any difference!' he spluttered belligerently.

'That's good, Alexander. I'm relieved to hear it. Just as long as we understand each other.' Helen let the dice roll to a halt and then hesitated for another moment before making her play. She rose from her seat and leaned forward, her fingertips splayed on the murky mahogany veneer of his desk. 'That's exactly what I wanted to hear today. I wouldn't really like our working relationship to become seriously unpleasant.'

'There's no reason why it should. We will have a decision to make and we will make it fairly and openly,' he said, his teeth locked together. The dice began to roll again.

'Great. It's just that the very new Employment Equality Act expressly forbids workplace discrimination on the grounds of sexual orientation, or victimisation for making a claim under the Act. It's all relatively untried at the moment but a person might be up forty grand for taking the trouble. I believe a company is also liable for the behaviour of its other employees.' Helen looked Fleming in the eye bluntly and stood upright, shrugging. 'Anyway, enough of displeasing thoughts,' she said, extending her hand. 'We have a deal, then.'

'We signed, didn't we?' Fleming replied, his voice low. He stood to take her hand and she shook his firmly and studiously.

'Pleasure,' Helen said breezily. 'Better get the troops to work and start checking out CP's notoriously reliable filing system before he leaves us for good.'

'Just treat McNally with respect. You'll get more work out of him with a softly-softly approach than if you behave like a dictator.'

'I'm no dictator but he will learn who is the boss here, at least for the next six months. I will not be gagged where he or anyone else is concerned. Leave running the newsroom to me. I'll get out good papers for you and if he doesn't like my style, he knows where the door is and he can close it on his way out.'

'He's a name and we don't want to lose him.'

'Speak for yourself, Mr. Fleming: you could get three solid juniors for what you're paying him. I won't have dead weight around me, waiting for me to fuck it up.' Helen raised a hand casually to forestall the coming protest. 'Apologies for the robust language. Don't worry, I won't do anything drastic, well, for the first six months at least.'

'I admire your confidence.'

'Thank you,' she remarked, adding her most engagingly sweet smile. 'I'm sure we'll bump along nicely, you and I.

You'll have my first progress report in four weeks, as you re-
quested. Until then, you can simply forget I'm here.'

Fleming's telephone rang and she took that heaven-sent
opportunity to leave his office. Outside the door, she realised
her palms were sweating. She was breathing too fast and her
pulse was elevated, but at least the dice had stopped rolling,
for the moment.

Niamh decided to give four months' notice or so, due
to a combination of claustrophobia from three adults living
in one small town house and an offer she couldn't refuse from
Matt. Helen had a three-day hangover after the engagement
party, and during it she bawled Georgie Lennon out of it so
badly for constantly putting apostrophes in the wrong places
that he nearly resigned. He accepted her grovelling apology
– given only when Philip gently called her to order – with his
customary good humour. At that particular interview, she
noticed a new earring in his left ear and wondered if he was
gay. She felt guilty for picking on one of her own and then felt
guilty for allowing her suspicion to colour her thinking. But,
fuck it, the apostrophes *were* in the wrong places.

Initially, Catherine was delighted that Niamh was planning to leave, even though she would be staying for another
few months until Matt's house was ready to move into, sometime between September and Christmas, builders and elec-
tricians willing. She liked the lodger but felt it would be nicer
and cosier for her and Helen to have the house to themselves
all the time. It seemed it would be easier to live together
without having to constantly censor conversations or check
on the movements of someone else before making plans for
a night in or a romantic dinner at home. Not that there was
much chance of either at the moment: Helen's working hours
had become truly ridiculous to Catherine, and Helen seemed
unaccountably obsessed with the office and its tortured pol-

itics to the exclusion of almost everything else. Catherine broached the subject quietly one evening but stopped pushing when it was obvious that she was pushing Helen's buttons. It became perfectly evident when Helen broke a plate on the kitchen worktop from sheer temper.

They were sitting companionably in the sitting room one night, watching a soap opera while Niamh slept upstairs. Helen got up to make a sandwich and Catherine followed her into the kitchen to stand with her hip against the worktop and arms folded in her usual pose, watching Helen as she moved around the kitchen and sniffed the contents of the fridge. Helen commenced slicing tomatoes, taking her time to ensure that each slice was exactly the same thickness as the preceding one.

'Want a beer with that?' Catherine asked, rooting in the fridge for one for herself.

'Yummy,' Helen replied.

'This is nice, the two of us being here, isn't it?' Catherine continued, removing the cap from one of the bottles with the opener she carried on her keyring.

Helen's slicing hand paused. 'Is that a loaded question, or what?' she said.

'I wasn't implying anything. I just thought it was nice for the two of us to be here together for a change.'

'For a change, eh? If that isn't weighted with a hidden agenda, nothing is.'

'Ah, c'mon, love. It's just that this is the first evening we've spent in the house together for nearly two weeks. I'd forgotten how wonderful it was just to sit quietly with you and watch telly.'

Helen finished her slicing and put the knife down. She took a long pull from the opened bottle, her dry throat working silently against the cloth of her open-necked white button-down shirt. 'Yes, it is nice. I'm tired,' she said weakly.

'Do you have to work so hard; such long hours? Surely there's something you can do to improve things. I can't see you surviving another few months of this, never mind the rest of your career. You'll get burned out and I'll never see you.'

'Maybe I should have joined the civil service then. Flexi-days, union hours, time off for illness, bereavement, jury service, divorces, weddings and watering the shagging house plants. The private sector is different, Catherine, and local newspapers are the modern equivalent of an Industrial Revolution sweatshop. Normal people don't work in them. I don't do what I do for money or because I want to make money for someone else. I do it because I love to write and I love asking questions and I love hearing other people's stories. Although there's precious little of that at the moment, now that I'm flying a desk and having nothing but flaming arguments with freelance photographers who never turn up or if they do, can't take a fucking caption properly. I just do the shit jobs that no-one else is available for. I'm not an editor: I'm a lackey.' There was bitterness and – what was more surprising to Catherine – even apathy in her words.

'Maybe you should start looking around for another job.'

'For what? I'm not qualified to do anything else. If I move to another paper it'll just be more of the same, only worse. We don't get civil service privileges like in-house who-you-know promotions and long-service increments. The newspaper business doesn't work like that. It's a business: the point is to make money, not write good journalism or win fucking awards.' She took another violent pull from the bottle.

'There has to be something you could do. Maybe you should take a couple of months off to think about it?'

'Yeah, sure, and who'll pay the mortgage while I'm

finding myself? Not you, that's for sure.'

Catherine was stung by the cold-hearted cruelty of the observation. 'I pay my way,' she said shortly.

'There'll only be two of us soon and the bills or the mortgage won't drop by a third. Your salary doesn't seem to stretch too far, does it? I have to keep this show on the road.'

'You're not on your own.'

'It seems like it sometimes. I'm the one who does the worrying. I'm the one who has to listen to you moaning about the disadvantages of living in the country. I'm the one who hardly has a family to speak to because of this relationship. I'm the one who works hard and comes home to an empty house and an empty bed because you're out playing with the girls.'

'Pity yourself, why don't you?' Catherine snapped back.

Helen picked up her empty plate in one hand and smashed it violently against the edge of the worktop. Catherine backed away in alarm as splintered fragments of pottery hit the floor.

'You know what you can do, don't you? You can go fuck yourself,' Helen said tightly. 'I'm going over to Philip's. I'm not spending what little free time I have listening to you moaning because I'm never here.'

A week later, Helen had calmed down enough to remember that she'd forgotten Catherine's father's anniversary. She made up for it by ringing Catherine at work, something she rarely did, and apologising. Catherine accepted the apology gratefully, glad to feel the slight thaw and willing to make a move in the same general direction.

'I'm definitely off on Sunday this weekend. Could you maybe take some time off and we'll go for a drive somewhere?' Helen continued. 'Maybe have a meal out, as well?'

'Sounds wonderful. I'll see what I can do. Maybe we

could head over to Achill or somewhere like that if the day is fine?'

'Sure thing, boss. I'm unlikely to meet anyone I'd know out there and that'd be just as well. I'm fed up of people trying to talk about their bingo local notes with me when I'm doing the frigging shopping,' Helen agreed.

'Yeah, right. The last time you went shopping you came home in a ripping temper with two six packs, two frozen pizzas and no toilet paper,' Catherine chided softly.

'Proves my point. All those people who think they know better than me how to run a newspaper distract me from my domestic duties. You'd think they have a share in the place, the way they carry on.' Helen paused, the palm holding the telephone sweating slightly. Identifying her own nervousness, she was alarmed a little. 'Lissen, Beeps, I'm really sorry I didn't remember about your dad. That was unforgivable. I know I'd be in a really serious snit if you forgot Caroline's anniversary – or our own – so I think I know how you must be feeling.'

'I said you're forgiven.'

'I know that, but one of my little faults is that I want to hear you say it more than once.'

'I said you're forgiven.'

'Now you sound like the proverbial broken record.'

'I said you're forgiven.'

'Messer.'

'I said…'

'I love you dearly,' Helen broke in. 'Is that enough to fix it?'

'You know it is,' Catherine replied warmly.

Helen hung up the telephone, then picked up the receiver again quickly and dialled Philip's extension. 'Mr. O'Connor, the acting editor would like to invite thee to a spot of lunch in our favourite 'ostelry, if you're not too busy today,' she said.

'Sounds a bit ominous to me. Are you sacking me?'

'Nah, just need some advice. Personal issue. Girly stuff,' Helen whispered.

'Emotional?'

'Yuck. I hate that word.'

'Commitment issues?'

'Philip, stop saying those things out loud! The Cougar knows it's me: my red light'll be lit up like a Christmas tree on her telephone. I can do without her smiling that superior little supercilious smile she practices in front of the bathroom mirror.'

'Alright so. Where d'ya want to meet?'

'TF at two. Don't say it out loud or she'll take a late lunch too.'

'Paranoid, as well. How very FBI codeword of you,' Philip said dryly.

Helen terminated the conversation with a hiss, then smiled to herself as she studied two jpegs on screen. They were very different pictures, but it was easy for Helen to pick one for the railway feature earmarked for page fifteen. There was no contest really: only one had a proper caption attached. Editorial decisions, she knew, were often made for the most obvious motives. The reading public, for some reason, always assumed there was a hidden agenda.

Over lunch, she skirted the issue and asked Philip about how much he'd sold his house for; how much of the purchase price Patti had settled for, and what he intended to do with the cash.

'Jesus, I feel like I'm in court!' he protested, but outlined that he intended buying a little bachelor pad, probably an apartment, when he found one that suited him and that he could afford. In the meantime, he was sharing a four-bedroomed house belonging to a friend of his… with two female students from the local campus of Galway-Mayo Institute of Technology. It didn't really suit, but it was cheaper than the going rate and he made up the difference by being a sort of caretaker.

'Anyway, it's only a temporary solution until I find something better,' he finished. 'It does have one advantage, however: it's on the other side of town from the ex, so at least we don't meet on the way to our respective workplaces.'

'Christ, I always hated sharing with students, even when I was one,' Helen recalled. 'Well, I know Niamh's a student, but she's nearly qualified now so it doesn't count.' An idea struck her. 'Hey, Niamh's moving out in a few months or so, or whenever the bold Matthew's house has been completed: what would you think about moving in with us? The rent's even cheaper than what you're paying now and I think meself and Catherine are easy enough to get on with. You could check it out with Niamh and let me know: she'd be honest and I wouldn't be offended if you decided not to bother.'

Philip looked dubious. 'But I work for you,' he protested. 'It could be a disaster. I mean, if you bawl me out over a garda brief I messed then I wouldn't make tea for you in the evening.'

'You are messing, I hope. And when have I ever bawled *you* out? For God's sake, Philip, you taught me everything I know about this town, most of what I know about the newspaper business, and anyway I only got this poisoned chalice because you weren't interested. You're my hero; I'd never shout at you,' Helen finished sweetly.

'After that bollicking you gave Lennon over his misplaced apostrophes, I don't believe a word of it. Tell you what, I'll think about it. Just one thing, though; if I do move in, that rug you have in front of the fireplace has to go. I don't know about living with you, but I certainly can't live with it.'

Helen punched him on the shoulder. 'Mighty! I'm

thrilled. Let me know when you make up your mind.' She continued munching the chicken and salad sandwich that, with a mug of strong black coffee, made up her lunch.

Philip swallowed a mouthful of tea. 'Now, what was it you wanted to talk to me about? Girly stuff, was it?'

'Ah, haven't got time for that now. Anyway, it's probably nothing apart from my imagination,' Helen said, twisting her lips around a lump of lettuce.

Unconvinced, he raised an eyebrow. Helen's mobile rang just at that moment. She shrugged, holding out her hands in a "what can I do?" pose. In reply, his smile was warm, if a little concerned.

The following Sunday was the first day of Summer and, for a true Irish wonder, it was actually warm. May Day meant a public holiday Monday, even in the newspaper trade, and Helen knew that the week's paper was well under control to the extent that she didn't even have to bring work home with her on the previous Friday evening.

She cried off a solo dinner appointment with her parents – they still hadn't made the colossal leap from having dinner with Catherine in Helen's to having dinner with both of them in their own home – in favour of keeping her promise. She even made a picnic, disregarding Catherine's protest that both of them would end up in bed with rampant Summer colds.

Ophelia's grey metallic paint actually glinted in the sun as they began the drive, despite the car's advanced age. Helen insisted on mooching towards Newport along the back roads, rather than taking the main road through the bustling, picturesque, but strangely unappealing town of Westport. Despite the consequential economic benefits, Helen thought this coastal town had developed too quickly. There were too many Summer homes and an excessively heavy reliance on the foreign and domestic tourism that could be as fickle as Western weather. Westport was a popular spot for hen nights and Christmas parties, and Helen had endured a few nights there, but she had never really warmed to the place.

In the little town of Newport, they crossed the bridge over the famous fishing river that flowed from the mountains down to the blue Clew Bay sea. One of Helen's earliest memories had been of a day like this, when she watched silvered fish catching the light as they strove to swim upstream to spawning grounds held in their folk memory. This was one of her dad's favourite angling spots, and when Helen and Caroline were young, he used to bring them both with him. They were easy with each other on days like that, and concentrated on maintaining the silence and not letting their shadows fall in case the fish saw them and grew canny enough to evade the flies her father expertly cast.

Helen thought she'd make a good angler herself now, if she had the time. She had learned her love of quietness on dewy afternoons, lying on the riverbank and reading a book, half-ignoring the background babble of running water and the occasional sizzle of the spinning reel. After the quiet hours, her dad always brought them to Newport House Hotel, where they sipped lemonade from grown-up glasses – rather than the bottle-and-straw method she'd favoured then – in the exhausted stateliness of a worn-out drawing room.

She told Catherine these childhood stories as she drove slowly on towards Mulranny, cleaving to the road that hugged the Northern coastline of Clew Bay. In the town, she hesitated, asking Catherine if she'd prefer a trip across the Nephin Beg range to Ballycroy and on to Belmullet, but Catherine demurred. She too had childhood stories and a persistent hankering for the rocky outcrops and straggling villages of Achill on such a fine day.

Helen drove across the Corraun Penninsula and across

the bridge at Achill Sound. On the island, clocks moved more slowly on quiet Sundays this early in the tourist season. The road was almost deserted. Helen was delighted with the barren tarred road as she negotiated the twists and turns that led to the village of Keel. They picnicked just beyond the village on the side of the road while Ophelia was safely tucked in to a farmer's gateway. When they looked South across the sea, Catherine's keener eyes could make out the shape of what she said was Inisbofin through the haze, although Helen claimed it was only the graceful hump of the nearer Clare Island.

Helen sighed violently, then leaned back against the turf, her rolled-up shirtsleeves creasing.

'What was that for?' Catherine said quizzically, wiping her lips with a raggedy piece of kitchen towel she'd unearthed in the bottom of the picnic bag.

'From, not for.'

'You what?'

'I was sighing *from* relief and contentment, not *for* anything.'

'Why?'

'Why what?'

'Why the relief and contentment?'

'Fair question,' Helen said, leaning forward again to rest her forehead on the crossed arms laid on her knees. 'Contentment, first. There's nothing really like this, is there? Sitting on someone's or no-man's land on the side of the road, with a tummy full from home-made grub that tastes so much better for being eaten in the open air; with no telephone's ringing and no-one to see and no-where to go; no panic; no emergency; no point to anything, for this moment, other than being here with you.'

'Sounds like a ditto so far. And the rest?'

'Relief? Well, I suppose I mean I'm relieved that we can just sit here, together, you and I, without pulling strips off each other. We seem to have been doing too much of that lately and I don't like it.'

'Me neither,' Catherine agreed, pausing to pick up the stray detritus of their haphazard picnic. 'I don't understand why we spark off each other so much these days. We used to be so alike. We even used to think alike and talk alike. I think we've just stopped talking properly, or something.'

Without looking, Helen reached across and placed her palm on Catherine's knee. 'I know I'm busy but that's no excuse. Sometimes, well, at times like this, I think maybe I'm just taking you for granted or something. Maybe I just think you'll always be there to come home to, when you mightn't be. I shouldn't expect that and I don't know why I do. Maybe I'm just behaving as if we're an old married couple when the truth is that we're not, and probably never will be.'

Clutching the wistfulness in Helen's tone, Catherine looked up, shielding her eyes against the sunshine in mock salute. 'What makes you say that, then?'

'Well, I don't really know.' Then Helen was silent. Her eyes were closed.

'D'ya know what I think? I think we're just getting accustomed to each other as individuals. The thing about being in a relationship is that even though you're in one, you're still an individual in other parts of your life. I mean, we're supposed to be a couple when we're together, but I wonder if sometimes we don't get too fond of being individuals when we're in situations where we have to act that way.'

'I don't quite follow you,' Helen said, glancing up in bewilderment before returning her forehead to her knees.

'Well, you're you, Helen, when you're at work or with your family and I'm me, Catherine, in the same situations. When we're together, we're us, Helen *and* Catherine. I suppose sometimes it's not too easy to make that kind of transition, not every day, not every time.'

'Do you love me?'

'What kind of a question's that?'

'The ordinary kind. The simple kind. Do you?'

'Yes, I do love you.'

'Enough?'

'For what?'

'To justify settling down with me, committing yourself to me, living with me and all that other boring crap.'

'Justify. That's a peculiar choice of work, but the answer is yes.'

'Do you fancy anyone else?'

'Fuck off, Helen,' Catherine replied heatedly. 'What are you looking for? Some stereotypical justification for the obvious fact that we're not getting along so well?'

'Answer me.'

'No, fuck you.'

'That's all right then. If you love me, want to be with me and don't hanker after anyone else, we'll be grand,' Helen smiled into Catherine's angry eyes. 'C'mon, Bubbles, I'm just messing.'

'You're not.'

'I am, sort of.' Helen looked out to sea. 'I don't want to fight with you. I have nothing to fight with you about. I just want you to be happy, but more than that and shame on me for wanting it, I want you to be happy with me. With *me*. Is that so wrong?'

Catherine shuffled closer until their upper arms were touching. Peeping down, Helen realised that the fine hairs on Catherine's forearm were stealing sunbeams from the gradually darkening blue of the skies. 'No, that's not so wrong. It's not even a bit wrong,' Catherine confirmed, putting an arm around Helen's shoulders. Helen started to cry, silently. 'What? What did I say? What's wrong?'

'Nothing,' Helen snuffled back. 'It's just that I find this

so hard. I find it so hard to need something from you, to need *you*. It cuts me up and I hate it, but at the same time, I know I couldn't do without you. And then I'm so busy and work is so fucked and I just can't seem to give you the time I should, and when I do have the time, I just rub you up the wrong way, or you're not even here to argue with, not that I can complain about you not being there when I'm not there most of the time.'

Catherine squeezed her arm. 'Shut up, you brainless woman. You're just being a silly moo, now. Yes, it pisses me off when you come home all tetchy and cranky and wound up tighter'n a watch-spring, but maybe I could handle it better instead of acting as if I'm the little woman who's been home all day with the sprogs, itching for a row. Eh?'

'I never think of you that way.'

'I wouldn't blame you if you did. Maybe if you could concentrate on separating that godawful office from your own hall door, I could concentrate on not harassing you as soon as you walk through it.' Catherine handed Helen her crumpled piece of kitchen towel. 'It's not too hygienic, I know, but you need to blow.'

Helen smiled warily, then took the proffered tissue and blew energetically. 'I think you're right,' she said. 'I just get the feeling sometimes that you haven't a clue what's it's like for me, and then I feel all isolated and ignored.'

'I do have a clue and you're not. Do you believe me?' Catherine held her eyes.

'Yup.' Helen gulped childishly, then rolled down her shirtsleeves ostentatiously. 'Will you drive home, Bubbles? I feel like letting the seat back, switching on the stereo and singing to the cows in the fields on the way there. I never got to do that because I'm always behind the wheel. I reckon it must be magic. Am I right?'

'You are. It is, but only if you love the driver.'

'I do.'

They gathered their belongings and stowed them in the car. Catherine slammed the boot lid and then caught Helen's sleeve. 'Hey, Helen,' she said shyly, 'maybe we'd be doing right to press ahead with that ceremony thing. I think it'd be good for us to get settled. It might make us more comfortable and confident with each other, the way we used to be.'

Startled, Helen looked at her in disbelief. 'After all this shit, you want to get on with that now?'

'No time like present, Confucius say.'

'Right so,' Helen said smiling. 'Let's get on to it next week. I'll set up an appointment with my solicitor about the house and we can have Mike and Evelyn over for dinner to discuss the arrangements. Oh, and Philip, of course... can't have any arrangements being discussed without the esteemed colleague being present.'

'Of course,' Catherine grinned. 'Y'know, if I didn't know better, I'd say I was part of a love triangle and that you'd a secret hankering for your subordinate!'

'Yuck,' Helen scowled. 'Ick! That's no way to talk about my surrogate older brother.'

They retraced their steps along the coast unhurriedly, finally arriving home in time for a late tea, a bottle of mature red and an unseasonably early night.

Catherine missed the appointment with Helen's solicitor, much to the embarrassment of both. Helen squirmed miserably in the waiting room for three-quarters of an hour before leaving after a muttered apology to the legal secretary. Catherine said she'd got stuck behind a double-artic on the way home from work. Helen was dubious, but Catherine protested enough to convince her it was a genuine explanation. The celebratory dinner was another story.

Mike Byrne and Evelyn arrived early, just as Helen

was in the middle of her shower. 'Get that, will you?' she yo-delled, intending the message to be received either by Catherine who was in the bedroom or Philip who was downstairs monitoring the saucepans. Philip made it to the door first, just as Catherine reached the third last step. Through the slightly open bathroom door and even over the low whisper of the still malfunctioning shower head, Helen could hear the doorbell ring a second time. 'Feck the pair of you, do I have to get out and do it myself, dripping wet?' she roared. Her simulated anger was rewarded by the sound of the door opening, so she returned to humming the latest KD Lang dit-ty and lathered conditioner all over her hair.

Downstairs, Philip was doing the deducing and the introductions. 'Hello, you must be Mike. And Evelyn, of course. I'm Philip, Helen's friend,' he said, extending a hand and holding the door open so the two visitors could make their way into the narrow hallway. He closed the door behind them and gestured towards the stairs on his right. 'Helen's in the shower but this is Catherine,' he said, glancing up.

Michael leaned forward quickly, extending his hand. 'We're so pleased to meet you at last, Catherine. We've heard so many good things about you from Helen,' he said, then smiled quizzically when Catherine failed to react. Philip cleared his throat and Catherine twitched. Focusing, she took Mike's hand and shook it slowly. 'Hi, Mike, nice to meet you too,' she said slowly.

Mike turned and indicated his fiancée. 'Evelyn, Catherine and Philip. Catherine and Philip, Evelyn,' he said politely. Evelyn shook Philip's hand and nodded warily in Catherine's direction. The circumspect gesture was returned. Philip and Mike exchanged a manly smirk to cover the moment.

'Ranger!' Helen yodelled from the top of the stairs. She was wrapped in a towel, her wet hair spraying droplets down the polished banister.

'Dunne Roamin'!' he returned, at roughly the same decibel. Mike and Helen traded high fives from where they stood while Philip and Evelyn bartered indulgent glances. 'Head into the sitting room where the gallant Philip and the gorgeous Katie will ply you with drink. I'll be down in half a sec.' Helen said, disappearing into her bedroom.

By the time she joined the three in the sitting-room, there were glasses in hand and cigarettes lit. Helen glanced at Catherine, surprised to see her smoking again, before ruffling her hair. 'So you've met the cause of all my troubles,' she joked, addressing Mike before she crossed the room to give Evelyn a warm handshake. 'Pleased to meet you again after all these years which, I must add, have been very kind to you despite your attachment to this fellow who's enough of a nuisance to age an angel.'

Mike laughed heartily. 'Still a messer, you. Evelyn, don't mind her. She hasn't changed a bit since the DIT snooker-hall days,' he said grinning. Helen helped herself to a glass of wine and sat on the floor at Catherine's feet, patting her knee comfortingly as she did so. She vaguely remembered Evelyn as a tall, short-haired and very attractive woman with obvious dyke potential and a quiet brand of charm, but hadn't made the connection between the name and the mental image when Mike had told her they were together and planning to get married. She hardly recognized the new Evelyn; this slightly plump, long-haired version wearing an engagement ring had taken her by surprise.

Catherine and Evelyn were very quiet, but still the meal was a success. Mike and Helen teased the other three unmercifully and Philip told some very risqué jokes to go with dessert. Initially, Helen had been concerned about Catherine's perceptible discomfort, but then dismissed it as she reached for the third wine bottle and poured herself another glass. She was tipsy and she knew it, but felt she deserved a night off from sobriety and responsibility for once. When Evelyn asked for the bathroom, Helen engaged in long, convoluted directions, and giggled with every half breath, until Catherine cut her off. 'I'll show her. I'm sure she wants to go before midnight,' she said sharply, heading for the door.

Mike, Helen and Philip remained around the table, re-telling anecdotes and cracking jokes at a mile a minute. Helen genuinely admired Philip's ability to just get on with people, even strangers. She felt it was one of the qualities that made him such a good journalist. He had the common touch that Helen constantly felt she lacked. She always felt strangely shy talking to strangers, even if her brusque and professional manner gave most of them the impression that she knew what she was doing well enough to do it successfully, even in her sleep.

Fifteen minutes after Catherine and Evelyn had left the table, Helen stretched lethargically and said: 'Well, gentlemen, now that the ladies have obviously left us for the sitting-room, I think it's time I disrupted them enough to unearth my special bottle of port. Anyone fancy a port to help the dinner go down?' she asked, surveying the men in turn through the dripping candles and clutter of dishes on the table. They both nodded, although Mike remarked: 'Jesus, Helen, if I drink much more Eve'll have to drive home, and in my state, that'd be worse than driving myself. We might have to take over your sofa if this shindig goes on much longer.'

'Not to worry, Ranger. It folds out into a bed, as my friend Philip here knows to the cost of his lumbar vertebrae,' she replied smoothly, then closed the kitchen door and walked down the hall. Before she got half-way, she heard a raised voice upstairs. It was Catherine's. Without pausing to think clearly, she climbed the stairs quietly and waited on the landing, breathing quietly. Her bedroom door was ajar.

'Eve, I didn't know it was you, but at the end of the day,

you were the one who left me without a word.'

Helen froze. Eve. Fuck. She'd never have made that con-nection in an age. The excessive quantity of wine she'd con-sumed that evening evaporated from her head in an instant.

'Look, Cathy, I didn't know it was you either. No-one ever used to call you Catherine except your mother, for God's sake! I wouldn't have come if I'd known. I'd have told Mike I was sick or something.'

'What are you doing with him, anyway. I thought you were gay. Fuck it, Eve, *you* thought you were gay!'

'I got tired of it.'

'Tired of me?'

On the landing, Helen's heart turned painfully in her chest at Catherine's melancholy tone.

'It wasn't like that,' Eve replied in a jagged, shaded voice.

'Might as well have been, for all the difference it made. You still left and you never gave me a chance. I would have worked it out with you. You would have been worth it.'

'It's too late now,' Eve said. 'I love Mike and I'm going to marry him. He takes care of me.'

'Is that enough?'

Realising she didn't want to hear the answer, Helen pushed the door hard enough for it to bang against the wall, and observed the two women sitting side by side on her bed. Catherine popped up quickly. 'Eve wasn't feeling too well so I brought her in to sit down,' she said, crimson guilt rising swiftly from her neck to her cheeks.

Helen eyed her levelly, then sniffed. 'Indeed. We're just at the port stage downstairs, ladies, if you'd like to join us.'

Eve stood up and brushed past Helen boorishly. 'I'm fine now. I'll just go back down and see how Mike's doing,' she said rudely.

Catherine also moved to leave, but Helen stood her ground and blocked the doorway. 'So that's the famous Eve,' she said coolly. 'Isn't it a small world?'

'I didn't know it was her.'

'Nor did I or she wouldn't be here. How long ago was it? Five years? More? It makes fuck all difference though, because it sounds to me as if you're still sweet on her.'

'You were listening to a private conversation!' Catherine accused.

'This is my house, darling, and private conversations between you and your ex-lovers in *my* bedroom are fair game. I'm waiting.'

'For what?'

'A denial.'

'Of what?'

''Of my statement that you're still sweet on that overweight girly.'

'If that's what you want, you can go fuck yourself, Helen. You either trust me or you don't.'

'Trust is an earned quality.' Helen replied, leaning towards Catherine threateningly. 'Now, we will both behave like gentlemen and join our guests at the table and we will say nothing more about this at this time. We will most particularly not give Philip or Michael the impression that there is anything wrong. If I'm as jealous and paranoid as you appear to think I am, then I think your conversation with Eve has given me adequate reason to be. We'll talk about this later because now is definitely not the time for a scene.'

'Good on you, Helen, for keeping up appearances,' Catherine sneered. 'You always get to make the rules, don't you, down to setting an appropriate time for giving me a bollicking.'

'Shut up. If you're not downstairs thirty seconds after me, I'll say you're ill, and two of them will believe me.' Helen turned on her heel and thumped down the stairs. After a couple of minutes, Catherine heard the kitchen door opening and Helen's voice, claiming that she'd mislaid the bottle of port and finally found it among the contents of her knicker drawer.

'Right. What's all this about, then?' Helen asked, surveying the reporters seated around the small conference table in her office.

Philip squirmed uncomfortably in his chair. 'Well, you know that the negotiations between the union and the owners broke down and the Labour Relations Commission have made a recommendation in our favour. The owners won't accept it and the union's calling for a ballot, although all chapels have to vote as individual units.'

'Yeah, I know that, I'm the mother of the chapel. I circulated the letter, remember?'

'That's the problem, really. You're an NUJ member but you're also part of management, even if your acting position is only temporary. I suppose what we really want to know is if you want to take part in the ballot.'

'Of course I do. I'm a member of this fucking union, after all. I presume it's a secret ballot, as usual.'

'Yeah,' he squirmed again, glanced at Liam and George, then added: 'We're calling a mandatory chapel meeting for Wednesday at 4.00 p.m. to discuss the issues first. We, that is, all of us would prefer if you didn't attend.'

Helen threw her pen on the A4 refill pad in front of her, then leaned back into her chair. 'I see. I'm the enemy now, am I? Not fit to sit in on a meeting of *my* chapel?'

'C'mon, Helen, don't be like that,' Liam said. 'You've got to see how awkward it would be for us to speak freely when we don't know for sure that you're not reporting back to the boss.'

'So I'm untrustworthy and a snitch, is that it? And you all feel the same about this?' She looked in turn at each face around the table. Philip tried and failed to meet her eye. She sighed, 'Go ahead then and have your fucking meeting without me, but I'll have to tell Fleming we'll miss the deadline next week because of it. There's fuck all I can do about that. I'll be voting though, the same as the rest of you. You might have the grace to let me know when that'll be. Now get back to work, the lot of you.'

One by one, George, Paula, Liam and Larry left the room. Philip didn't stir. 'That includes you,' Helen snapped.

'Ah, Helen, please, there's no need for this.'

'Look at it from my point of view. I was one of you a few weeks ago. We're all still on the same side here. You know I'm no management snitch and you could have backed me up. I was depending on you.'

'They were all thinking the same way. There was nothing I could do.'

'That makes you a sheep, Philip. I thought you had more balls.'

Philip rose and strode furiously towards the door, but turned back before he got there. Standing over Helen, he put a hand on her shoulder. She shrugged it off angrily, and looked into the middle distance.

'Remember this, Helen. If I stay on-side with the rest, at least I'll know what's going on. I don't shit on my friends for the sake of politics. I never have. I thought you knew that much about me by now.'

Helen sniffed cynically but didn't reply. When he left, she turned it over astutely. He'd as much as promised to feed her information to keep her ahead of events, not that it'd be much use if she was the first *Recorder* editor to preside over a strike. She picked up the telephone and made an appointment to see Fleming that same afternoon.

By the time she arrived home, Catherine had started

dinner and lit a small fire to take the chill out of the evening. In the week or so since the post-dinner middle-of-the-night screaming match that had ended abruptly when Niamh arrived home and Helen took Catherine to bed, they had lapsed into a prickly rapprochement that was as much about passion as anger.

Helen flung her briefcase into a corner, flopped down on the living room sofa and accepted a whiskey from Catherine gratefully, as well as the lingering kiss that went with it.

'Well, darling, how'd it go?' Catherine asked, leaning on the counter that divided the room while keeping a weather eye on a bubbling saucepan of spaghetti.

'Basically, I'm fucked. Fleming's not prepared to break ranks with the rest of those blood-sucking owners and pay up something on the quiet. He said he'll find out the result of the ballot, and if it's unanimous he'll know I didn't vote "the company's" way. Meanwhile, if it's not unanimous, the rest of them will know I voted against industrial action and their perception that I'm in bed with management will be confirmed. I'll never get a decent day's work out of any of them again. My life will be hell, either way. Fuck that. Now, what's for dinner?'

'Spaghetti Bolognese, your favourite; there's a bottle of Chianti in the fridge to go with it.'

'Divine. As last meals of the condemned go, that beats all.'

'What are you going to do, Helen.'

''Haven't a fucking clue. I can only hope the boss class relent and agree to follow the LRC recommendations, with a few extra demands for increased productivity thrown in. I'm out of my depth here. I don't know how to play these games, but even if I did, I don't think this one is winnable.'

'Poor sausage.'

'Still, it's good to have you here to listen to me moaning. Didn't run off with any women today, then?'

'No, apart from your mother.'

Helen spluttered whiskey over the rim of her glass. 'Come again?'

'Can't. Still too shagged after last night.'

Helen wiggled her eyebrows suggestively. 'Hmm, true, true. Now what was that about my mother?'

'She telephoned today and chatted me up for half an hour.'

'You exaggerate, surely.'

'Not really. She wanted to know how you were and how you were getting on. I told her you were having a shit time at work, but that I was looking after you and making sure you were eating properly and all that stuff. She even asked how I was getting on at work, and wondered if she could pop into the office the next time she's in Ballina to visit your Great-Auntie Whatsit.'

'Margaret. The blessed woman's name is Margaret, as in Cantankerous Ould Biddy.' Helen took another sip from her glass. 'Sounds promising. At least they're speaking to you, which is more than can be said for that flute of a brother of mine.'

'I'm likeable, aren't I? I'm sure Andy'll come 'round too, given time.'

'Famous last words. I couldn't give a shit about him but I miss my little chats with Maria. Hey, did I tell you she sent me a card at the office? She even wrote the address and posted it herself obviously, judging by the fact that the stamp was on the back of the envelope. She said she misses me and wonders why I don't call any more. I wish she was old enough to make up her own mind.'

'If she was, you'd be fifteen years older and I mightn't fancy you half as much.'

Helen smiled. 'Like 'em young and fit, do you?'

'Nah, not really. Just like you.'

'Ditto. When's dinner? I'm starving. I thought we could go for a walk later and watch the sun go down. I might even pull you behind some bushes for a quick snog.'

'Wait 'til you eat first… it mightn't be that good!'

'I'm sure it'll be delicious, as is anything that's made by your fair hands.'

'Flattery'll get you most places.'

Helen sidled into the kitchen and put her arms around Catherine's waist, peering into the steaming saucepan over her shoulder. 'I'm counting on it,' she said.

Catherine served up dinner and said casually: 'Oh, I'm not sure if I mentioned this to you already, but I'm popping home this weekend. Mam was wondering if you'd be coming as well.'

'No can do, sweetheart. I've some work to catch up on over the weekend but you fire ahead.'

'I was going to anyway,' Catherine said sharply. 'I have to see my family now and again and I don't need your permission.'

'Chill, chill. I didn't mean it like that.'

Partly mollified, Catherine sat down and picked up her fork. 'Right,' she said grumpily, then added. 'Oh, Niamh rang. She's staying over with yer man tonight.'

'Won't be long now until she's gone. It'll be strange. Sometimes I think of her as being like a connector thing that stops us sparking off each other all the time. I wonder will we kill each other when she leaves?'

'Unlikely,' Catherine replied. 'I'll do you first and that means that I'll survive.'

Helen laughed. 'You'd want to be quick! Seriously though, I wonder should we start looking around for an equally broad-minder lodger with a job that keeps him or her out of our hair for sixteen hours out of the twenty-four in every day?'

'No, Helen. We'll be fine on our own. I'll cook dinners and serenade you with amazing riffs, and you can be a corporate whiz down at the paper and finish the study shelves to make space for my books here.'

'Sounds like bliss,' Helen said, trying to twist spaghetti strands around her fork but failing. 'I never could get the hand of this. Must be lacking in manual dexterity, I suppose.'

Catherine snorted. 'Not my experience,' she said.

Helen glanced at her curiously, nonplussed for the moments before the penny dropped. 'Catherine Lacey,' she said finally, 'you have a dirty mind.'

'Jesus, where did you appear from?' Helen said in amazement, then gestured at six-year-old Maria. 'My, my, how you've grown, Tinkerbell. Come in, come in. It's great to see you both. What are you doing here?'

'Andy's gone to Bundoran for the day to play golf with Frank and Nora's gone off on a day trip with the ladies' club to Dublin. We were at a loose end.' Mary smiled and then hugged Helen while Maria danced up and down, holding Helen's hand. 'It's good to see you. You look fantastic!' she continued.

'Yeah, took up swimming and lost some weight.'

'And are those highlights I see in your hair?'

Helen blushed. 'Yeah, Catherine persuaded me. Waste of money because I keep my hair so short,' she growled, opening a bottle of lemonade for Maria and switching on the kettle. 'Mary, will Andy go ape-shit if he finds out?'

'I'd imagine so. Not much chance of keeping it a secret though.'

'Hey, hang on, Tinkerbell. Don't be putting the bottle on your head like the wino man down the town. I've some straws around here somewhere that I keep just for you.' Helen rooted the straws from the back of a cupboard and opened the double doors into the garden. 'C'mere, Maria, see that bit of white fluff down there? No, over there by the shed? That's Tiddles. Well, that's not her real name. We were waiting for you to visit and think up a proper one. She's adopted us and she'd love a cuddle.'

'Mam, Mam, look. It's a kitten. Can I?' Maria jumped up and down.

Mary peered at the snow white kitten and nodded. 'Alright, but leave the bottle of lemonade and wash your hands when you come in.'

Maria followed the paving stones down to the shed door, bent over and put her hand out gently. No-name Tiddles eyed her warily for a second, then stuck her tail up in the air and started to wrap herself around Maria's ankles.

Helen smiled and went back into the kitchen to make coffee.

'Catherine not around?' Mary asked.

'Nah. Gone to the city to see her folks and won't be back until late tomorrow night. I was just catching up on some work and I was dying for a reason to take a break.' She stirred milk into the two mugs and gestured at the sofa. 'So, what news, Maid Marion?' she enquired.

'Just the usual. Now that I took at you right, girl, you look tired.'

'Yeah, I suppose.' Helen filled her in at length, cradling her mug in both hands, and then finished up with a bright '... so as you can see, all's well on the professional front.'

'And the personal?' Mary asked.

Helen squirmed uncomfortably, then put down her mug. 'Ah, c'mon, Mary, you really don't want a proper answer to that,' she said.

'I wouldn't ask if I didn't. Did I ever tell you that my youngest sister, Katie, is gay?'

'The one in London?'

'Yeah. It was obvious even when she was very young. She's living with some English woman called Andrea. They both work for the same company and she's very happy. Andy never really liked her. I wonder why that might be…?'

'Jesus, Mary, but you're full of surprises today. First you turn up on my doorstep with that gorgeous daughter of yours and now you casually announce the secret you've been hiding in your family closet. What next?'

'Nothing. No more surprises, I'm afraid. So, now that we've avoided the matter for another minute or so, how are you and Catherine?'

'Hard to tell. Everything was going fairly swimmingly, just the usual ups and downs, but I'm beginning to wonder if we'll stick it out. Something's not right, but as usual when it comes to relationships, this eejit here just can't put her finger on it.'

'Have you talked to her about it?'

'Yes and no. I don't quite know what I'm trying to say; she gets defensive and we just end up finding something else to argue about. I'm so up to my neck at work just now that it's tempting to simply let it slide for a while until I can figure it out on my own.'

'Not good policy,' Mary said firmly. 'Hang on a sec, I'll just check on my sproglet.' Maria was engrossed in the friendly little kitten and was unwilling to return to the kitchen, even for a bottle of lemonade and a cuddle from her aunt. 'Well, maybe you should take a holiday,' Mary said, when she sat down again, then held up her hands to make peace. 'Sorry, I forgot. Work comes first. It always did with you, Helen. Did you ever think that maybe that was why things didn't work out for you before.'

'Before? What do you know about before?' Helen asked in genuine amazement.

Mary tapped the side of her nose in a conspiratorial gesture. 'I understand more than you might think, even from a distance. You and … what *was* her name again… Diana? You were together a long time in the States, I think, and you came home in a mighty hurry to mope around your mother's house in a snit for weeks, looking like you'd found a shilling and lost a pound.'

'I applaud your insight… and your understanding,' Helen said, smiling. 'She drank too much. I got tired of it in the end so I left.'

'And did you try to talk to her about the effect her drinking was having on you, or on the two of you?'

'Not really. I didn't figure it out for ages, and by the time I did, she was too far gone, I suppose,' Helen said, then shrugged. 'It mightn't have worked out anyway.'

'Ever the optimist,' Mary said softly. Helen nodded slowly in reply. 'Listen, Helen, I might sound like a daft old biddy here, but the key to it all is communication. Getting married or moving in together is only the start of it, not the end, obvious as that might sound. I don't know the girl at all, but I do know that if you think there's something off and you don't talk to her about it, you might lose her. Homespun wisdom and undoubtedly clichéd, but true nonetheless.'

Their conversation was cut short by Maria's return. She tried coaxing, but the little kitten stayed at the back door, unwilling to risk being trapped. 'Why won't Lily come in?' she asked petulantly.

'Lily? Is that her new name?' Helen enquired. Maria nodded. 'Well I think Lily might be a little afraid because she doesn't know her new family so well yet. She's been sleeping on a cushion in the shed for the last three nights and this is the first time she's come so close to the house,' Helen continued. 'I think you've done her a lot of good, Maria. Maybe she'll trust us a bit more now that you've been so kind to her.'

This appeared to satisfy Maria, who hopped onto Helen's lap. Helen put her arms around her and the child lay back. She could smell the clean childhood scent from the small head resting just under her chin. Helen hugged her hard and Mary smiled.

'How's Andy doing?' Helen asked.

''He's really sad that his school friend has gone to heaven and he's sad about you too,' Maria piped up before her mother had time to answer.

'Why's he sad about me?'

'I dunno. He said you and him had a fight and that's why you don't visit us anymore. I wish you didn't have a fight and then you and Lily could come to my house and stay in the spare room.'

Helen laughed at the mental picture of a long journey to Cork, Lily perched on Ophelia's dashboard, sporting a typical feline sneer aimed at the outside world. 'I don't think Lily'd like the car just yet,' she responded. 'But maybe when Daddy and I make up I'll come on my own to see you and we can go feed the ducks.'

'I've tried to get your *frere* to speak *avec vous*, but there's no shifting him yet,' Mary said. Mystified, Maria looked up at Helen but stayed silent.

'Tell me something I don't already know,' Helen said, and then sighed heavily. 'I think we made a clean breast of it at Johnny's funeral, so to speak, and I doubt there'll be much of a reconciliation for a long time to come. I accept that. There's not much left to say on either side without loss of face, anyway. Personal pride can be a very dangerous characteristic, and principles can be a form of moral bondage. I have more than enough of both.'

'Interesting point of view. I suppose I'm glad you're so philosophical, but I just feel that life's too short and your family's too small to let this fester.'

'Sorry, Mary. I appreciate why you're trying but I've resigned from the post of Dunne family mediator. The pay was wicked, the conditions were worse, and it was a thankless job. I tried keeping them all happy and failed. Time to move on.'

'Speaking of moving on, it's time I shifted myself.'

'Ah, can't you stay another hour? I wanted to bring Maria down to the office to show her my name on the editor's door. And I believe they're doing that Mississippi Mud Pie she likes so much in Crosbie's on Saturdays.'

Maria smiled pleadingly at her mother and Mary nodded.

'Is that a "yes" I see before me?' Helen declaimed, then tickled her niece 'C'mon, Maria, let's bundle her up in a sack and throw her in the back of Ophelia before she changes her mind.'

Catherine returned home just as the main news bulletin was ending. Helen, stretched on the sofa soaking up the sports results, hit the off button on the remote control and bounded to her feet when she heard the key in the door followed by the unmistakable sound of Catherine's bag hitting the wooden floor in the hall, just beside the stairs.

Sticking her head around the sitting room door, she blew a kiss in Catherine's direction and asked: 'How about a cup of coffee for a weary traveller?'

Catherine smiled crookedly, stretched her arms over her head, and groaned. 'Jesus, yes, cooffeeeeee, please!' she said.

Helen hugged her gently and kissed her thoughtfully on the lips. 'I missed you,' she said modestly.

'I missed you too.'

'That's all right, then,' Helen let her go, then looked into her eyes deeply. 'I'll put the kettle on.' Catherine followed her into the kitchen, her boots knocking on the floorboards. 'So, how was your weekend?' Helen asked.

'Good. The mater families sends her best, as do the lads. I went out for a few pints with Eilish last night in The George. They had a couple of drag queens on and it was a laugh.'

Helen paused in the act of reaching into the fridge for the milk. 'Eilish? Do I know her?'

'Don't think so. I worked with her for a few years ago. Met her on the street when I was shopping in Dun Laoghaire on Saturday afternoon. Didn't know she was gay until our third cup of coffee. We had a good giggle at what we had in common and met up with a few of the old gang that night. Ended up at a house party somewhere in Kimmage until four in the morning. I think I remember even smoking a reefer at one stage. You would have enjoyed it.'

'Yeah, I would… well, some of it, anyway. Seems like we haven't been out-out for yonks. Maybe we should both go up some weekend soon and have the crack?' Helen said.

'Name the day and I'll be up for it,' Catherine said through the early stages of a mammoth yawn. 'Feck, I'm shattered. Any bikkies to go with that?'

'Ah, head on in and sit down. I'll bring them in.'

'On a plate, I'll bet.'

'Eh?'

'You always put the biscuits on a plate,' Catherine replied briskly, patting Helen on the shoulder before wandering away.

Helen was just arranging four chocolate digestives on a plate when she heard the sound of the television being switched on.

CHAPTER EIGHT

CROSSED WIRES

Feeling sweat trickle from under her hairline towards the collar of her shirt, Helen brushed the drop away irritably. It was too hot; it had been too hot for ages. She sighed heavily, then looked across her desk to where Niamh slumped, sobbing softly.

Helen drummed her fingers on the desk impatiently for a moment, and then pressed the speaker button on her telephone. She hit a three-digit extension. It rang twice.

'Yeah, Helen?'

'Hold my calls for an hour, Claire, will you? Oh, and tell Mac I'll talk to him and the sales ladies about that colour supplement after four instead.'

'Okay.'

Helen hit the speaker button more gently the second time. 'Now, tell me exactly what happened,' she said softly, opening a drawer, locating a packet of tissues and pushing them gently across the desk with her fingertips.

Niamh took one and sniffled. 'You know it all already.'

'Then tell me again, just so I've got it straight.'

Niamh shrugged. 'I came home for lunch, just this

once, to make sure that Lily was all right after her trip to the vet. When I got there, Lily was fine and then I heard his voice coming from upstairs, so I just went up and opened the door without thinking.' Niamh stopped speaking and took a tissue out of the packet.

'And then what?'

'I saw them and I ran downstairs to stop myself from killing him.'

'Good move. And then?'

'He came down, wrapped in my dressing-gown and said… and said… "It's not what you think".'

'The bastard.'

'So I hit him. I made his nose bleed and, God, it felt good. Then I left and told him to leave his key behind. I hope I never see the fecker again.'

'Come on, you're engaged to him. I think that's hardly likely.'

'He's fucking slept with someone else in my bed, in your house, for God's sake. I doubt there's much more we have to say to each other.' Niamh crumpled the damp tissue and rolled it between her palms.

Helen leaned back in her chair, rested her elbows on the armrests and surveyed Niamh's dark bent head over a steeple of fingers. Her expression was concerned, but also speculative. Niamh looked up and saw it.

'What? What?'

'I think there's a little more to this than meets the eye. You're not telling me everything, are you?' Helen asked, swivelling in her chair to take in the view from her office window. There was a heat haze rising from the street outside.

Niamh half-grinned sadly and replied with a question of her own: 'What makes you think that?'

'Instinct, you poor petal,' Helen said, leaning forward and crossing her forearms on the desk. 'Tell me. You say you

want advice about what to do now and yet you're not prepared to tell me what really happened. I can't read your mind.'

Niamh sobbed and then continued: 'It's all my fault. I
should never have told him.'

'Told him what?' Helen's telephone rang. She whipped
up the receiver before the first ring died away. 'I said hold
my calls, for Christ's sake!' she said abruptly, then listened
intently for a few moments. 'Understood, but I need about
half-an-hour or a little more.'

'Problem?'

'The petty cash of problems compared to your bankrupt state, my love,' Helen responded, starting to frown. 'So?
What should you never have told Matt the pig?'

Despite herself, Niamh smiled, then blushed. Helen
looked perplexed and spread her hands in defeat. Niamh
false-started and paused to take a deeper breath.

'You remember that time it was all off with Matt and
me? Early last year? Well, I went to Galway for a weekend
with some old friends, and I slept with someone. We had a
conversation last week about honesty being vital to a marriage so I told him.'

'And he thought he'd get you back, except this time he'd
score higher for sleeping with another woman in your own
bed after giving you an engagement ring. How piggy can a
pig be?'

'I knew I shouldn't have told him.'

'Explain to me why you think it's your fault that he can't
keep his dick in his trousers while he's committed to you?'

Niamh reached and took another tissue. She blew
air through her fringe, then ran the fingers of both hands
through her long hair. 'That person I slept with in Galway. It
was only a one-night stand. It didn't really mean anything to
me at the time… but it did to her.'

'Her? Is my hearing going? Are you telling me you slept

with a woman?' Helen yelped, and at Niamh's slow nod, added: 'Jesus Christ and the holy extended family!'

They sat, both breathing heavily through a long silence. 'Have I shocked you?' Niamh asked finally in a low voice.

Helen laughed aloud, her shoulders shaking with genuine amusement. 'I'm unshockable, Niamh, but I'm as sure as fuck surprised. I really thought they didn't come much straighter than you.'

'Don't let the high-heels and long hair fool you, cave-woman,' Niamh said acidly. 'I didn't know it was going to happen. I didn't know she was gay. I was drunk. We were both drunk. It just happened and then afterwards I just couldn't stop thinking about it. Not about her exactly, but about it. I think I might be bisexual and I told Matt that too, but that I was still prepared to marry him if he'd have me. He said it was all right… in fact, I thought at the time that the whole thing turned him on a bit.'

'Yuck. The quintessential male fantasy of two women being naughty together. How like a man. As for the bisexual bit, some of the greatest dykes on the planet have trotted out that old line at one time or another, including me.'

Without warning, Niamh started to sob again, just like a child 'Sorry,' Said Helen quickly. 'I'm supposed to be trying to help, not make fun of you.' She stood up, walked around the desk and gripped Niamh firmly on the shoulder. 'Come on,' she said.

'Where're we going?'

'First, I'm going to bring you home because you're not fit to drive in that state. If Matt's still there with the harlot – which I very much doubt… I mean, it's hardly likely he hopped up to bed for seconds, complete with a bloody nose – I'll turf the little fuck out on his ear and add a good kick in the arse for good measure, once I extract the house key from him. Okay?'

'Okay. I don't want to stay there on my own though.'

'Let's see.' Helen tapped her teeth with the index finger of her free hand, then squeezed Niamh's shoulder again. 'I'll ring Catherine. I think she's a half-day today and if not, maybe Philip could call around. He's not working today either. I'll fill them in and...' Noticing the horrified expression on Niamh's face, she added: 'No, eejit, not the whole story. Not the bit that makes you blush, just the bit about him being a cad and a rake. What they don't know can't sicken them. C'mon, dry your eyes and make a happy face until I get you out of here. I don't want the staff thinking I'm the type of domineering butch that makes little girls cry.'

As it happened, Matt was gone by the time they arrived at the house. Helen parked Niamh on the downstairs sofa, handed her a stiff shot of whiskey and was on her way back upstairs when Catherine arrived home.

'She's in the front room,' Helen whispered. 'She's very upset and I don't think it'd be right to leave her on her own. Will you stay because I've got to get back to work soon?'

'Of course,' Catherine replied quietly, squeezing Helen's shoulder warmly and kissing her on the cheek as she reached for the door handle. 'Oh, by the way... nah, it's all right, I'll talk to you later.'

Helen went back upstairs, opened the window in Niamh's room and completely stripped the bed, her teeth grinding. 'The little fucking bastard,' she said under her breath as she ripped the under-sheet from the mattress. When all the bedclothes were on the floor in an untidy pile, Helen sat on the bed for a moment, catching her breath. Through the open door, she could hear murmured voices from downstairs, and an occasional muted sob. She was very angry. She picked up the bedclothes, pounded down the stairs and flung open the back door. Lily, sleeping quietly on one of the kitchen chairs, meowed in alarm. 'It's all right, puss,' Helen said, scratching the cat behind an ear with her free hand. 'I'm just throwing out the rubbish.'

On her way back to work, Helen stuck her head in the door, said goodbye to Niamh and beckoned to Catherine. Outside in the hall, she said: 'Keep an eye on her but give her space. If she wants a nap, put her in our room. I've stripped her bed and left the window open to air the room. I rang Philip and he's coming around later to change the locks. See you.'

When Helen returned home in the evening, Philip was cooking dinner. She and Catherine made up the bed with a full new set of bedclothes. 'Shite,' Helen said, scratching the back of her neck and looking at the plain blue duvet cover. 'I should have bought something more flowery and girly to cheer her up.'

Catherine punched her on the shoulder playfully. 'Give it up, will you? It's fine. At least it's clean.'

Gradually, life at McHale Road returned to what passed for normal. On the third evening after what they were all starting to call 'The Incident', the telephone rang during *Coronation Street*. Helen, working upstairs in the study, whipped up the extension quickly, half-thinking that it might be her mother with another Sunday lunch overture. It wasn't.

After listening for a few moments, Helen sighed heavily. 'Matthew, she doesn't want to talk to you. You know that already so why do you keep ringing? If you don't get the message soon I'm going to have to change the number as well as the locks.'

'Just let me talk to her, even for a minute. If I could just get her to listen, get a chance to explain…'

'Sorry. Matt, she said no and she means it. You broke a trust that was sacred to her. There's nothing to explain and I've got to go now anyway. Don't telephone this house again or I'll have to contact the guards.'

'Jesus, you dykes are all the same,' Matt said nastily. 'You look after each other, don't you? It's all your fault, anyway. You turned her. I bet there's a regular old threesome going on in that house. I'll get to her at work if you won't let me talk to her and, by Jesus, I'll make sure everyone knows what's going on.'

'Listen to me, you homophobic, malicious little fuck!' Helen spat, her patience at an end. 'If I hear a word that I can trace back to you, I'll personally beat the living shit out of you myself. Leave Niamh alone or you'll find yourself in a heap of trouble. I mean it so don't push me. Now fuck off, you little twerp.'

By the time she hung up, Catherine was standing in the open doorway. 'Jesus, what's going on?'

'Three guesses.'

'Matt?'

'Right first time, sweetheart.' Helen swivelled on her computer chair to face the door. 'Everything all right?'

'Yeah, fine.' Catherine sat on the edge of the old sofa on one side of the room. 'Listen, I'm going to head up to Dublin this weekend. There's a bit of a gig on in The George that I might go to with Eilish and a few of the women. You can come if you're free.'

Helen chewed her bottom lip thoughtfully for a few seconds. 'I'm not free, as it happens, but I thought we were spending this weekend on our own together anyway. Niamh's heading away to her mother's for the weekend. Why don't you stay here and we'll go for a drive or something if the weather's as good as it is now?'

'Nah. Anyway, I've already sort of half-promised; it wouldn't be fair to let them down. When're you working? Maybe you could come up for one night even?'

'Shit, it's only Wednesday and I'm already knackered,'

Helen replied. 'I've got a meeting tomorrow with the reporters about the pay claim and I've to report to the bollix
Fleming on Friday. The Chamber dinner's on Friday night
and I was just going to flake out on Saturday. I dunno about
driving all the way to Dublin for a few pints, driving home
on Sunday and then getting back into another shite week the
following morning. No. I'll pass this time, but I will go with
you sometime soon. I promise.'

'You said that the last time.'

'I know, but the last time the fucking secondary school
went on fire and it was all hands on deck. Sometimes things
happen without appointments. We might not be an emergency service but we do have something in common with
them. Things happen and other plans get fucked out the window. That's the life. I'll go with you soon.'

Seeing Catherine's non-committal and seemingly un-
concerned shrug, Helen continued: 'Hey, Bubbles, don't do
that. You know there's nothing I can do, but if you want to go
ahead and enjoy yourself, then fire away.'

'Is that supposed to make me feel guilty for leaving
you?'

'I didn't mean it like that: I meant that I'm not going to
hold you back. If I try, you'll resent it and eventually resent
me. I can't stop you doing what you want to do and, to be
honest, I don't think there's much point trying at the moment.'

'What?'

Helen took a long, slow deep breath and swivelled to
and fro for a moment. 'You've been behaving what I class as
a bit strange since that time Evelyn was here. We're no further on with our plans and, every time the subject comes up,
you're too busy to talk about it. You go to Dublin more often too, and I sometimes think you're nearly as well pleased
when I can't go with you. That might not be the way it is, but

that's how it looks to me.'

'That's not the way it is,' Catherine said truculently. 'Every time I want to do something, you're busy. You've very little time for me because of the crack at work, and now you want to punish me for making my own arrangements. You're behaving as if it's all my fault.'

'As if what's all my fault?'

'I don't know.'

Remembering her sister-in-law's advice, Helen turned in the chair and looked out the window: it was a warm Summer's evening and the light was beginning to turn golden with the hint of an impending sunset. 'You may not know, but I do.' She turned to face Catherine and looked into her eyes. 'We're drifting, you and I. I don't like it and I want to do something about it now, before we reach the point of no return.'

Catherine snorted and smacked her palms on her knees. 'Would you ever cop on?' she said jocularly. 'That's bullshit. We're just busy, that's all. We're doing fine and you know it.'

'If I did, I wouldn't be sitting here trying to have this conversation with you. Why won't you let me in? Have we come so far so soon that the tables have completely turned? Here I am now, trying to get you to talk about us, about how we feel about each other, and you're treating me as if I'm the clown.'

'Don't be so fucking dramatic,' Catherine said sharply. 'As far as I'm concerned, we're fine.'

'I'm not so convinced. Sure, the sex is great, but then it always was, wasn't it, right from the very beginning? But you can't build a life on that, purely on what you do in bed. Sex on its own isn't an adhesive; we need something else to keep us stuck to each other.'

'And what's that?'

'I'd give my eye-teeth to know,' Helen replied softly and broodingly, her words followed by a stretched, tense silence. Eventually, Catherine stood up and moved over to the window to stand with her hands in her pockets beside Helen's chair.

Without looking at Helen, she said: 'Don't worry.'

'I can't help it. I love you and that's that. It hasn't been the same since Eve was here. I know that much, and I don't believe you don't know it too.'

'Believe what you must. All I know is that this is my home… when you're here.'

Catherine went to Dublin on her own in the end. Helen spent the weekend at home alone but joined Philip for a few pints on Saturday night. He was in truly great form and, although he denied it, Helen suspected there was a new woman on the scene. They were celebrating his successful bid on a flat in one of the snazzy new town centre apartment blocks, and with 'sale agreed' in the bag, Philip was looking forward to being master of his own household once again. Before she even explained, Philip said he knew the offer of a room in her house wasn't open any more, not since The Incident, and that he was happier to have his own place at last anyway.

As they relaxed over matching pints of Guinness, watching soccer on the pub TV, Helen pondered why anyone would possibly think they were such good friends. She and Philip really had nothing much in common, apart from broad minds, occupations, and senses of humour that sometimes bordered on the zany. All that aside, there was nothing obvious to indicate why they liked each other so much. In a chaste, brotherly sort of way, she even loved him. Since finding out she was gay, he even managed to treat her both as one of the lads and as a woman as well.

'You're lookin' at me funny,' Philip said suddenly. 'Stop

doing that or people'll think you fancy me.'

'Sorry,' Helen replied, snapping out of her temporary reverie. Returning her attention to the television screen, she moaned: 'Oh, fuck. Is there no end to my sorrows… United have fucking scored.'

'Two minutes ago. Where've you been?'

'Thinking about you.'

Philip snorted into his pint. 'Fuck off,' he said. 'Is there something you need to tell me: are you perhaps, transforming yourself into a straight woman who fancies older men *and* wants to put the make on a subordinate? They have a name for that, you know: it's called sexual harassment.'

Helen laughed merrily. Philip cocked an ear for a moment and then commented: 'What a sweet sound that is. I haven't heard you laugh like that for weeks.'

'Not much to laugh about at the moment, I'm afraid. Phil, can we talk business for a sec?'

'Come on, Helen, it's Saturday night! I'm off duty and so are you. Well, you should be…'

'Please. Is the strike going ahead? I really need to know. I don't expect them not to because of me, but if they do, I'm finished.'

Philip drained his pint and put the glass back on the bar, dead centre in the middle of a beer mat. 'Your round,' he said shortly.

'Okay,' Helen said, waving a hand at the barman and indicating their two empty glasses. 'I'm sorry,' she said then. 'I shouldn't have asked. I know Fleming's been in touch with the regional newspaper association this week but he won't tell me anything, the bastard.'

'Listen, I'm not giving you details, but most of us are on your side.'

'Apart from McNally and the Cougar, I suppose.'

'No prize for guessing that. We've agreed with the union recommendation to refer the whole shebang to the Labour Relations Commission, if you must know. From what I know of that wonderful body, the RNA'll use any delaying tactic they can. It'll take months to get a recommendation and, by then, you'll either be home and dry or you'll be out of here. And this conversation never took place.'

Helen rewarded him with a tiny, relieved smile. 'Thanks, Philip,' she said simply. 'That's one less thing for me to worry about, for the next few weeks at least. I owe you.'

'No, you don't. Think of it as a quid pro quo for helping me out when Patti and I broke up. Always remember, youngster, that what goes around in life, comes around.'

Helen's reply was disrupted by the shouts of the bar's other customers. Glancing at the television, she remarked acidly: 'Two-nil. The jammy Anglo bastards.'

'Ah, c'mon Helen, even you must be due a few days off sometimes!' Catherine said roughly.

'Yes, I am and, yes, I will take the time but, no, I'm not going to that load of crap.' Helen continued weeding the pots of herbs on the patio while Catherine stood in the doorway, arms folded.

'Why not? You might learn something. You might even enjoy it.'

'I would not enjoy it under any circumstances. All that sort of thing is good for is to provide a comfortable forum for a crowd of whingeing, underemployed dykes to rant about patriarchy, the politics of penetration, penis envy and probably where to get decent pot. Lesbian workshops, my arse. That's about the only work most of them'll ever hear about.'

'Please.'

'If these bastarding chives don't flower soon I'm fucking them in the bin.'

'Would you do it for me?'

Helen straightened and squinted into Catherine's eyes. 'Why? Are you asking me to do it for you?'

'I suppose I'll have to ask.'

'Then I'll do it. I don't like it but I'll do it for you,' Helen said grumpily.

Catherine laughed, wrestled her off the patio and down onto the grass. Lily, who had been sleeping calmly in a patch of sunlight with the tip of her tail touching her nose, ambled over to join them. Catherine, on top, kissed Helen hard, then giggled when Lily's purring nose almost got in the way. 'I'll pack, I'll drive. I'll do everything. All you have to do is come with me and hold my hand so I can show you off,' Catherine said.

'Show me off to whom?'

'You know. The girls. They'll all be jealous of my handsome newspaper editor.'

'Acting.'

'Hmmm?'

'Acting editor. And we won't be telling them that, either. For the information of the attendance, I'll be just yet another underemployed, moaning dyke with too little to do but plenty to say. Understood?'

'Roger that.'

Helen grunted. 'I'll roger you, wench,' then tickled Catherine unmercifully until their positions were reversed. 'Now, in payment for being so accommodating, I suggest you resign yourself to paying in kind, and this afternoon would be very convenient, thank you. Up the stairs now, like a good girl.'

She let go and Catherine stood up, heading obediently for the door. Stretched on the grass, with the cat snuggling into her neck, Helen watched her go. When she reached the doorway, Catherine turned around, stuck her tongue out cheekily and ripped open her shirt provocatively.

The cat wasn't pleased to be dumped so unceremoniously.

It was a quiet week anyway, so Helen simply packed up Ophelia on Wednesday evening and followed the little yellow Micra to Dublin because Catherine was staying over on Saturday night and Helen had to be home for a work function by eight. They drove to a house in Kimmage where Catherine knew some people and said they'd have a room for a few days, apparently because it was more convenient to UCD than Bray. The standard of hygiene was of the student variety. Helen, unimpressed and worried about the safety of the two cars, suggested a B&B or hotel in central Dublin instead, but Catherine ticked her off for being unnecessarily fussy. Helen gave in, as she almost always seemed to do these days, and joined the Kimmage housemates for a takeaway around a wobbly kitchen table. There were six of them altogether and, apart from Catherine, she was the only gainfully employed person in the room, even though they were all over twenty-five or so.

The evening broke up at about 3.00 a.m., following several cans of cheap lager and a couple of violent videos. Helen was tired the next day, but dutifully rose early and drove Catherine to Belfield where she spent most of the day trailing around the campus in the sunshine, in between watching Catherine help organise maudlin workshops for about eighty non-taxpaying dykes. To Helen, the toddlers in the conference crèche looked like the more sensible participants but, wisely, she kept her mouth shut, shook hands with shaven, intense women when introduced, and otherwise maintained an air of uninvolved nonchalance. Catherine thought she was doing it on purpose – which she was – and said so. Helen demurred strongly but she knew that she really did hate all this earnest, well-meaning claptrap that had nothing to do with the real life she lived in a medium sized town outside the Pale.

Despite all the rubbish she made herself listen to in the morning, it was the Dublin-centred West Brit attitude of the facilitators that she found most irritating. Most of them didn't even seem to know where Castlebar was, never mind why any self-respecting lesbian would want to live there. For something to do while Catherine was busy in the afternoon, Helen joined a workshop on Lesbian Images in Modern Culture, and ended up having a massive squabble about the popular media and its treatment of women with the facilitator. Helen's bitter and dismissive retorts to unreasoned arguments she simply wouldn't entertain drew curious glances from the participants. She was fed up and just wanted to hurt someone. Anyone.

On Thursday night, they drove out to Bray to visit Catherine's family, and passed a pleasant enough evening there. Helen even brought the boys out bowling to a place in Stillorgan, an experience that all four of them really enjoyed, while Catherine stayed home to keep Maggie company. Driving back to Kimmage later, Catherine suggested a couple of pints in the city, but Helen pleaded tiredness and they went back to the hang-out instead. There was no-one at home but Catherine had a key.

When she produced it, Helen looked at her curiously and said nothing, but Catherine pretended not to notice. Just when they were settling down with coffee in the tacky, under-furnished sitting room at the front of the house, Helen switched her mobile on. The phone rang almost immediately. It was Philip.

'Helen? Where are you? Have you heard a radio news lately?'

Helen glanced at her watch. It was well after eleven. She knew Philip wouldn't ring so late unless it was important.

'No, not tonight. I'm in Dublin. What's up?'

'Something major. I can cover it, but I need to know what you want. There's been a bus crash outside Charlestown. Fifty-five teenagers and four adults on their way back to town from a European camping trip; three dead, twenty-eight injured, nine seriously, and the driver's critical. Went off the road on the Dublin side an-hour-and-a-half ago. No other vehicle involved. It's a mess out here. I've been trying to get hold of you for ages.'

Helen stood up, adrenaline pumping, 'Anyone with you from our side?'

'No, but the nationals are beginning to arrive and all the locals are here already. What kind of pix do you want? Nearly all the freelances are here so I can take my pick.'

'Loads, but nothing too gory,' Helen said. 'Get me shots of the bus from every angle, plus shots of emergency vehicles, ambulance men carrying stretchers, that kind of thing. Tell 'em to get body shots if they can, but I may not use them. Call out George and Liam, and Cougar if she's not drunk. Get them to talk to as many kids and parents as they can; ring the bus company for a statement, and try to get something out of the guards at the scene. Is the fire brigade there?'

'Yeah. Four units. They're having to cut some of the kids out of it but I can't see what's happening exactly because there's a cordon set up and we've been moved back.'

'Look for Tommy Coffey. He'll be wearing a white helmet and he'll have ACFO on the back of his jacket. I hope he's on duty tonight: he'll talk.'

'Anything else?'

'Yeah, get the name of the dead and injured. Philip, I'm really sorry, but it'd be over by the time I got there even if I left now. Hold the fort and I'll be back tomorrow for the mop up.'

'Can do. See you.'

'Yeah, I'll ring you in the morning when I'm on the way. I'll ring the rest and we'll meet up at the office at noon, if you don't hear from me.'

'Right, Helen.'

When she hung up, Catherine pressed her for details until she didn't have any more to give. 'I'm sorry, Katie, but I've got to get back tomorrow,' Helen said. 'This is a big one and I've got to be there to make sure we're covering all the angles, and some the competition doesn't think of in time. What day is tomorrow? Friday. Friday. Okay, a day or two for the post mortems means the funerals'll probably be on Monday or Tuesday. Thank God the *Connaught Telegraph* goes to print a day before us!'

'Jesus, Helen, that's sick!' Catherine spluttered.

'I know. Look. I'm really sorry there are people killed and injured, but I have a job to do and I have to do it the best way I know. This is a big story for us and I have to do it justice.'

'You mean you have to sell as many papers as possible.'

'That's not what I said,' Helen replied, puzzled.

'No, but that's what all this means,' Catherine continued, sickened. 'You're a vulture like the rest of them, making a living by picking over the bones of other people's miseries. Why can't you just leave them alone.'

'Because it's my job to report the facts and to inform the public.'

'If it's been on the radio, the public already knows.'

Stumped for a riposte for once, Helen changed tack. 'Anyway, I've to leave early tomorrow. Are you coming with me?'

'No. I might as well stay the weekend. Yet again, Helen, what we're supposed to be doing together is fucked up because of your job. I'm staying here. I don't want to be around you while you do this kind of work, anyway. It brings out something in you I don't really like.'

Helen took the rebuke with stoicism. 'I know, but that's who I am,' she said, and went to bed.

Everyone knew – or knew of - someone who'd been on the bus when it crashed. At the meeting on Saturday, Philip silently handed over two compact discs of photographs and a list of names provided by the Gardai once all the families had been notified.

Adam Murphy was listed as dead at the scene. Helen dropped the page and reeled back from the desk, her chair spinning across the floor. 'Oh, Jesus, not him, not him: not the one fucking teenager I actually know,' she said softly. Philip touched her on the arm but she shrugged him off, the face of her neighbour's child, her part-time gardener and car washer, filling her vision.

She pulled the chair back to the desk and sat down slowly. 'Oh, Jesus,' Helen said again. 'He was such a lovely young fellow too.' After a few moments, during which the other reporters shifted uncomfortably in their chairs, Helen coughed and started the meeting. It was a long one, filled with arguments about what was fitting to write and what was not, in the very special circumstances of such a clear community tragedy. With Catherine's criticism still echoing in her mind, Helen decided to be cautious and allocated safe angles to the team. They looked at the pictures for a few minutes, trying to decide on the most appropriate shots, until Helen turned off the computer during an argument about whether or not it was fair to show a recognizable body covered in blood and broken glass, even if a black bar was superimposed on the face. 'I'm sorry. I just can't do this today,' she said. 'Let's leave it at that.' She looked at Philip, George, Laurence, Liam and Paula in turn. Not one of them gave her an argument.

In the early evening, while the sun was still shining,

Helen dressed carefully in a dark suit, white shirt and sil-ver cufflinks. She walked slowly along the street as far as the closed door of the Murphy house. Three men stood in a semi-circle in the garden, smoking. None of them spoke to her. There was a black crepe ribbon on the door, and the key was in the lock, but Helen knocked quietly anyway. Adam's father answered, his eyes red-rimmed and angry.

'What do *you* want? Your crowd didn't get enough out the Charlestown Road?' Billy said furiously.

Helen stepped back in anxiety; this was not what she had expected. 'Mr. Murphy,' she said calmly. 'I've come to say how sorry I am about what happened to Adam and the rest of the kids. I know it's no comfort to you, but it's all I can do.'

'Fuck off,' he said succinctly, and was on the point of closing the door in her face when Adam's mother, Myra, ran from the kitchen and stopped him. 'Billy, don't,' she said. 'It's not right to do that, even to her.'

Puzzled at the way Myra had put it, Helen repeated her message of condolence. Billy walked back into the house, but Myra shook Helen's hand and invited her in. 'No, thank you, Mrs. Murphy; you've enough to contend with at a time like this without making soft chat with the likes of me. I just wanted to tell you how much I liked Adam, and how sorry I am for the trouble that has come to your door. He, and you, deserved more out of life.' Helen said, then squeezed the be-reaved woman's hand before turning away.'

As she reached the front garden gate, she heard the single muttered word 'dyke' rising behind her. Turning, she stared at each of the three smoking men in turn, while they examined their cigarettes or kicked at innocent blades of grass in a successful attempt to avoid catching her eye. Sad-dened and tired, Helen decided not to respond and closed the gate quietly on her way out.

Catherine returned from Dublin on Monday evening, hung over and a day later than promised, but Helen, being so busy with a bumper post-accident edition of the *Recorder*, hardly noticed. After a few words on the telephone to Helen at the office, Catherine went straight to bed. Accompanied by Philip and Niamh instead, Helen went to Adam's removal in her personal capacity, leaving it to Georgie Lennon to either surreptitiously take notes at the back of the church or cajole written notes out of the local parish priest. He hated the task and begged Helen not to make him do it, but she reminded him severely that he was a reporter, and his job was to report as instructed by her.

Sitting in a crowded local church during the brief removal service, Helen reflected on how much she hated her job sometimes and did her best to ignore the sounds of weeping from the top pews. Adam's relatives filled the first few pews on the right, and behind them were crowds of teenage boys and girls, pale, pink-eyed and obviously shocked. Helen started to think about Caroline, then deliberately changed her train of thought when Philip reached over to pass her a tissue and hold her hand. She hadn't realized that she'd started to cry.

Deciding not to have a drink in the local football club bar with the rest of the funeral crowd, Niamh and Helen went straight home and made coffee before turning in for the night. Taking off her jacket and massaging the back of her neck, Helen sighed heavily, then looked Niamh in the eye.

'And how are you doing?' she asked.

'Me?' Niamh said, taking a long gulp of hot coffee. 'I'm fine. At least I'm alive.' She smiled thinly.

'Yeah, but I mean how are you since The Incident? We never really talked about it much and I think we should have. I mean, if there's any advice you need about the gay thing… sorry, the bisexual thing… you only have to ask.'

Niamh put down her mug. 'I'm all right. I'm getting over it much quicker than I thought I would. It'd probably have been madness to marry him anyway when I'm not quite sure what way the wind's blowing. Anyway, I've exams to concentrate on and, when they're over, I might start looking for a job somewhere else.'

'I'd be sorry to see you go, but try Dublin: there're loads of babes up there, if that's what you're after,' Helen said.

Niamh chortled, but Helen continued: 'I'm serious. I'm not trying to convince you or anything, and I'm certainly not recruiting, but you might just like to explore the possibilities. And, God knows, there are far more possibilities in cities than in this godforsaken kip. You're not allowed to be a lesbian in this town… well, you are, but just as long as no-one gets to hear of it. I should know: I think my filthy secret's making its way into the open air and I can scent trouble on the wind.'

'Are you trying to scare me off?' Niamh asked coquettishly, then fluttered her eyelashes at Helen suggestively.

Almost unaccountably, Helen blushed. 'Stop doing that. I'm nearly married. And no, I'm not trying to scare you, I'm just trying to tell it like it is. Now stop messing; I'm going to bed.'

Upstairs, Helen watched Catherine sleep for a long minute by a dim bedside light before undressing and climbing into bed. As she curled up behind her lover, Catherine stirred and mumbled indistinctly.

When she was close to sleep herself, Helen pulled the sleeping body closer to her. 'I love you,' she whispered in Catherine's ear.

'Love you too,' was the reply, followed by a soft, whistling snore.

As Helen ate breakfast the next morning, Catherine careered into the kitchen to grab a mug of coffee before heading to work. 'Whoa, whoa, there, girl. Where's the fire?' Helen said, smiling as she spooned up the last of her cornflakes.

'C'mon, c'mon,' Catherine urged the kettle, then glanced at her watch in anxiety. 'Shit, I'm going to be late again.'

'Indeed. So what else is new? Listen, I've set up an appointment for the solicitor's on Friday, you know, to discuss the joint ownership business. He said he'll stay late so we're set for half-past-six, if that's okay.'

'Yeah, fine, whatever.' Catherine shovelled sugar into her mug and stirred furiously.

'Sugar? Since when did you start taking sugar in coffee?' Helen asked, rolling down her shirt sleeves and examining the buttons.

'Since I stopped having time for breakfast, that's when. Oh, sweetie, I'm thinking of taking a couple of weeks hols shortly, so can we link up later to see if the end of September or early October would suit? I need a break from this treadmill and so do you,' Catherine said, searching the kitchen drawers for her car keys.

'Sounds great. I'll see what the story is at work. A week or two weeks?' Helen asked, picking up her jacket.

'Two, I think. One week is fuck all use. Where are my fucking keys?!' Catherine replied, still rooting mercilessly through the cutlery drawer.

'Catherine.'

'What? I can't find the bloody yolks…'

'Catherine,' Helen said again in an even tone.

Impatiently, Catherine turned, a rebuke on her lips, to see Helen standing there with a key ring swinging from her outstretched index finger.

'Your keys, my love, were on the kitchen table, where you left them last night.'

Catherine grabbed the keys, threw on a light jacket and

made for the door, blowing Helen a quick kiss. 'See you to-night. I'll have to make up the time so I'll be late.'

'See you,' Helen repeated, but the door had already closed.

Catherine rang at the last minute to say she couldn't make the solicitor's appointment. Helen, who took the call on her way out the door, put the telephone down angrily, then picked up the receiver again and rang her solicitor to apologise. After that, she ranted at Niamh for twenty minutes before picking up her briefcase in temper and throwing it down the back garden, narrowly missing Lily who was tip-toeing up the garden path on her way home for tea.

'Why am I always the gobshite?' Helen asked the startled cat conversationally.

'Because you look like one,' Niamh replied from the kitchen.

'Hah, bloody hah.'

'C'mon, where's your sense of humour gone?'

'You stole it.'

'Temper, temper, D'ya want some of this?' Niamh indicated the grill pan filled with enough sausages and rashers for two.

'Might as well, seeing I'm not getting any better offers for dinner this evening. Give me a minute to get out of these clothes.'

Niamh pulled the tea-towel from the draining board and covered her eyes. 'Not here, please, or you'll drive me mad with lust.'

'Fuck you and the dyke you rode in on,' Helen retorted sourly.

'Go on upstairs and put on your fluffy slippers if it'll cheer you up. This'll be ready in ten minutes and I've a bottle of plonk a grateful patient dropped into A&E for me today as well. Is that not an offer you can't refuse?'

'All right, then.' Helen picked up the cat and carried her inside, dropped her on the floor and filled her bowl full of kitty kibble from the cardboard box on the worktop. Lily purred happily, but wound her body around Niamh's ankles instead. 'Typical,' Helen continued. 'I feed that yolk but you're her favourite. Bet she just wants a rasher. Cupboard love, that's all you get from cats.'

'Meow,' said Niamh, making scratching motions with her free hand.

'Right,' said Helen. 'Fuck the pair of you. I'll change for dinner like a gentleman and meet you here in eight-and-a-half minutes.'

They were three-quarters of the way through the bottle and deep in conversation about the health service when Catherine finally made an appearance, two hours later. Neither Niamh nor Helen noticed when she opened the door, but Helen raised her glass when she heard the sound of Catherine's bag hitting the tiled floor. 'Welcome to this week's debate, which is about the scale of medical inflation and value for money in the health sector,' she said.

'Anything to eat? I'm starving,' Catherine said without really acknowledging either of them.

'Sorry, we've just finished and Lily's eaten the scraps,' Niamh said.

Catherine sat into the chair opposite Helen heavily, then reached for the bottle and Helen's wine glass. As she poured, she slopped red wine on the surface of the table. Helen looked into her face, concern lighting her eyes.

'Are you okay?' she asked.

'Fine, fine, never better,' Catherine responded.

Helen noticed that her pupils were dilated and her movements sluggish. 'You look funny or something. Have you been drinking?'

'What is this, the Spanish Inquisition?'

'You know you shouldn't drink and drive. Apart from the possibility of the guards catching you, you could kill yourself, or someone else.'

Catherine stood up, walked around the table and breathed directly into Helen's face. 'See. No alcohol. And don't be so goddamn prissy.'

'Hey, go easy, Catherine. She's just concerned about you,' Niamh interrupted.

'Who asked you for an opinion?'

'Enough said. I'm out of here.'

'Off you trot, then,' Catherine sneered dismissively. 'Stay out of what you don't understand, Niamh, and that includes our relationship.'

Helen smiled an apology as Niamh picked up her wine glass and left the room.

'What are you smiling at?' Catherine asked rudely.

'Give it a rest, will you? What do you think gives you the right to come in here and treat both of us to that fucking attitude?' Helen countered.

'I live here.'

'When it suits you.'

'Meaning?'

'You come, you go. I don't know where you are half the time, not that it's any of my business anyway,' Helen said, raising a hand to forestall Catherine's obvious protest.

Taking Helen's glass, Catherine left the table and slouched on the little sofa in the living area of the room. She pulled a cigarette out of her pocket, lit it and puffed energetically. Silently, Helen contented herself with drawing a pattern in the wine spillage on the table with her index finger. After a few moments, she sniffed suspiciously, then looked up. Catherine was reclining, eyes closed, the cigarette still in her mouth.

Moving quietly but with purpose, Helen whipped the cigarette out of her mouth and threw it into the sink. 'Hey, hey! Give that back!' Catherine shouted as Helen turned on the tap.

'No fucking way! No-one smokes pot in my house, and that include you. You can do what you like outside the door, but this shit does not happen in here. Do you understand me?'

'It was only a little reefer, you sanctimonious prig.'

'And not the first one you've had this evening, by the look of it.'

'You should try it; it might mellow you out a little and stop you being so serious all the time.'

Helen sat down in the armchair opposite. 'Please, Catherine, let's stop this now. Is all this because you didn't want to go to the solicitor? Just say it out and be done with it. If you're under pressure at work, say so. Just don't come home, insult me, insult Niamh and then insult my intelligence by smoking pot in our home. That's not much to ask.'

Catherine started to cry. 'Oh, shit, what have I said now?' Helen asked, climbing over the coffee table to sit beside her. 'Jesus, stop bawling like that; you're scaring me. What's going on?' There was no reply, so Helen put her arms around Catherine and simply held her tightly until the tears ebbed.

'I miss you,' Catherine snuffled quietly. 'I want us to be like we were. I want your attention but all you have is time for work, Philip, Niamh, your mother and that fucking cat…'

'Stop, stop. That's not true. I've booked the last week in September and the first week in October for us to spend some time together. Two clear weeks. No emergency will get me back to work, I promise. We'll potter around the country. It won't even matter if it's raining because I'll be with you.'

'D'you mean it?' Catherine asked tearfully.

'Yes, I do,' Helen replied earnestly, using her thumb to

wipe a wayward tear from Catherine's cheek. 'If that's all it takes, I can do it. Now I'm going to make you some tea and a sandwich, and you're going upstairs to sleep off whatever poison you've put into your body.'

'You can talk. You're a smoker.'

'True,' Helen smiled, 'but at least nicotine's legal.'

August was a dead month in the newspaper. Helen hated it when the courts, local authorities and all the other regular events disappeared from the diary, only to be replaced with festivals at every crossroads and agricultural shows in what seemed like every one-horse town. She was always relieved during the first week of September when the regular merry-go-'round started up again: by the end of that first week, when the pressure started to build again, she always wondered why she'd felt relieved in the first place. This year was no different.

Helen knew she'd been doing well in the job, but she still shivered a little when Fleming told her the time to advertise the permanent editor's post was approaching quickly. She still hadn't clearly decided whether or not to go for it and, if she didn't get it, what to do next. She felt like a circus performer juggling in a style beyond her abilities, waiting for the inevitable ball to drop.

Meanwhile, Philip closed the sale of his new flat and that turned out to be an occasion of great celebration and general debauchery. No-one spoke above a whimper in McHale Road for two days after the flat-warming, such was the high standard of the triple hangover. Helen, cautiously skirting whatever it was that was between her and Catherine, waited for the last week of September and their holidays with genuine enthusiasm, buoyed with confidence that a little time together as an ordinary couple again was what they needed. She suspected that if she could get as far as the last week of

September, everything was going to be absolutely fine.

One evening, scenting the end of the year's Indian Summer, Helen sat out in the back garden, waiting for the dew to fall before giving in and sitting indoors. It was a stereotypical autumn evening, warm and carrying a soft hint of the damp, wet Winter to come, but still enough to heat Helen's body down to the bones. Lily was on her knee and Catherine was sitting outside as well, reading a book. They exchanged slow sentences from time to time, Catherine reading from her book, Helen murmuring softly in reply. It was almost idyllic until the telephone rang. Picking up the receiver, Helen reminded herself how much she hated telephones and almost resolved, then and there, to have the implement removed from the house permanently. This time, it really was her mother.

After the usual preliminaries – Nora asking after Catherine and Helen replying politely on her behalf – the conversation turned to more general matters.

'Of course, you're going to be busy for the next few weeks now,' Nora said.

Helen's stomach churned slowly. 'I'm always busy, but why would I be more busy for the next few weeks?' she asked.

'Ho, ho. Call yourself a journalist, you. Have you not seen the news? It was all over the airwaves at six o'clock. An election's been called.'

Nearly dropping the receiver, Helen recovered enough to squeak: 'But we're only in the middle of the term.'

'Doesn't matter. They lost their majority on the tax amnesty issue. The Government want to bring it in; the Opposition think it's not fair, and the three Independents turned their coats. We'll all be off to the polls before October's out.'

'Oh, fuck.'

'Helen, your language.'

'Sorry. It was just that I'd planned to take holidays and

now… 'Through the open back door, Helen saw Catherine raise her eyes from her book. Their eyes met, then Catherine closed hers and shook her head slowly from side to side. She dropped her book, picked up the cat and strolled slowly down the garden.

There was no argument, no row, no angry words exchanged in haste. Helen told her that the situation had changed; Catherine shrugged and said she wasn't really surprised. After discussing the development calmly and rationally, Helen agreed that it would be best for Catherine to take her two-week break and use it to visit home. That would leave Helen free to concentrate on the election campaign without any distractions, and would also mean that Catherine would be contented enough.

'And, on the quieter days, I could come up and visit you there,' Helen added.

Catherine nodded. 'Sounds like the best we can do under the circumstances. An election was something you just couldn't predict, I suppose.'

'Well, normally I can, or at least I get a tip-off from someone in the know. This time, I wouldn't have figured those three TDs would cross the floor for a moral issue like a tax amnesty. I don't think anyone would have. I've a lot of work ahead of me for the next month or so, but it'll be great if I know you're with your mum and being looked after.'

'I don't need anyone to look after me.'

'I know, I know. It's just a butch thing; I have to make sure the wifie is cared for, etc., etc.,' Helen said, smiling. Catherine didn't smile in return. 'I'm really sorry, Bubbles. I know how much you were looking forward to our fortnight, just as much as I was if not more. I'll do what I can to get some time, and we can trip the light fantastic in the fleshpots of Dublin at weekends, if nothing else.

Two weekends later, Helen arrived late and she knew it. Very late. Catherine was already half-way down her third pint when she appeared and was distinctly tiddly, if not quite merry. Helen sniffed the atmosphere and decided she didn't like it. She went to the bar for a rock shandy but Catherine was deep in conversation with someone else by the time she got back to her seat. Helen fished in her pockets quietly for cigarettes and offered one to the stranger, mainly as a way of making sure she was noticed.

Catherine looked at her. 'Oh right, Helen, this is Aifric. She's up from Galway with a soccer crowd for the weekend. Aifric, this is Helen.' The stranger nodded in her direction, not quite meeting her eye. They went back to their conversation.

'Aifric. Now, what sort of a jaysus name is that?' Helen mused to herself, casting her eye over the sparse crowd in the student bar of the Belfield campus that was home to the concrete jungle of University College, Dublin. 'And what, pray tell, am I doing lurking around a student hangout on a Friday night? And why am I being introduced as 'Helen', rather than, 'Helen, my partner?' Questions, questions. It was late and she was tired. Her eyes were bloodshot from night-driving.

Aifric and Catherine remained locked in conversation, their mutual body language automatically excluding her. The surface of the table was sticky from old beer and Helen had a vague suspicion that she was sitting on some antique chewing gum. After an hour or so, she yawned obviously and leaned over to put her hand on Catherine's arm. 'Sweetheart, I'm shagged out. Any chance we could head off shortly?'

Catherine looked at her obliquely, and sighed. 'All right, Helen, I coming when I've finished this.' She indicated her still one-third full fourth pint. Helen nodded and relapsed into silence.

When they got up to leave, Catherine leaned across the table and kissed the stranger on the cheek. 'Jesus, she's tall,' thought Helen, shaking Aifric's hand and saying goodnight while looking up at the young five-foot-ten woman warily.

Catherine was silent on the way home to her mother's house and Helen had the impression she was sulking. 'Is there something wrong, sweetie?' she asked eventually.

'No. Yes. Not really.'

'That's three different answers… ant to pick one?'

'You're always so fucking pedantic,' Catherine spat.

'Hey, hey! Easy, Catherine.'

'No, I won't. It's all pedantry and seriousness with you lately… the job and the mortgage and the bills and this fucking car that never works properly.'

Helen stopped the car outside the house, pulled up the handbrake and switched off the engine. 'Hey, you go easy on Ophelia if you know what's good for you. Where is all this coming from?'

'Fuck it, I'm young. I just want to have some fun and all you want to do is go home and watch a fucking video.'

'For your information, madam, I do not want to watch a fucking video. I just need some sleep. If you were listening to me at all this week you'd realize I've been up to my eyes at work. I haven't had a night off for nine days. Look at the time: it's two in the morning and I've been on the go since half-past six. There's a shagging general election on, or does what happens in this country pass you by in a haze of drink and cannabis?'

'So that's it. You're pissed off because I smoke a little hash!'

'Oh, fuck this. I don't give a fuck what you do with your time when I'm not around but, when I am here – and you know I do my damnedest to be with you when I can – I expect a little fucking consideration from you, instead of this selfish, juvenile carry-on. Grow fucking up!' Helen got out and slammed the door.

Catherine got out on the other side. 'What the fuck gives you the right to tell me to grow up? Are you out of your fucking mind? I do what I want, when I want.'

'Clearly, but you're drunk.'

'So fucking what?'

'Sleep it off. We'll talk in the morning.'

'We will in our arse. We'll talk now.'

'No way. I'm not having a fucking screaming match with you in the middle of a suburban street at two in the fucking morning. We will talk in the morning when you're sober and I've had some sleep. We're just sparking off each other. Now let's calm the fuck down and go inside before your mother wakes up.'

'Sensible Helen, always thinking of how things might look,' Catherine sneered.

'Give me your keys.' Helen stood straight with her hand stretched out, her breath condensing in frosty October air. 'Give me your keys, Catherine. I don't want to fight.'

'You never do,' Catherine's voice was quieter but menacing. 'You never even try to get things sorted. All you do is let them run until they become bigger than they might have been.'

'I do try,' Helen said, dropping her hand to her side. Then she asked: 'What does that mean?'

'I don't know. I need time to think. We need to talk. We need to sit down and talk about where we're going.' Catherine ran a hand through her hair. 'Aifric's asked me out. She said she fancied me before she knew you and I were together.' There was something wishful in her tone that made Helen's stomach flip over once with anxiety.

'And?'

'And what?'

'And what did you say?'

'I said we'd been together for a couple of years.'

'That's not really a definitive answer, is it?' Helen asked, leaning back against the car and feeling faintly suffocated.

'No, I suppose not.' Catherine kept her eyes down. There was a long, very uncomfortable silence. Helen waited for more explanations but nothing further was forthcoming. Catherine looked towards the house. 'Come on in, Helen. It's cold, we don't need to discuss this on the street now, do we?'

'How long has this been going on?'

'There's nothing going on.'

'Yet.'

Catherine did not reply. Helen exhaled heavily and thought carefully before replying. Eventually, she said: 'Well, you seem to need time to think and I don't believe I want to be around you while you do that. Go inside. I'm going home. Ring me.'

'Don't go, Helen, we can't talk about it.'

'No, not now, Bubbles, there's no point. I'm going home.' She kissed Catherine lightly on the cheek. 'Ring when you're ready. We'll talk, okay?' Helen got back into the car and drove slowly away, nodding at Catherine through the driver's-side window. She drove back through Dublin and stopped at an all-night petrol station near the city limits, parked under the floodlights and told the attendant she was going to have a kip. By the time she arrived home, it was 7.30 a.m. and there was a taste of Winter in the air. Helen went straight to bed.

Chapter Nine

Another Country

Over the following couple of days of that October week-end, the pieces fell slowly into place, clicking together comfortably like a child's puzzle. There had been changes over the past weeks that she had noticed, half –noticed and ultimately ignored, Helen reflected when the blazing heat of her anger faded to tepid despondency. Catherine had stopped talking about their future plans; on several occasions, she had avoided the serious discussion they were planning to have about making their living arrangements legally permanent. With a sense of surprise, Helen remembered at least three broken solicitor's appointments. She refused to trust her memory but then her diary confirmed it. Questions travelled around and around in her head, her thoughts jumping non-sequentially from one point to another, and they were questions that only Catherine could answer truthfully. Why had she agreed so easily to take holidays and go home as soon as the General Election was called? Why had Aifric never been mentioned before, even casually, although it seemed she had been on the scene for a while? If there was something going on, why had Catherine even mentioned it? Was it a way of making Helen do the dirty work? Or was it a kind of plea, an attempt to repair the damage almost before it was done?

Above all, Helen spent most of those two days looking at the telephone. Yes, it did ring, but it was never Catherine.

On Monday, she went back to work and allowed herself to be caught up in the organised hysteria of a newspaper office during an election. For Helen, the election was a small miracle, an excuse to ignore the toothache in her heart, to reach beyond it into that methodical, plodding part of her personality that served her so well professionally. There were candidates to be interviewed and shadowed on the canvass; vox pops to be organized to assess the mood of the disparate electorate in various Mayo towns; analysis pieces to be written and editorials to be composed, not to mention the witty colour pieces reflecting the mad circus realities of an Irish election. There was also all the usual work to be done too. Even in time of elections, the courts, local authorities and sports fixtures still went on as usual and, of course, there was the usual quota of nutters who called into the office with individual axes to grind or a severe dose of religious mania. Helen co-ordinated the efforts of her willing team – even the Cougar sobered up enough to be a real asset – read the copy churned out by everyone from the knowing Philip to the politically naïve George, and binned the more obviously partisan party press releases. It was Thursday before the paper was out and Helen had the need to breathe and the time to consider her personal situation with even a modicum of calm reflection.

On Thursday night, she was getting ready to go out on a night marking that no-one else was available for – the sleep-inducing AGM of the local Association for the Mentally handicapped – when the telephone rang.

'Get that, Niamh, will you? If it's for me, tell whoever it is that I'm on my way out the door,' she called down the stairs from her bedroom. Helen continued rooting around for a spare tape for her Dictaphone, but froze when Niamh shouted: 'It's for you. It's Catherine. I told her you were going but she wants to talk to you. Pick up, will you?'

Helen looked at the telephone beside her bed as if it was a new invention. Reaching out a hand, she carefully picked up the receiver and held it to her ear. 'Hello,' she said, enunciating the word clearly, and heard the muffled click that was Niamh hanging up.

'Hello, Helen.'

'I'm on my way out.'

'I know. Rodgers the lodger said. I just wanted to catch you because I'm on my way out too and I didn't want to ring too late.'

'Well, you caught me.'

'So I did.'

Helen could hear Catherine's slow breathing as she waited for the next move in this verbal game of chess. She had been a journalist for a long time, and her skill at listening to silence, waiting for someone to talk, came in useful in other situations.

'I just wanted to see how you were doing.'

'I'm fine.'

''Okay. Are you coming up this weekend?'

'Depends.'

'On.'

''Circumstances.' Helen recalled those last words from another, very different conversation two years before. She swallowed hard. 'What do you want to do?'

'I want to talk to you. Things have changed. I don't know what's going on. Will you come up?'

Helen sat down on the bed. 'Okay. I'll be there at nine tomorrow.'

'Nine, great.'

'Do you want to tell me what this is about so I can have time to think about it too?'

'No, not over the 'phone. Neither of us has the time. I'll see you tomorrow.'

'See you so.'

Helen waited five long seconds for the click that meant Catherine had hung up. She sat motionless for a few minutes before resuming her search for the Dictaphone tape. She found it in the drawer of Catherine's bedside locker along with the usual night-time detritus of life. As she pulled the tape out of the back of the drawer, an envelope fell to the floor. Helen picked it up, glancing at it. It bore the Irish harp used by most Government departments and was postmarked six weeks previously. She could tell by the tattered flap that there was a sheet of paper inside.

Helen stood with the envelope in her hand, vacillating. Reading the letter would be an invasion of privacy, one she wouldn't tolerate herself. Strictly speaking, whether it was a demand for money from the Revenue Commissioners or a pension statement or a blank page, Helen knew she had no right to check. She sat back on Catherine's side of the bed, weighing up the ethical pros and cons. 'Principles be damned,' she said aloud finally, and took the sheet of paper from the envelope to open it up.

The letter was very short and to the point, signed by some half-illiterate minion in the Department of Environment headquarters in Dublin. Catherine's application for a transfer back to Dublin had been duly noted and they would be in touch in due course when a vacancy arose. Helen slowly folded the letter and slipped it back into the envelope before carefully placing it back exactly where she had found it, closing the drawer quietly and deliberately. She put the tape she'd found in her Dictaphone and went to work.

At the meeting, her hand moved automatically across

the pages of her notebook but she didn't really hear a word. She felt sick to the point of throwing up. Afterwards, she threw her bag in the car and walked from the hotel down to Crosbie's where she sat for ninety minutes looking into her pint of Guinness, oblivious to the easy conversations that went over and around her. She went home, boiled the kettle and sat down, forgetting to make the coffee she thought she wanted.

Then she threw up.

When Helen arrived on Friday night she made the usual polite noises to Maggie Lacey and deposited a bottle of Chardonnay – her contribution to Sunday dinner – in the pantry before going upstairs. She could hear gentle guitar chords coming from the quaint drawing room on the first floor so she stuck her head around the door. Catherine was sitting in darkness, bent over the guitar, so close to the fireplace that the flames licked alternate shadow and orange afterglow on her face. She looked around, put down the guitar and stood up, shifting from one foot to the other. Helen walked into the room and Catherine's arms lifted for a hug.

'That doesn't seem like the kind of hug you give to someone who's going to be dumped,' Helen quipped.

Catherine hugged her tighter before letting go. 'It's not like that.' She turned away and poured from an already opened bottle of red that was warming beside the hearth, handing a glass to Helen. They clinked glasses without making a toast. Helen folded her coat meticulously over a worn armchair and sat in front of the fire, ankles crossed and arms around her knees. Catherine, after a moment, joined her and they sat side by side in silence. Helen said nothing for about a quarter of an hour: nor did Catherine. Both of them simply sat there, looking into the flames and periodically sipping wine from their glasses. Eventually, Helen lost her professional patience.

'So, Bubbles, are you going to let me in on what's going on?'

'I've been thinking about it but I don't really understand what's happening.'

'Well, that makes two of us then.' Helen paused. 'Do you really not know what's going on here?'

'No. Something isn't right, though.'

Helen thought for a moment. 'Okay, we'll do it this way. I'll be the journalist and ask the questions and you can give me whatever answers you can. That way we might actually find out what the difficulty is.'

Catherine's slow smile in the firelight made Helen want to groan with craving. 'All right, Helen. Nothing else is going to work tonight. Let's try it.'

Helen thought for a few minutes before beginning. 'Right. First off, do I bore you?'

'No.'

'Do you still love me?'

'Yes… but not as much as I did.'

Helen rarely cried but she felt silent tears sliding down her cheeks in the following moments. Trying to control herself, she said: 'Jesus, Catherine, that hurts!'

'I know, Helen, but it's the truth.'

'Do you still want to buy a new house with me for both of us?'

'No.'

'Are you looking for a job in Dublin?'

Catherine's head came up quickly. 'Yes. How did you know?'

'I'm asking the questions. Is there someone else?'

A pause. 'No.'

'You hesitated too long. I don't believe you.'

Catherine shrugged. 'I can't make you believe me.'

'Are you saying it's over between us? Is that what you're saying? Because, if it is, you've broken your most important promise to me. Catherine, damn it, you promised me you wouldn't do this. You promised me that if things were going wrong you'd tell me in time to give us an opportunity to fix it. You promised.'

'It's not over. I'm not breaking any promise to you.'

'Jesus, if it's not over then what is it? In the last five minutes you've said you don't love me as much as you did, you don't want to buy a house with me when we've talked of nothing else for months and you're looking for a job on the other side of this island. If that's not over, what is?'

'I never said I didn't love you enough.'

'Don't patronise me,' Helen said bitterly.

Catherine started to cry and the sound almost broke Helen's heart. She reached out and cradled Catherine in her arms, kissing the special spot where hair grew softly on her temple. 'Don't do this to us, sweetheart. You know we have everything going for us. Don't throw it all away because some bit of skirt with no job and no prospects temporarily takes your fancy.'

'It's not like that. It's nothing to do with Aifric.'

'I never mentioned a name.'

Catherine closed her eyes, breathing shallowly. 'It's not like you think. She just likes me. I haven't done anything.'

'If you mean you haven't slept with her, fine, I believe you, but there are plenty of other ways of having an affair without screwing your brains out.'

'Don't, Helen.'

Helen sat upright. 'Don't what? Don't tell you how I feel? You're pulling the carpet right out from under my feet and I don't get a chance to say something? I'm fucked if I'm going to make this easy for you.'

'It's not easy for me either. I don't want to hurt you.'

'Famous last words, Catherine.'

'I just need time to sort myself out. Can't you do that? Can't you give me a little time without hassling me? I can't cope with all this.'

'And I can? You must be joking.' Helen sipped her wine and reached for the bottle to replenish the empty glasses. 'I don't know what the fuck's going on here but I love you and I want you so I'll give you a chance to get your shit together and talk to me properly. Is that what you want to hear?'

Catherine was really bawling. 'Yes. Just don't leave me. I don't think I can sort anything out if you leave me.'

Helen's hardening heart melted and she pushed away the physical feeling of sickness. She cuddled Catherine, whispering endearments until the tears stopped. They stayed there in relative silence for over an hour.

After eleven, Helen glanced at her watch. 'Come on, love, there's no point sitting here over a dying fire. Let's go to bed and sleep on it. You never know, it might seem better in the morning.'

Catherine look up. 'Oh, Jesus, yes, I'd better hit the bed. I'm helping out at that conference tomorrow. I've to be in Belfield at eight-thirty.'

'What conference?'

The second in the series of lesbian workshops. I told you about them. They're on tomorrow and Sunday.'

'Fuck. Catherine, can you just not leave it? We'd both be better employed staying at home and sorting this mess out.'

'I can't. I promised I'd be there to help register everyone and organise the rooms.'

'Please, Catherine. Ring in sick or something.'

'No, I can't.'

'All right. I'll go with you then.'

Catherine glanced up in surprise. 'You hate that wim-mimy stuff. You'd hate it. You did the last time.'

'What you really mean is that I stick out like a sore thumb because I'm bound to be the only woman there with a decent job, apart from the lecturers or facilitators or whatever the fuck you call them.'

'Don't be so dismissive. These things are important.'

'Oh, all right. I'm only messing. Come on, let's go to bed and I'll give you a lift in the morning.'

They got ready for bed in silence, conscious of the sleeping household. Side by side, they brushed their teeth in front of the mirror in the freezing first-floor bathroom, then padded quietly on naked feet up to Catherine's room.

The camping bed had already been set up beside Catherine's single bed. Helen started to climb into it but Catherine touched her arm when the springs started to creak with Helen's weight.

'Don't, Helen. Sleep with me tonight.'

Helen looked up, smiled through the heaving in the pit of her stomach and nodded. 'Okay, if that's what you want?'

'It is.'

Catherine took off her nightshirt and got into bed. Helen hesitated, then switched off the bedside light and removed her pyjames. They lay down, both facing the same way, Helen's arm around Catherine, her stomach fitting exactly into the small of Catherine's back. They rested quietly, silent but wakeful. Helen felt herself warming from the scent of her lover and the closeness of their bodies. She put her free hand on Catherine's chest, feeling the regular thump of her heartbeat.

'We'll sort it out,' Helen whispered. 'You know I love you. You're everything to me and I'd give up anything just to have you. Just pick up the ball and keep running until you get to the try line. I'll be there when you do.'

'I'm sorry, Helen. I just can't get it clear in my head. Help me?'

Helen thought she heard physical longing in the words

and kissed the back of her neck, slipping the edge of her tongue along Catherine's neat hairline. 'I just can't resist you,' she said.

'I never really got that impression.'

Helen went rigid. She was stung and it hurt but laid over the aching place was a thick film of bittersweet emotional desire. She clasped Catherine tighter and bit her neck gently. 'I can show you,' she said, hating herself.

Catherine turned in her arms and held Helen's face in her hands, boring into her eyes in the dim street-lamp light that peeked through the ill-fitting curtains and threw a thin slash of light across the room. 'Show me,' she said slowly.

Looking at her, Helen knew words were pointless. Her words were having no impact. Snuggling closer, she pressed closed lips against Catherine's and felt them opening under her touch. Helen had never eaten an oyster but when Catherine's lips opened like that, she was always reminded of an oyster shell opening under water, revealing soft, slippery wetness. Helen groaned as their tongues tenderly intertwined: she felt as if they had never kissed before and as if they had been kissing forever. She broke the kiss, wriggled until Catherine lay half under her and put one arm under her shoulders. 'I'll show you,' she said quietly.

Leaning down, she let her wet open mouth rest on Catherine's and waited until Catherine's tongue probed and met hers before kissing back, softly. Catherine's arms snaked around her waist and pulled her closer until their nipples touched. Catherine's were already hard and tight. Still kissing, Helen ran fingertips lightly across Catherine's forehead and the side of her face before flicking her tongue quickly along the corner of Catherine's mouth. Catherine's hips began to move and she moaned softly. Helen pulled away and waited until Catherine lifted her head from the pillow, searching for her lips. When it happened and her head was held tightly between Catherine's hands as she devoured the kiss, she leaned down with all her weight, parted Catherine's legs with her own and turned her sideways.

With Helen's neatly padded hip pressed against her, Catherine was watchful, silent and unmoving. Helen slipped two fingers into her own body and moistened them slowly and carefully while Catherine watched, hardly breathing. Helen slipped her damp fingers around one of Catherine's nipples and began to rock her body backwards and forwards, each movement teasing the fiery patch of wetness against her hip. Catherine gripped her arms and clenched her thighs around Helen's hips. Her breathing began to labour.

Helen was in no hurry. She maintained her slow, careful rhythm for a long time until the sheet beneath their bodies grew wet with the sap sliding out of Catherine's musky body.

Then Helen lay along Catherine's body, mouth to mouth, chest to chest, toe to toe. Somehow, the slight difference in their heights disappeared when they were like this. Helen pressed one thigh between Catherine's legs and began sliding up and down slowly against her while her tongue and mouth teased the lonely nipple.

Helen was open and slavering but something in her didn't want to be fucked, didn't want to feel the delicious sensation of Catherine's fingers sliding into her body to where they belonged.

Catherine moaned softly but regularly, a tempo matched by Helen's movement. When she said just one work, 'Please,' Helen slipped off her body, cradled her against her own chest, and reached around her hip, lips against Catherine's ear.

'This is me, only me, fucking you,' she whispered, sliding her fingers around the wetness until she found the hard, throbbing place that begged for serious attention. She fucked hard but slowly, growing hotter with pleasure when Catherine's body began to undulate against her own. She felt Catherine climbing quickly until she reached the plateau where Helen knew she could keep her for a long time. Catherine slipped one redundant hand under Helen's arm and sought the steaming, boiling cavern.

'No,' Helen said, her hand pausing and resting firmly against Catherine.

'Yes,' Catherine replied, expertly sliding three fingers into Helen's body.

Helen quivered, remembering other times they had made love like this and the rare occasions when concentration and circumstances led to them both being fucked over a simultaneous, razor-sharp edge. Her helpless body betrayed her; her body closed with relief around fingers and tightened as Catherine began to fuck her with a slow, sombre tempo.

She sighed deeply and resumed stroking Catherine firmly where she felt it most. They matched each other, move for move, stroke for stroke, each increasing the rhythm and pressure in easy, unhurried steps. The only sound in the room was ragged, uneven breathing and the faint cry of a far-away ambulance. No words of love were spoken. Not even one.

Catherine, always the one with the shorter fuse, came explosively, strangling a cry in her throat before it was born and drawing her knees to her chest. As she came, she plunged her fingers deeper into Helen and kept them there, her fingers still while the rest of her body sweated and heaved. After a time, she grew quiet and her breathing slowed. Helen started to pull away.

'No,' Catherine said. Slipping her hand out of Helen's body, she turned around, lay cradled in Helen's arms and sucked her fingers while her other hand went back down to consuming heat. Helen tensed as fingers pushed against her demandingly.

'Come for me. I want you to come for me too.'

Vanquished by her own longing, Helen surrendered and lay unresisting as Catherine fucked her harder and harder, falling, falling, falling, turning over and over in pitch dark nothingness. In the moments before she fell, Helen's heart, so full, began to crack. The cracks widened and small pieces fell away, like old plaster on a wall, as she careered downwards. She knew. Afterwards, she would wonder how she could possibly know.

When she slowly quietened, Catherine moved to kiss her on the lips. Helen turned her head abruptly.

'Well, at least we can still do that much,' Helen said brusquely in her daytime tone of voice. There were tears flowing from her eyes but in the dark, Catherine couldn't see. Her body ached and throbbed, keeping time with her pulse. 'It's late. We need to sleep,' Helen added, turning her body to the wall, excluding the usual cuddles they awarded each other as a cover for the vulnerability of their mutual afterglow.

'Goodnight, Helen.'

'Goodnight.'

When Helen woke it was dark and there were still tears on her face. She had been crying in her sleep. She opened her eyes dreamily and felt nothing during the one short moment it took for reality to cleave in. She lay there, her back to the sleeping Catherine, her body scrunched up and rigid against the urge to wail.

After enduring tedious workshops throughout the next day, Helen drove back to Bray, and they got something to eat in a local pizza restaurant before spending the evening in a pub, talking and talking but getting nowhere. As Helen tried to verbalise, her mood swung sharply between despair, elation and anger. She was drinking vodka, a spirit to which she was unaccustomed, and fought her need to express vicious resentment. They went home late and slept in the same bed, Helen with her face turned to the wall just like the night before.

On Sunday morning, they fought long and hard. Helen was infuriated and would have used long nails if she possessed them. She felt she was fighting for her life but all she could get out of Catherine were non-committal replies, tears and a plea for a month alone to sort herself out. The fight terminated abruptly when Helen stopped pacing the room and hit the wardrobe so hard with her fist that her knuckles bled. She looked at them, surprised and weakly perturbed by her own violence. She no longer recognised herself. She was becoming someone she didn't know.

'That's it. I'm going home,' she said. 'There's no point staying here. We're just tearing each other up, doing this. You want a month, fine. Have it. Just remember I'll be there at the end of it; I'll be the one you fucked over without a logical reason. Why can't you just finish it? Are you so unkind that you'll leave me strung up like this when you really want to finish me off? Who the fuck are you, anyway?'

Catherine did not object. Helen looked at the stranger sitting on the bed and was on the point of continuing her rant when Maggie knocked and opened the door.

'Lunch's ready,' she said, bustling in and stopping abruptly when she saw Helen's hand. 'What happened?'

'I cut my finger trying to open that blessed sash window,' Helen said jocularly. 'And it hurts like crazy.'

'Oh, come on, love, I've some TCP in the bathroom. We'll get you fixed up,' Maggie said, turning to go.

Helen looked searchingly at Catherine for a long moment. Catherine didn't look up but there was a lock of hair on her forehead that made Helen's knees weak.

'Okay, Maggie,' she said, walking out of the room, 'but I warn you, I'll scream and scream when you put the TCP on it. Mothers are so cruel!'

After lunch, they walked through the basement door and sat in the rare October sunlight on front-door steps, breathing in the scent from next-door's bay tree. Helen had already packed and her bag was in the car. Maggie was perturbed at her unplanned departure but Helen invented a professional summons.

'Are you going back to work? You can still stay with me,' Helen said, picking a few bay leaves surreptitiously.

'No, I'm not. I've gone sick and looked for a career break for six months. I need the time.'

'Are you staying here?'

'I don't know.'

'Jesus, Catherine, do you think I don't need to know where I'll be able to contact you?'

'Ring here. If I'm not around mother'll get me the message.'

More silence. Helen was all talked out. She stood up and put her hands in her pockets. 'All right. I'm off,' she said austerely.

Catherine walked her to the car. Helen's senses were heightened. She could smell the sea as if her feet were trailing in it and the sound of the key in the car lock was too loud. Standing with the open door between them, she paused. Catherine was crying. Helen lifted one hand and rested it on the side of Catherine's face, tears filling her own eyes.

'Catherine, my beloved one, this is not goodbye. This is not goodbye, it's simply *au revoir*.'

Catherine did not reply. Helen sat into the car and drove away without any added prevarication. She didn't wave or look behind, but paused for a moment at the top of the street, dispassionately observing the diminished figure of her life's blood in the rear-view mirror.

She turned right into the line of Sunday traffic and drove home slowly.

Philip was a rock of sense. 'Can I be honest?' he asked, when Helen told him the complete story on Tuesday evening, as she twirled a cold and half-empty mug of coffee between her hands unhurriedly. She nodded.

'It sounds to me like you're fucked,' he said succinctly. 'She's either playing away from home or she wants to. Cut your losses, Helen. She's not worth this kind of torture. No-one is.'

Helen half-smiled wishfully into the mug. She hadn't eaten or slept for two days and yet she felt full but still un-utterably weary. 'You're right, Philip. I know you're right but that doesn't make it easy. I don't want to let her just walk away from me. I can't. I won't. I said I'd give her a month. I promised.'

'Nobody could hold you to a promise exacted in the circumstances you've just told me,' he said forcefully. 'You know you won't be able to stick a month of not knowing what's going on.'

'No, I won't. The past two days seem like they've lasted a year,' she said, 'but I have to give her a chance. I have to try. I'd like to think she'd do the same for me if I was in her shoes. I promised, Philip. I promised I'd never walk away if there was anything left to save. I gave her my word and I have to keep it.'

'Yeah, right. And she promised you she wouldn't do this, wouldn't fuck you over without warning. But she's doing it to you and you're letting her.'

'I know, but neither of us will gain anything if I buy into a point-scoring competition based on she-broke-her-promise-now-I'll-break-mine.'

Philip sighed heavily and leaned back into the cocoon

of the battered couch in the corner of Helen's study. 'It still sounds to me like you're fucked.' He paused. 'Maybe you could use this time to think about what you want. What do you want?'

'Her,' Helen said simply. 'Just her. Just to be sure of her the way I was up to a few weeks ago. I want to be happy the way I was, happy so I know it at the time: the kind of happiness that makes you sit up, day after day, and say to yourself "I'm happy". Not the kind that you only think was happiness when you look at it in retrospect. I have to wait for as long as I can. She's worth that, damn her. There's nothing else I can do.'

'All right, Helen. There's no talking to you, I can see that. You're obviously going to do what you have to do, but how are you going to fill the time, for Christ's sake?'

'Same way I've done the last two days. Work, drink, lack of sleep, work, drink...' her voice trailed off for a moment. 'Was it like this when Patti left? Did it feel like this?'

'Like what, Helen?'

'Empty. Weightless. I was lying on that couch last night, trying not to think myself into a crying jag, and I assumed the law of gravity had simply disappeared. I felt so weightless I thought I was going to float up into the air on a cloud of my own pathetic misery.' She smiled. 'Good line, eh?'

'Yeah. Good description too. Yes, it did feel like that. I know you're going to hear this a lot, but it doesn't last. You will get over it. You will also hear that line about there being plenty more fish in the sea. It's true. There are. Even if you don't find one, you'll learn to live with it. Or, rather, without it.'

'What "it" are you talking about, you dirty old man? You think I can't live without sex?' Helen asked, her shadowy grin almost, but not quite, touching tired eyes.

Philip blushed. 'I didn't mean that!' he protested.

'Honestly, all you young ones think about nothing but sex, sex, sex. And as for you queer… sorry, gay people… you're the worst. Sure, everyone knows you do nothing but have sex all day and all night, in the supermarket, in the office and, if you're not doing it, you're thinking about doing it to or with somebody's daughter or sister. It's common knowledge.'

Helen's short burst of almost-laughter tinkled in the room, quite like the circle of tin angels powered by night-lights she'd enjoyed at Christmas as a child.

'That's better,' Philip said firmly. 'Look, only you can know what's best for you. If you insist on putting yourself through a month of this, fine, but don't expect me to sit here listening to you for another twenty-eight days. I have better things to do with my time than provide a shoulder for a young but unavailable dyke to cry on.'

'Like what, for example?' Helen asked.

'Like making you toast,' he commented, standing up. 'C'mon Helen, you know she's not worth starving yourself for. You're sick, God love you, and you need some tea and toast.' He put his hand on the door handle. 'C'mon, Helen.'

'All right, Philip. Tea and toast it is. Just the thing for a breaking heart. Whenever anyone sings that line asking what's become of the broken-hearted, I'll be sure to remark that they're being force-fed invalid food in their own homes by a local reporter.'

Helen worked hard in the succeeding days, putting in extra hours and not even indulging in the traditional bout of moaning when unpopular jobs were shoved her way because none of her team was willing to do them. Everyone was looking at her funny, she decided. They knew there was something wrong and she wondered why even the Cougar hadn't tried to pry some juicy details out of her. She suspected that Philip had had a quiet word and warned them off, but she couldn't prove it and when she confronted him about it, he cheerfully denied it. She worked hard and hit the bottle with a vengeance, drinking top-shelf spirits every night until she fell asleep, close to unconsciousness. Whether she was at home or in the pub, Helen drank the evening hours away with single-minded determination to achieve a respite, however temporary, from the half-formed and less understood thoughts crowding her head.

Every morning, she greeted the dim October sunshine with slitted eyes and a massive headache, but she still turned in on time and worked like a demon. She more or less gave up eating altogether apart from occasional munchies-attacks in the middle of her regular evening's labour of drinking herself into a calm stupor. Her alcohol intake was phenomenal: she could drink half a bottle of Jack Daniel's in a night and never get falling-down drunk, rowdy, or weepy. Just dangerously calm. Niamh gave her wide berth after commenting on the drink on the fourth evening on the binge.

'What are you at, Dunne? Trying to find out what the inside of an empty bottle looks like?' she said conversationally one evening while tucking into pizza and garlic bread in front of the sitting-room fire and *Emmerdale*.

'Mind your own fucking business,' Helen replied bitterly, her voice already lowered a couple of half-tones from whiskey, Benson & Hedges and late night. 'I'm spending my own fucking money and my own fucking time.'

'Well, sorr-ee. I just thought you'd lost the power of speech over the last week.'

'I don't talk when I don't have anything to fucking say.'

'Helen, if you'd just tell me what's wrong, I might be able to do something to help, even if it's just to listen,' Niamh put down her plate. 'It might help just to let it out, have a good cry or something. This isn't like you.' She indicated the bottle on the coffee table. 'Why don't you just start talking and see where it leads? You'll probably feel better if you do.'

'No thanks, Niamh. Bawling is not for me. It never has been. Maybe that's the trouble.' Helen sighed heavily, picked up the bottle and her glass and stood up. 'I'm off to bed. If the 'phone rings, tell 'em to get and be fucked. In exactly those words. Goodnight.'

'Goodnight, Helen. Sleep well.'

'Some fucking chance.'

Later that night, Niamh sneaked into Helen's room and tiptoed across to where she lay, shoes still on, one foot on the floor. The bottle was on the bed, empty. Niamh lifted the stray foot onto the bed. Helen, still half-dressed, shifted and turned into the empty side, curling her body around a spare pillow. Niamh took Helen's spectacles off, and paused for a moment to tidy a wayward curl on her forehead pensively. She closed the open book that lay on the bed and picked up the bottle and glass before turning off the light and departing quietly. She left the door open half a crack, just in case.

Helen was just reaching for a glass in the evening about a week later when the telephone rang. She looked at her watch. 'Fuck it,' she said, assuming it was the office and picking up the extension in the kitchen. 'What now?'

'Helen.' It wasn't a question.

'Yes. Who's this?'

'Aifric.'

'Oh.'

'Catherine told me what happened. I just rang to see if you were all right.'

'I'm fine.'

'Really?'

'Yeah, really.' Helen blew air through pursed lips noisily. 'Oh, for fuck's sake, what do you really want?'

'Hey, I'm just being friendly. I thought you could use

someone to talk to.'

'I have people to talk to already.'

'I know that, Helen. I just wondered if you were okay.'

'Like I said. I'm fine.' Something about the background noise sounded familiar. 'Where're you ringing from?'

'Catherine's.'

'Very cosy then.'

'It not like that.'

'What is it like then? Go on, tell me. No, let me guess. You're the shoulder to cry on and eventually you'll get what you want, if you haven't already. Do I win a prize?'

'It's not like that.'

'So you said.'

'Would you be very upset if it was like that?'

Helen paused, her fingers whitening as she tightened her grip on the telephone and leaned her forehead against the wall to bolster her weakening knees. 'Upset is irrelevant. If it's over, it's over. That's life and I'll move on. I always do. I hope you'll be very happy together.'

'She's worried about you.'

'Yeah, right. I can see that. She's so worried about me that she couldn't even let the corpse go cold. Is she there?'

'Yes.'

'Now that makes me angry. I can see it now. You're on the telephone to break the wonderful news that my lover is sleeping with you. She hasn't the balls of a flea on a moth-eaten moggy, and you're just doing the dirty work. How does it feel to be so manipulated by an expert?'

'Helen, come on. Is it too much to expect that you'd be reasonable about this? People change.'

'Not that much and not that fast. How long has it been going on?'

'Since Tuesday.'

'And the rest.'

'I'm telling the truth.'

'And I'm the king of Siam.'

'Helen, please. Listen, do you want to talk to Catherine about this?'

'No, not about this. Not about anything, now I come to think of it.'

'It's just that we were wondering if you'd like to come up for a weekend. Catherine says we can all work this out. There's no reason why we can't still be friends. You need to keep in touch. There's nothing for you down there and Catherine is worried that you'll be lonely.'

'Aifric, would the pair of you ever get up the yard? I don't need pity from either of you. I have my own life to lead.'

'Well, if you change your mind, let us know.'

'Sure,' Helen replied sarcastically. She paused. 'There is one thing.'

'What's that.'

'Tell her I want my pocket watch back. It's in the jewellers being repaired. I'll pick it up sometime when I'm in Dublin.'

'I'll tell her.'

'Goodbye.' Helen put the receiver down quietly and covered her face with her hands for a moment. Turning swiftly, she drew back her foot and kicked a hole in the flimsy kitchen door at about knee height. By the time Niamh arrived downstairs, Helen was laughing and rubbing her bruised toes.

'Jesus Christ, did you just do what I think you did?'

'Yep, and it felt fucking great! If that was on a rugby pitch it would've been a perfect drop goal. Three points and Ireland win a famous victory over the Springboks.'

'Holy God, will you look at the size of that hole? It'll take more than a bit of wood filler to fix that!'

Helen, still chuckling, turned on the tap and filled

the tumbler with water. She took off her Claddagh ring and dropped it onto the sink tidy, rubbing her fingers on her shirt afterwards. 'Niamh,' she said quietly, her back still to her housemate. 'Are you doing anything tonight?'

'Nothing much. What're you offering?'

'Let's go swimming.'

'You're on.'

Helen turned and looked into Niamh's eyes. 'Thanks.'

'For what?'

'You know for what. I don't know what I'd do without you sometimes. Having you here helps, just now.'

'Ah, would you go on out of that?' Niamh replied, blushing. 'C'mon, you lumbering drunk, let's get kitted out and see if there're any babes down at the pool.'

Helen spluttered her drink of water all over the place.

At the end of the following week, Helen cooked dinner for Philip and Niamh as a sort of gesture of appreciation for their support. Philip joked that if all the support Helen need-ed was someone to accompany her to the pub, he was game every time. At about 2.00 a.m. the two of them faced her on the couch and, drunk as lords, started quizzing her. Helen thought she was on *Mastermind*.

'What the fuck is this?' she joked after the tenth ques-tion about women and relationships. ''Helen Dunne, your two minutes on your specialized subject of yourself starts now'' or what?'

Despite the jokes, she did her best to explain. Philip and Niamh were drunk enough to blurt out the most outrageous stereotypes about butch dykes, lipstick lezzers and lumber-jack shirts. Helen was, at various points, rolling around on the floor, tears running down her face.

'What? What did I say?' Philip asked, confused, when he expressed the view that sex between women was obviously very sensitive and tender.

Niamh caught Helen's eye and they both laughed knowingly before Helen disabused him gently and recommended some light reading.

Later, she washed up the dishes – breaking one because she was drunk – and climbed the stairs to bed. The silence in her bedroom hit her hard. She'd packaged up Catherine's stuff the morning after Aifric telephoned and sent it to Dublin on the train, including her own heavy silver Claddagh in a plain white envelope tucked down the side of the box. Helen missed the ring and constantly fiddled with the obvious dent on her ring finger.

The nights when the silence was broken only by the sound of her own breathing were the hardest to bear. She missed Catherine: she missed the warm body on the other side of the bed, and missed the two of them curling up together, their bodies shaped like lumpy question marks. She was still finding it hard to sleep but had replaced drinking with frenetic exercise overnight. It helped. Her tired body found it easier to rest. Still, she knew she would wake in the early hours to find her head on a damp pillow. She cried in her sleep most nights.

Helen missed having someone to talk to in the mornings, and the drowsy conversations in the middle of the night when both of them woke. Often, she turned around, her mouth open to say something inconsequential, before she realised that Catherine was no longer there. It felt like a slap in the face every time.

Helen left the hole in the kitchen door unrepaired as a reminder to her of how destructive her anger could be. She left it there as an indication too that she would never allow herself to be that angry with Catherine again. As the days trickled slowly by, she reined herself in tightly and was surprised by her gradual liking for solitude: for cups of coffee drunk standing at the kitchen window, looking out at the few potted plants on the patio she'd made herself; for a quiet hour to read newspapers uninterrupted on Sundays; for the freedom to do as she pleased without having to consider what Catherine wanted.

Philip sidled into the office and over to her desk. 'No, O'Connor, I will not do some of your work. Fuck off and do it yourself,' Helen said without lifting her head.

He spread his hand theatrically. 'What? Here I come to do you a favour and you just assume I'm looking for something?'

Helen smiled up at him. 'Well, you usually are.'

'Not true.'

'Okay, what's the favour then?'

'I, Philip O'Connor, reporter of this parish, am the proud possessor of not one, but two press passes to... ta-dum,' he said, imitating a drummer beating a flourish on cymbals.

'Get on with it, fuckwit. I've got to get this finished before my 2.30 appointment which is why I'm working over lunch again.'

'Never mind. It could be worse,' he whispered. 'You could be unemployed. Maybe Fleming fancies you... a lot of men do lust after the unobtainable.

'Ick. Well, if he does, he's got a funny way of showing it. That bastard is determined to lick me into shape. I feel like I'm in the army. Someday you'll come in here and I'll be the one standing to attention and saluting Him indoors,' Helen whispered back.

'Hmm, lick you into shape, eh?' Philip muttered, waggling his eyebrows.

'Jesus, you have a mind like a sewer,' Helen laughed. 'C'mon, Pip, I'm busy. Tell me what you've got press passes for.'

'For nothing less than the forthcoming, long-awaited, eagerly anticipated…'

'Tell me or I'll screech right now.'

' rugby match between Ireland and the Barbarians. Would you do me the honour of accompanying me to Lansdowne Road on Sunday?'

Helen jumped up, climbed on her desk and executed her mad *Riverdance* manoeuvre. Hopping down energetically, she hugged Philip and kissed him on the cheek, making a loud smacking sound. 'O'Connor, I love you. You're the only man for me. I'll drive and buy you pints all day, I promise.'

Philip had a few days' holidays and was staying over in Dublin, so Helen rang Catherine's to be told she'd moved out to share a house in Dolphin's Barn. Helen took the address and telephone number. She rang the new number but Catherine wasn't there. Helen left a message with a stranger that she'd call late on the way home from the match to collect her pocket watch.

Philip and Helen had an absolutely brilliant day at the mismatched fixture set up to raise money for charity by two of the Irish international players. The *ad hoc* Babas showed their usual flashes of brilliance, and regular turnovers led to fascinating counter-attacks and the wide running Helen loved to watch and analyse. Technically, it wasn't great rugby but Helen loved it. This was different to the Five Nations Championship: Helen loved not caring who won or lost. She loved the sheer occasion of it and the good humour on the East Terrace. It was cold but the slanting afternoon sun was shining onto the hordes of supporters. Once they were settled in a spot near half-way with a good view of the white sticks at either end, Helen reached under her coat like a magician and produced a quarter-pint flask of Jack Daniel's. She and Philip had a good nip apiece to get them going and keep them warm.

Something like one-hundred-and-thirty points were scored that day. The Irish team was beaten out the gate but no-one cared and the applause was raucous when the referee blew the final whistle. Nobody wanted the game to end and Helen was so happy she didn't want to leave the old, familiar dump that was Lansdowne Road. After the match, Philip pulled her out onto the pitch and made her stand on the try-line under the posts at the Havelock Square end. 'Now,' he said, 'you can always say you stood on this hallowed turf. Remember this day, young Dunne. There won't be many more days like this one.'

The crowd finally dispersed and, after making their way to the city centre, they went for a meal with some of Philip's old buddies. Charlie, a stockbroker, was about fifty but looked younger. Billy, a plumber, was about the same, but Tony had to be fifty-five if he was a day. The four had all gone to the same school and, over the years, they maintained a tradition of meeting up once a year for a lads' night out. They were great crack. Helen was treated like a proper lady, but declined when they asked her to go clubbing later that night.

Philip was mock affronted. 'Oh, I see, you're too groovy to be seen with a bunch of old fogies like us, I suppose,' he complained. 'C'mon, it'd be fun.'

'Would you ever feck off, the lot of you,' she replied. 'I have to get back for work in the morning. And, Philip, for God's sake, will you not use words like "groovy". The women will think you're ninety.'

'That's gratitude for you,' he said, appealing to the three men seated at the table. 'The women will think no such thing. Anyway, there's just one in particular I'm interested in and she knows for a fact I'm not ninety.'

'O'Connor, you dog! I knew it! Who is she? What's she

like? Can I meet her?'

'Well you could if you stayed.'

Helen's face fell. 'Oh, boy, I wish I could, but I can't be late for work tomorrow, you know that.' She brightened suddenly. 'Never mind. Come up to my office and see me sometime. I want to hear every little detail.'

'I never kiss and tell.'

'Kissing? Kissing already? I have to meet this woman!' Helen got up to leave. 'Sorry, lads, but I must go to hell or to Connacht this evening. Thank you for a lovely time.'

Their riotous goodbyes followed her out of the restaurant. Helen was still smiling happily when she got back to the car and found the slip of paper with Catherine's address in the door pocket. She found her way eventually through a tight warren of identical streets but was unimpressed with Dolphin's Barn: she was no snob, but this was far too much like Kimmage for her liking. She pulled up at a small mid-terrace red-brick house and locked Ophelia securely. The doorbell didn't work, Helen discovered. She knocked.

Catherine answered the door after a few moments. 'Come in,' she said.

Helen stepped into the hallway and followed Catherine down a dark, dingy passage to an untidy sitting-room that smelled like a bedsit.

'Sit down.'

She sat cautiously, checking the cushion first for possible disgusting objects, and pulled out her cigarettes.

'Coffee?'

Helen nodded. Catherine left the room, returning with two mugs and a small brown paper parcel.

'There's your watch.'

Helen realised she had yet to speak. She felt as though she were standing somewhere, watching herself with wary, unforgiving eyes. Expelling smoke, she said: 'Thanks. How much do I owe you for the repair?'

'It's okay. I'll pay for it.'

Helen shrugged. 'Suit yourself,' she said.

Catherine sat down, crossed her legs and then un-crossed them. She couldn't seem to sit still. Helen offered her a cigarette. She took one. They smoked in silence. Helen stubbed out her cigarette on a saucer, obviously used as an ashtray, sitting on one end of a sticky little table marked with grey mug rings. She sat back.

'How are you?' she asked, immediately realizing she didn't want an answer.

'I'm okay.'

'And Aifric?'

'Fine too. She's out. I asked her not to be here.'

'Very sensitive. Thank you for that. When did you move in here?'

'Two weeks ago. There're three students and us.'

'Hmm. Are you working?'

'No. Career break, remember? I'm hoping that by the time I'm due to go back my transfer will be through.'

'Yes, that would be best.'

'How's Philip?'

'Great. We just watched the Babas trounce the Gaels to-day. We got absolutely steamed on whiskey up on the terraces but then he fed me to sober me up properly.'

There was a very long and very strained silence. Helen broke it. 'I suppose that's what you'd call a pregnant pause,' she said softly, looking up. Catherine's eyes were red-rimmed and puffy. 'Hey, what did I say?'

'I never thought it would be like this,' Catherine said slowly.

'Nor did I. However, the best laid plans of mice and men...'

'I don't know how you can be so philosophical.'

'It's a recent development. I didn't have any choice. I have to get on with it.'

'I know, but it could have been so different.'

'True.' Helen looked into her eyes and her heart started rattling hard against her rib cage. 'I gather freedom isn't all it's cracked up to be then.'

'I never thought it would be like this,' Catherine repeated. Helen felt the early warning prickle of unwanted tears and took a very deep breath before swallowing hard.

'Never mind. These things happen. Sometimes the game isn't worth the candle.' She marvelled at how easily she had been trapped into cloudy sympathy yet here she was, mouthing clichés and trying to ignore the heady hammering in her chest.

'I suppose I'm still in shock about how quickly it happened,' Catherine replied.

'Now that I do understand. Look, Catherine, I don't know why it happened but it did. Move on. I won't come here again. I'm obviously upsetting you.'

Catherine shrugged, tears gathering at the corners of her eyes. Helen simply couldn't bear it. She wanted to reach over and cuddle her and the ferocity of that desire made her stand up abruptly and reach for her keys. 'I need to get going.'

'Okay.' Catherine looked up. 'The lads from the house are in The George. I know it's the wrong direction but would you give me a lift? I don't want to be here on my own.'

'Ah, c'mon then; that's not much to ask.'

Helen drove in complete silence. She had nothing and everything to say and didn't trust herself enough to open her mouth even to ask for the time. Catherine's head was bowed. She looked smaller somehow. At a red traffic light near Christchurch, Helen sneaked a glance sideways just in time to see a tear falling from Catherine's face onto the back of the finger still bearing a silver Claddagh ring. Helen looked back at the traffic, shaking. The light turned green. She hit the accelerator. After driving maybe a hundred yards and without making a conscious decision, Helen swerved out of the line of traffic into a laneway behind the civic offices. She stopped, pulling the handbrake hard enough to rip it out of the floor. Catherine looked up in alarm.

Staring blindly through the windscreen, Helen spoke. 'Right. That's it. If I'm a fucking eejit then I might as well be hung for a sheep as a lamb. I don't know what the hell you were trying to say back there and I don't know if I give a damn. I'm probably going to kick myself around the county for this latter, but I have to say it; if you want to give it another go, I'm willing.'

Catherine burst into noisy, choking sobs; her hands covered her face and tears spilled through her fingers. Touching her own face, Helen's fingers came away wet. She undid her seat-belt and turned sideways, putting a hand on Catherine's shoulder gently.

'It's all right. Don't cry. Please. You're breaking my heart. Don't cry.'

Catherine's sobs began to slow. She took her hands away from her face. 'I don't know how you can do this, after all I've put you through. Why? Why are you offering me this?'

'Because I'm a fool most probably but also because I love you. I can't just amputate my heart. I know you're not happy. You were with me. I know I'm not happy but I was with you. QED, I'm asking. Yes or no?'

'Yes.'

Helen leaned back and closed her eyes, her hand slipping from Catherine's shoulder to take one of the hands in her lap. Catherine hung on tightly, still crying. 'Right. Obviously, there are a few things that have to be sorted out first. Come back to me and we'll discuss it then,' Helen said.

'What things?'

'Well, Aifric springs to mind.'

'Oh, fuck. I didn't mean that to happen. It was just… well… I was fucked up and she was there and I didn't have the strength not to.'

'I don't want to discuss that now. She gets the bullet or you can forget about it. No negotiation. I won't share you. I can't. I'd do without you first. I mean it.'

'I'll talk to her.'

'Talk all you want but do it. Immediately. I'm not hanging off a cliff for you for long.'

'Jesus, Helen, it won't be easy. She has feelings too.'

'Don't care. You made the mess; start cleaning it up now. I'm not fucking about.'

Catherine squeezed her hand. 'Okay. What else?'

'No drugs. Ever again. Do you hear me? They're fucking up your head and they're changing your personality. Don't tell me you're not on them. I could smell grass in that house. If you need help with that, I'll find you someone.'

Catherine looked into her eyes. 'Okay. I don't know how all that started. I just want to get clear of this and start all over again. With you. Can I have a hug?'

Helen leaned across the gear stick and kissed her gently and courteously on the lips with only the slightest pressure before pulling Catherine into her arms. Catherine cried on for another ten minutes. Helen stayed still and waited until she was quiet before mopping Catherine's face with a tissue and fixing her fringe back into place.

Catherine smiled weakly. 'Stay and have a drink with me. You could go in the morning.'

'No. I have to go. I have a lot to do and I can't even talk to you until this is sorted out. I won't stay in that house.'

'Why not?'

'The combination of students, dirt, cannabis, God

knows what other illegal substances and the retuning Aifric with the prospect of a row… it turns my stomach.'

'I'll ring you.'

'Do that. And remember that if you fuck me over once more, that's it. It's going to take me a long time to get over what happened. There is no quick-fix solution so don't kid yourself that there is.'

'I won't. I'm grateful for this chance. I'll make it up to you.'

'Well, you can try. Now, c'mon, you silly woman, I'll bring you to the corner and you can go off to enjoy your pint.'

Before Catherine got out of the car, Helen kissed her on the cheek, pausing to inhale the special scent that always addled her head. She waved and beeped the horn; Catherine turned to wave back.

Driving home through heavy Sunday evening traffic, Helen started thinking again, distractedly running through the conversation and her impressions. She felt almost nothing. She was roughly numb and it surprised her. Helen had expected elation or, at the very least, a quiet sense of satisfaction at an achievement. There was nothing fitting once her heart stopped hammering. She thought that maybe it couldn't be repaired but there was still a thin vestige of tepid hope. Nothing more. She considered ringing Philip on his mobile but didn't because he'd say she had done something very stupid. Helen decided to keep silent until she figured out the way the wind was really blowing before definitively proving to Philip that she'd been a complete arse.

The shrill sound of the telephone jerked her awake. Surfacing from under her quilt, Helen reached out a hand for the receiver and squinted in alarm at the luminous dial of the bedside clock. It was four-thirty the following morning.

'Jesus Christ, who's dead?' she barked into the telephone, her heart thumping with fright.

She could hear nothing on the line but buzzing. 'Who is this? Oh, I get it, a funny 'phone call at half-four in the morning. Ha bloody ha. Now fuck off,' she put the telephone down. It rang again almost immediately. Helen switched on the bedside lamp, hauled herself up in bed and snatched up the telephone.

'What?'

'You leave her alone.'

'Who the fuck are you? Aifric, is that you? Are you drunk or stoned or both? Either way, you're out of your fucking mind.'

'I said leave her alone. I'm warning you. I know you were here because the watch is gone. When I got back she said we were finished. She's been crying all night. I got it out of her in the end though. You want her back, don't you? She's upset. Why can't you just leave her alone?'

'None of your fucking business. She's over twenty-one and she can pick her own friends. You're not her jailer.'

'You stay away from us or I'll fucking kill you. Do you hear me? Stay away. Leave her alone. She doesn't want you.'

Helen hung up. Her hands were shaking. Niamh tapped on the bedroom door, opened it without waiting and stuck her head around it.

'I heard shouting. Are you alright? Jesus, you're white in the face. Will I get you tea or a drink? What happened?'

Helen closed her eyes for a moment. Opening them, she said evenly: 'It's all right, Niamh, go back to bed. It was just some crank with a great line in smut. He just got on my goat.' She took the 'phone off the hook. 'There. That'll settle the little bastard.'

Niamh looked dubious so Helen continued in a New York drawl: 'Move along, folks. The show's over. Nuttin' to see 'round here, folks. Move along there.'

Niamh smiled. 'Jesus, that scared the shit out of me. I thought it was burglars and you were trying to beat them about the head with the poker!'

'Twas nothing so dramatic as that. Merely a fuck-wit with more money and time than brains. I'll report it to the guards in the morning. Now go to bed.' Helen switched off the light and Niamh retreated. Sitting up in bed, Helen started shaking again. Her skin crawled uncomfortably. She wondered what exactly was going on in the Dolphin's Barn house and worried that Catherine wasn't safe. Helen knew, however, that she couldn't telephone back. Worried sick, she was both helpless and impotent. She didn't sleep and went to work at first light, letting herself into the office even before the streets had been cleaned of their Sunday night take-away dross.

Helen dozed on the couch on Monday evening. The house was quiet. Niamh had gone for a swim but, after a disturbed night, Helen was knackered and unable to put one foot in front of the other by the time she got home from work. She hadn't eaten all day and was in a heightened state of continuous alarm. She felt sick and her stomach constantly churned like an out-of-control washing machine. Through her half-sleep, she willed the telephone to ring. Eventually, it did. Helen leaped up, hurdled the back of the couch and grabbed it.

'Catherine, is that you? Are you all right?'

'Yes, it's me.' Catherine sounded weary, her voice slow and hard to hear.

'Did that bitch touch you? Did she lay a finger on you? What happened? Are you okay?'

When Helen paused for breath, she could hear the unmistakable sound of crying. 'Oh love, tell me what happened. Come on, now, tell me. It'll be all right if you just talk to me.'

Through the tears, Catherine's voice, choked and unfamiliar, mumbled: 'She's so hurt. It wore me down. I couldn't do it to her.'

'But you could to me,' Helen snapped.

'I'm sorry.'

'Sorry? Sorry? What are you saying? Sorry for what?'

'I can't do it. I can't find my way back to you. Not yet.'

'Hang on the bell a minute! What did you give her, a lifetime commitment after three fucking weeks or what? Where do I come in?'

'Helen, please. Wait a second. Listen to me. She's awful hurt. She's fragile. I can't do it when she's like this. Please be patient with me. You're stronger. It's just going to take a little time.' Catherine's words were beginning to slur.

A wave of nausea hit Helen hard, mingling with a rip tide of rising anger. 'You're drunk,' she said tonelessly. 'You're drunk and you're asking me for time I cannot give you. I don't have it to give you. I'm not strong. You've broken me. We have to finish this now. I can't do this anymore. There's no fight left in me. My life is enough of a mess and if I don't stop this now I'll never recover from you.'

'No, Helen, don't say that. Don't say it!' Catherine's voice rose. 'Don't leave me. I need you now more than I ever did. We can get it back if you wait for me.'

'We have to finish this now,' Helen repeated.

'No, no, no,' Catherine wailed. 'Give me a chance. Just one chance. Don't. I need you. I can't do it without you.'

'You'll learn. The same way I'm learning. I can't parley with you anymore. There's fuck all point. This is just tearing my guts out. If you won't finish this, I will. I'm hanging up now. Don't ring me again.'

'Wait. Please, Helen.'

'For what, Catherine? For a half-chance of an infinitesimal possibility that I'll ever be able to trust you again? No,

Catherine. No.'

'But if you could just...'

Helen could hear Catherine still speaking as she hung up. Holding the receiver three inches above the telephone, she dropped it into its cradle, steadying herself with one hand against the wall while she contemplated the splintered hole in the bottom panel of the kitchen door.

It was over.

CHAPTER TEN

PARTING SHOT

Dear Catherine,

It's difficult to know why I'm writing this letter and, at this point, I don't even know what it's going to contain or if I'm even going to post it. I've just spent the evening waffling with Michael Byrne – remember him? And that disastrous dinner? Maybe that was the beginning of the end, only I couldn't or wouldn't see it like that at the time – over a pint and your name came up as it usually does, somewhere between the antics of our political masters and the price of raw fish.

So why am I writing? I suspect it's probably got some-thing to do with all the words that have been left unsaid be-tween us, and all the unfinished business that didn't simply go away when I hung up on you without even saying goodbye. I suppose you could look on this as one last throw of the dice, one final toss. I don't really have anything left to lose. I've lost you, after all. What's a little more loss of pride between two people who used to be friends?

I've been busy but, somehow, there's always enough time to think. At times, it's difficult to know what to think, except to wonder where it all went wrong. Catherine, you know that I can be the most self-possessed of people, but what you and I have done has broken something fundamental in me that I can't repair without you.

I've been thinking back over the events of the last couple of years and, by and large, my memories are very happy ones. We were so close, we had so much in common and we shared all our little ordinary hopes and dreams… or so it seemed at the time. Maybe we were too close but, whatever the reasons, somehow we managed to throw it all away. Somehow, this is where we've ended up.

I suppose I've given you the impression that the Last Chance Saloon has been closed forever. It's not. I've tried so hard over the last couple of months to shut up the shop and be done with it, but I still think you're worth another calculated risk. In time, the guards will raid my little saloon and I'll lose my licence, but I'm keeping it open for you now just the same. You used to be somebody I liked, not the pale, faded reflection I last saw, and that's why my saloon's still open for you.

In a strange way, this gesture has a lot to do with self respect. If I'm going to fail this particular test, I need to know now that I did my very, very best. When I'm 93, toothless and strapped to a commode, I'd like to be able to tell the cute nurse's aide that, yes, I did love someone and I lost her, but I gave it my very best shot.

And this is my best shot. I'm willing to go that extra mile, to take another risk. Are you? While I have the feeling that what we had is irretrievably broken and smashed beyond re-pair, I still think we could fashion something worthwhile from the scattered pieces.

This letter is probably a final goodbye, one I should have said before I hung up on you that day. If you've had enough, if this really is goodbye, then I have to thank you. Thank you for the happiest time of my life and for the most challenging chapter of my life so far. Thank you being, for a while, my best friend, my sister, my lover.

What we shared was infinitely special and I know being with you has changed me, and that I'll carry one jagged-edged little piece of you with me forever, wherever I go. That melancholic reality leaves me now in a strangely happy but discontented place. I'll always know that you taught me to appreciate simple things, like the stars on crisp and clear Winter nights, for example, even if now I must learn to appreciate the darkness.

If I'd never met you, my life would have been very different. Not only are you part of my past, but that piece of you I'll be carrying will also be part of my future.

Thank you for all the morning kisses and evening cuddles; for all the warm words once spoken in earnest; for all the tickles and wrestling matches and naff walks in the rain, listening to raindrops falling from the branches above. Thank you for all the laughter and most of the tears; for allowing me to look deep inside your strong and willing heart during the darkness of our nights. Essentially, Catherine, what I'm trying to say is that it was all worth it. Sure, I have my regrets: everyone does eventually. There are times I'd like to live over again properly, with the benefit of my new and amazing twenty-twenty hindsight, but it was all worth it. I hope you never forget that either.

A few weeks ago, I thought you were just a bad habit, an addiction, and what I needed most was to forget you and get the rest of my life back on the rails. But, to me, you're not just a habit. You're the positive to my negative: the white to my black, the missing piece of my life's jigsaw.

We hit a stone wall and couldn't get through it or over it, but I still think there's a slight chance we might find a new direction, a previously untried way of getting around it. Every logical thought in my head is telling to me to have sense: to cut my losses and run like hell as far away from you as it's humanly possible to get, but my heart has its own route to follow and I'm prepared to tag along a little more.

I'll be under that clock at Eason's on Saturday afternoon at three. Maybe I'll just be taking a half-hour break on the way to somewhere else and maybe not. That's for you to decide. I'll be there because I think you're worth one last half-hour of my life. If, however, there's any doubt in your mind, please don't show up. I'll wait. Those thirty minutes will tick away and when they're finally gone forever, I'll be able to make a start at tying the broken threads of my life back together.

Enjoy your drink in my Last Chance Saloon, Catherine. The guards have turned a blind eye here for a long time, but I've got a tip-off that they'll be raiding at half-past three on Saturday. After that, I think I'll get out of the trade; maybe it's not really for me after all. I'll be selling up, packing up and moving on but, as I said, I'll be carrying a little piece of you with me. I suspect it'll be hard to carry, for a while.

I hope you realize that I've never been as honest with you as I am now. There is nothing here for you to read between these lines; there is no hidden agenda. I'm writing this and making you this offer because my life is no dress rehearsal and I'll never have the chance to live this day over again. If this is a mistake, then I'm prepared to make it and learn from it rather than avoid it.

Somehow, it seems appropriate to me that all this should finish on the steps under the clock; after all, that's where it really started. I'll be waiting there in the same place, just like I did that first day; two similar days like bookends, the first and last pages of our chapter.

I came across a quotation the other day… "The weariest nights, the longest day, must sooner or later perforce come to an end." Depressing? No, not really. If this is my last goodbye to you, Catherine, if this really is the end, then thank you for spending the longest day with me. In my heart, I know it's already dusk and that day is drawing to a close.

If you think you have enough left in you to light the darkness, then do it. The option is still there for you. The Last Chance Saloon is still open now but the time for messing is truly over. In a sense, your decision is irrelevant. I just feel I owe you this one last twirl on the merry-go-'round before I walk away with my honour intact. You know me and my sense of honour; I think no higher of any other moral standard. I owe this to you.

Now this debt of honour is paid. Take it or leave it. Thank you again, and I'm sorry. I'll miss you. May the road rise to meet you, Bubbles, and good luck.

Helen

EPILOGUE

Dublin city centre was packed with what seemed like the same harassed pre-Christmas shoppers. Bald heads skirmished with punk haircuts, and vexed mothers wielded loaded pushchairs as if they were battering rams. The O'Connell Street clock above her head tolled the half hour with little joy.

Helen glanced up at the familiar face of the clock, then squinted through rain-splattered spectacles into empty distance. She dropped her half-smoked cigarette, crushing the still-red coal deliberately under her heel. Indifferently, she kicked the butt off the step onto the wet pavement.

Helen took one deep breath and glanced at the broad strip of sky above the street, then started walking slowly towards O'Connell Bridge. She walked several measured steps, watching her feet strike the paving ahead, then glanced up to study the stream of oncoming faces dispassionately. She stopped walking suddenly, her hands in the pockets of her coat, and waited until the familiar figure approached and blocked her path.

'Catherine said you'd be here. I didn't mean to be late.'

'Oh,' said Helen.

'Anyway, I thought you might have waited a little longer.'

'No point.'

'Are you sure?' asked Niamh.

Printed in Great Britain
by Amazon